Wonder Cat Kyuu-chan 5

Story & Art by Sasami Nitori

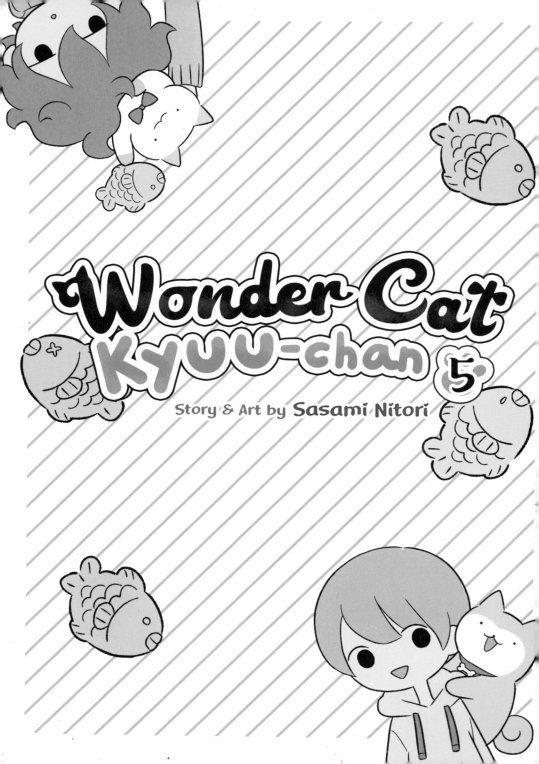

Wonder Cat
Kyuu-chan

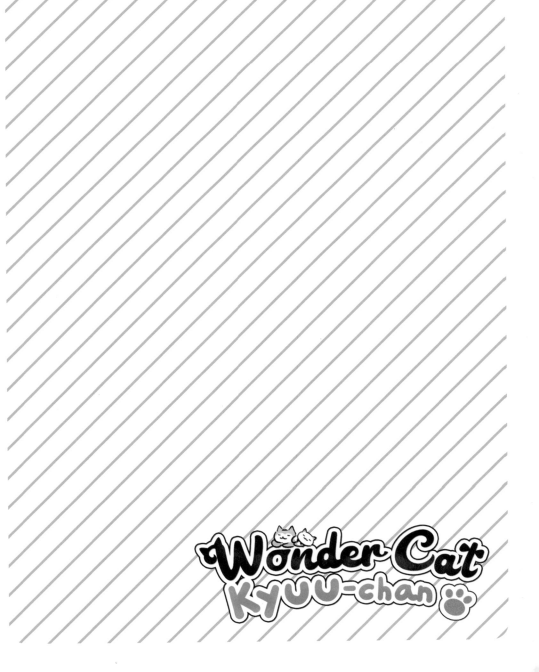

SUPER-HOT DAY

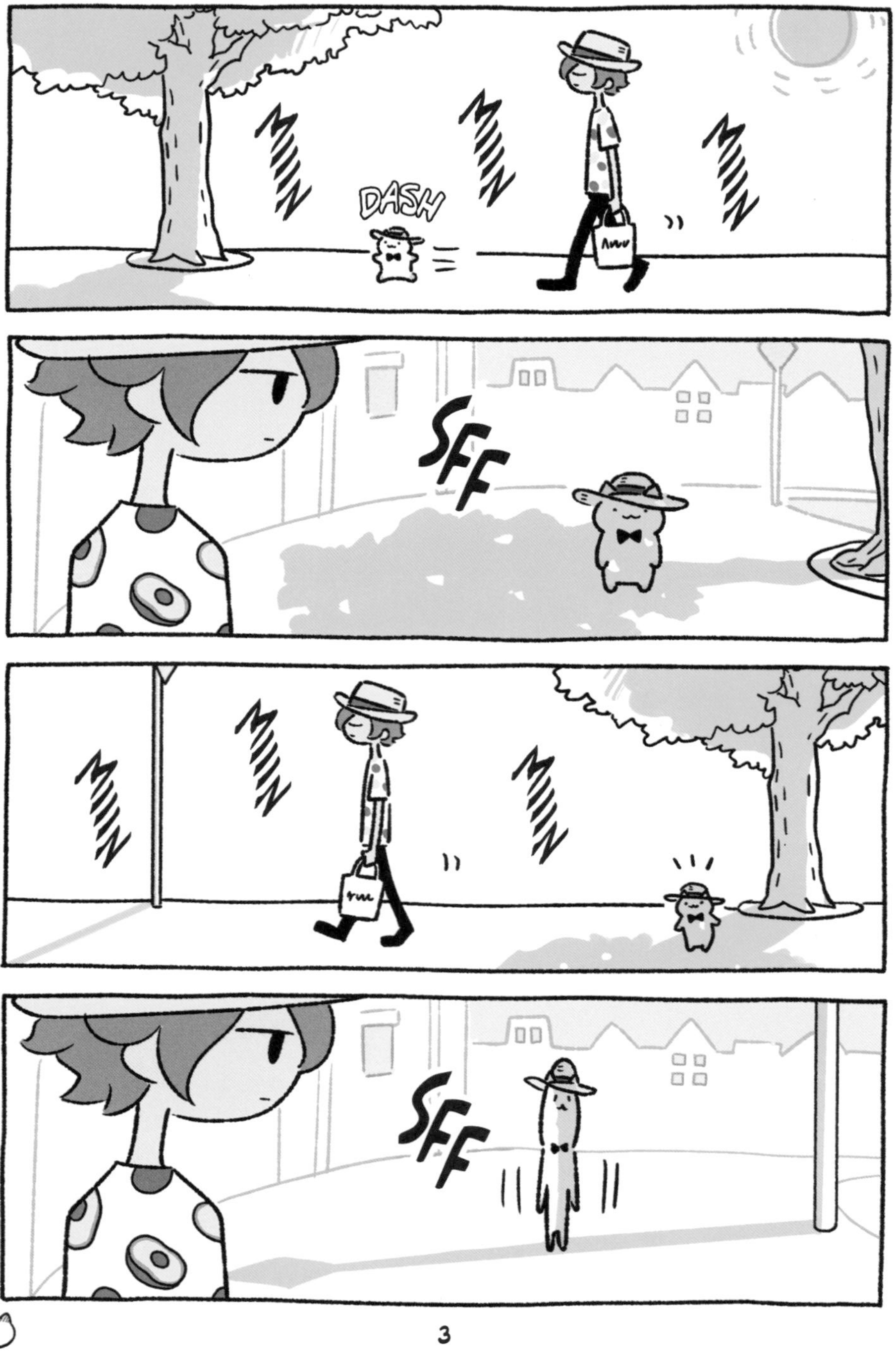
MIIIN
MIIIN
DASH
MIIIN
SFF
MIIIN
MIIIN
MIIIN
SFF

WIND

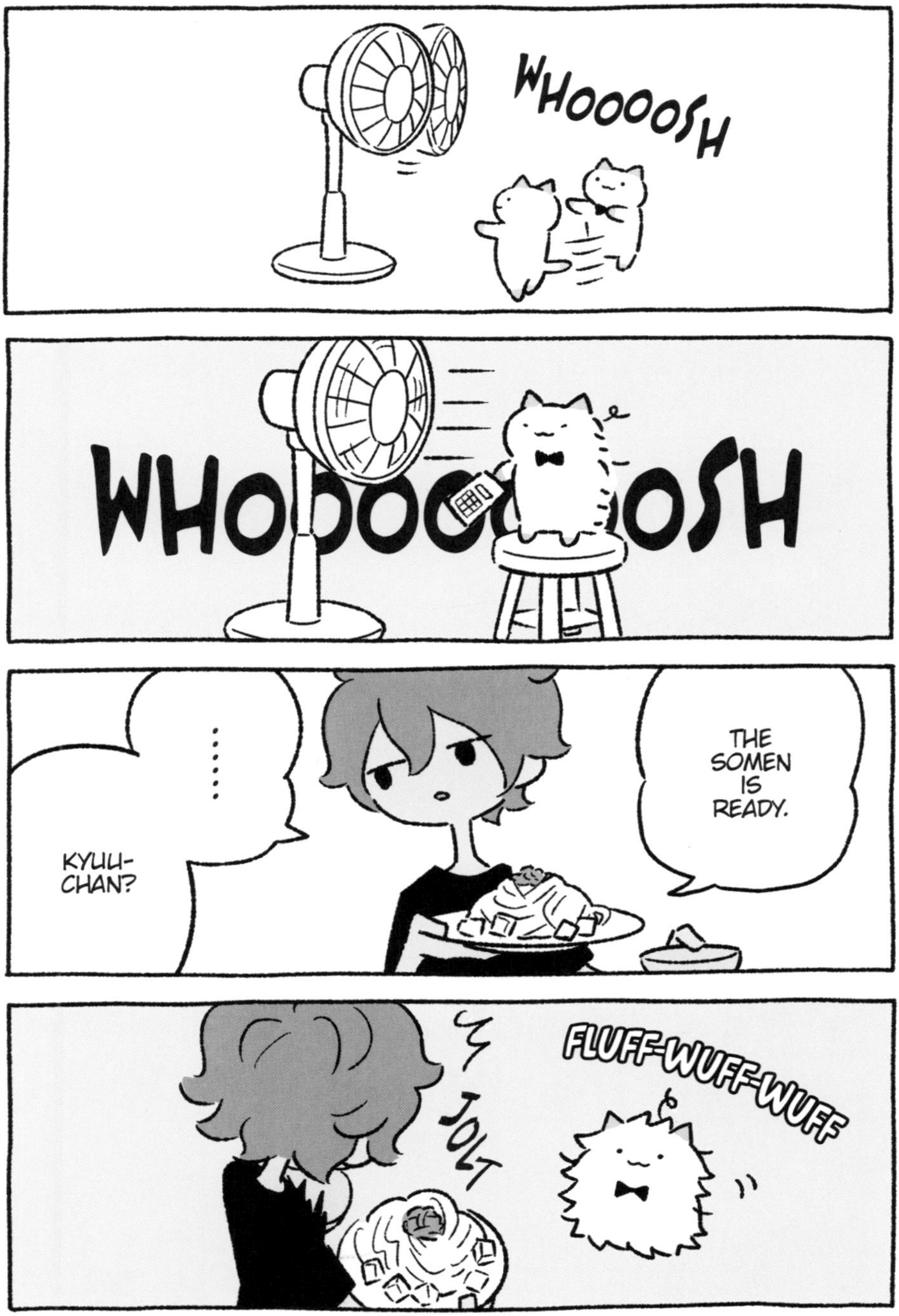
WHOOOOSH
WHOOOOOOSH
THE SOMEN IS READY.
......
KYUU-CHAN?
FLUFF-WUFF-WUFF
JOLT

WIND CHIME

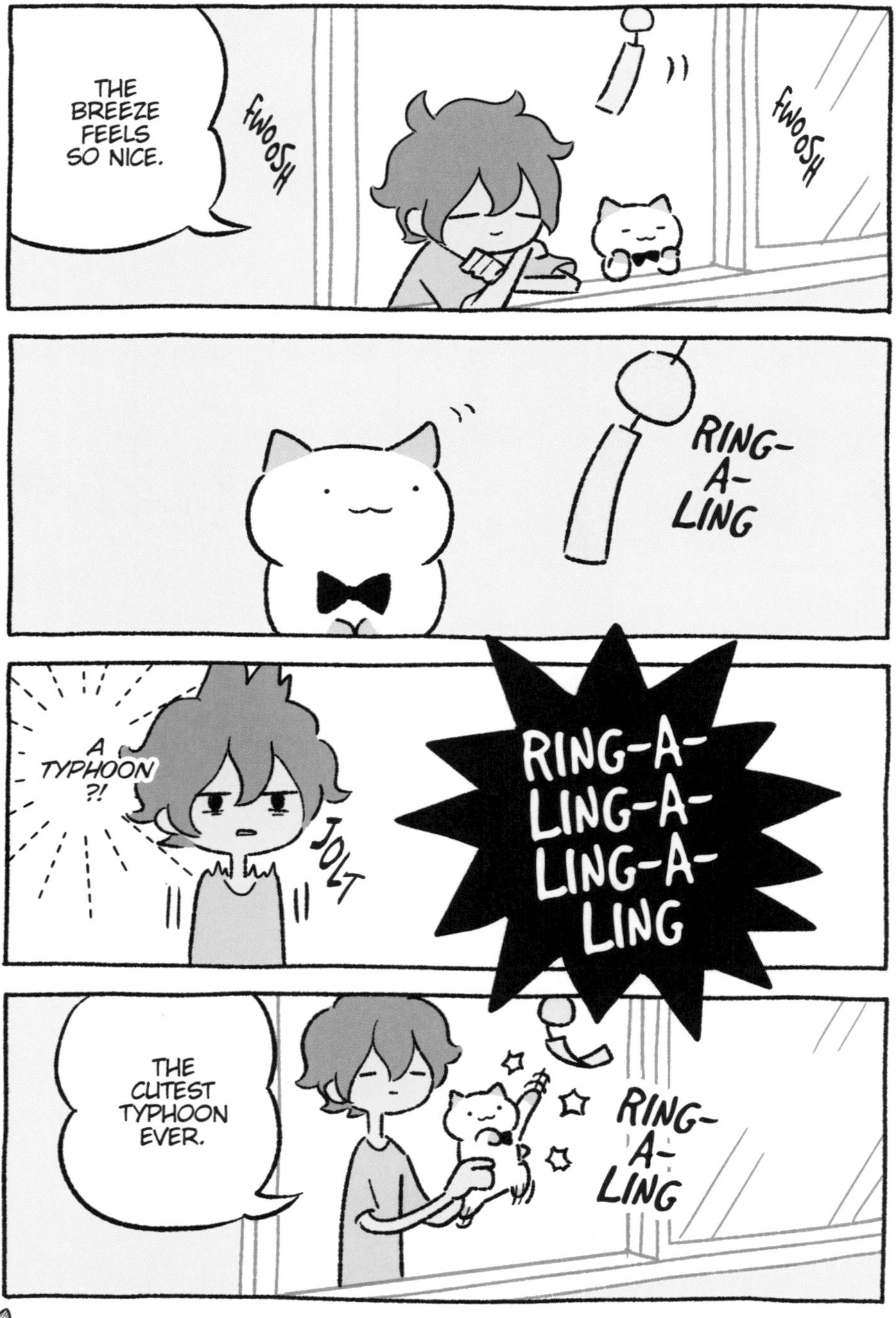
FWOOSH
FWOOSH
THE BREEZE FEELS SO NICE.
RING-A-LING
RING-A-LING-A-LING-A-LING-A-LING
JOLT
A TYPHOON?!
RING-A-LING
THE CUTEST TYPHOON EVER.

POCKIN ICE POPS

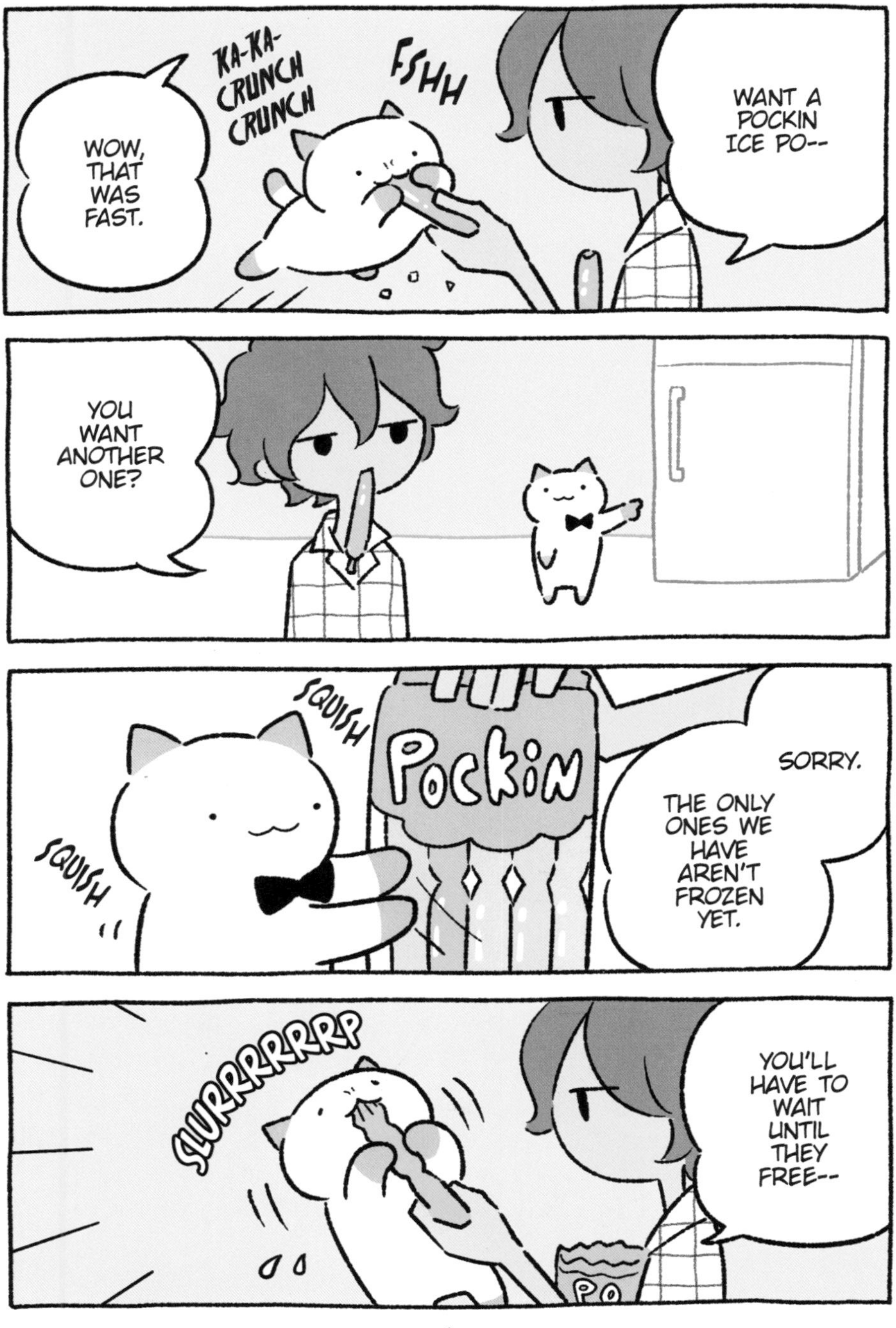
WANT A POCKIN ICE PO--
FSHH
KA-KA-CRUNCH CRUNCH
WOW, THAT WAS FAST.
YOU WANT ANOTHER ONE?
SORRY.
THE ONLY ONES WE HAVE AREN'T FROZEN YET.
Pockin
SQUISH
SQUISH
YOU'LL HAVE TO WAIT UNTIL THEY FREE--
SLURRRRRRP
PO

WON'T GO HOME: MONA-CHAN

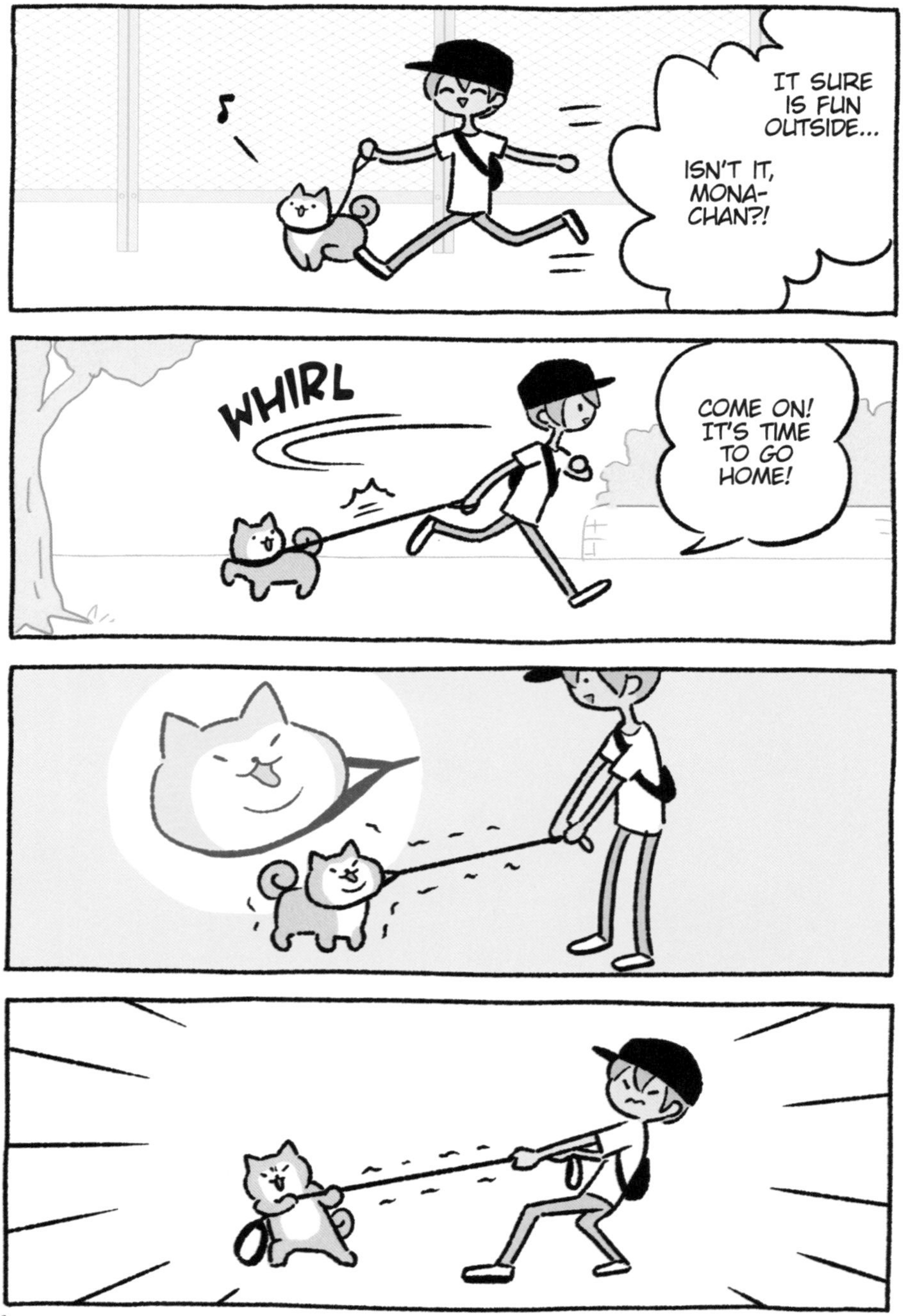
IT SURE IS FUN OUTSIDE...
ISN'T IT, MONA-CHAN?!
WHIRL
COME ON! IT'S TIME TO GO HOME!

WON'T GO HOME: KYUU-CHAN

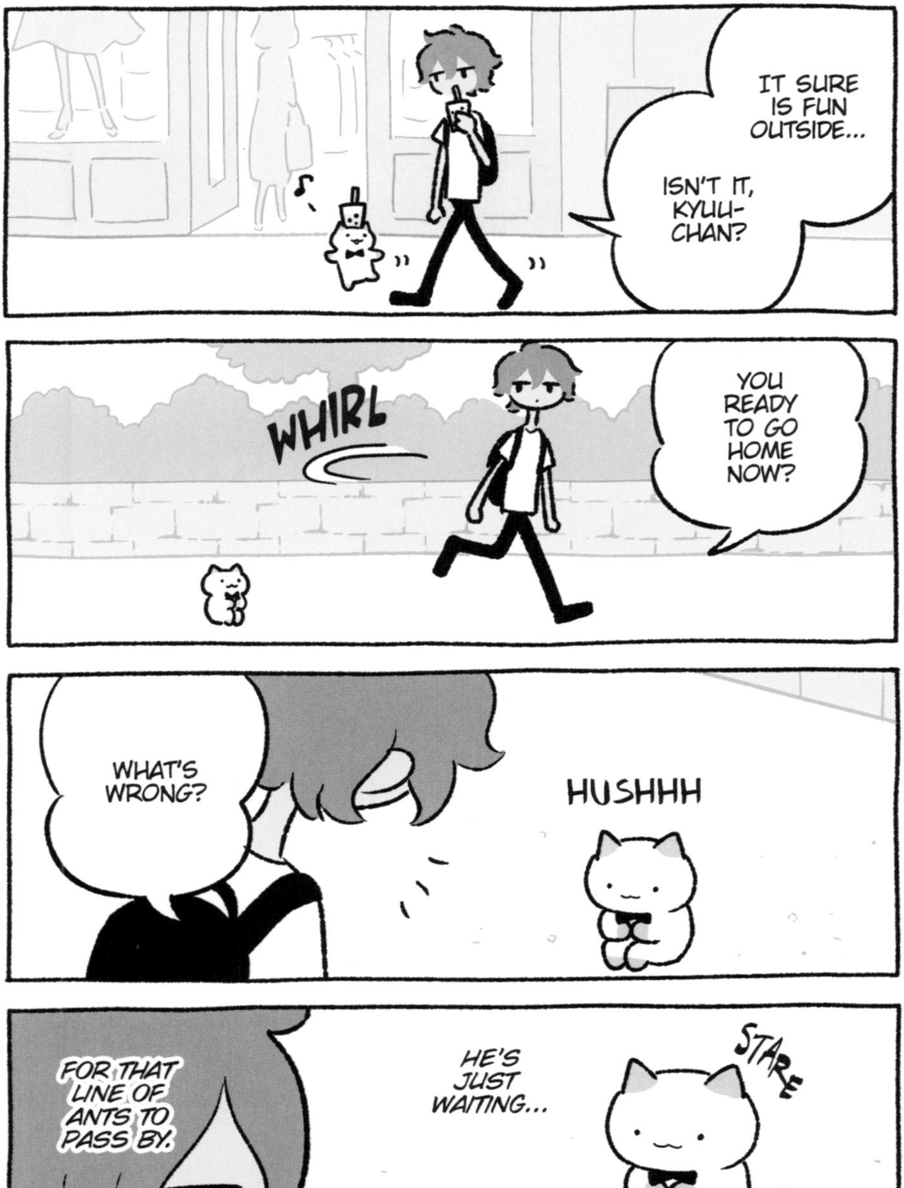
IT SURE IS FUN OUTSIDE...
ISN'T IT, KYUU-CHAN?
YOU READY TO GO HOME NOW?
WHIRL
HUSHHH
WHAT'S WRONG?
STARE
HE'S JUST WAITING...
FOR THAT LINE OF ANTS TO PASS BY.

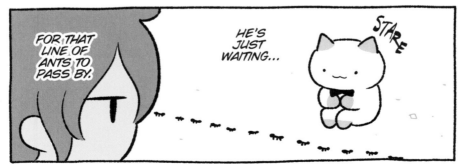

NEW SOCKS

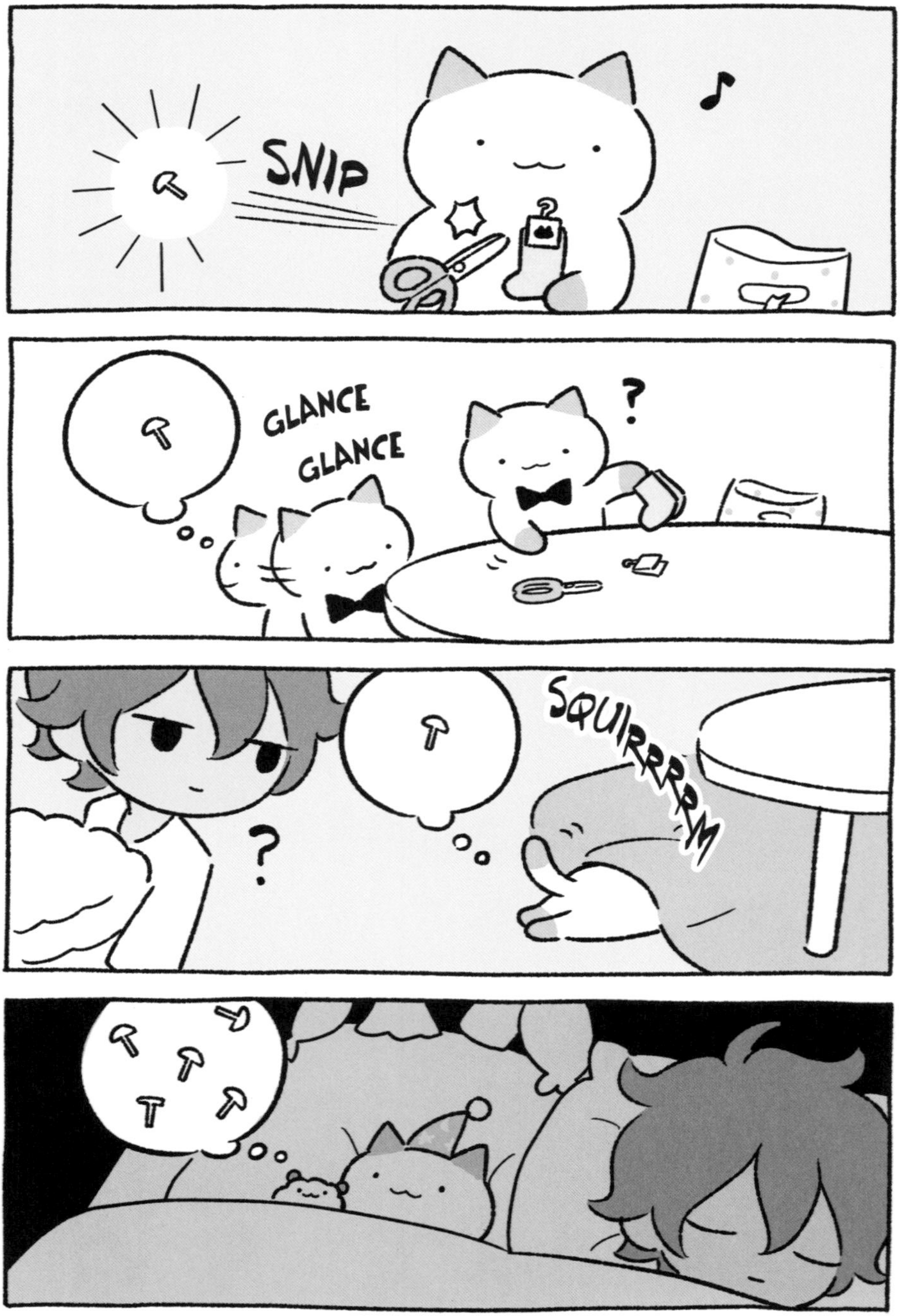
SNIP
♪
GLANCE
GLANCE
?
SQUIRRRRRM
?

WITH A WARNING

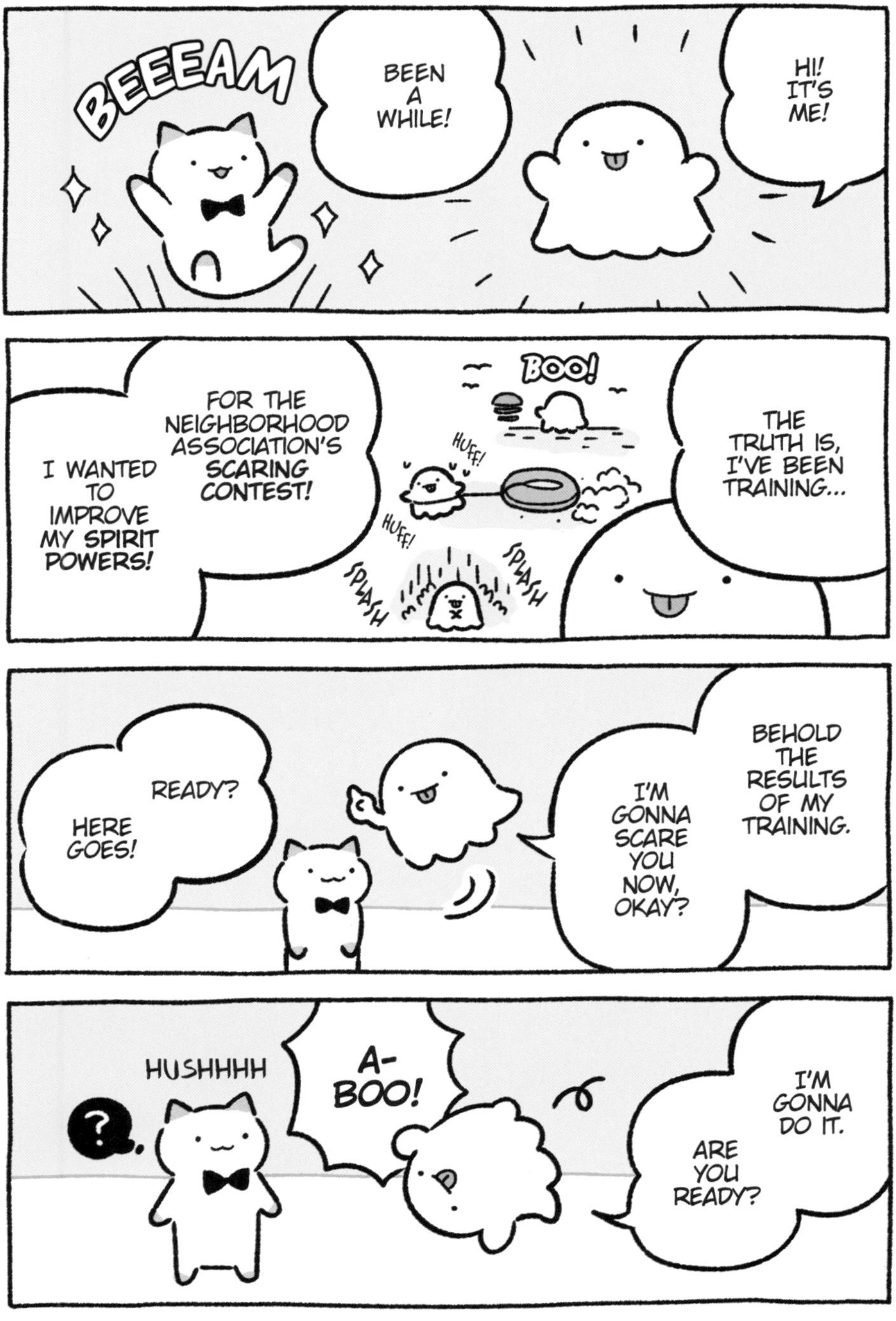
HI! IT'S ME!
BEEN A WHILE!
BEEEAM
THE TRUTH IS, I'VE BEEN TRAINING...
BOO!
HUFF!
HUFF!
SPLASH
SPLASH
FOR THE NEIGHBORHOOD ASSOCIATION'S SCARING CONTEST!
I WANTED TO IMPROVE MY SPIRIT POWERS!
BEHOLD THE RESULTS OF MY TRAINING.
I'M GONNA SCARE YOU NOW, OKAY?
READY?
HERE GOES!
I'M GONNA DO IT.
ARE YOU READY?
A-BOO!
HUSHHHH
?

SPIRIT POWERS: LEVELED UP

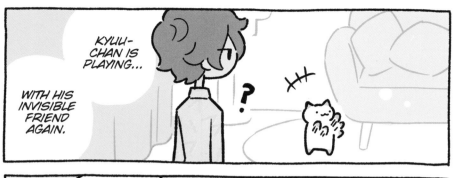

KYUU-CHAN IS PLAYING...
WITH HIS INVISIBLE FRIEND AGAIN.
I'M GONNA PLAY A TRICK ON YOU!
HM? YOUR FRIEND IS HERE?
POINT
I STILL CAN'T SEE THEM.
I CAN'T TOUCH THEM.
FSH
FSH
ACK!
BOP
I TOUCHED THEM!
IT FELT LIKE A CUSHION.
H-HOW DID THAT HAPPEN?

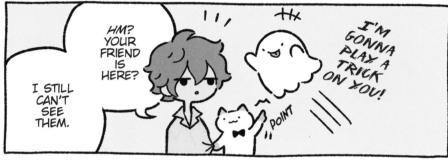

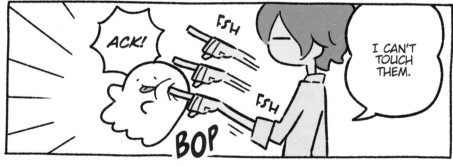

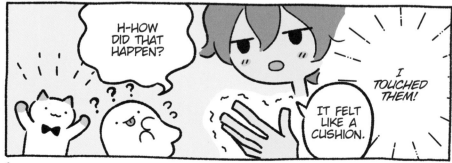

CUSHION

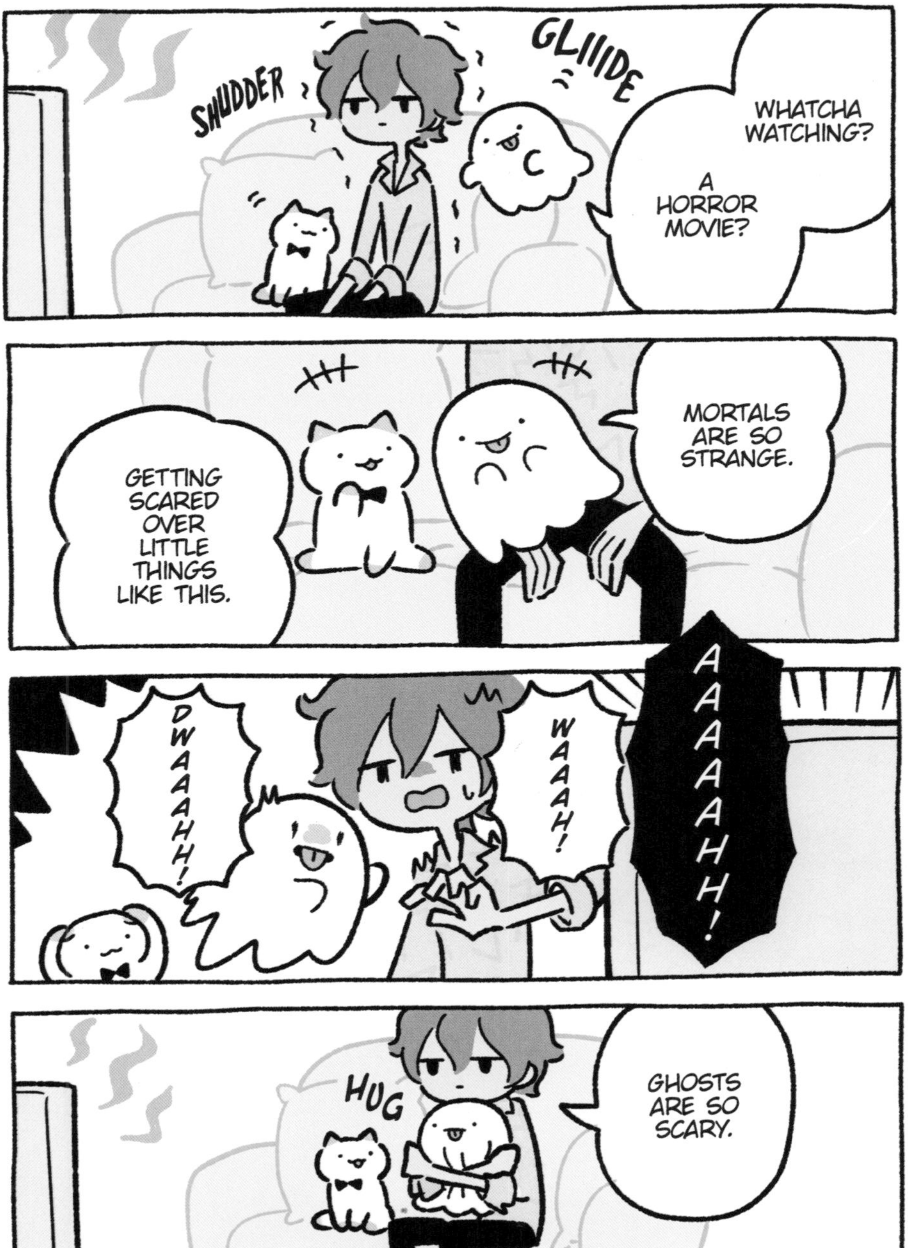
WHATCHA WATCHING?
A HORROR MOVIE?
GLIIIDE
SHUDDER
MORTALS ARE SO STRANGE.
GETTING SCARED OVER LITTLE THINGS LIKE THIS.
AAAAAAAH!
WAAAAH!
DWAAAAHH!
GHOSTS ARE SO SCARY.
HUG

SCARING CONTEST

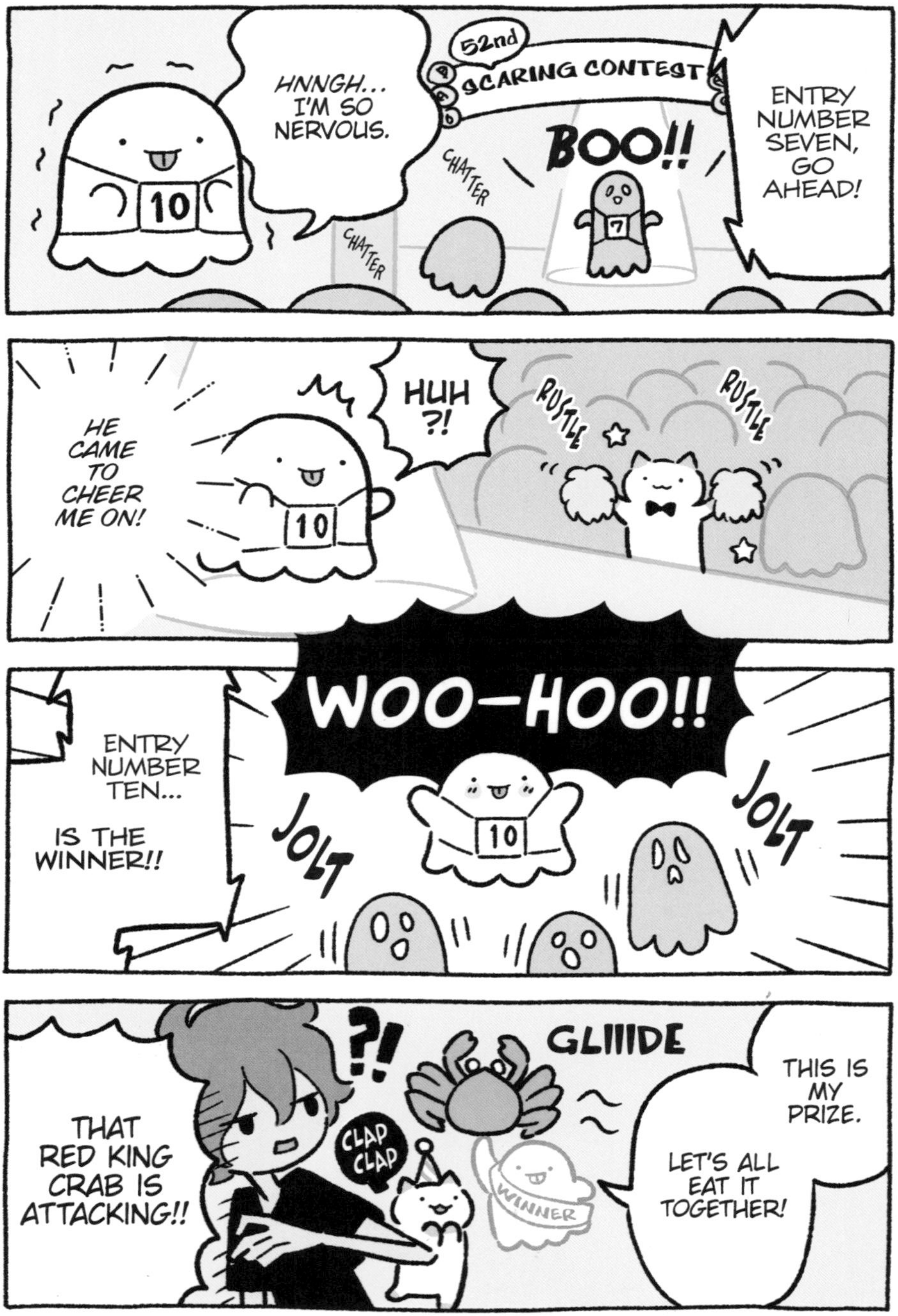
ENTRY NUMBER SEVEN, GO AHEAD!
52nd
SCARING CONTEST
BOO!!
CHATTER
HNNGH... I'M SO NERVOUS.
CHATTER
RUSTLE
RUSTLE
HUH ?!
HE CAME TO CHEER ME ON!
WOO-HOO!!
JOLT
ENTRY NUMBER TEN...
IS THE WINNER!!
JOLT
GLIIIDE
THIS IS MY PRIZE.
LET'S ALL EAT IT TOGETHER!
?!
CLAP CLAP
WINNER
THAT RED KING CRAB IS ATTACKING!!

BOWING

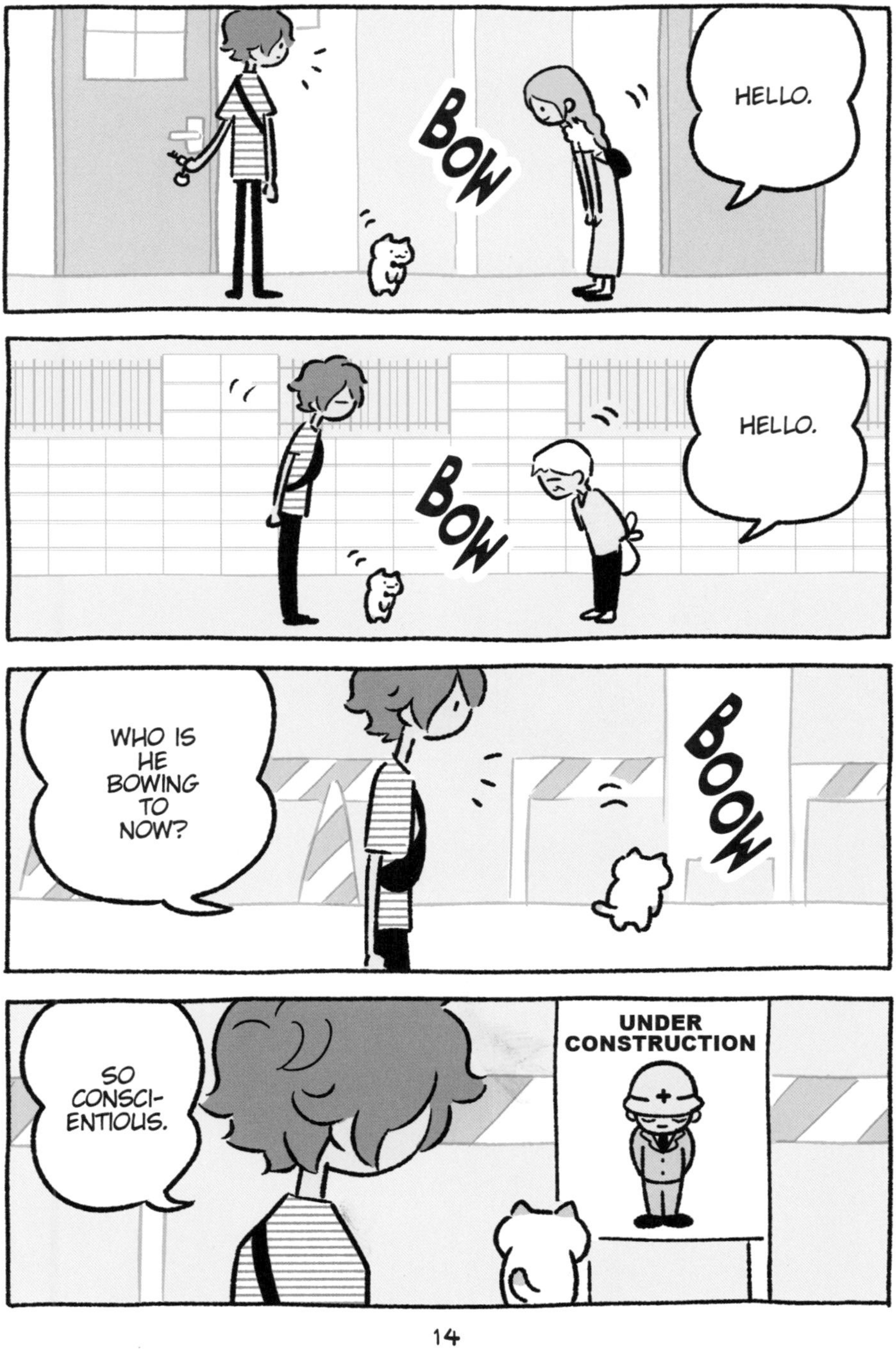
HELLO.
BOW
HELLO.
BOW
BOOOW
WHO IS HE BOWING TO NOW?
UNDER CONSTRUCTION
SO CONSCI-ENTIOUS.

SOFT BODY

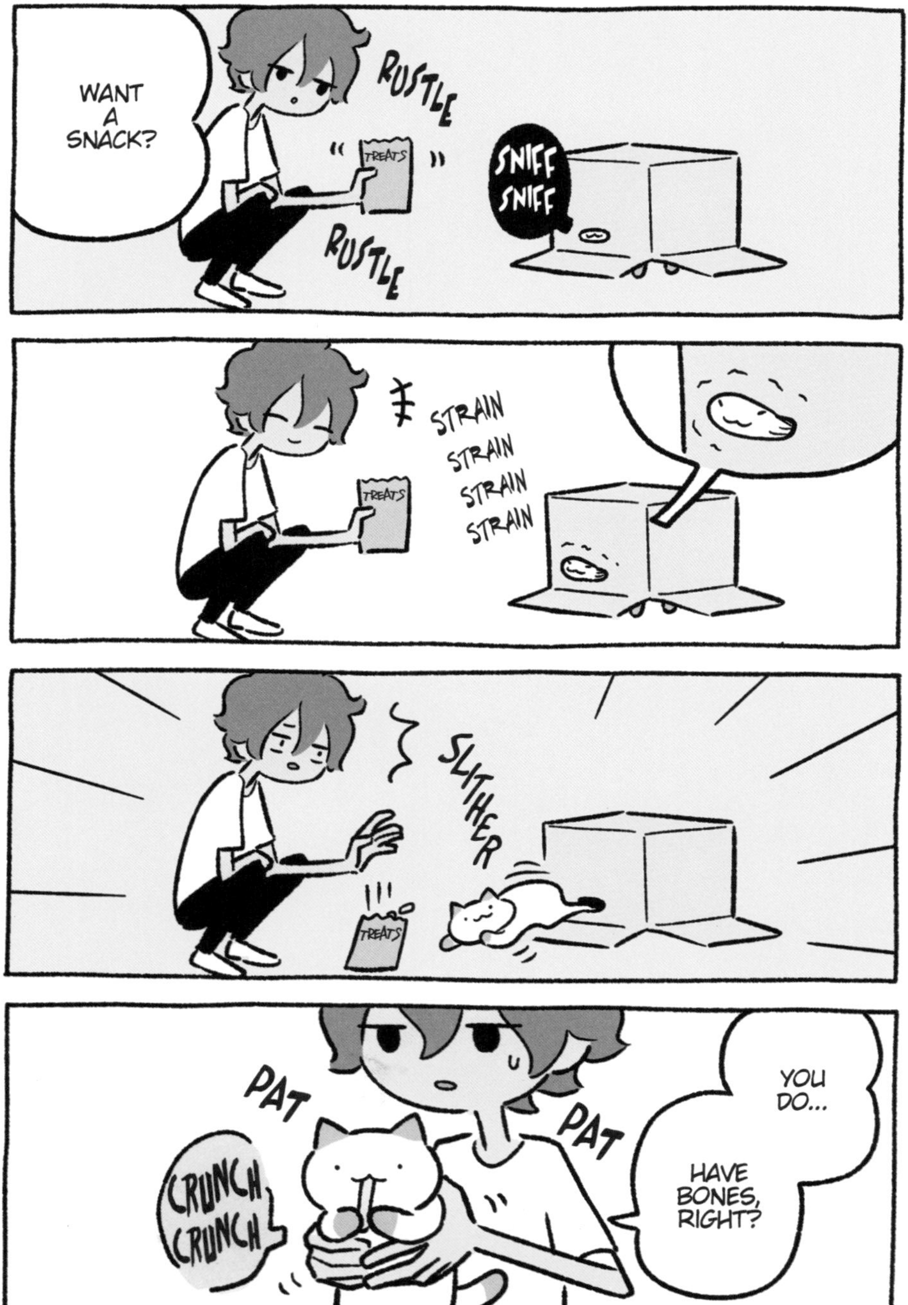
RUSTLE
SNIFF SNIFF
TREATS
WANT A SNACK?
RUSTLE
STRAIN
STRAIN
STRAIN
STRAIN
TREATS
SLITHER
TREATS
YOU DO...
HAVE BONES, RIGHT?
PAT
PAT
CRUNCH CRUNCH

PACKAGE PICKUP

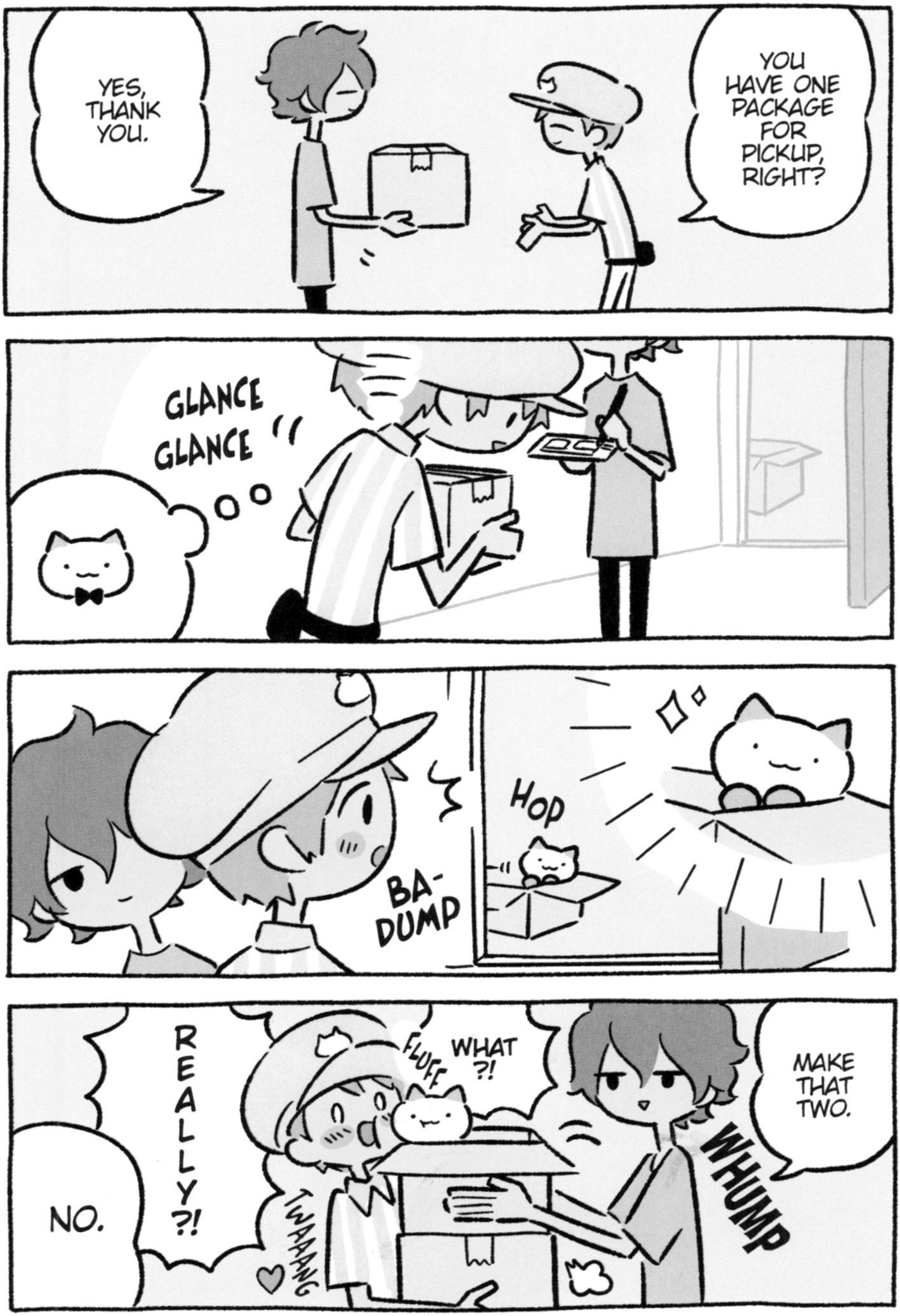

YOU HAVE ONE PACKAGE FOR PICKUP, RIGHT?
YES, THANK YOU.
GLANCE GLANCE
HOP
BA-DUMP
MAKE THAT TWO.
WHUMP
WHAT?!
FLUFF
REALLY?!
TWAAANG
NO.

STARING

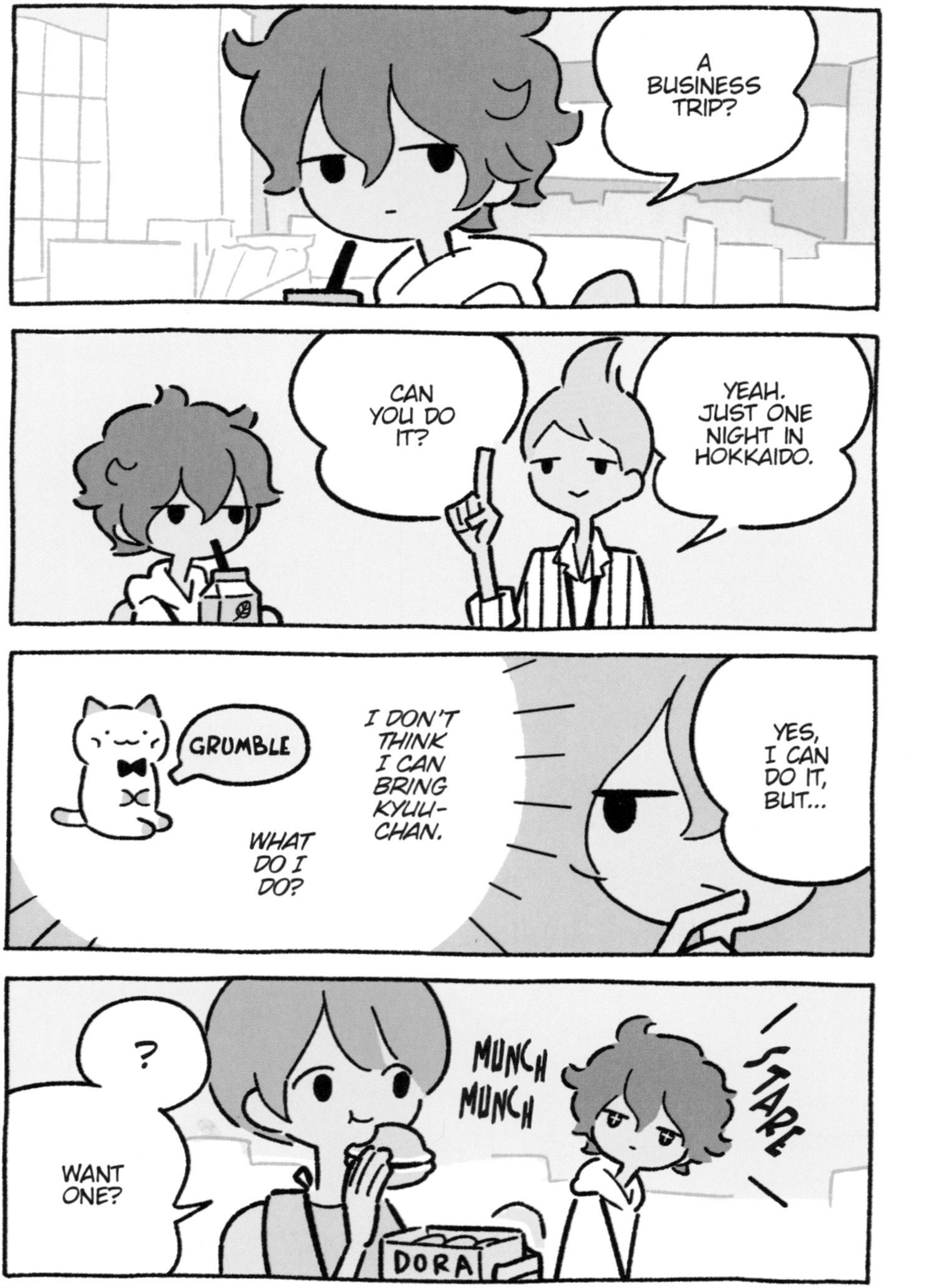
A BUSINESS TRIP?
YEAH. JUST ONE NIGHT IN HOKKAIDO.
CAN YOU DO IT?
YES, I CAN DO IT, BUT...
I DON'T THINK I CAN BRING KYUU-CHAN.
WHAT DO I DO?
GRUMBLE
STARE
MUNCH MUNCH
?
WANT ONE?
DORA

DELIGHTED

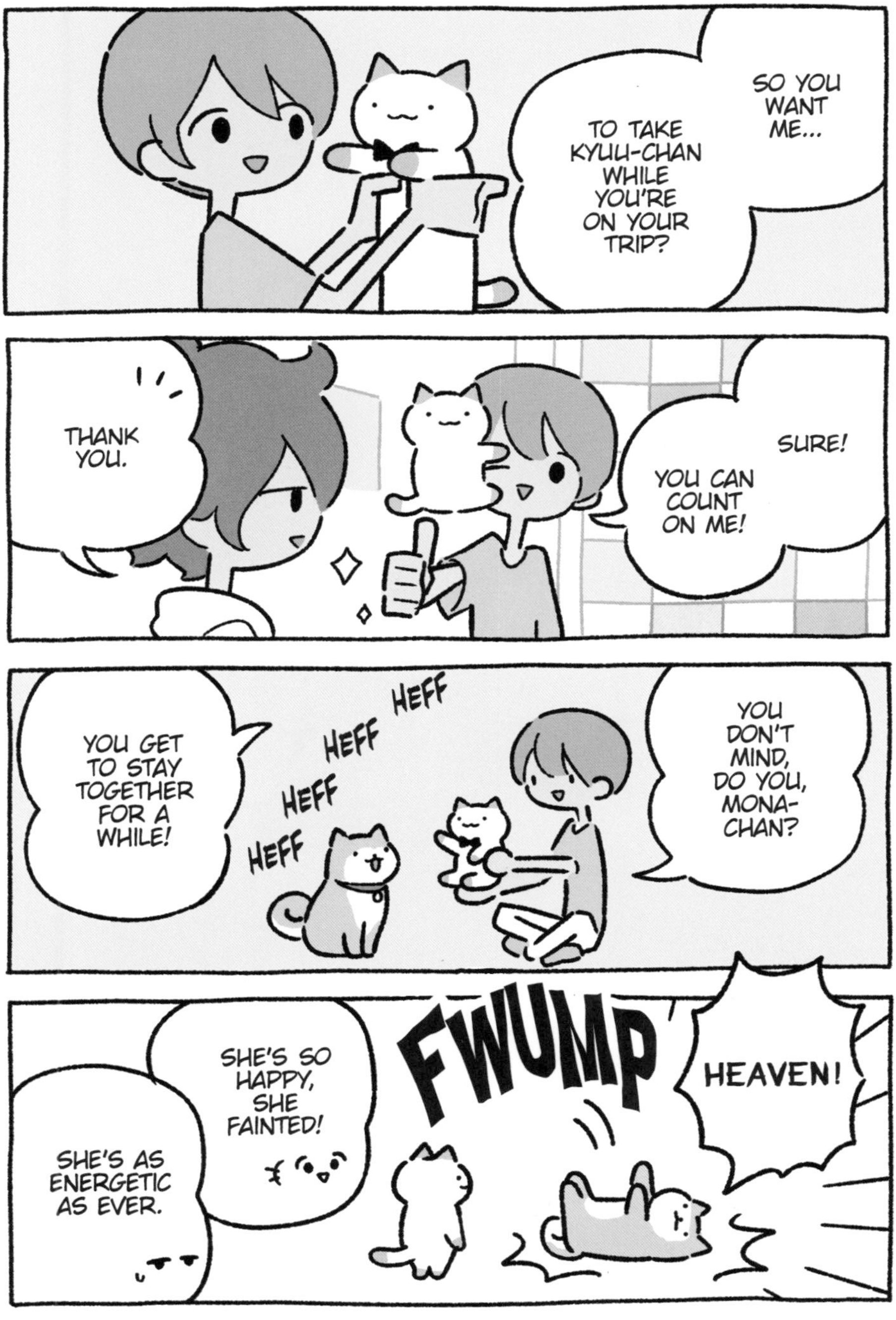
SO YOU WANT ME...
TO TAKE KYUU-CHAN WHILE YOU'RE ON YOUR TRIP?
SURE!
YOU CAN COUNT ON ME!
THANK YOU.
YOU DON'T MIND, DO YOU, MONA-CHAN?
HEFF
HEFF
HEFF
HEFF
YOU GET TO STAY TOGETHER FOR A WHILE!
HEAVEN!
FWUMP
SHE'S SO HAPPY, SHE FAINTED!
SHE'S AS ENERGETIC AS EVER.

EXCITEMENT

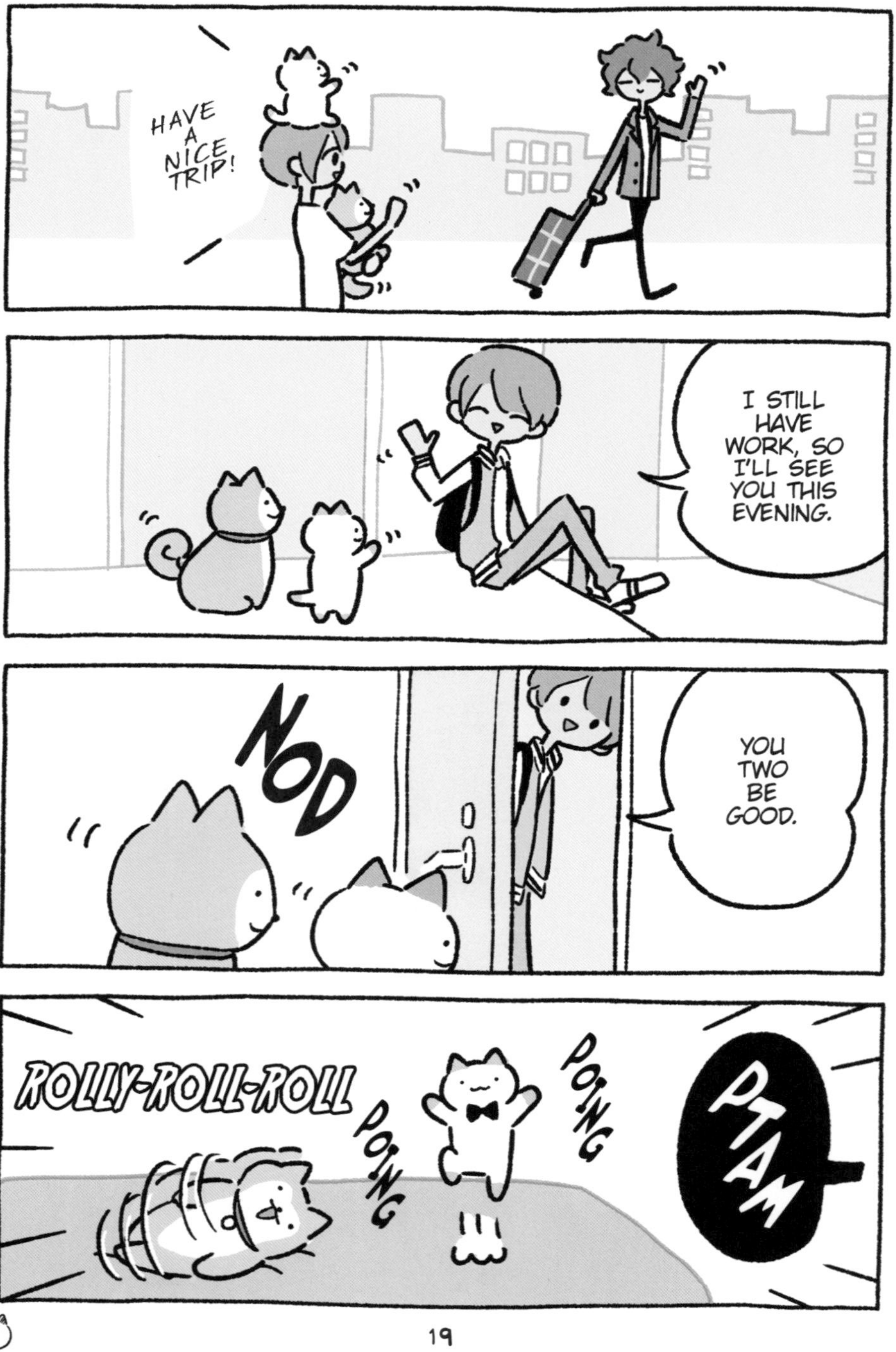
HAVE A NICE TRIP!
I STILL HAVE WORK, SO I'LL SEE YOU THIS EVENING.
YOU TWO BE GOOD.
NOD
PTAM
POING
POING
ROLLY-ROLL-ROLL

ENEMY ATTACK

CLONG
BOING
BOING
WHAP
BOING
BOING
TOSS
TOSS
WHAM
RRRRR
BEEP
WHRRRR
JOLT

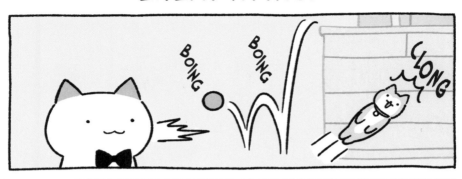

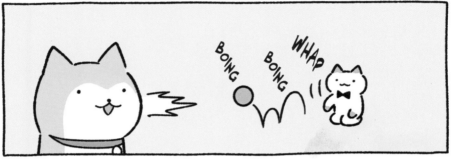

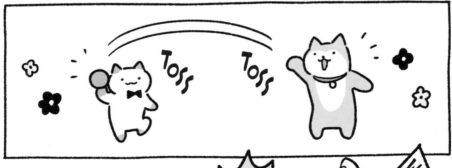

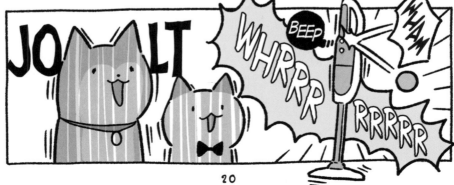

HERO

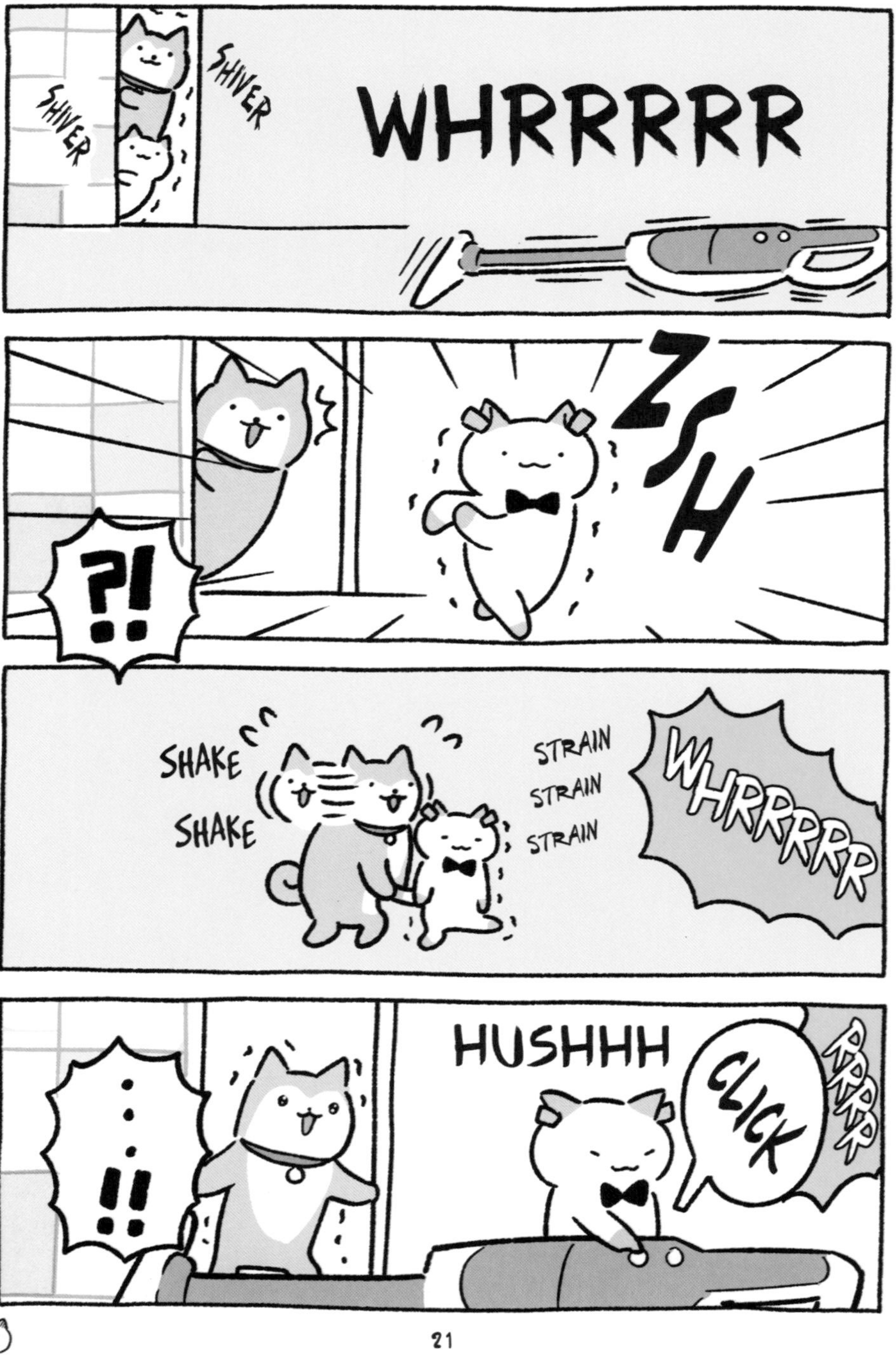
WHRRRRR
SHIVER
SHIVER
ZSH
?!
WHRRRRRR
STRAIN
STRAIN
STRAIN
SHAKE
SHAKE
RRRR
CLICK
HUSHHH
...!!

MEANWHILE

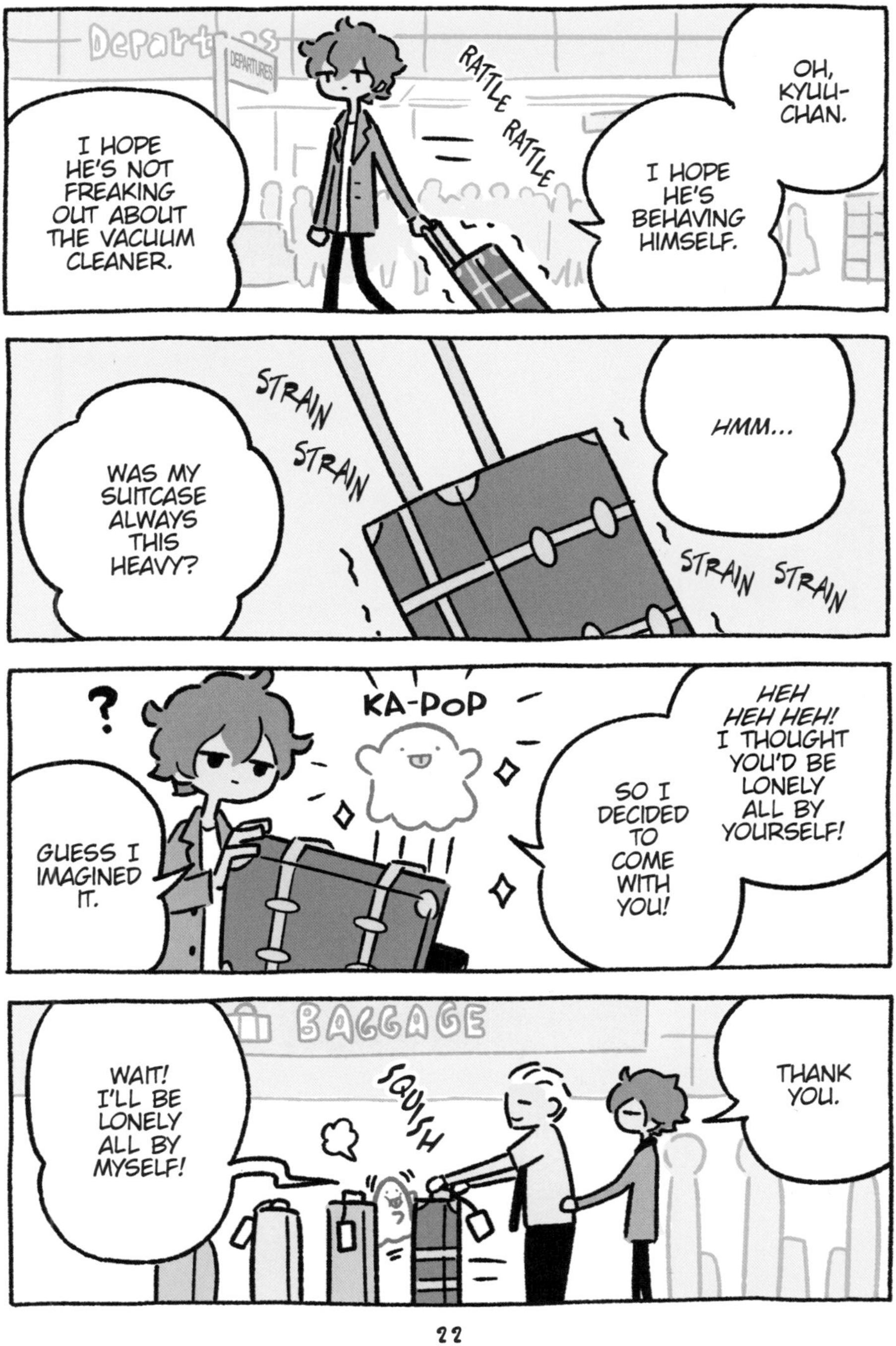

Departures
DEPARTURES
OH, KYUU-CHAN.
I HOPE HE'S BEHAVING HIMSELF.
RATTLE RATTLE
I HOPE HE'S NOT FREAKING OUT ABOUT THE VACUUM CLEANER.
HMM...
STRAIN STRAIN
STRAIN STRAIN
WAS MY SUITCASE ALWAYS THIS HEAVY?
HEH HEH HEH! I THOUGHT YOU'D BE LONELY ALL BY YOURSELF!
SO I DECIDED TO COME WITH YOU!
KA-POP
?
GUESS I IMAGINED IT.
BAGGAGE
THANK YOU.
SQUISH
WAIT! I'LL BE LONELY ALL BY MYSELF!

INITIATION

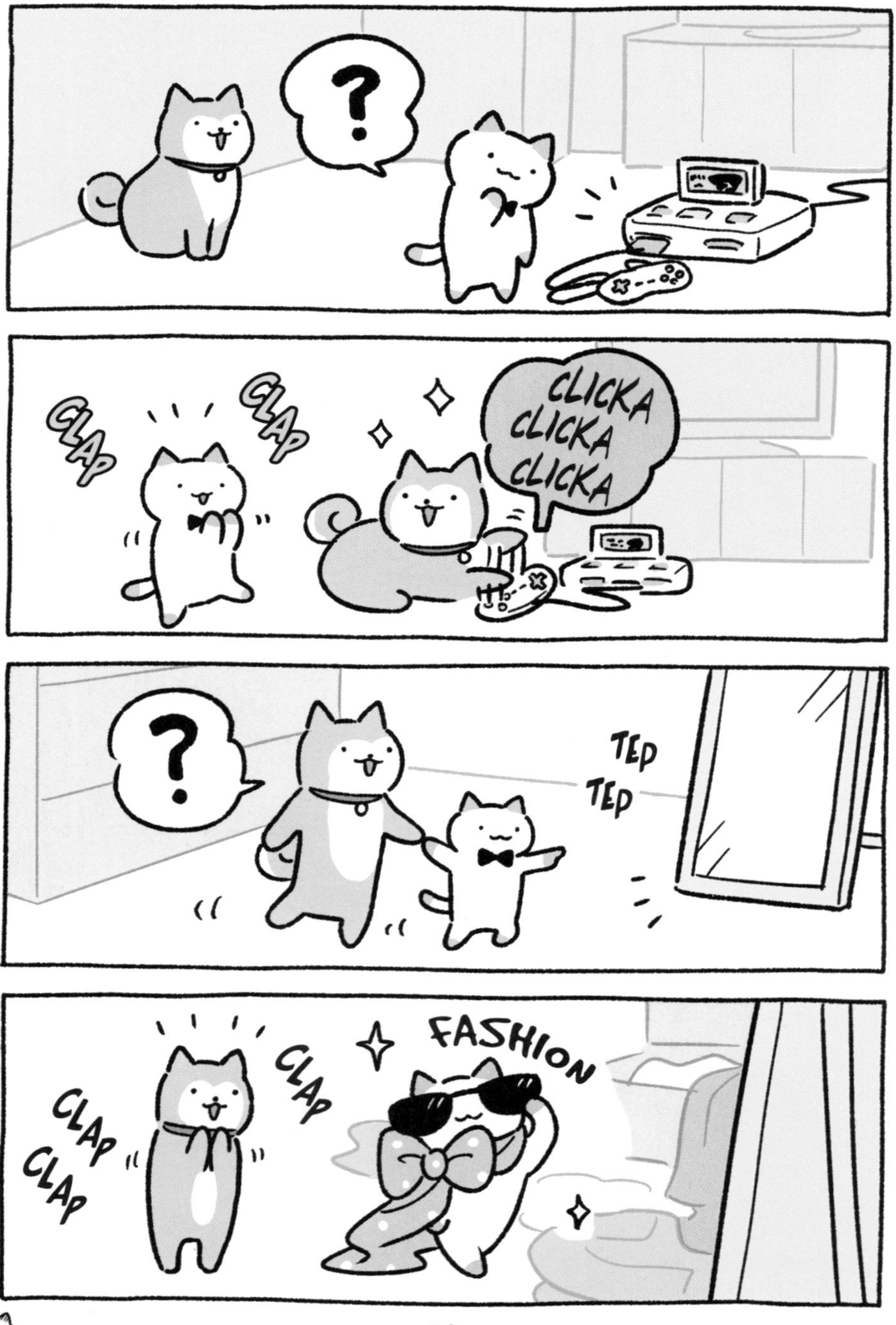
?
CLICKA CLICKA CLICKA
CLAP
CLAP
TEP TEP
?
FASHION
CLAP
CLAP
CLAP

GOOD BEANS

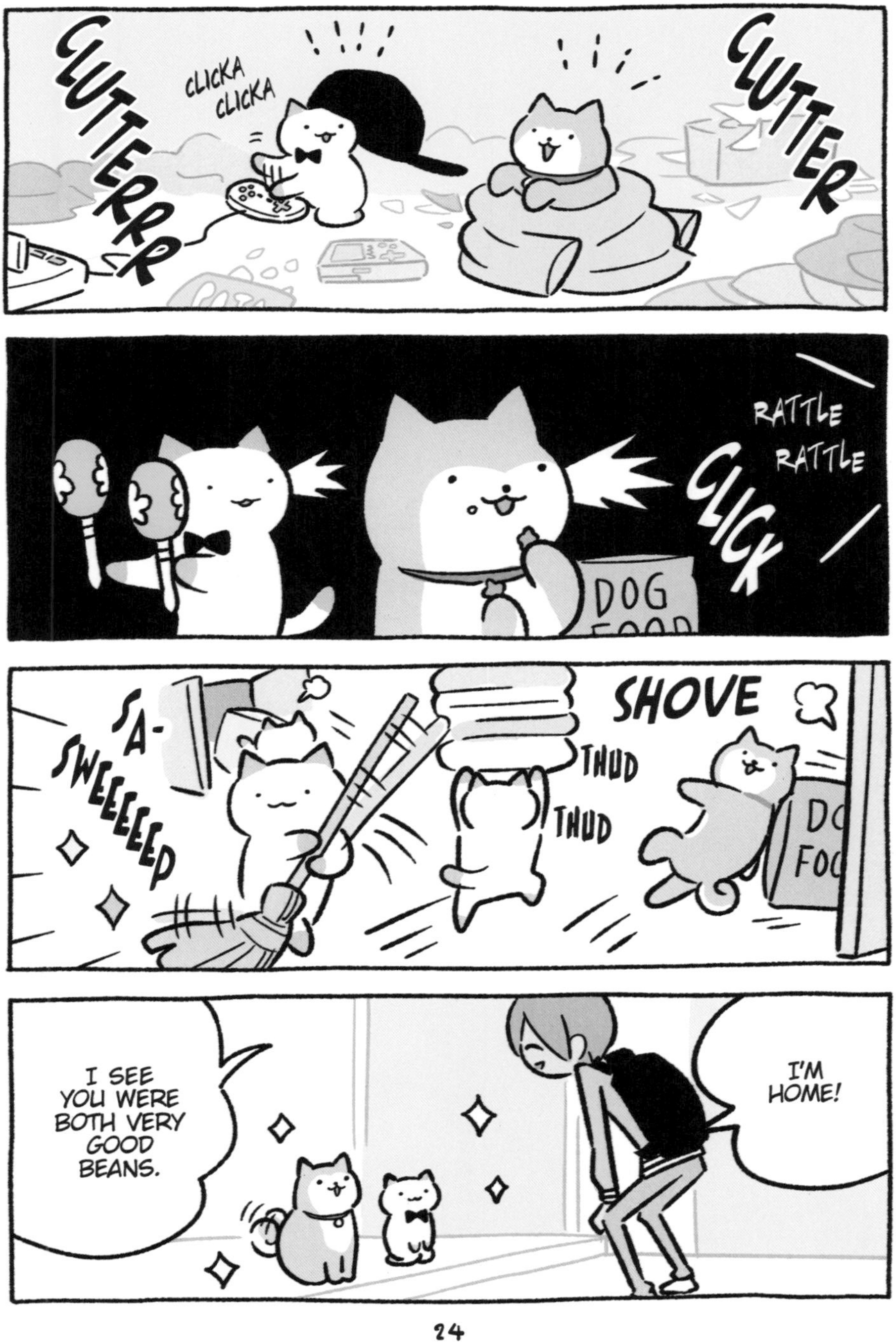

CLUTTER
CLICKA CLICKA
CLUTTERRR
RATTLE RATTLE
CLICK
DOG
SHOVE
THUD
THUD
SA-SWEEEEEEP
I'M HOME!
I SEE YOU WERE BOTH VERY GOOD BEANS.

WATER GAMES AND BATH TIME

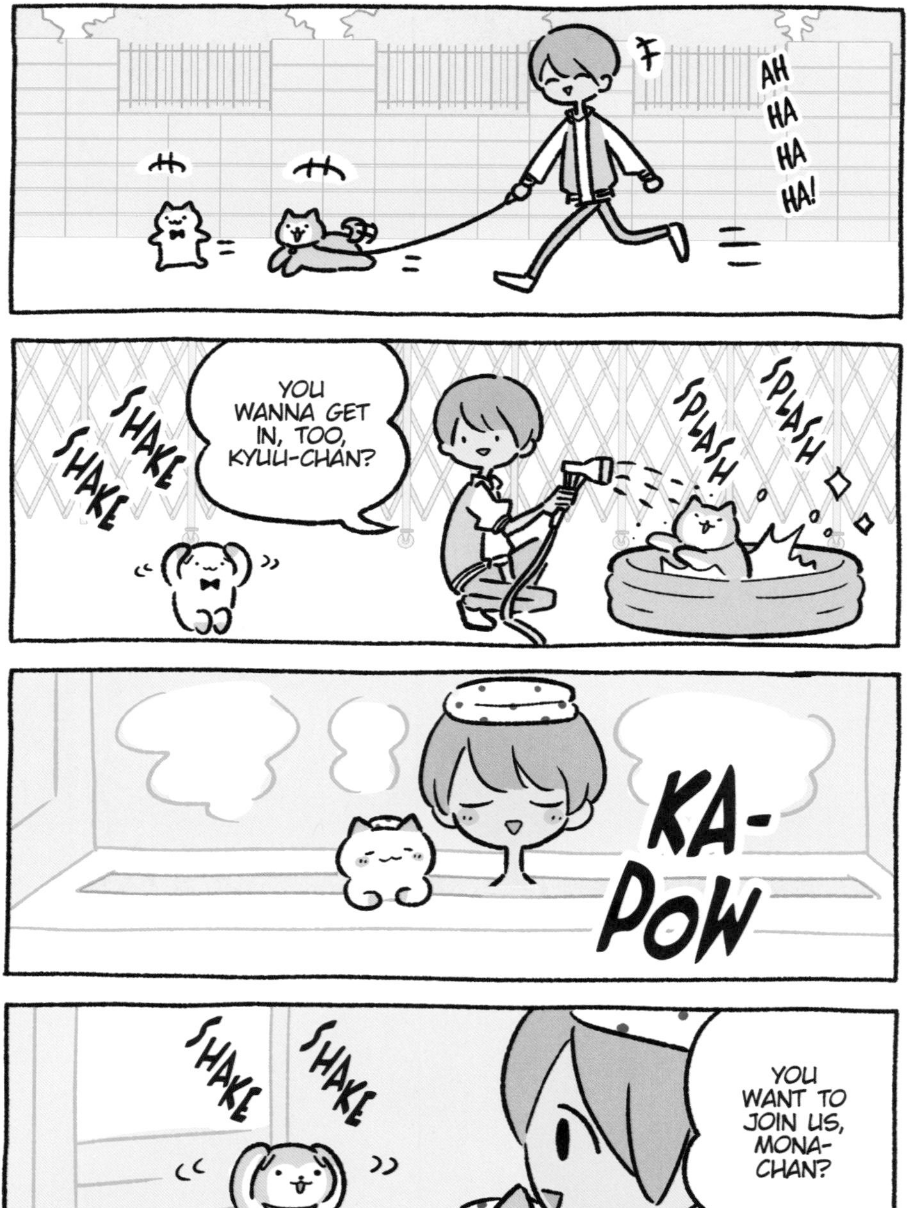
AH HA HA HA!
SPLASH SPLASH
YOU WANNA GET IN, TOO, KYUU-CHAN?
SHAKE SHAKE
KA-POW
YOU WANT TO JOIN US, MONA-CHAN?
SHAKE SHAKE

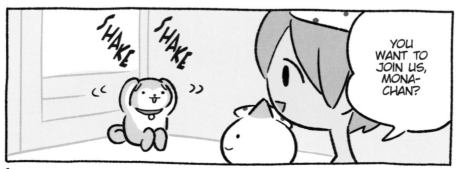

WAITING

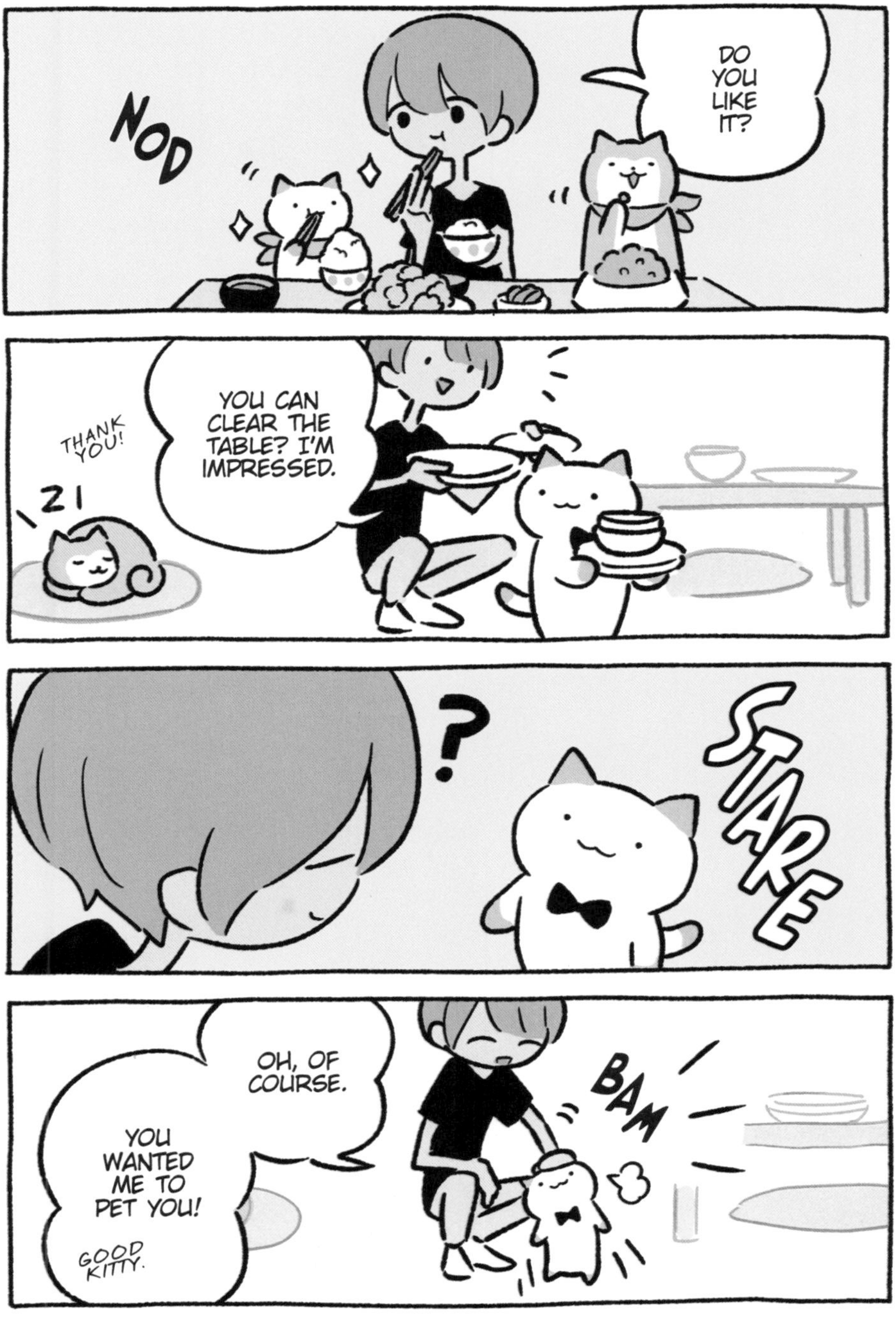
DO YOU LIKE IT?
NOD
YOU CAN CLEAR THE TABLE? I'M IMPRESSED.
THANK YOU!
STARE
?
BAM
OH, OF COURSE.
YOU WANTED ME TO PET YOU!
GOOD KITTY.

DON'T CRY

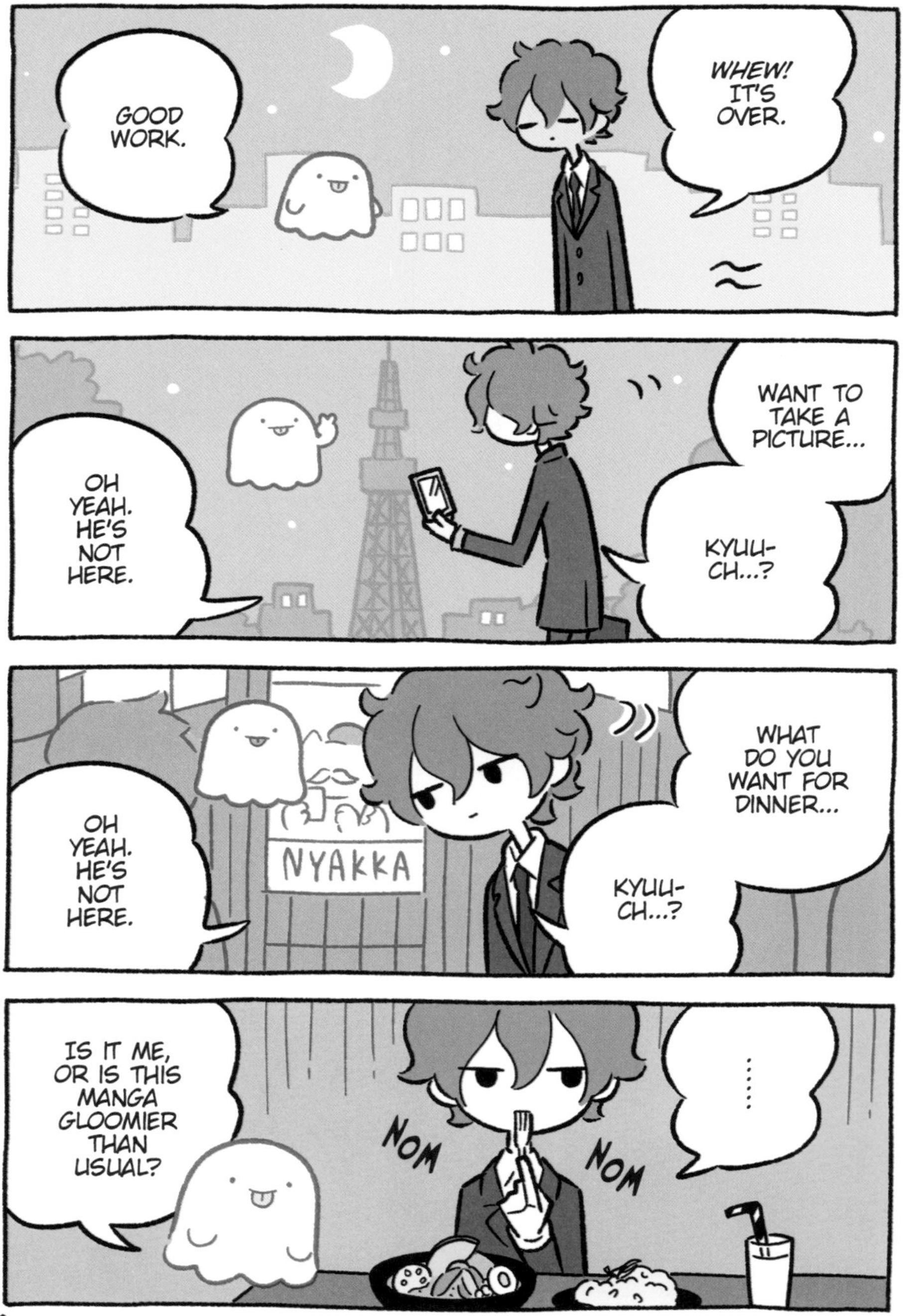
WHEW! IT'S OVER.
GOOD WORK.
WANT TO TAKE A PICTURE...
KYUU-CH...?
OH YEAH. HE'S NOT HERE.
WHAT DO YOU WANT FOR DINNER...
KYUU-CH...?
NYAKKA
OH YEAH. HE'S NOT HERE.
......
NOM
NOM
IS IT ME, OR IS THIS MANGA GLOOMIER THAN USUAL?

FEELING JUST A LITTLE BETTER

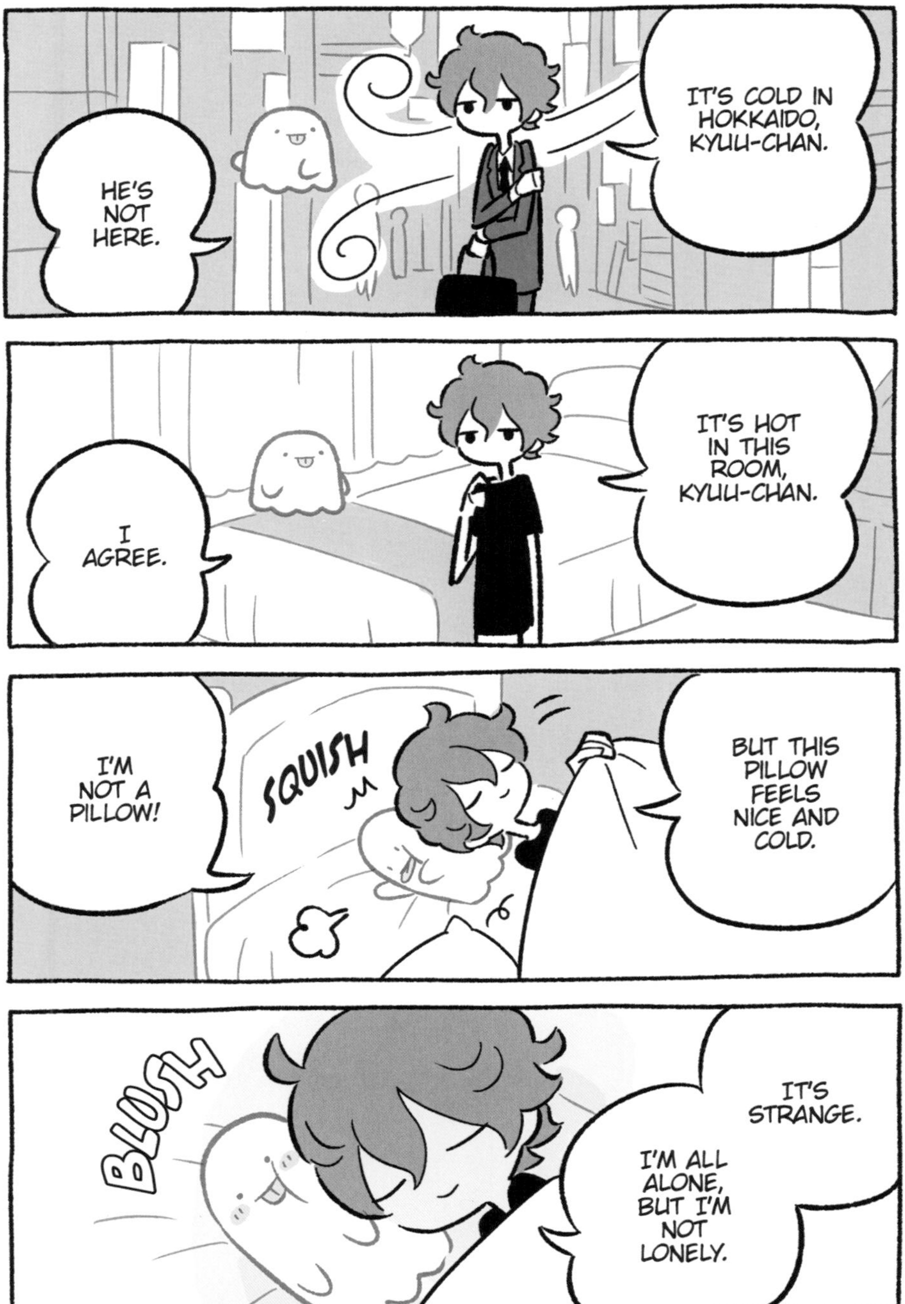
IT'S COLD IN HOKKAIDO, KYUU-CHAN.
HE'S NOT HERE.
IT'S HOT IN THIS ROOM, KYUU-CHAN.
I AGREE.
BUT THIS PILLOW FEELS NICE AND COLD.
SQUISH
I'M NOT A PILLOW!
IT'S STRANGE.
I'M ALL ALONE, BUT I'M NOT LONELY.
BLUSH

TIRED

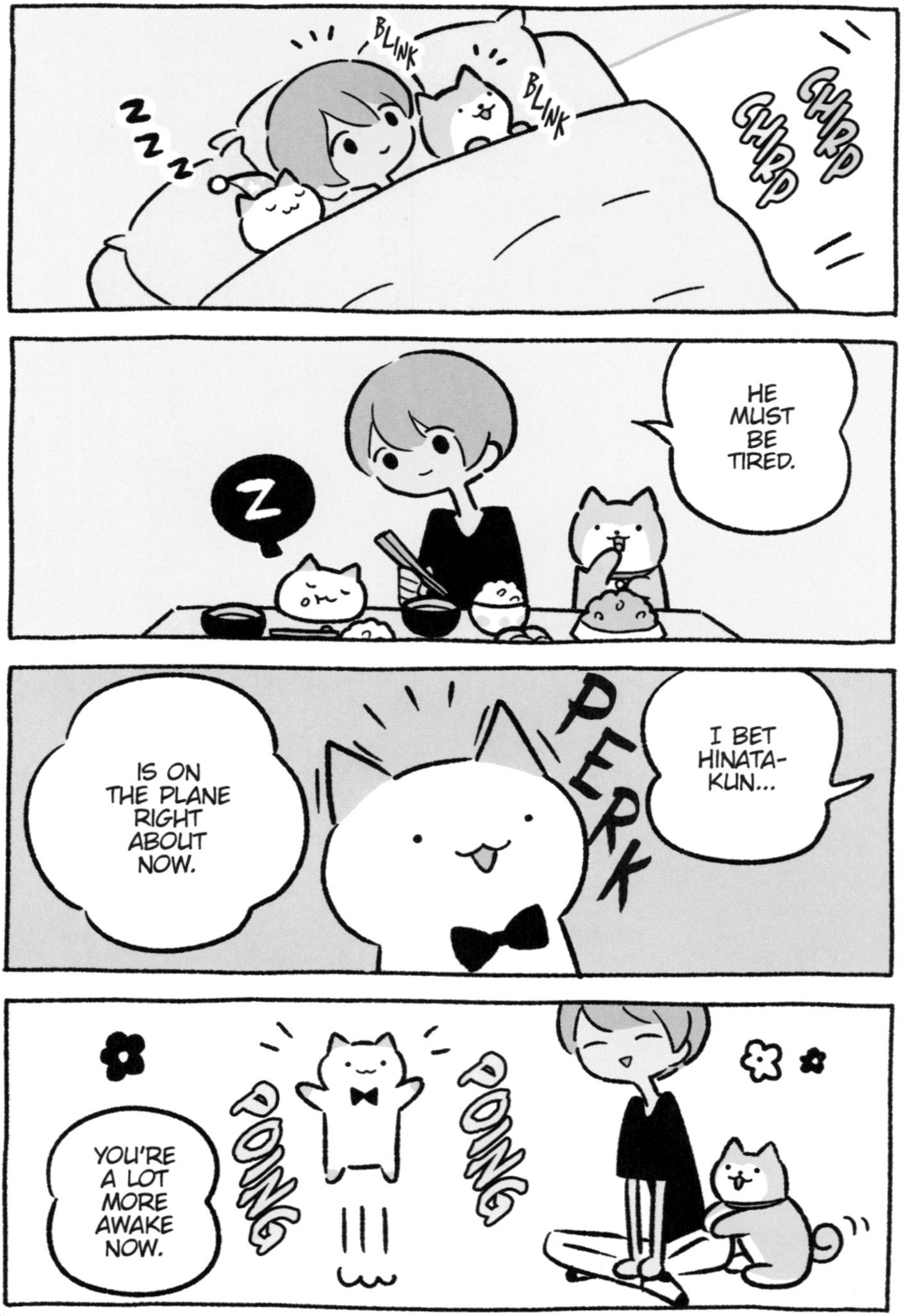
CHIRP
CHIRP
BLINK
BLINK
ZZZ
HE MUST BE TIRED.
Z
I BET HINATA-KUN...
PERK
IS ON THE PLANE RIGHT ABOUT NOW.
POING
POING
YOU'RE A LOT MORE AWAKE NOW.

MOTIVATED

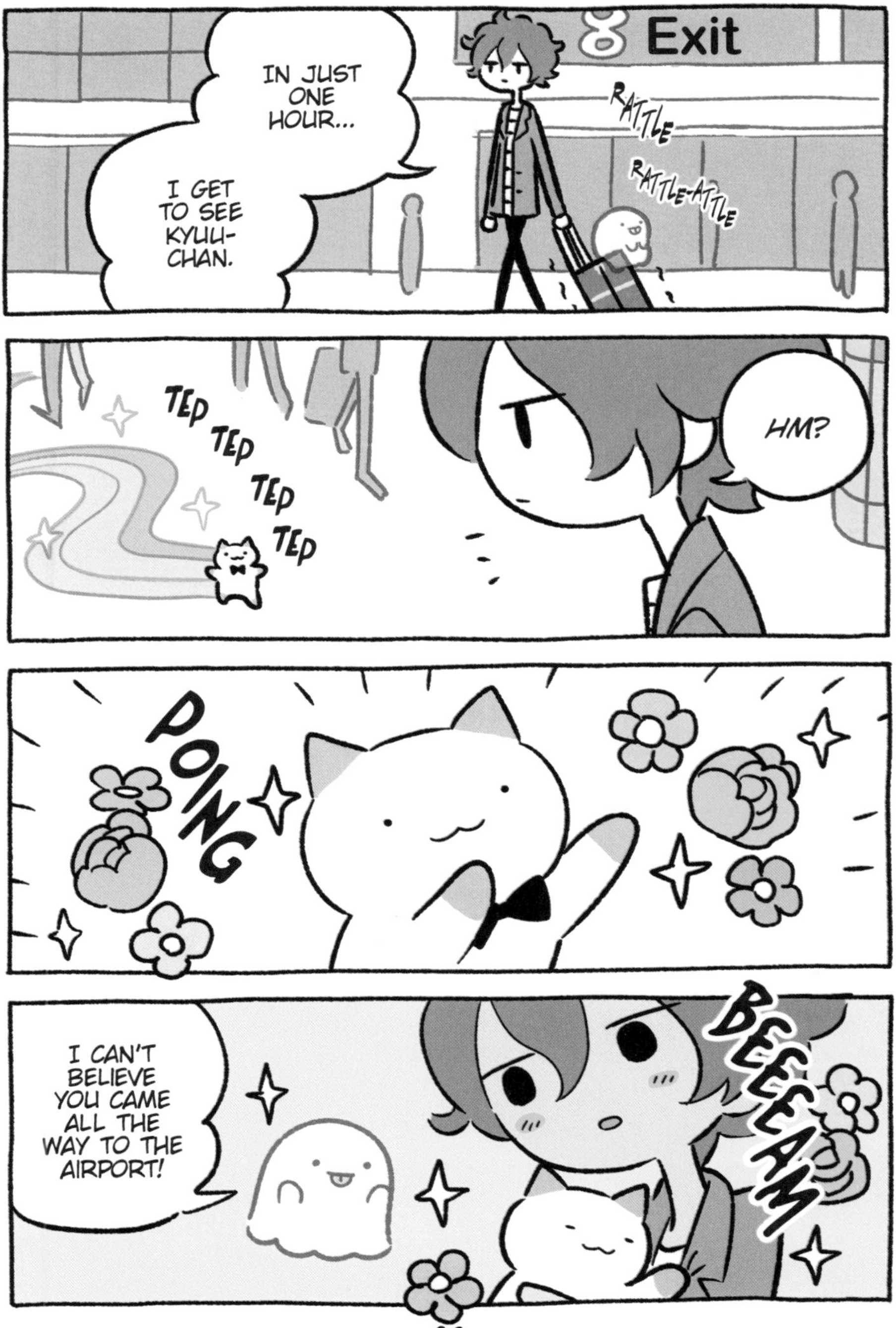

8 Exit
RATTLE
RATTLE-ATTLE
IN JUST ONE HOUR...
I GET TO SEE KYUU-CHAN.
HM?
TEP TEP TEP TEP
POING
BEEEAM
I CAN'T BELIEVE YOU CAME ALL THE WAY TO THE AIRPORT!

THE TRUTH

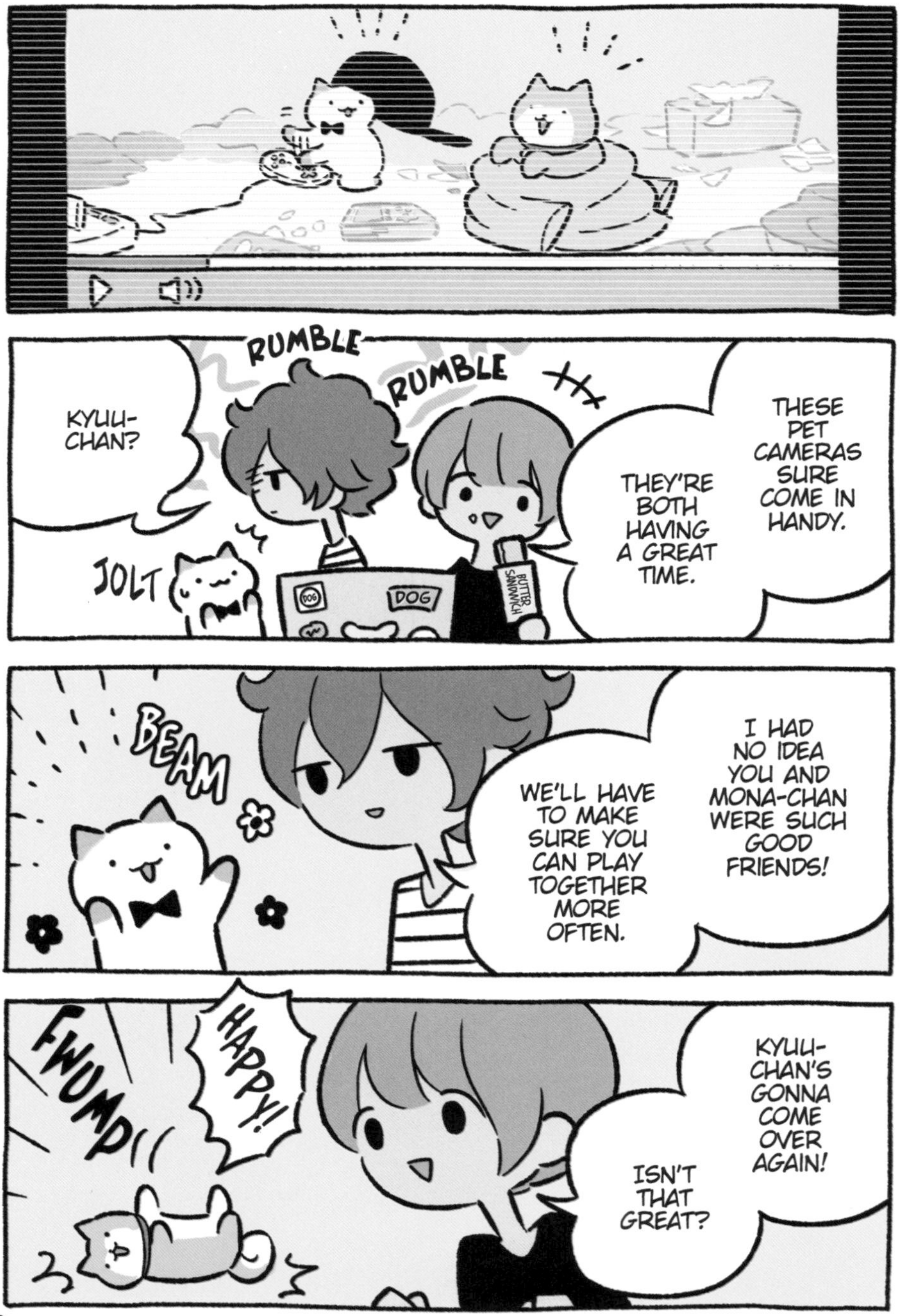

THESE PET CAMERAS SURE COME IN HANDY.
THEY'RE BOTH HAVING A GREAT TIME.
RUMBLE
RUMBLE
KYUU-CHAN?
BUTTER SANDWICH
DOG
DOG
JOLT
I HAD NO IDEA YOU AND MONA-CHAN WERE SUCH GOOD FRIENDS!
WE'LL HAVE TO MAKE SURE YOU CAN PLAY TOGETHER MORE OFTEN.
BEAM
KYUU-CHAN'S GONNA COME OVER AGAIN!
ISN'T THAT GREAT?
HAPPY!
FWUMP

SENSE OF SECURITY

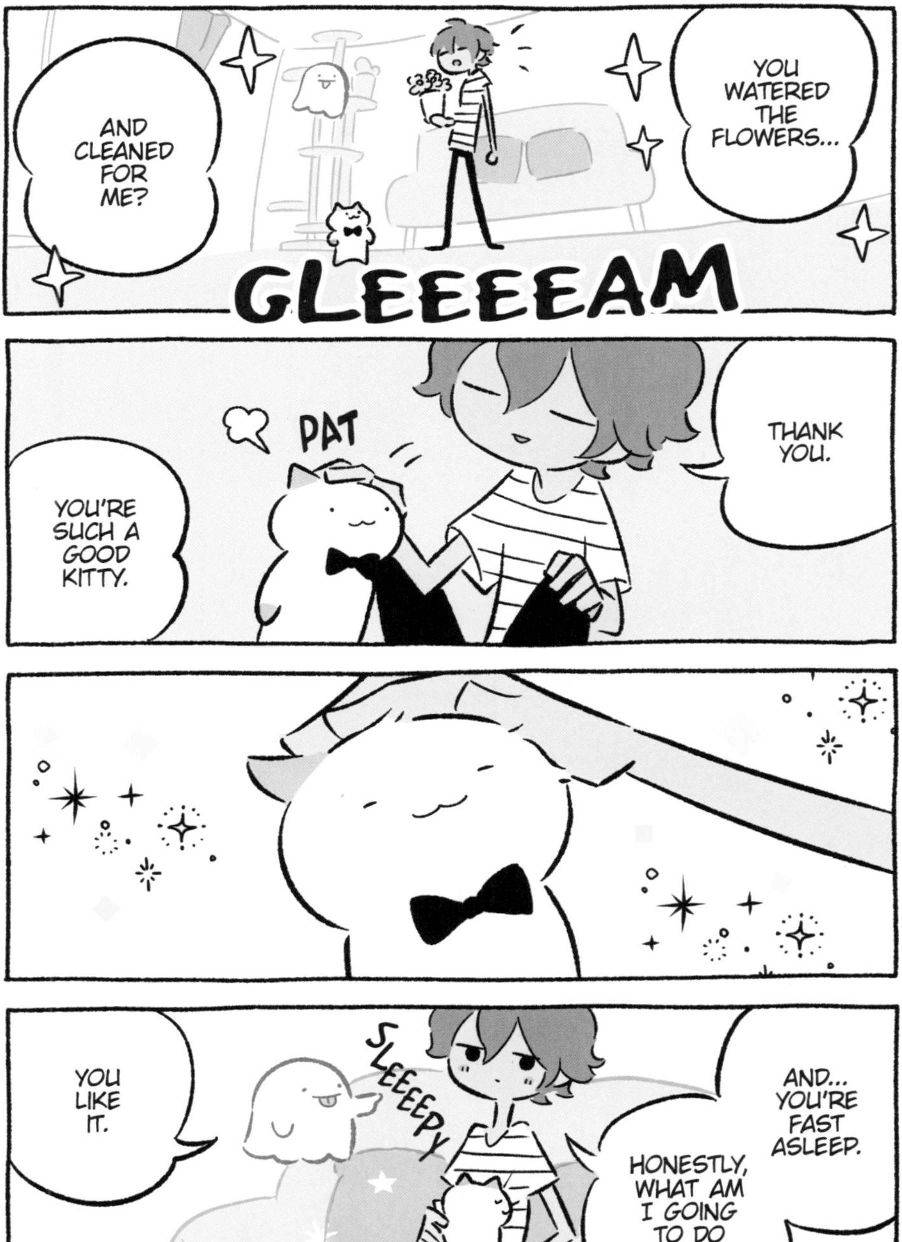
YOU WATERED THE FLOWERS...
AND CLEANED FOR ME?
GLEEEEAM
THANK YOU.
PAT
YOU'RE SUCH A GOOD KITTY.
AND... YOU'RE FAST ASLEEP.
HONESTLY, WHAT AM I GOING TO DO WITH YOU?
SLEEEEPY
YOU LIKE IT.

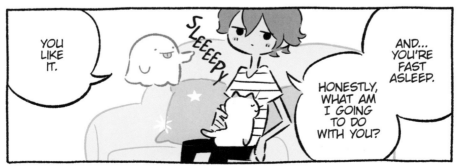

AGAIN SOMEDAY

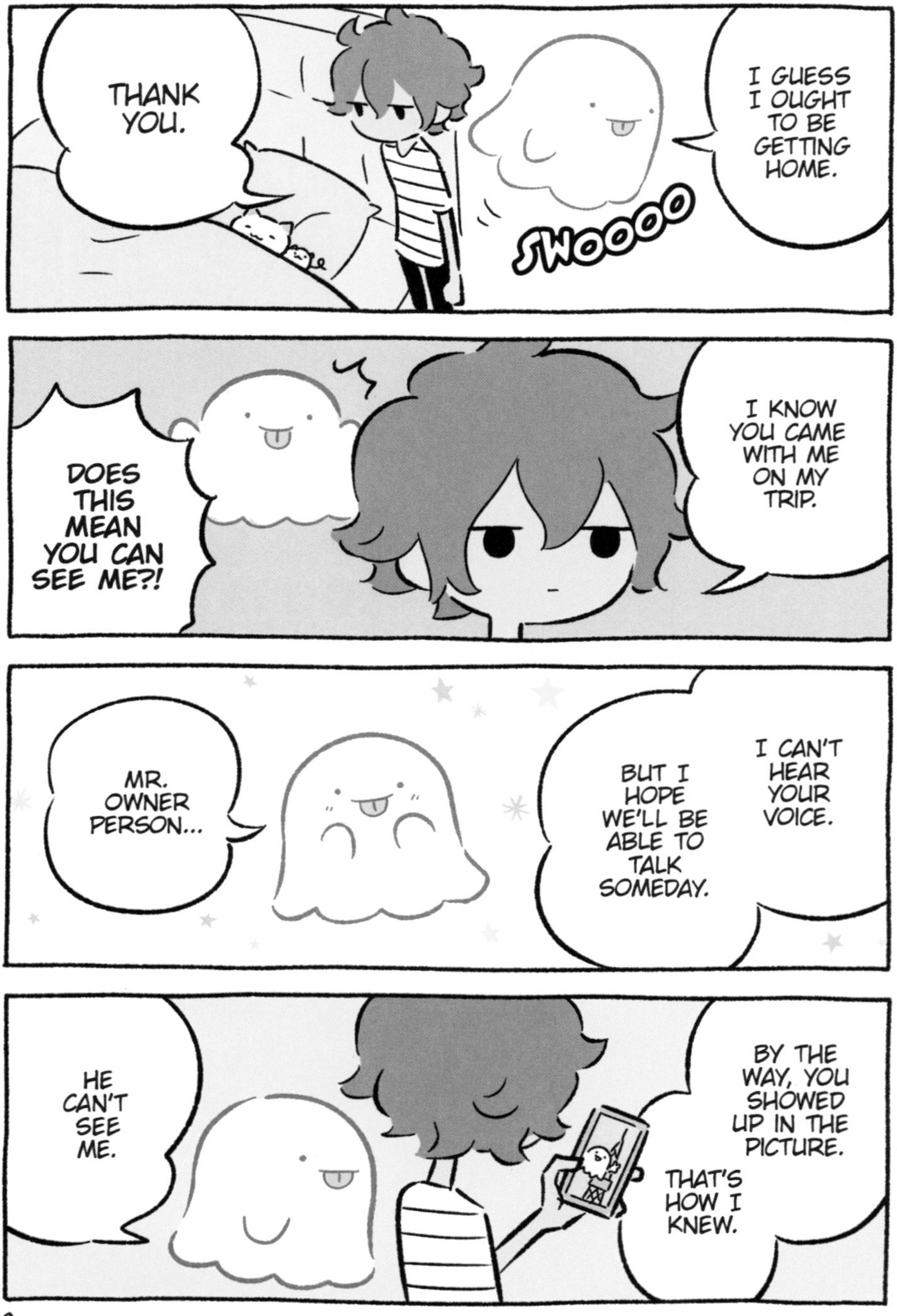
I GUESS I OUGHT TO BE GETTING HOME.
SWOOOO
THANK YOU.
I KNOW YOU CAME WITH ME ON MY TRIP.
DOES THIS MEAN YOU CAN SEE ME?!
I CAN'T HEAR YOUR VOICE.
BUT I HOPE WE'LL BE ABLE TO TALK SOMEDAY.
MR. OWNER PERSON...
BY THE WAY, YOU SHOWED UP IN THE PICTURE.
THAT'S HOW I KNEW.
HE CAN'T SEE ME.

OOSHIMA-SAN-STYLE EDUCATION

YOU'RE WORRIED ABOUT KYUU-CHAN WHILE YOU'RE GONE?
WANT ME TO TAKE CARE OF HIM?
THAT BIRD'S JUST WINGING IT.
HAHA!
HAHA!
JUST WHAT ARE YOU IMAGINING?
NO, THANK YOU.

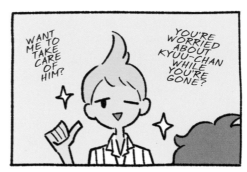

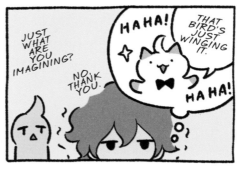

BUBBLE TEA

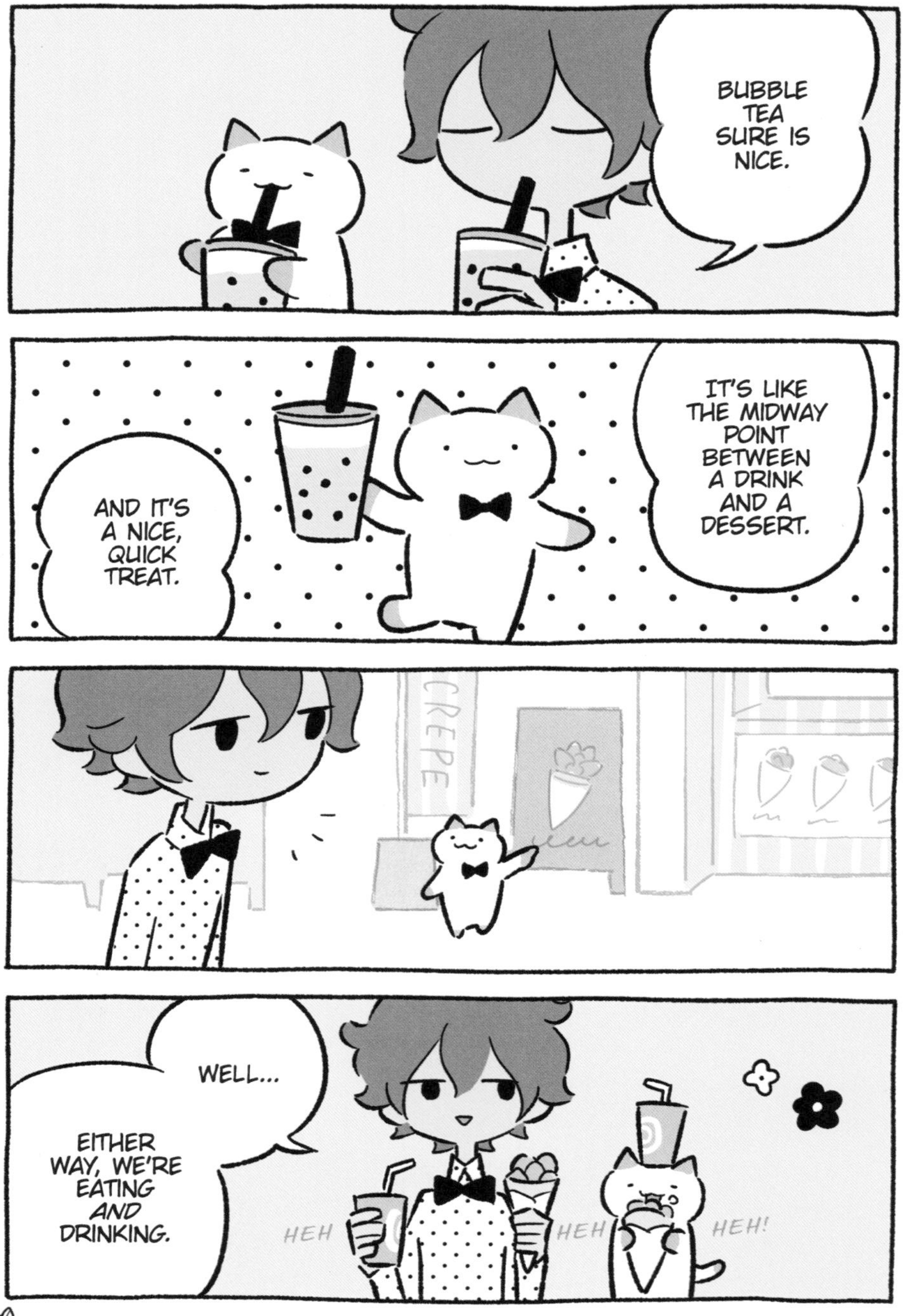
BUBBLE TEA SURE IS NICE.
IT'S LIKE THE MIDWAY POINT BETWEEN A DRINK AND A DESSERT.
AND IT'S A NICE, QUICK TREAT.
CREPE
WELL...
EITHER WAY, WE'RE EATING *AND* DRINKING.
HEH!
HEH
HEH

TURKISH ICE CREAM

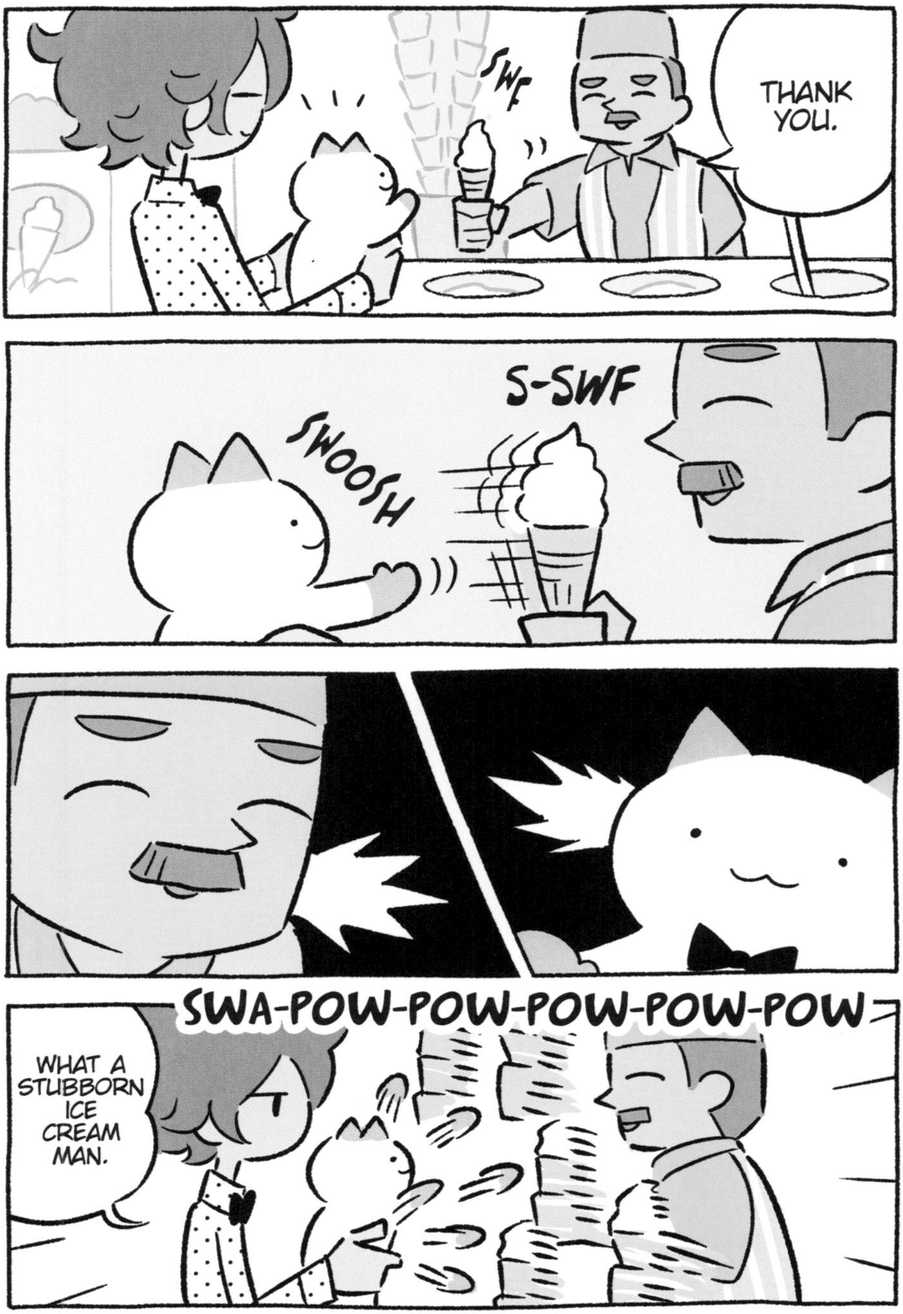
THANK YOU.
SWF
S-SWF
SWOOSH
SWA-POW-POW-POW-POW-POW
WHAT A STUBBORN ICE CREAM MAN.

DONUTS

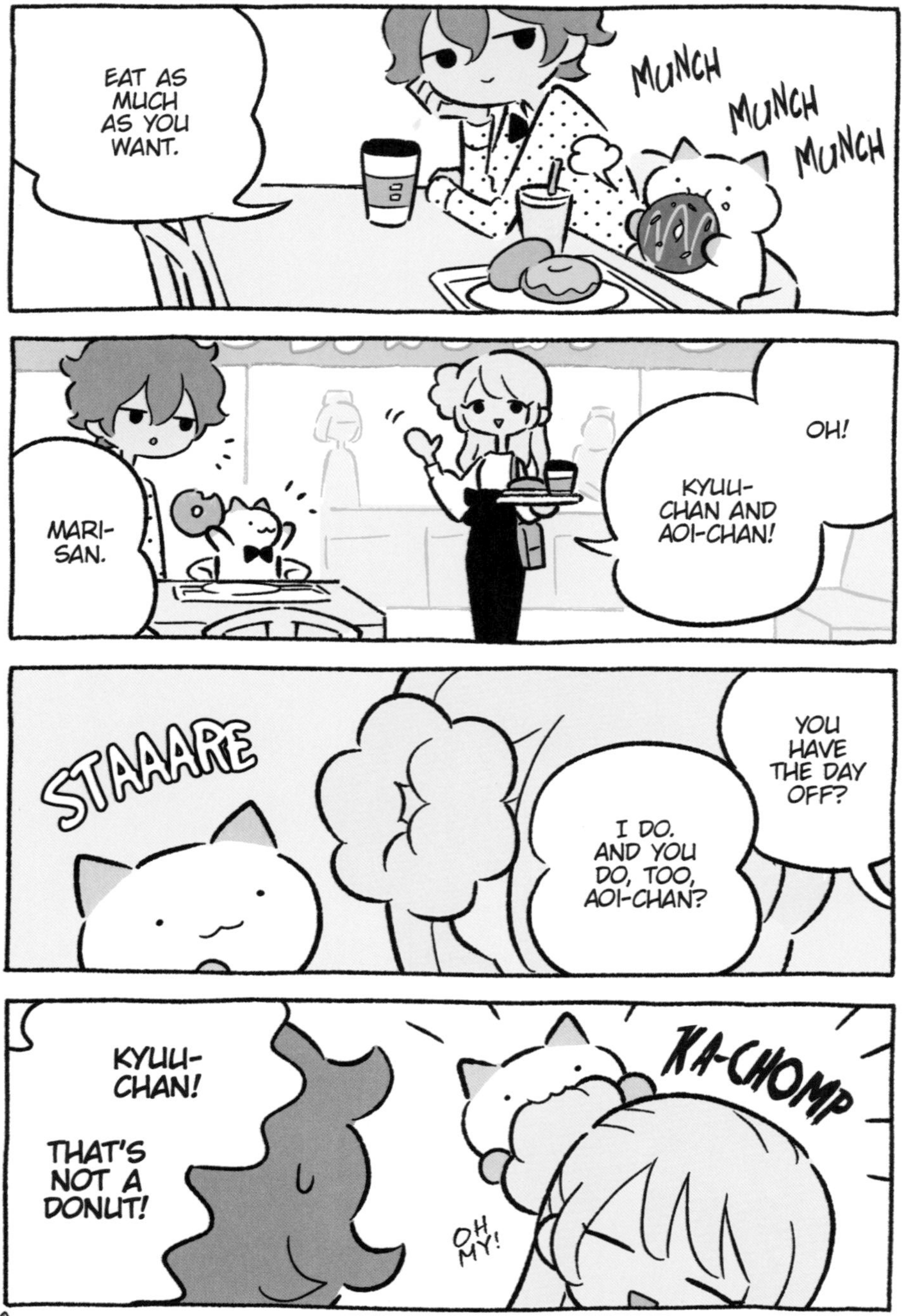
MUNCH
MUNCH
MUNCH
EAT AS MUCH AS YOU WANT.
OH!
KYUU-CHAN AND AOI-CHAN!
MARI-SAN.
YOU HAVE THE DAY OFF?
I DO. AND YOU DO, TOO, AOI-CHAN?
STAAARE
KA-CHOMP
OH MY!
KYUU-CHAN!
THAT'S NOT A DONUT!

HOW IT STARTED

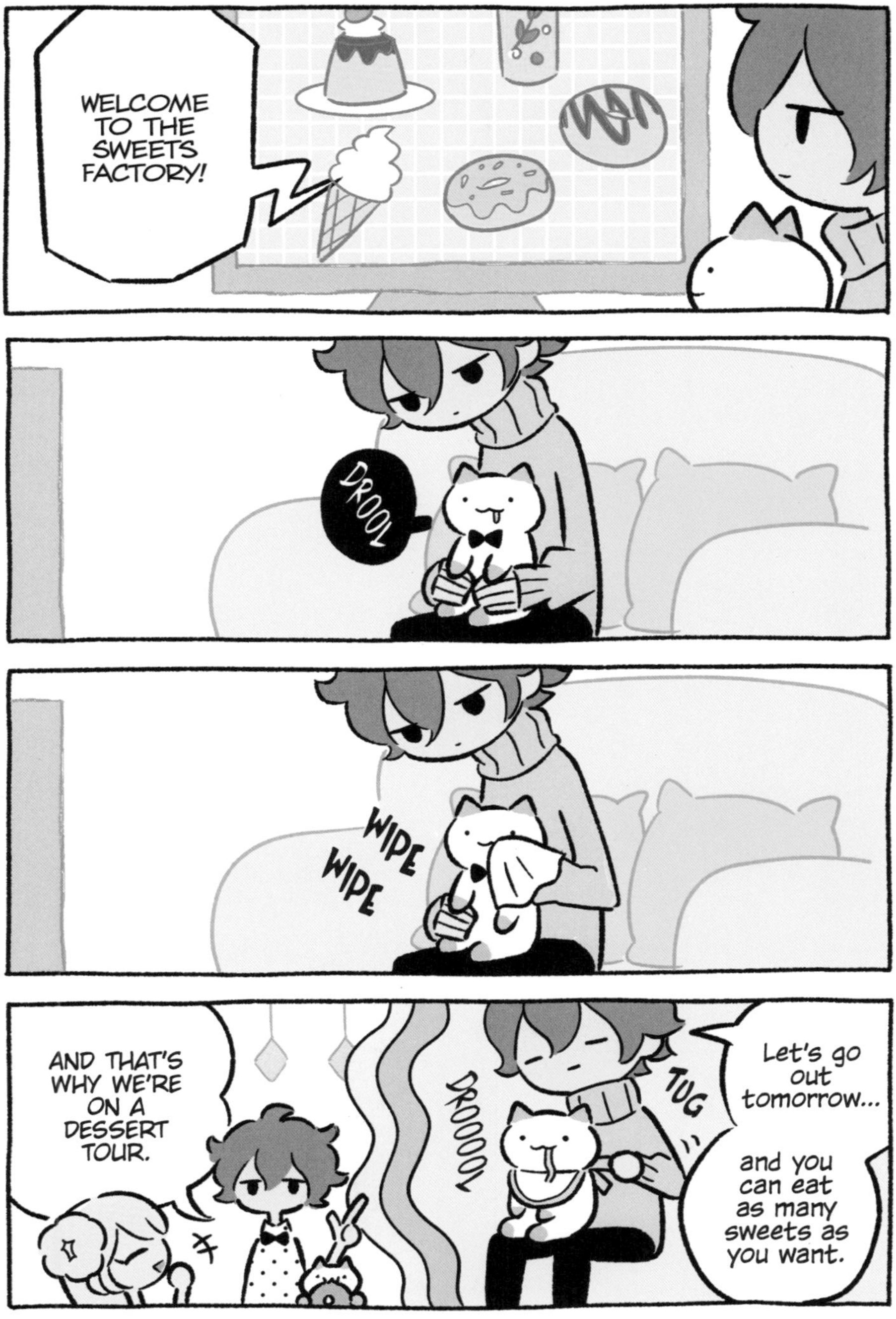

WELCOME TO THE SWEETS FACTORY!
DROOL
WIPE WIPE
Let's go out tomorrow...
and you can eat as many sweets as you want.
TUG
DROOOOOL
AND THAT'S WHY WE'RE ON A DESSERT TOUR.

COLLECTING INFORMATION

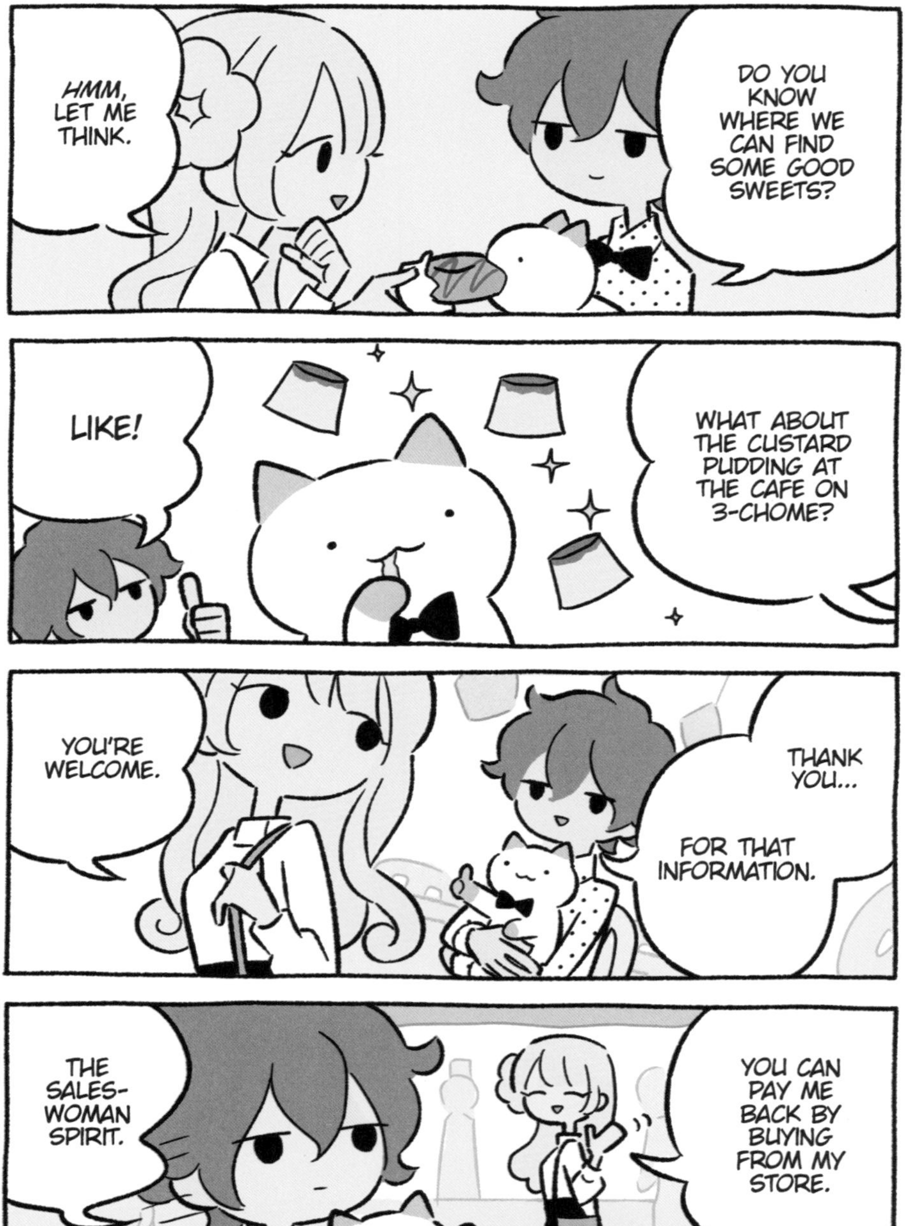
DO YOU KNOW WHERE WE CAN FIND SOME GOOD SWEETS?
HMM, LET ME THINK.
WHAT ABOUT THE CUSTARD PUDDING AT THE CAFE ON 3-CHOME?
LIKE!
THANK YOU...
FOR THAT INFORMATION.
YOU'RE WELCOME.
YOU CAN PAY ME BACK BY BUYING FROM MY STORE.
THE SALES-WOMAN SPIRIT.

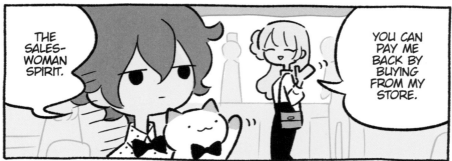

SOLID FLAN

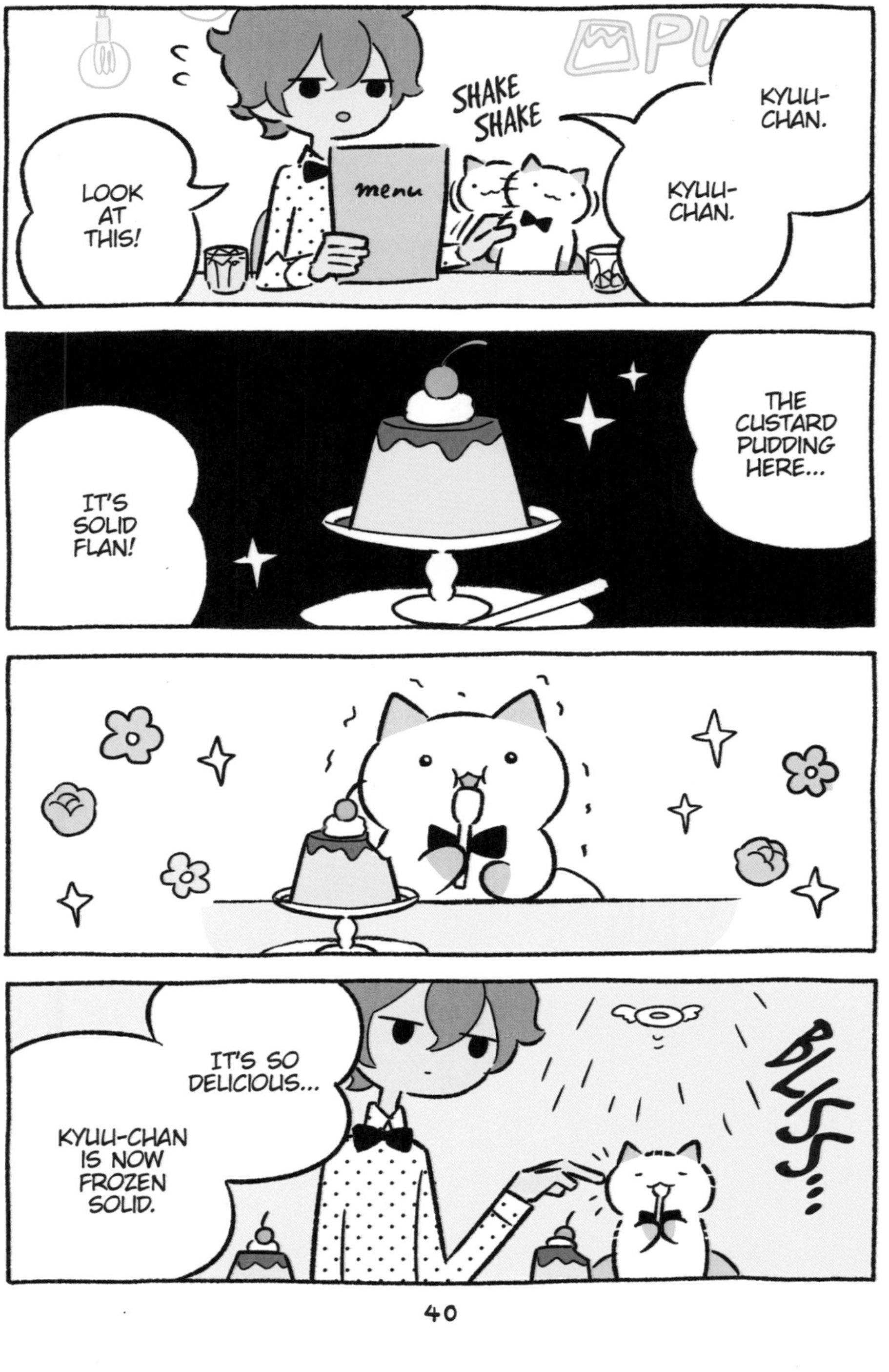
KYUU-CHAN.
KYUU-CHAN.
SHAKE SHAKE
LOOK AT THIS!
THE CUSTARD PUDDING HERE...
IT'S SOLID FLAN!
BLISS...
IT'S SO DELICIOUS...
KYUU-CHAN IS NOW FROZEN SOLID.

COLLECTING INFORMATION: CONTINUED

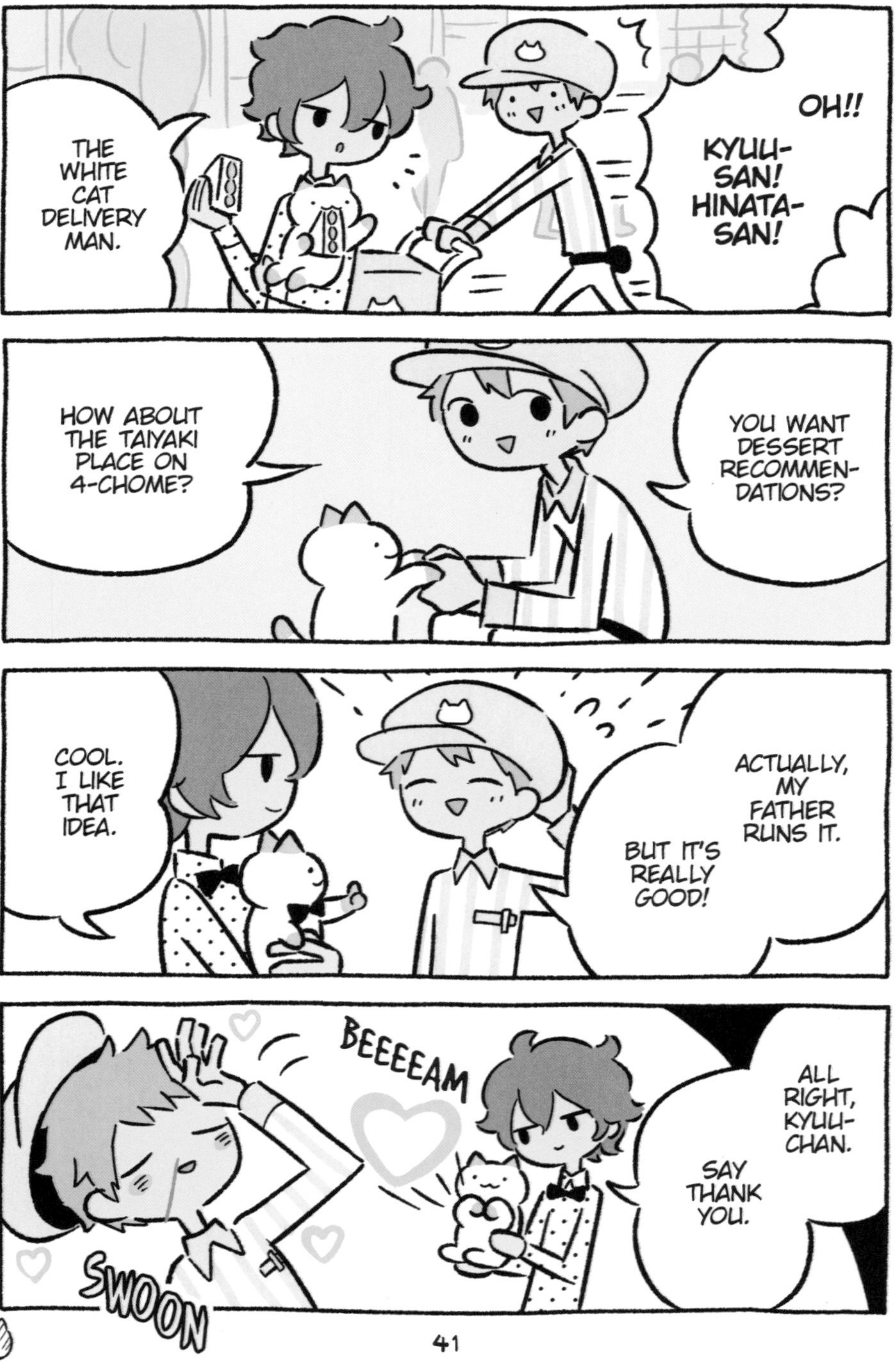
OH!!
KYUU-SAN! HINATA-SAN!
THE WHITE CAT DELIVERY MAN.
YOU WANT DESSERT RECOMMENDATIONS?
HOW ABOUT THE TAIYAKI PLACE ON 4-CHOME?
ACTUALLY, MY FATHER RUNS IT.
BUT IT'S REALLY GOOD!
COOL. I LIKE THAT IDEA.
ALL RIGHT, KYUU-CHAN.
SAY THANK YOU.
BEEEEEAM
SWOON

TAIYAKI

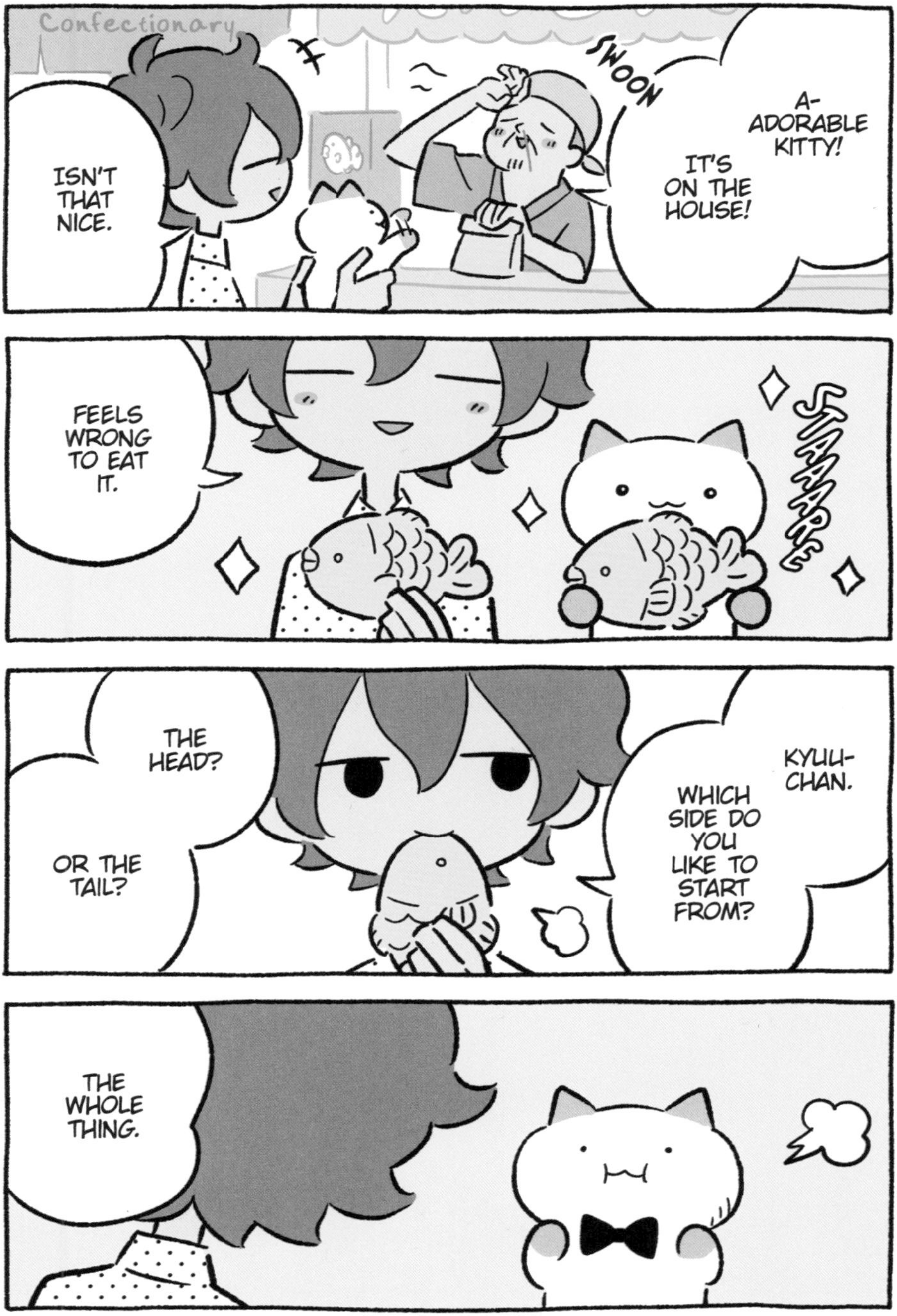

A-ADORABLE KITTY!
IT'S ON THE HOUSE!
SWOON
Confectionary
ISN'T THAT NICE.
STAAAARE
FEELS WRONG TO EAT IT.
KYUU-CHAN.
WHICH SIDE DO YOU LIKE TO START FROM?
THE HEAD?
OR THE TAIL?
THE WHOLE THING.

SOUVENIRS

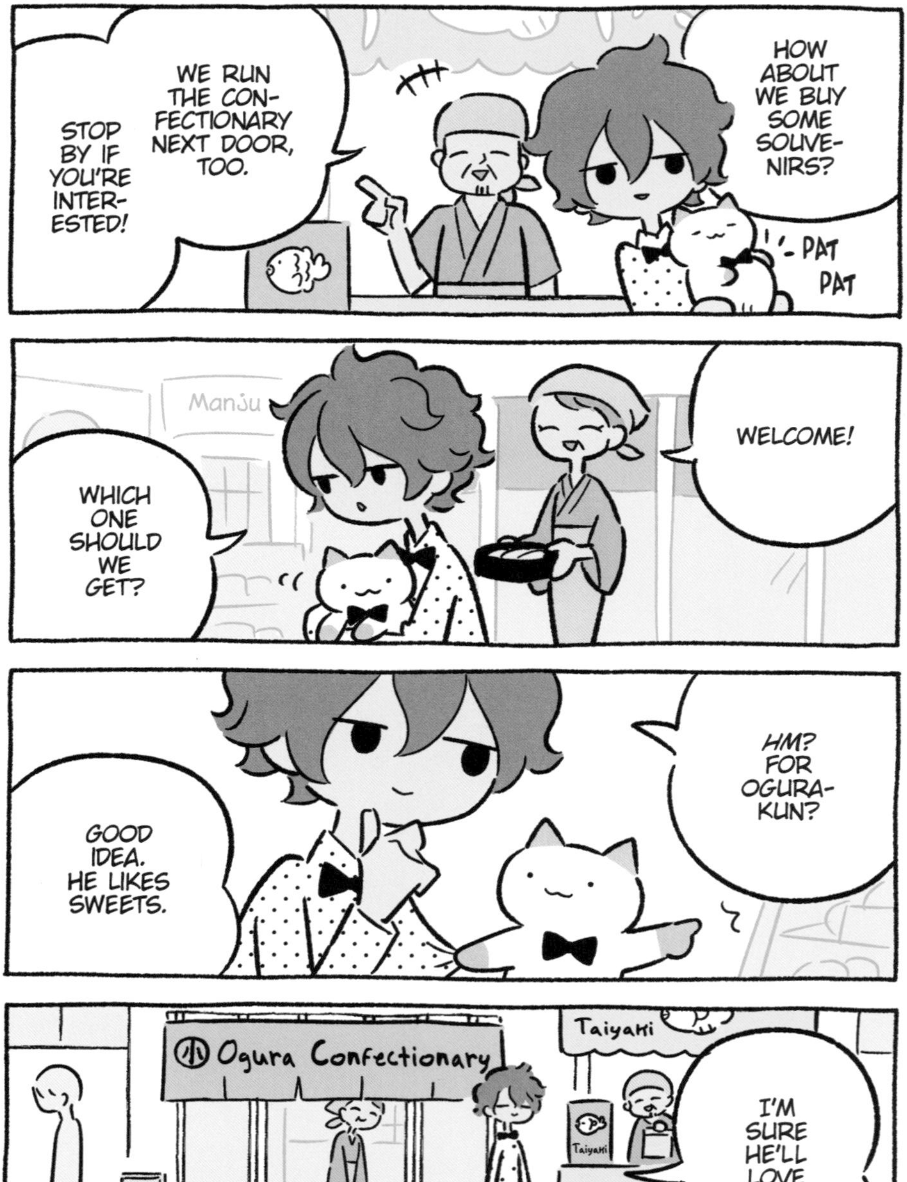
HOW ABOUT WE BUY SOME SOUVE-NIRS?
PAT PAT
WE RUN THE CON-FECTIONARY NEXT DOOR, TOO.
STOP BY IF YOU'RE INTER-ESTED!
WELCOME!
Manju
WHICH ONE SHOULD WE GET?
HM? FOR OGURA-KUN?
GOOD IDEA. HE LIKES SWEETS.
Taiyaki
I'M SURE HE'LL LOVE IT.
Taiyaki
Ogura Confectionary
Ogura

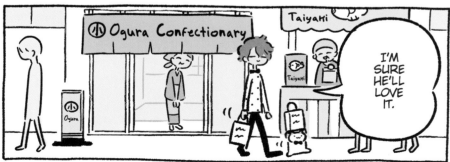

SHARING

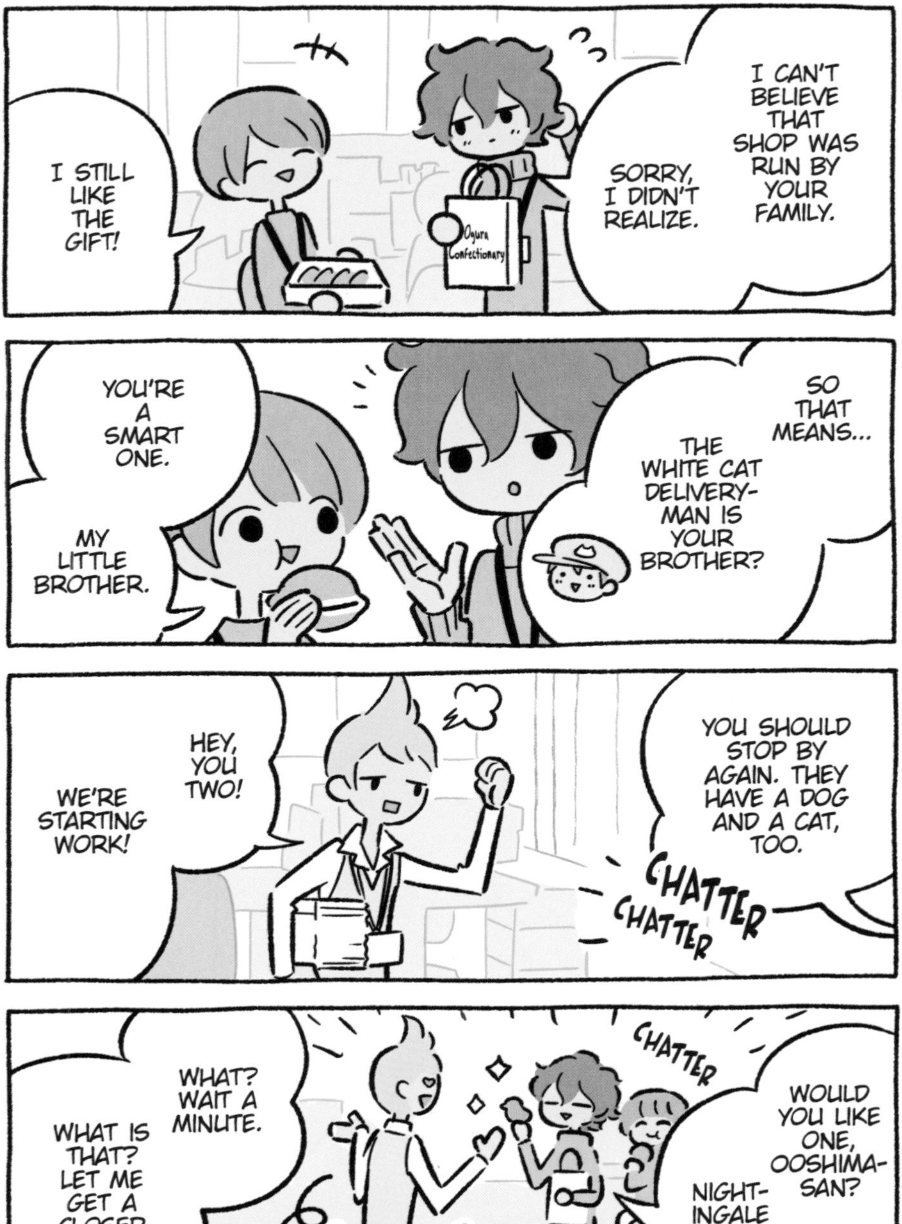
I CAN'T BELIEVE THAT SHOP WAS RUN BY YOUR FAMILY.
SORRY, I DIDN'T REALIZE.
Ogura Confectionary
I STILL LIKE THE GIFT!
SO THAT MEANS...
THE WHITE CAT DELIVERY-MAN IS YOUR BROTHER?
YOU'RE A SMART ONE.
MY LITTLE BROTHER.
YOU SHOULD STOP BY AGAIN. THEY HAVE A DOG AND A CAT, TOO.
CHATTER
CHATTER
HEY, YOU TWO!
WE'RE STARTING WORK!
CHATTER
WOULD YOU LIKE ONE, OOSHIMA-SAN?
NIGHT-INGALE MANJU.
WHAT? WAIT A MINUTE.
CHATTER
TOSS
WHAT IS THAT? LET ME GET A CLOSER LOOK!

ESPECIALLY FOR KYUU-CHAN

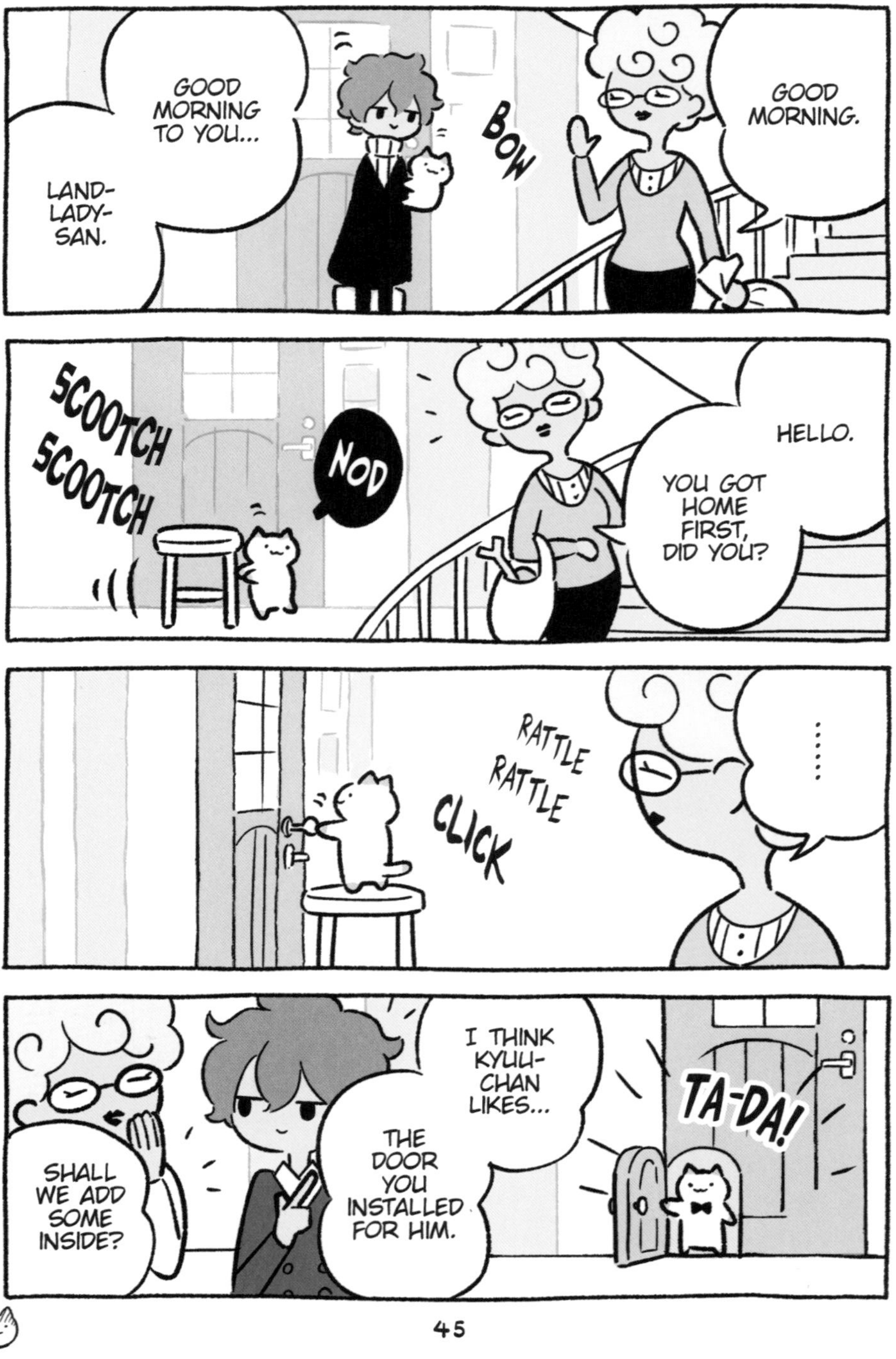
GOOD MORNING.
BOW
GOOD MORNING TO YOU... LAND-LADY-SAN.
HELLO. YOU GOT HOME FIRST, DID YOU?
NOD
SCOOTCH SCOOTCH
......
RATTLE RATTLE
CLICK
TA-DA!
I THINK KYUU-CHAN LIKES... THE DOOR YOU INSTALLED FOR HIM.
SHALL WE ADD SOME INSIDE?

RAMEN

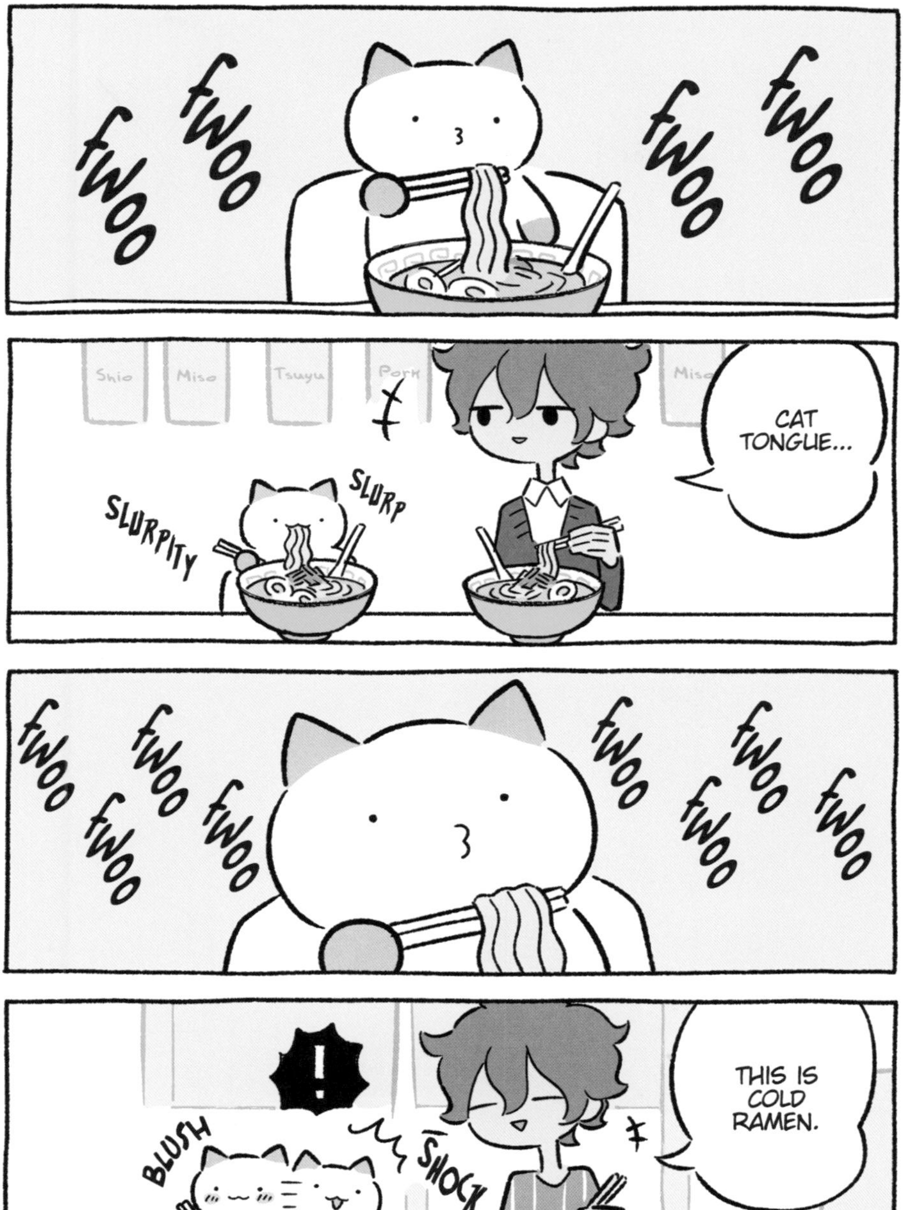
FWOO
FWOO
FWOO
FWOO
Shio
Miso
Tsuyu
Pork
Miso
CAT TONGUE...
SLURP
SLURPITY
FWOO
FWOO
FWOO
FWOO
FWOO
FWOO
FWOO
THIS IS COLD RAMEN.
!
SHOCK
BLUSH

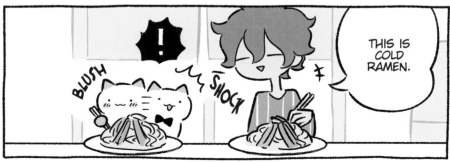

CURRY

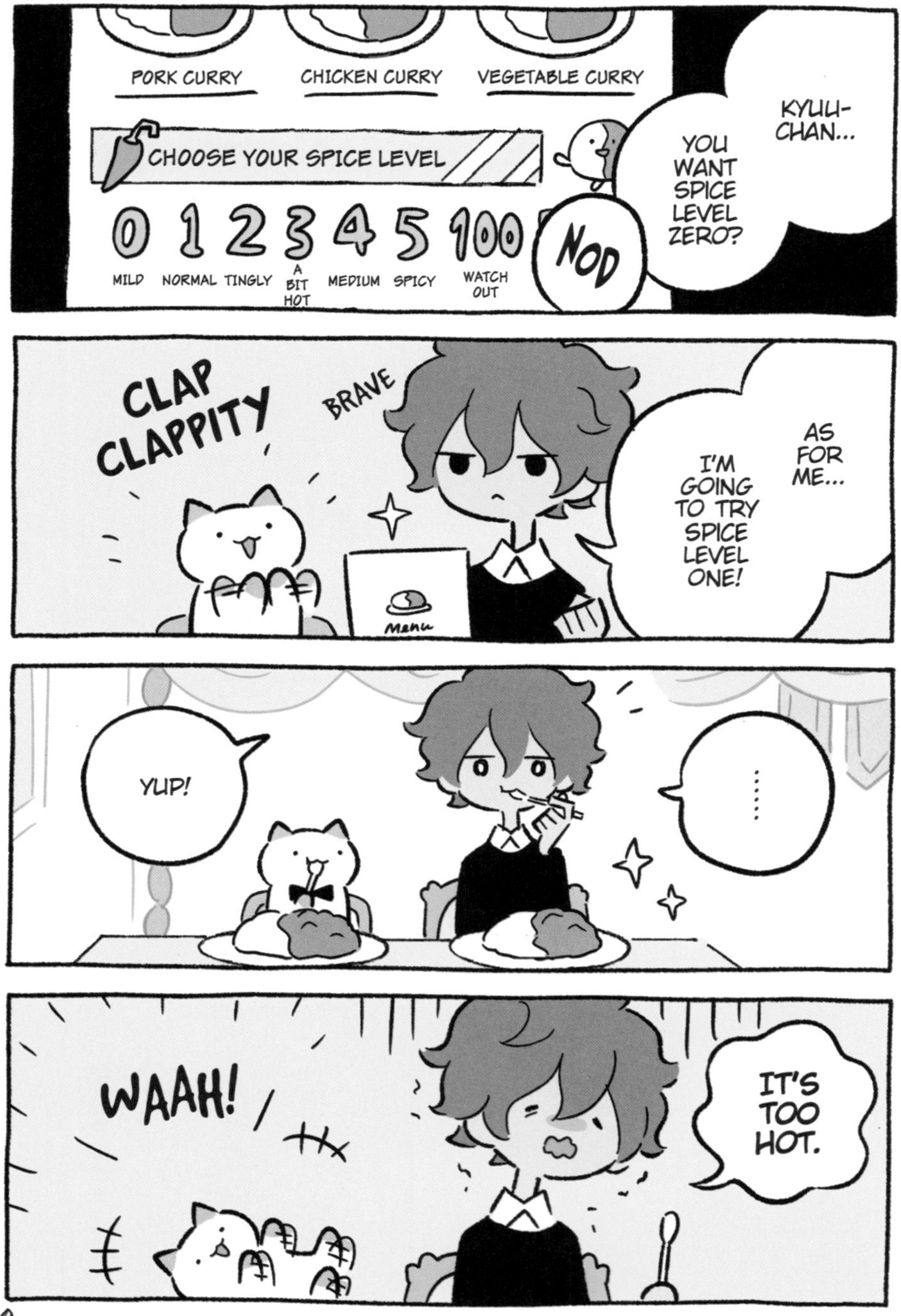

KYUU-CHAN...
YOU WANT SPICE LEVEL ZERO?
NOD
PORK CURRY
CHICKEN CURRY
VEGETABLE CURRY
CHOOSE YOUR SPICE LEVEL
0 MILD
1 NORMAL
2 TINGLY
3 A BIT HOT
4 MEDIUM
5 SPICY
100 WATCH OUT
AS FOR ME...
I'M GOING TO TRY SPICE LEVEL ONE!
BRAVE
CLAP CLAPPITY
Menu
......
YUP!
IT'S TOO HOT.
WAAH!

WELCOME

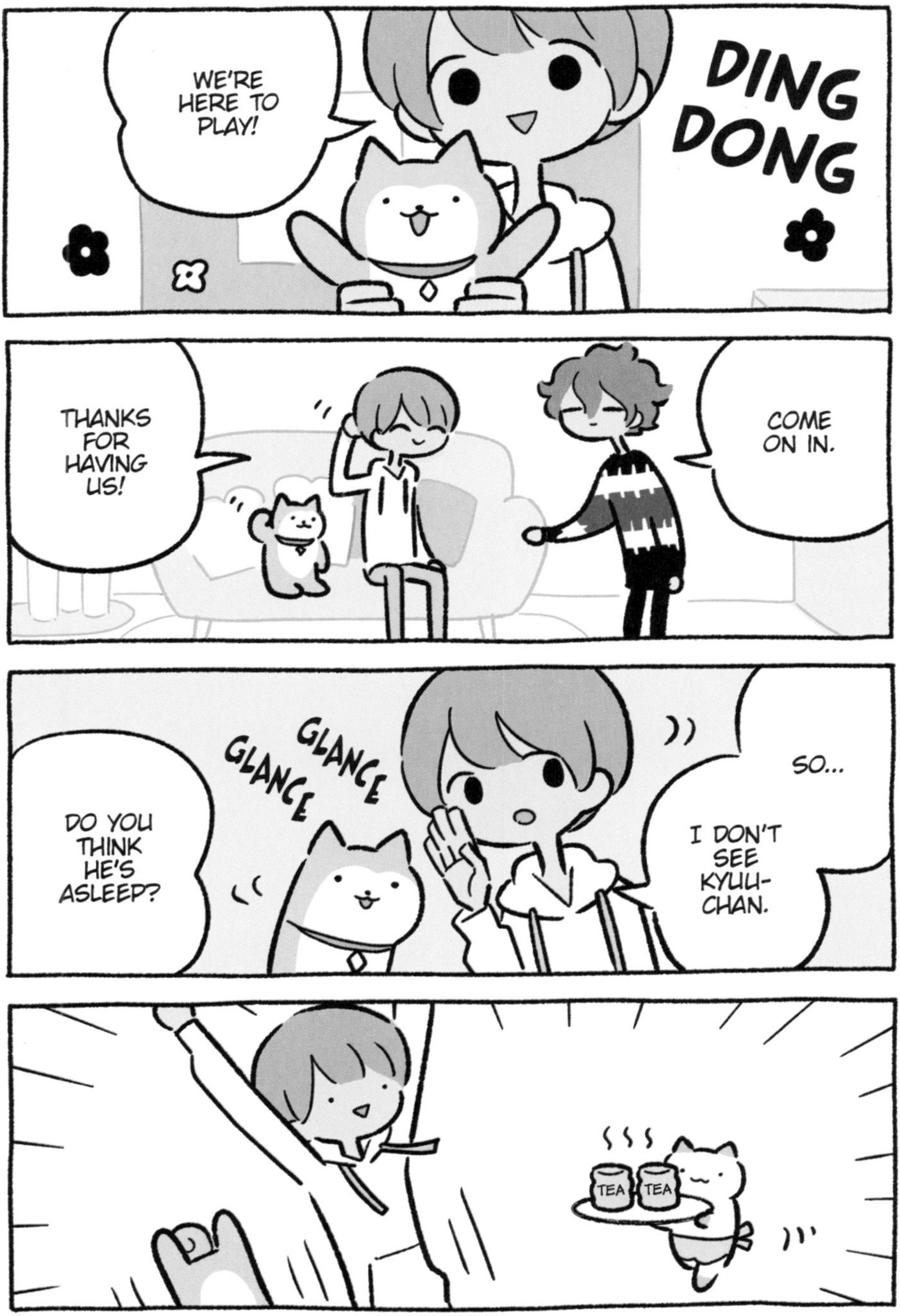

DING DONG
WE'RE HERE TO PLAY!
COME ON IN.
THANKS FOR HAVING US!
SO...
I DON'T SEE KYUU-CHAN.
GLANCE GLANCE
DO YOU THINK HE'S ASLEEP?
TEA
TEA

EXTRA SPECIAL

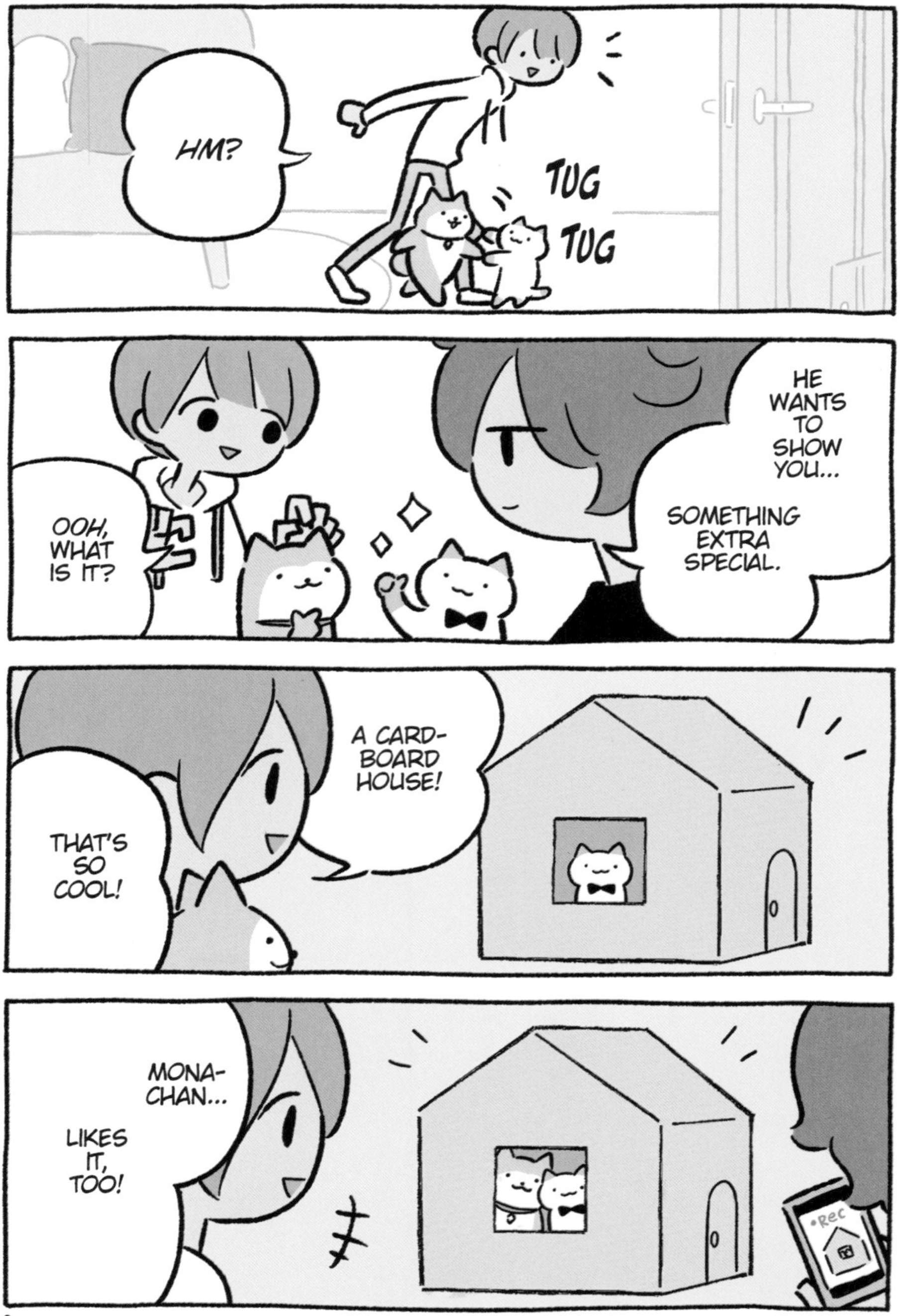

TUG
TUG
HM?
HE WANTS TO SHOW YOU...
SOMETHING EXTRA SPECIAL.
OOH, WHAT IS IT?
A CARD-BOARD HOUSE!
THAT'S SO COOL!
MONA-CHAN...
LIKES IT, TOO!
Rec

FOR YOU

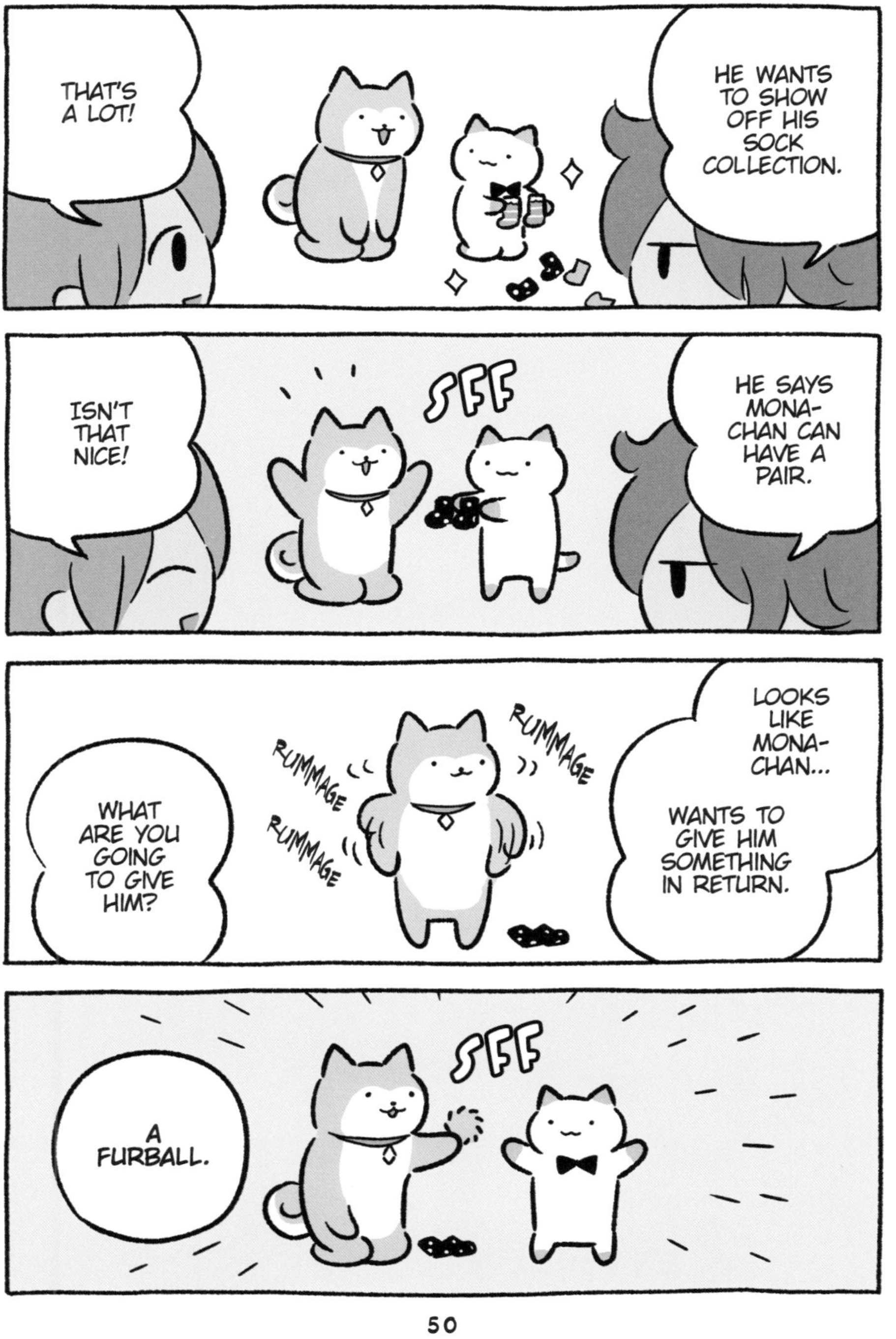

HE WANTS TO SHOW OFF HIS SOCK COLLECTION.
THAT'S A LOT!
HE SAYS MONA-CHAN CAN HAVE A PAIR.
SFF
ISN'T THAT NICE!
LOOKS LIKE MONA-CHAN...
RUMMAGE
WANTS TO GIVE HIM SOMETHING IN RETURN.
RUMMAGE
RUMMAGE
WHAT ARE YOU GOING TO GIVE HIM?
SFF
A FURBALL.

MEETING THE FAMILY

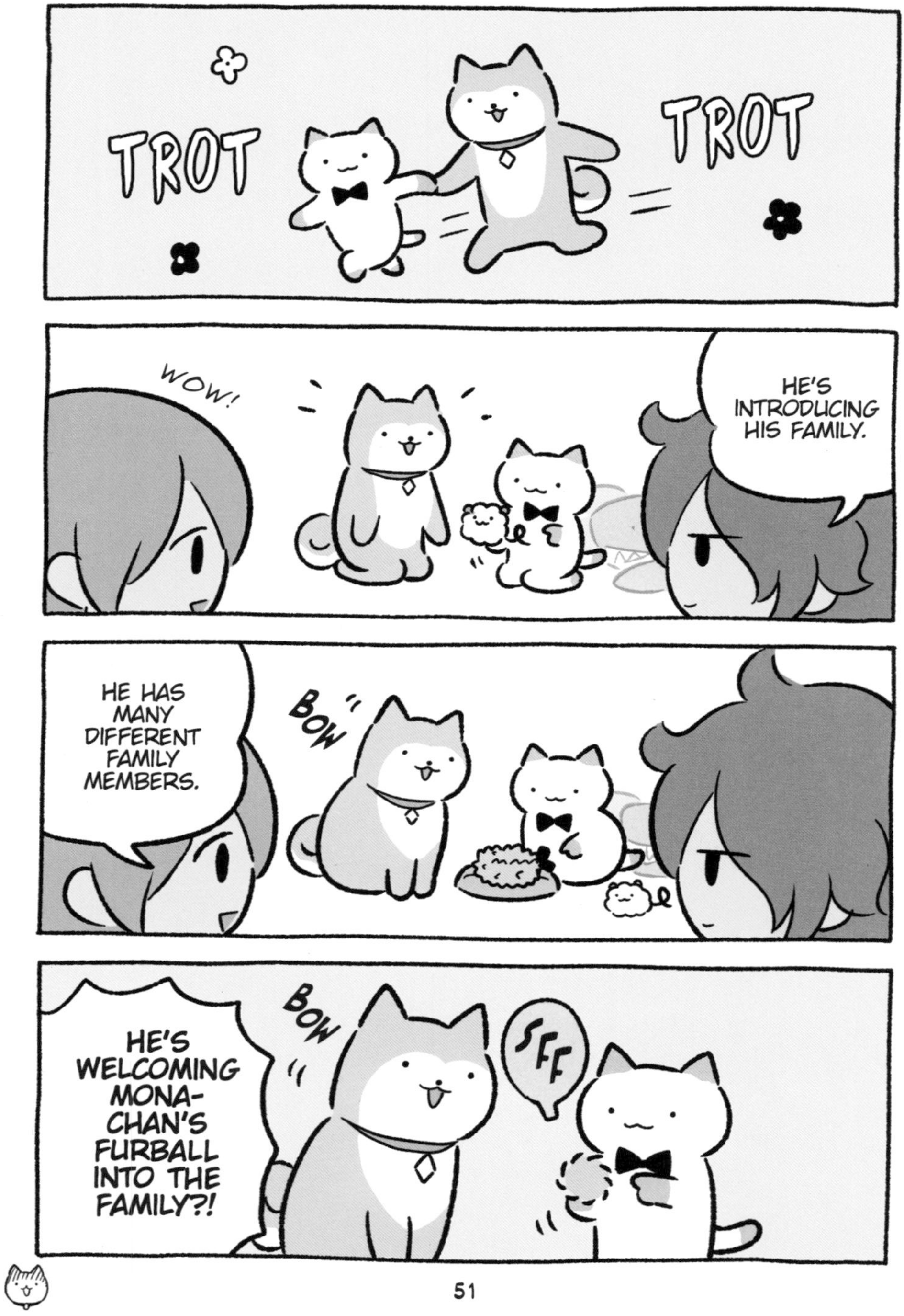
TROT
TROT
HE'S INTRODUCING HIS FAMILY.
WOW!
BOW
HE HAS MANY DIFFERENT FAMILY MEMBERS.
SFF
BOW
HE'S WELCOMING MONA-CHAN'S FURBALL INTO THE FAMILY?!

DINNERTIME

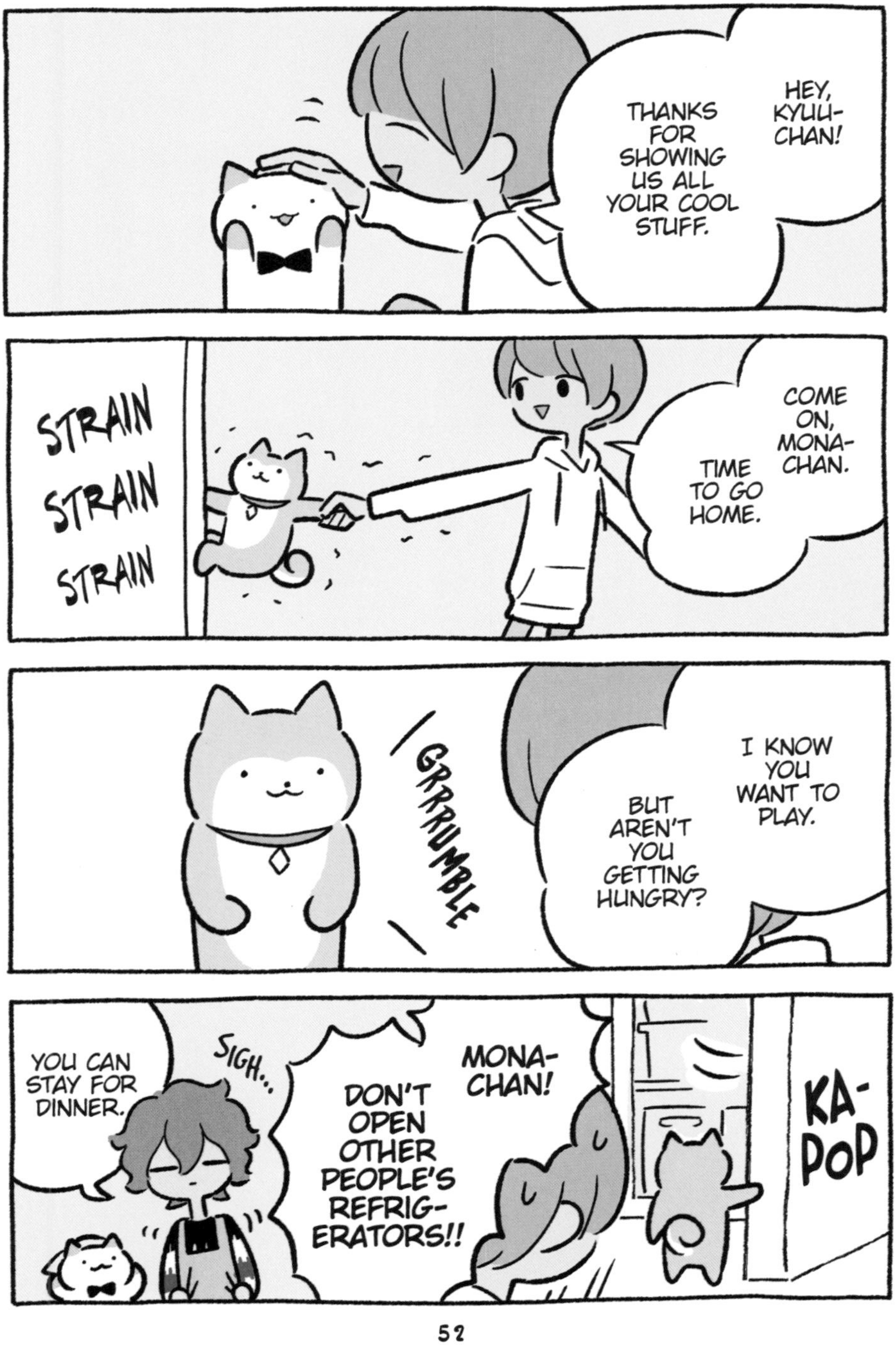
HEY, KYUU-CHAN!
THANKS FOR SHOWING US ALL YOUR COOL STUFF.
COME ON, MONA-CHAN.
TIME TO GO HOME.
STRAIN STRAIN STRAIN
I KNOW YOU WANT TO PLAY.
BUT AREN'T YOU GETTING HUNGRY?
GRRRUMBLE
KA-POP
MONA-CHAN!
DON'T OPEN OTHER PEOPLE'S REFRIGERATORS!!
SIGH...
YOU CAN STAY FOR DINNER.

TREASURE

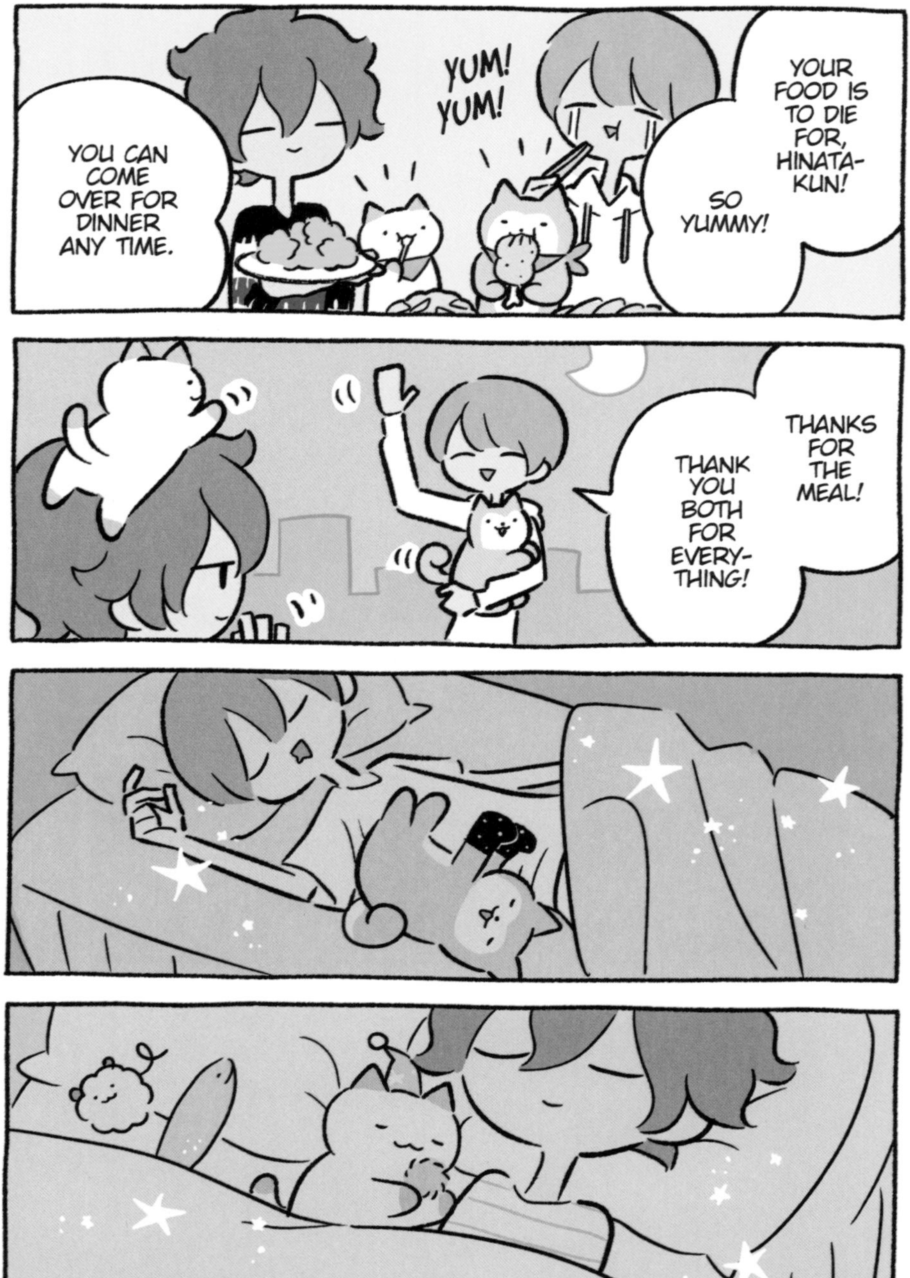
YOUR FOOD IS TO DIE FOR, HINATA-KUN!
SO YUMMY!
YUM! YUM!
YOU CAN COME OVER FOR DINNER ANY TIME.
THANKS FOR THE MEAL!
THANK YOU BOTH FOR EVERYTHING!

CHEESE TEA

THIS IS GOOD, HUH?
SLURRRP
GULP
GULP
Cheese
TMP
PAPA?
Cheese

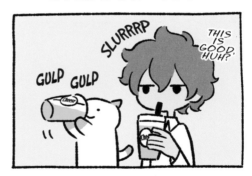

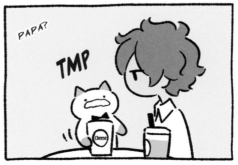

THE BUN SWITCH

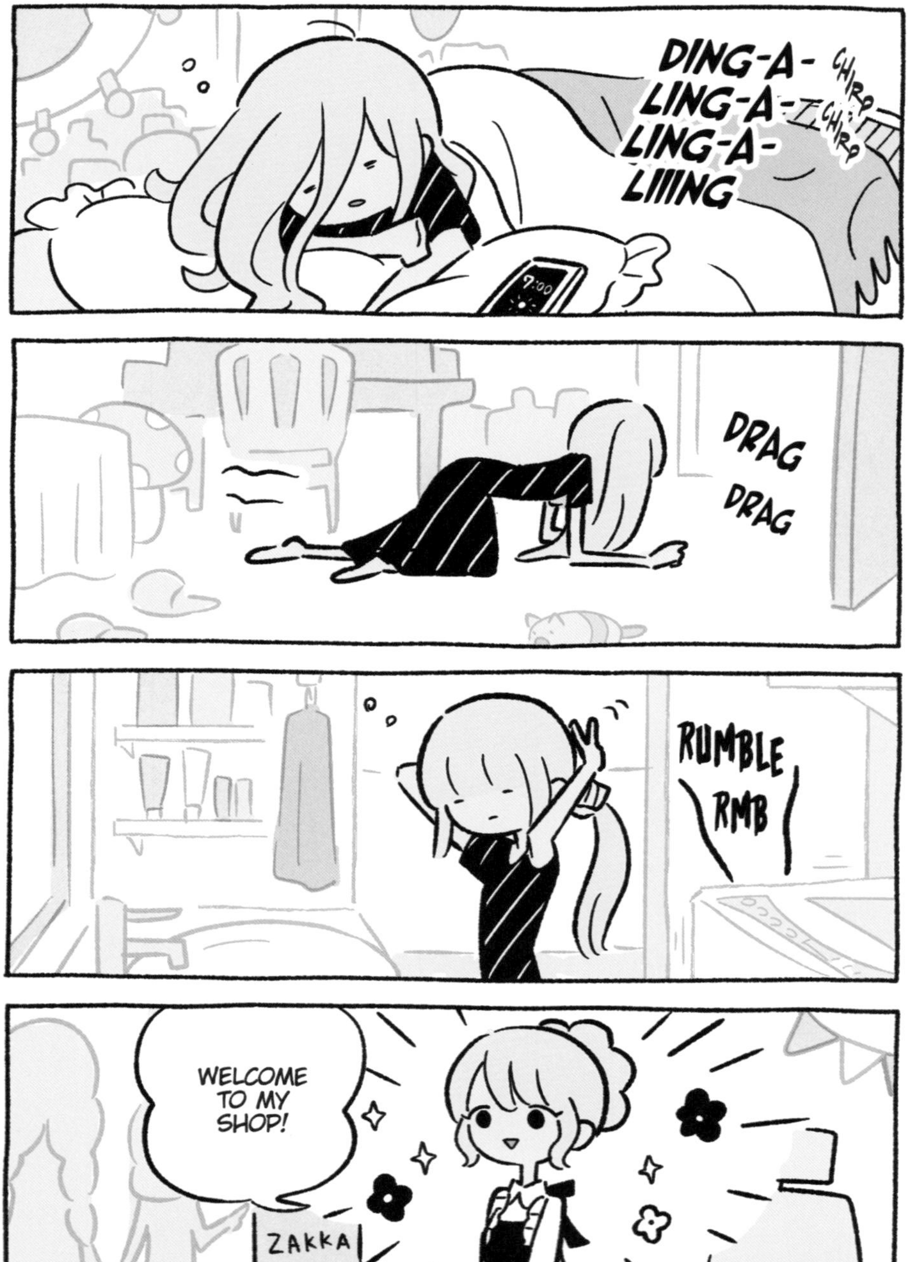
DING-A-LING-A-LING-A-LIIING
CHIRP CHIRP
DRAG DRAG
RUMBLE RMB
WELCOME TO MY SHOP!
ZAKKA

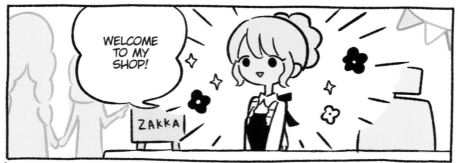

BAG

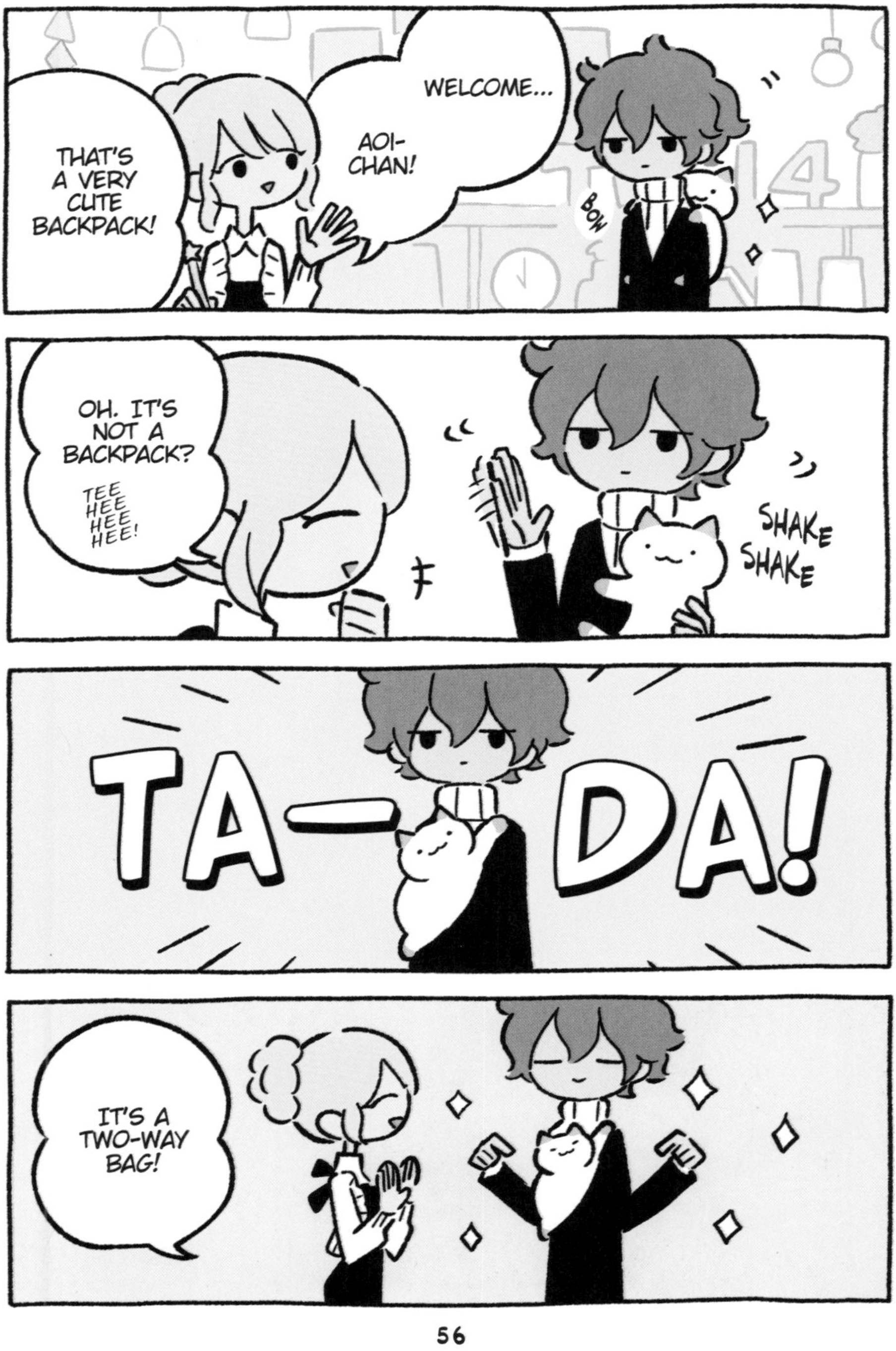
WELCOME... AOI-CHAN!
BOW
THAT'S A VERY CUTE BACKPACK!
SHAKE SHAKE
OH. IT'S NOT A BACKPACK?
TEE HEE HEE HEE!
TA-DA!
IT'S A TWO-WAY BAG!

THE TETRA FAMILY

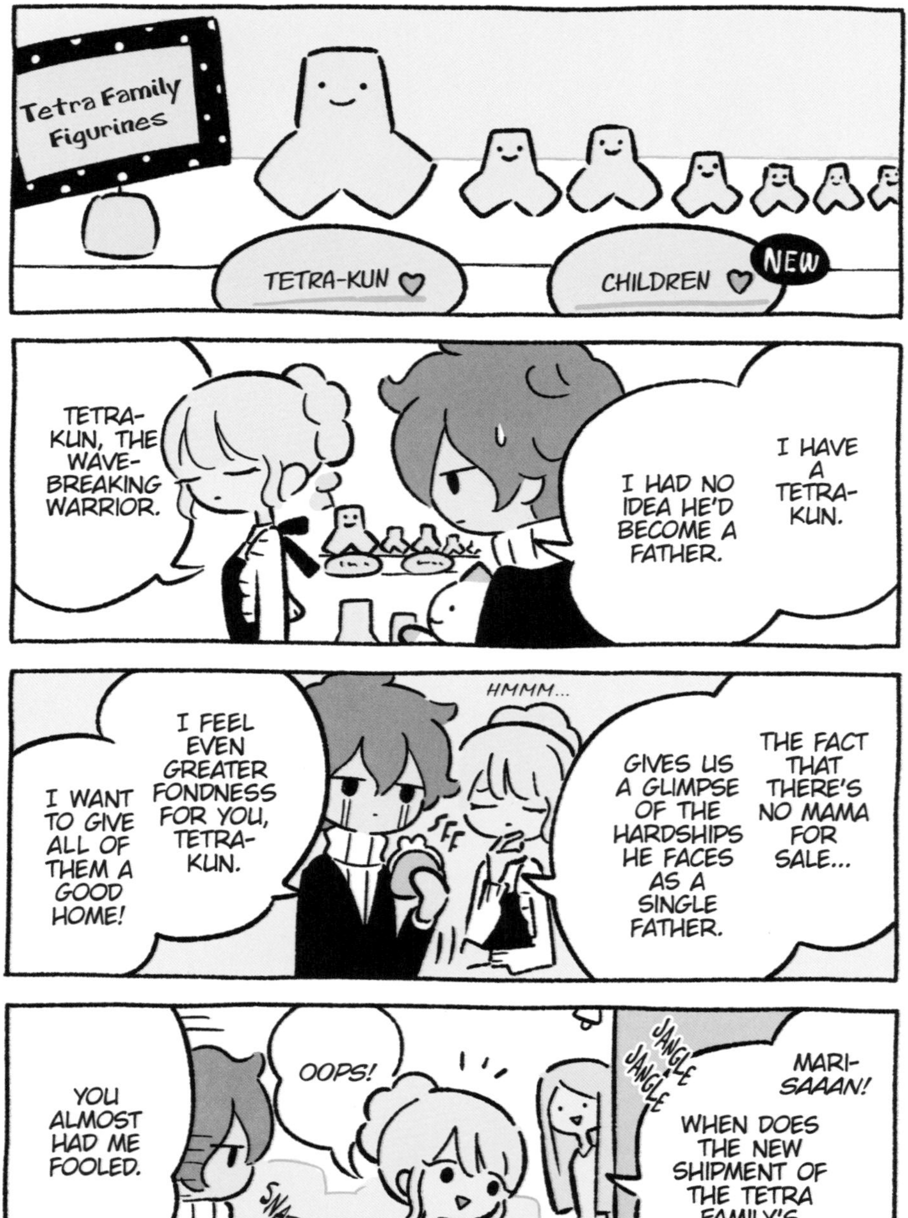
NEW
CHILDREN
TETRA-KUN
Tetra Family Figurines
I HAVE A TETRA-KUN.
I HAD NO IDEA HE'D BECOME A FATHER.
TETRA-KUN, THE WAVE-BREAKING WARRIOR.
HMMM...
THE FACT THAT THERE'S NO MAMA FOR SALE...
GIVES US A GLIMPSE OF THE HARDSHIPS HE FACES AS A SINGLE FATHER.
I FEEL EVEN GREATER FONDNESS FOR YOU, TETRA-KUN.
I WANT TO GIVE ALL OF THEM A GOOD HOME!
JANGLE JANGLE
MARI-SAAAN!
WHEN DOES THE NEW SHIPMENT OF THE TETRA FAMILY'S MAMA ARRIVE?
OOPS!
SNATCH
YOU ALMOST HAD ME FOOLED.

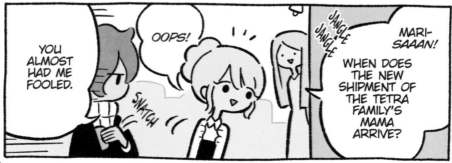

BIG SOFTY

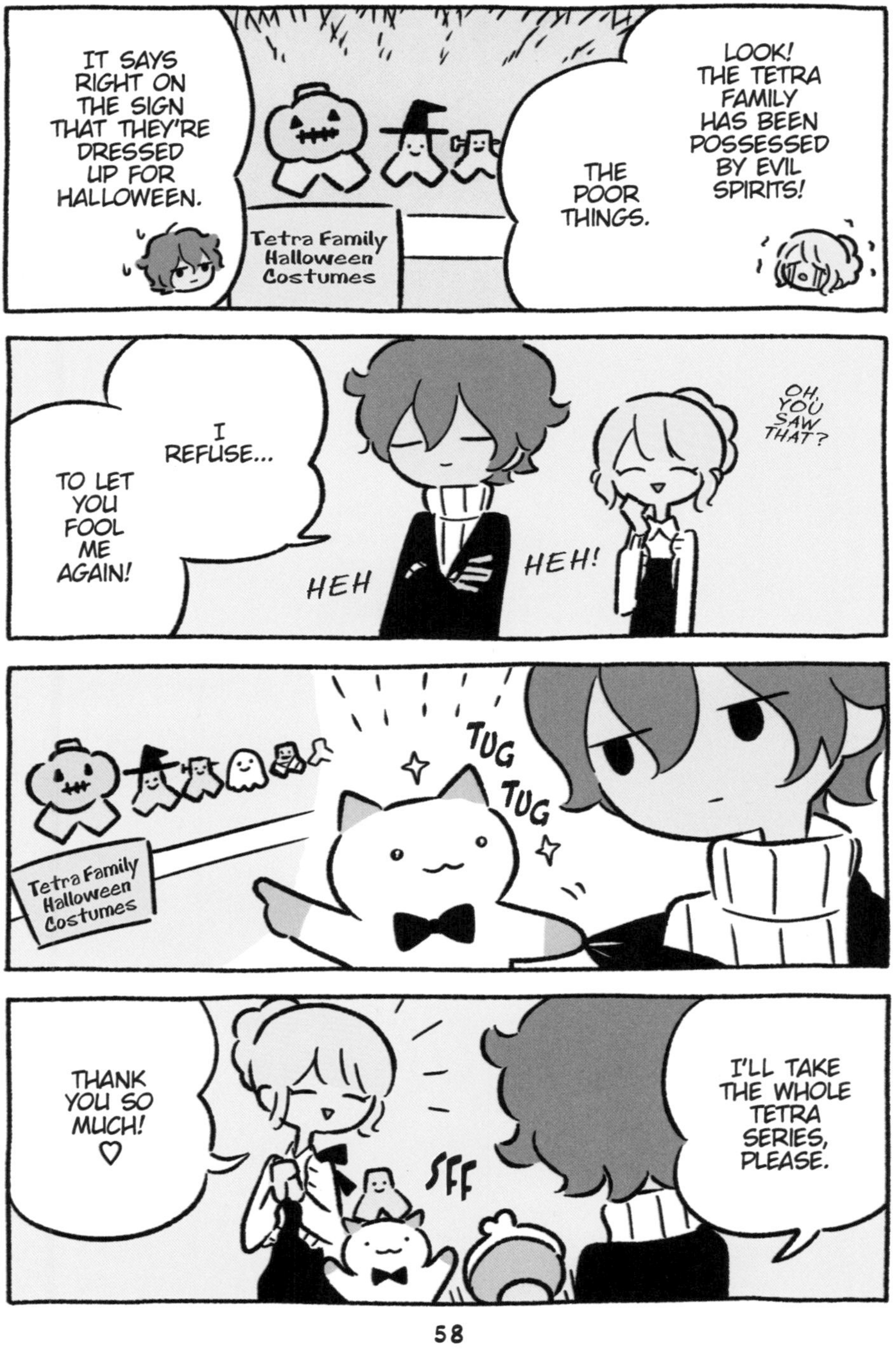
LOOK! THE TETRA FAMILY HAS BEEN POSSESSED BY EVIL SPIRITS!
THE POOR THINGS.
Tetra Family Halloween Costumes
IT SAYS RIGHT ON THE SIGN THAT THEY'RE DRESSED UP FOR HALLOWEEN.
OH, YOU SAW THAT?
HEH!
HEH
I REFUSE...
TO LET YOU FOOL ME AGAIN!
TUG TUG
Tetra Family Halloween Costumes
I'LL TAKE THE WHOLE TETRA SERIES, PLEASE.
SFF
THANK YOU SO MUCH! ♡

CUTE POSE

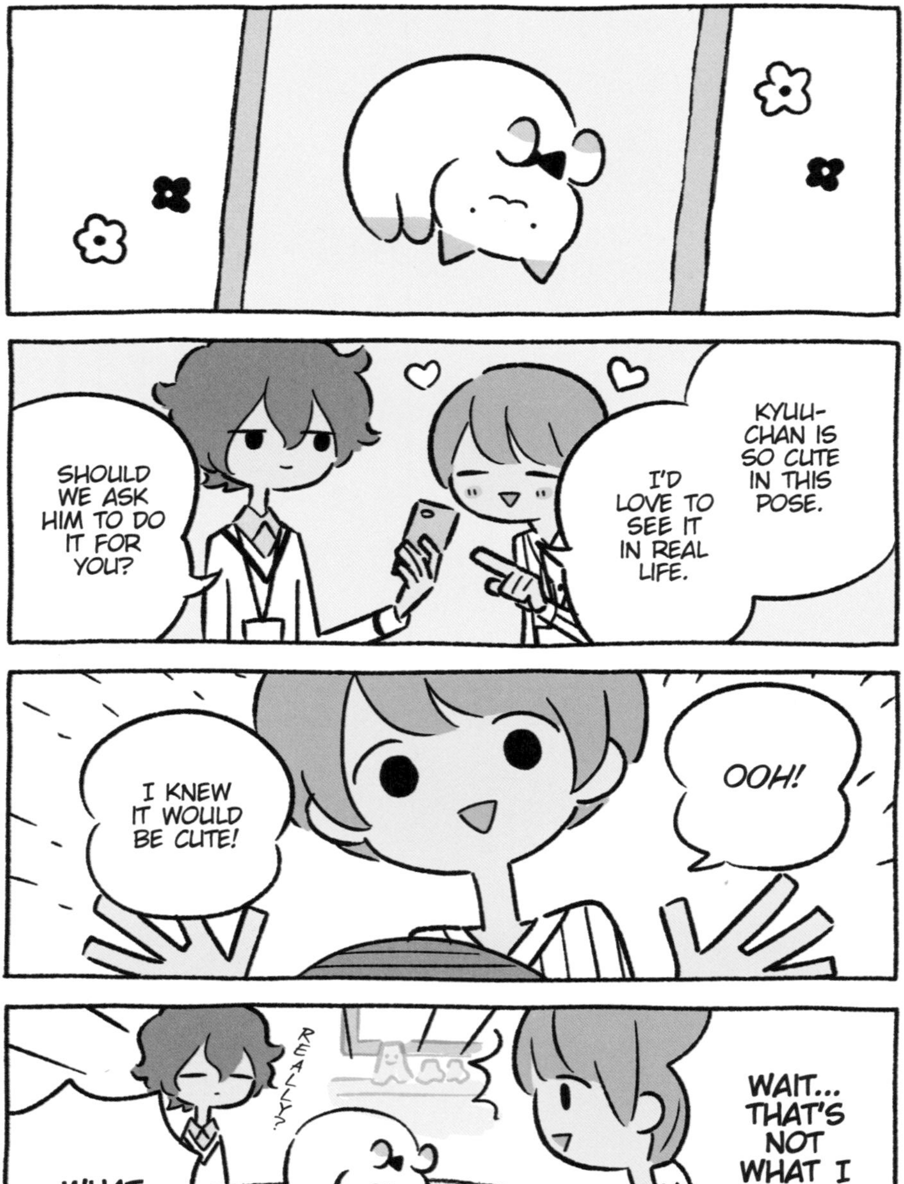
KYUU-CHAN IS SO CUTE IN THIS POSE.
I'D LOVE TO SEE IT IN REAL LIFE.
SHOULD WE ASK HIM TO DO IT FOR YOU?
OOH!
I KNEW IT WOULD BE CUTE!
WAIT... THAT'S NOT WHAT I EXPECTED!
REALLY?
WHAT BALANCE!

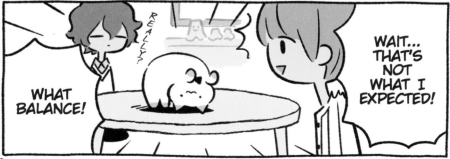

DRILLS

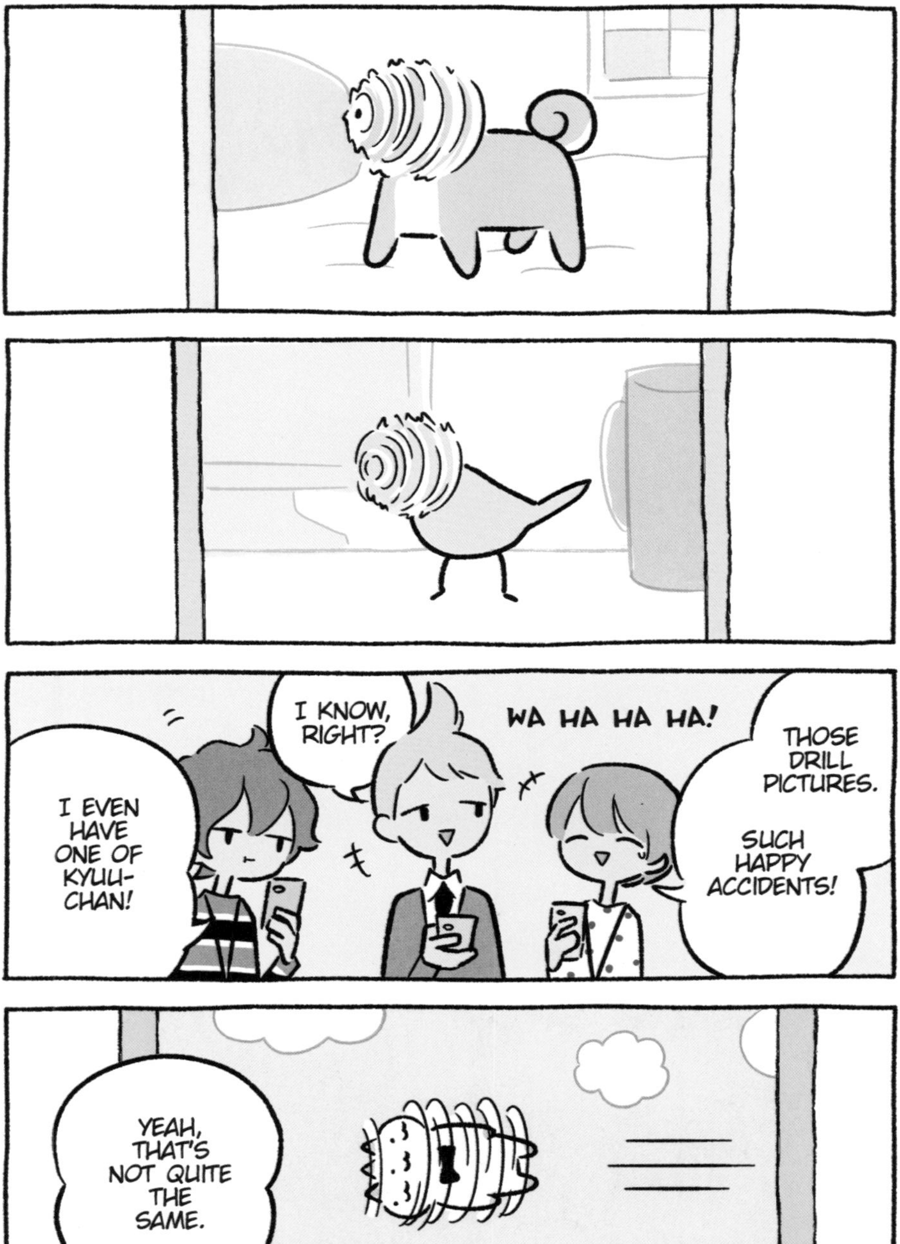
THOSE DRILL PICTURES.
SUCH HAPPY ACCIDENTS!
WA HA HA HA!
I KNOW, RIGHT?
I EVEN HAVE ONE OF KYUU-CHAN!
YEAH, THAT'S NOT QUITE THE SAME.

LEAVE IT TO ME

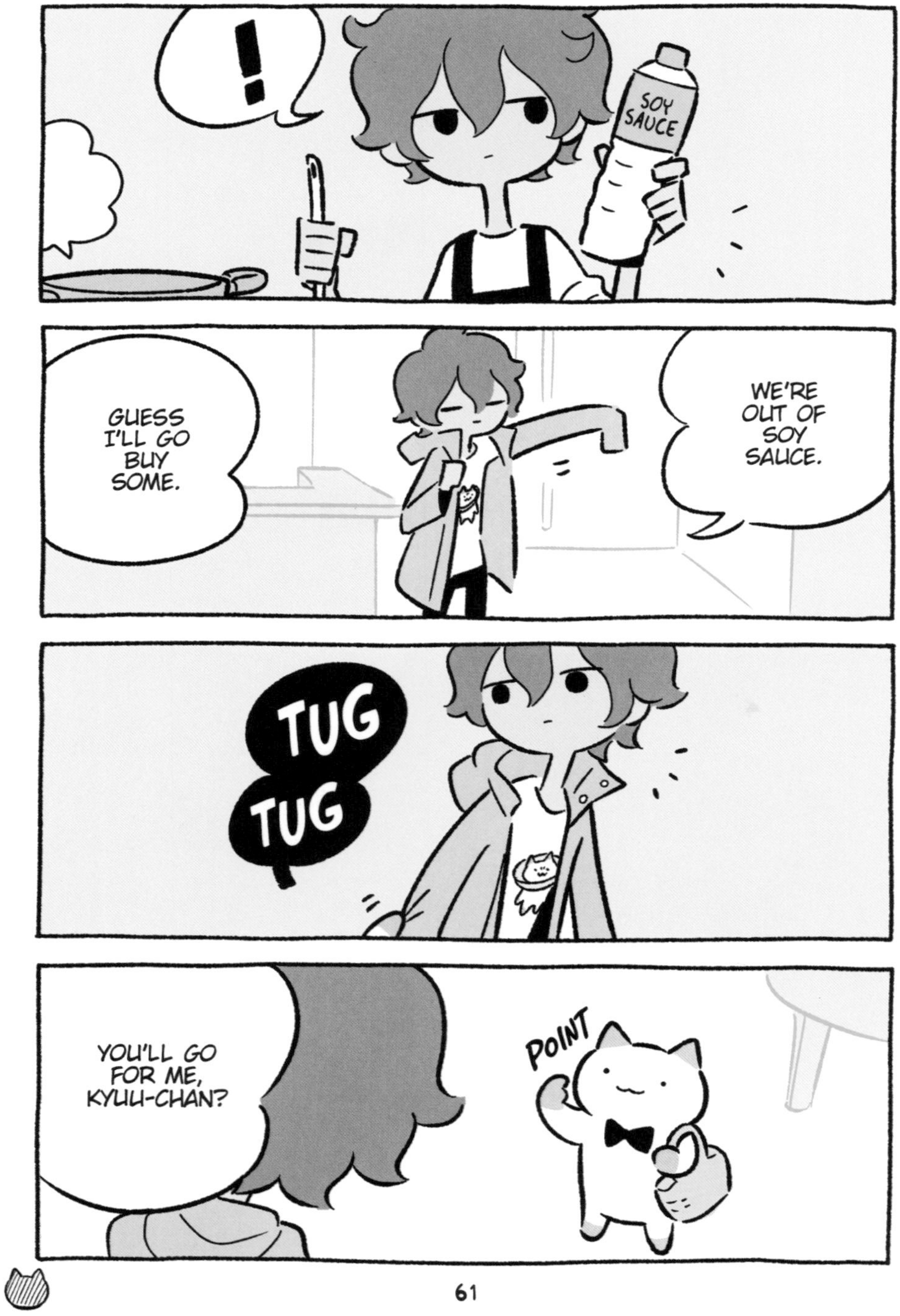
!
SOY SAUCE
WE'RE OUT OF SOY SAUCE.
GUESS I'LL GO BUY SOME.
TUG
TUG
POINT
YOU'LL GO FOR ME, KYUU-CHAN?

ERRAND BOY

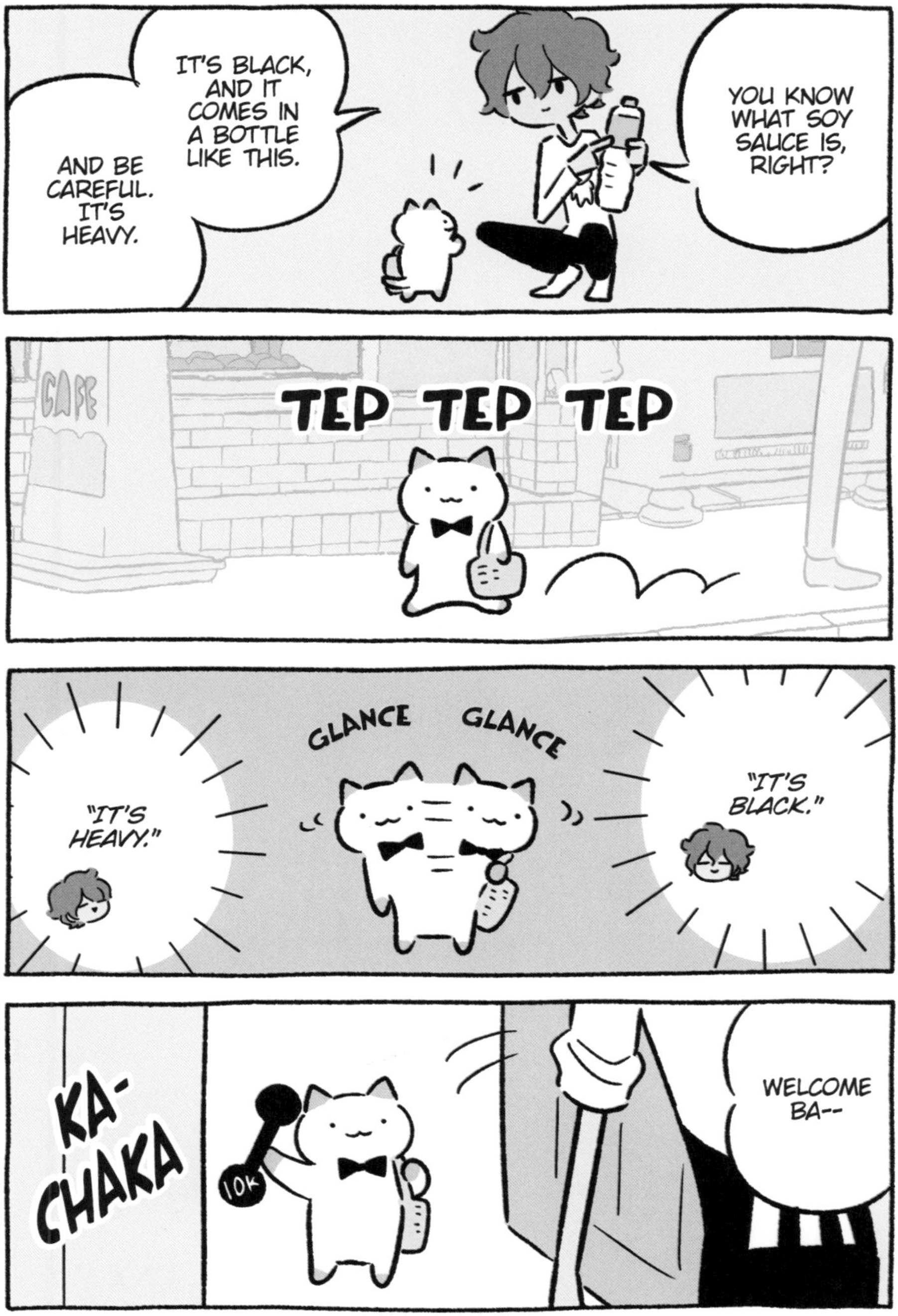
YOU KNOW WHAT SOY SAUCE IS, RIGHT?
IT'S BLACK, AND IT COMES IN A BOTTLE LIKE THIS.
AND BE CAREFUL. IT'S HEAVY.
TEP TEP TEP
"IT'S BLACK."
GLANCE GLANCE
"IT'S HEAVY."
WELCOME BA--
KA-CHAKA
10K

ERRAND BOY REDO

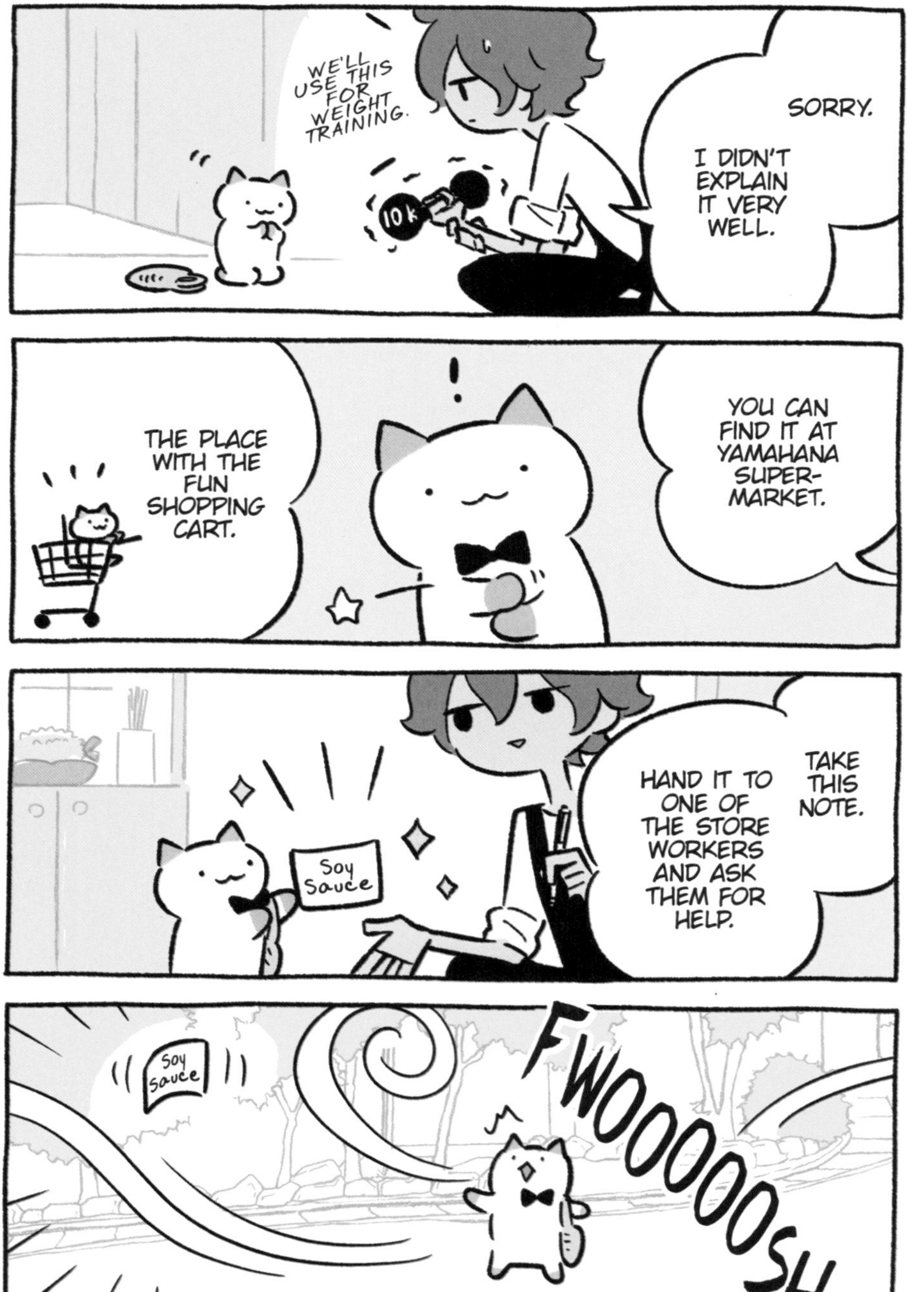
SORRY.
I DIDN'T EXPLAIN IT VERY WELL.
WE'LL USE THIS FOR WEIGHT TRAINING.
10k
YOU CAN FIND IT AT YAMAHANA SUPER-MARKET.
THE PLACE WITH THE FUN SHOPPING CART.
TAKE THIS NOTE.
HAND IT TO ONE OF THE STORE WORKERS AND ASK THEM FOR HELP.
Soy Sauce
FWOOOOOOSH
Soy sauce

SHOPPING NOTE

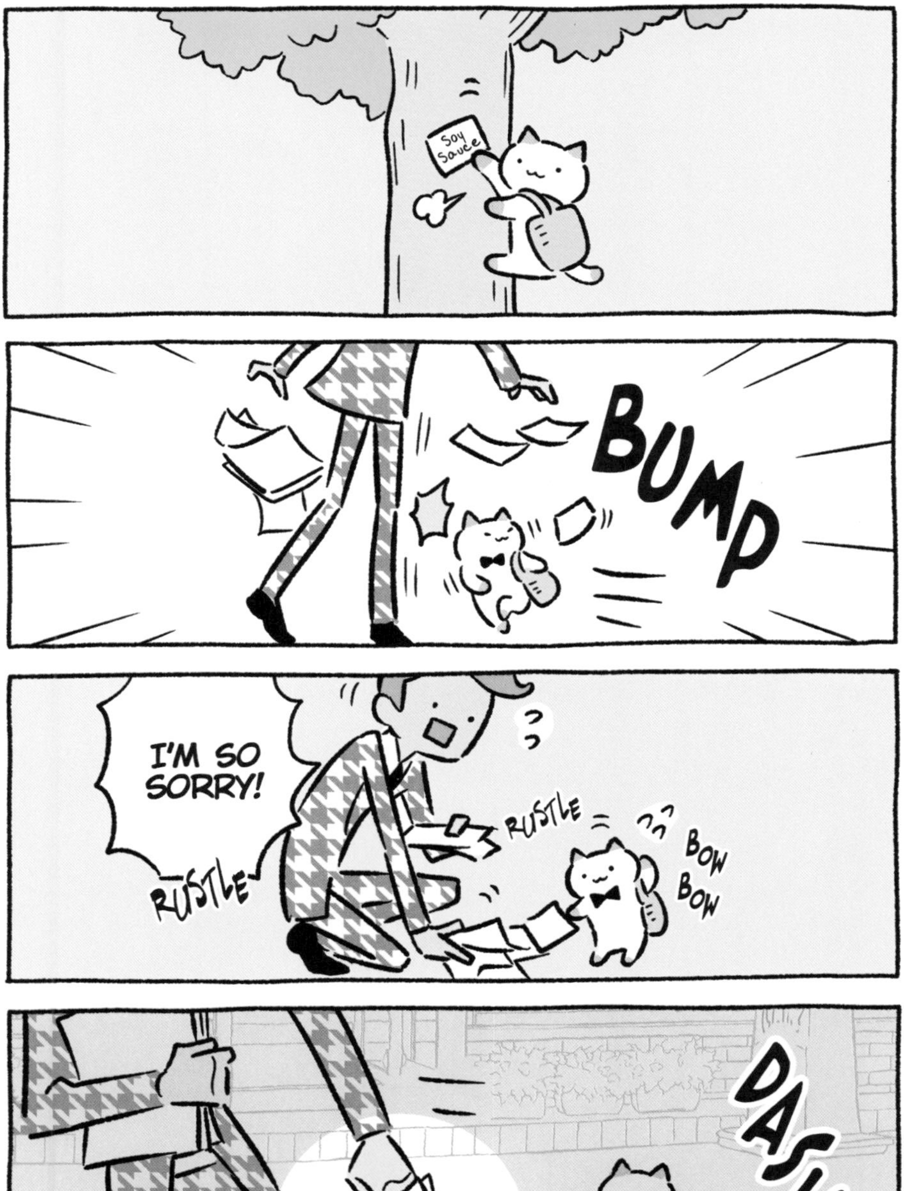
Soy Sauce
BUMP
BOW BOW
RUSTLE
I'M SO SORRY!
RUSTLE
DASH
Soy Sauce

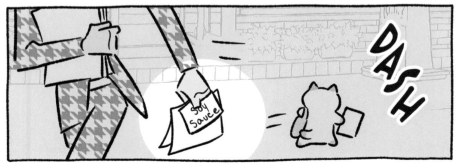

BREAK TIME

WORN OUT
RE LAXED
OH, PART-TIMER!
PUT THE HALF-PRICE STICKERS ON THESE!
YES SIR!
HALF PRICE
HALF PRICE
HALF PRICE
HALF PRICE
BREAD

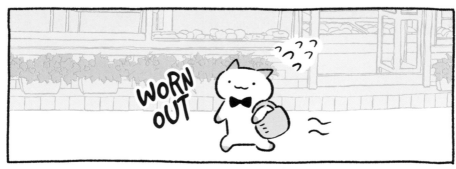

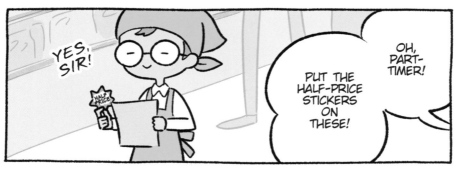

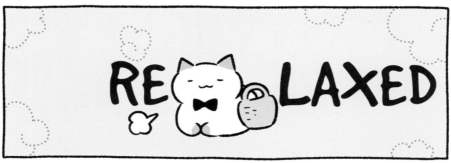

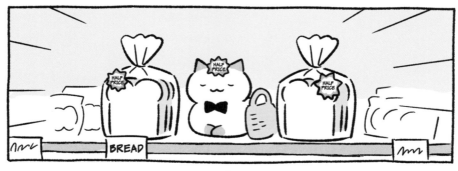

THE WRONG NOTE

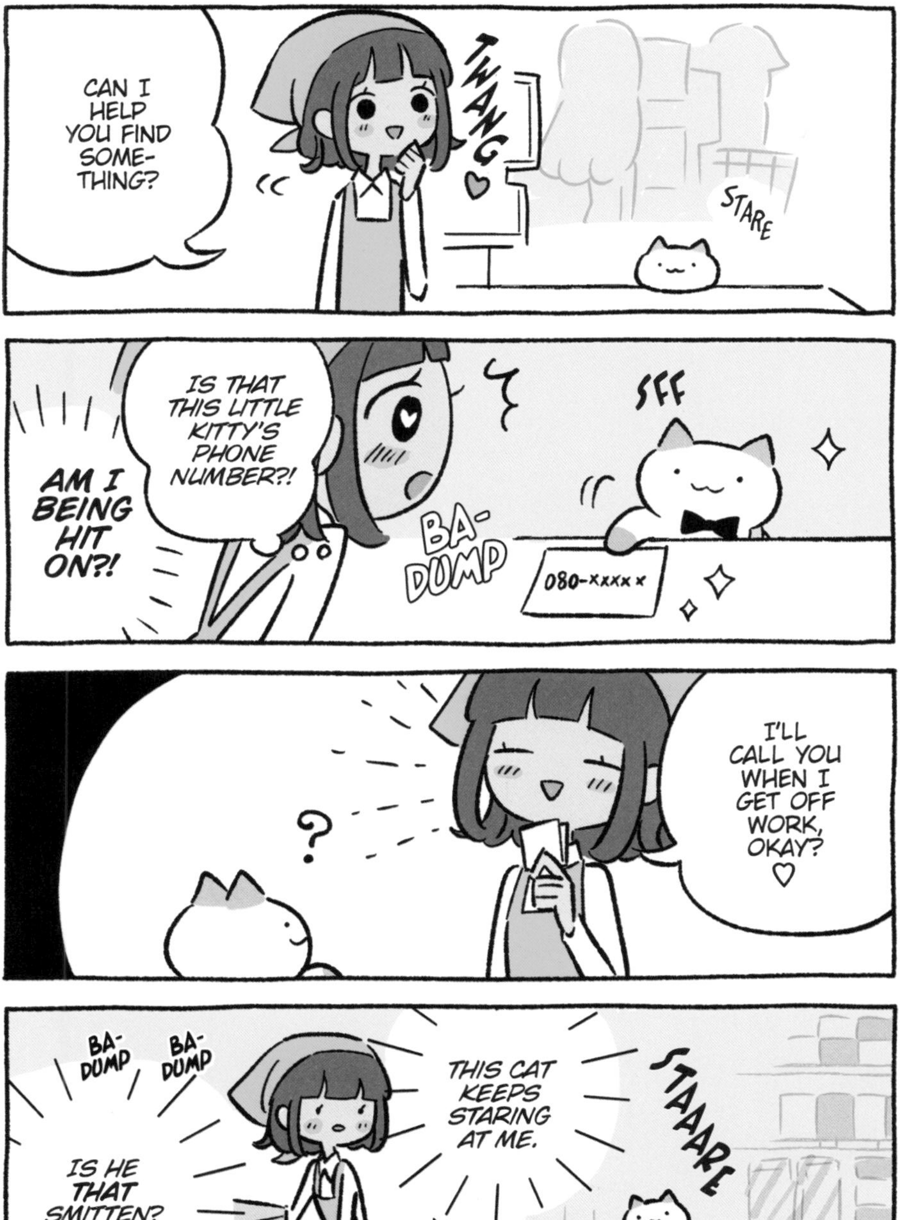
TWANG
STARE
CAN I HELP YOU FIND SOME-THING?
SFF
IS THAT THIS LITTLE KITTY'S PHONE NUMBER?!
BA-DUMP
080-xxxxx
AM I BEING HIT ON?!
I'LL CALL YOU WHEN I GET OFF WORK, OKAY? ♡
?
STAAARE
THIS CAT KEEPS STARING AT ME.
BA-DUMP
BA-DUMP
IS HE THAT SMITTEN?
BA-DUMP
BA-DUMP

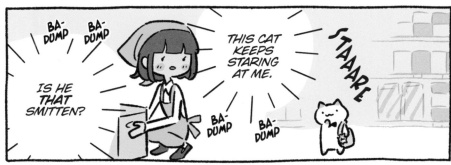

DISCOVERY

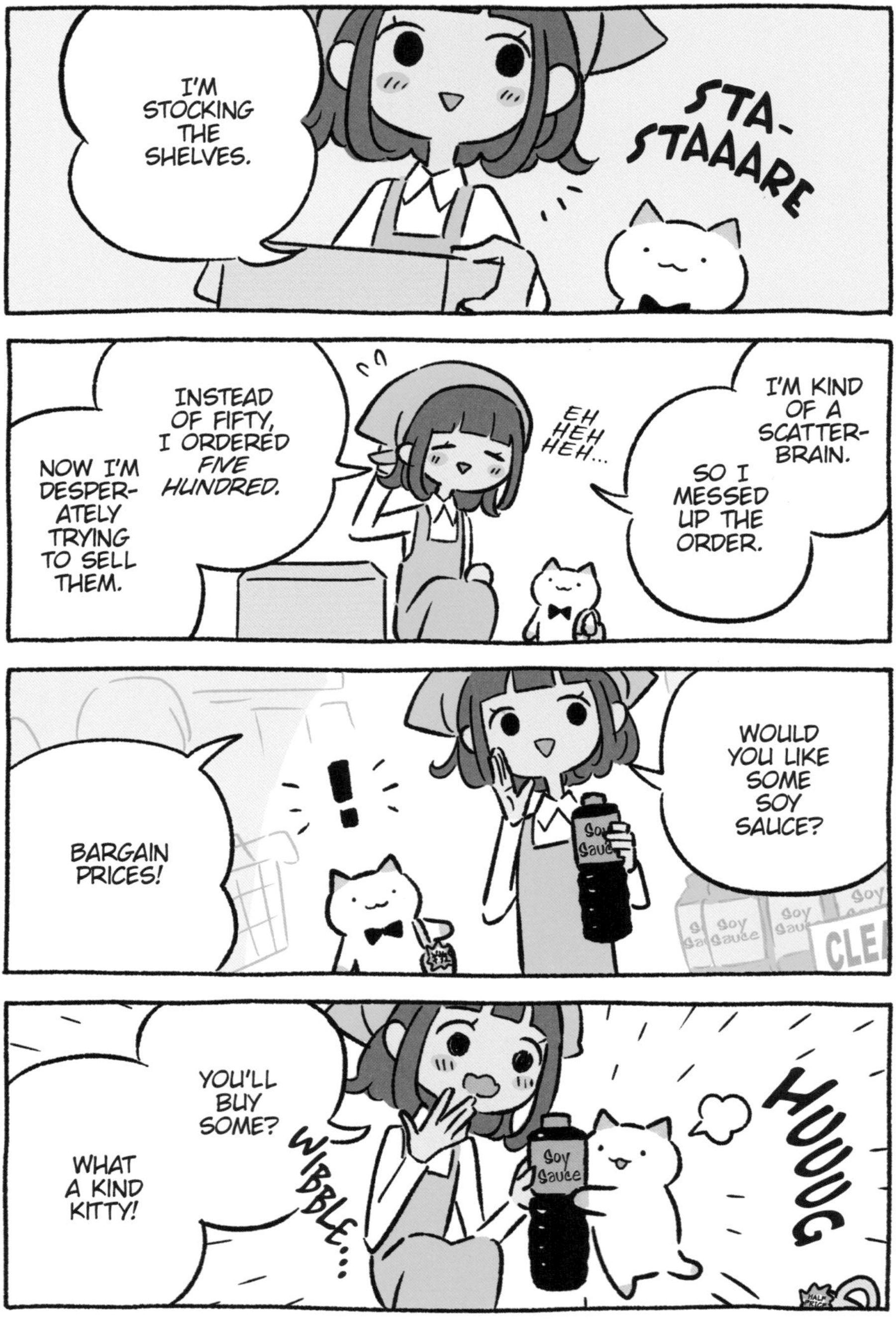
STA-STAAARE
I'M STOCKING THE SHELVES.
I'M KIND OF A SCATTERBRAIN.
SO I MESSED UP THE ORDER.
EH HEH HEH...
INSTEAD OF FIFTY, I ORDERED *FIVE HUNDRED.*
NOW I'M DESPERATELY TRYING TO SELL THEM.
WOULD YOU LIKE SOME SOY SAUCE?
Soy Sauce
!
BARGAIN PRICES!
Soy Sauce
CLEA
HUUUG
YOU'LL BUY SOME?
Soy Sauce
WIBBLE...
WHAT A KIND KITTY!
HALF PRICE

PHONE NUMBER NOTE

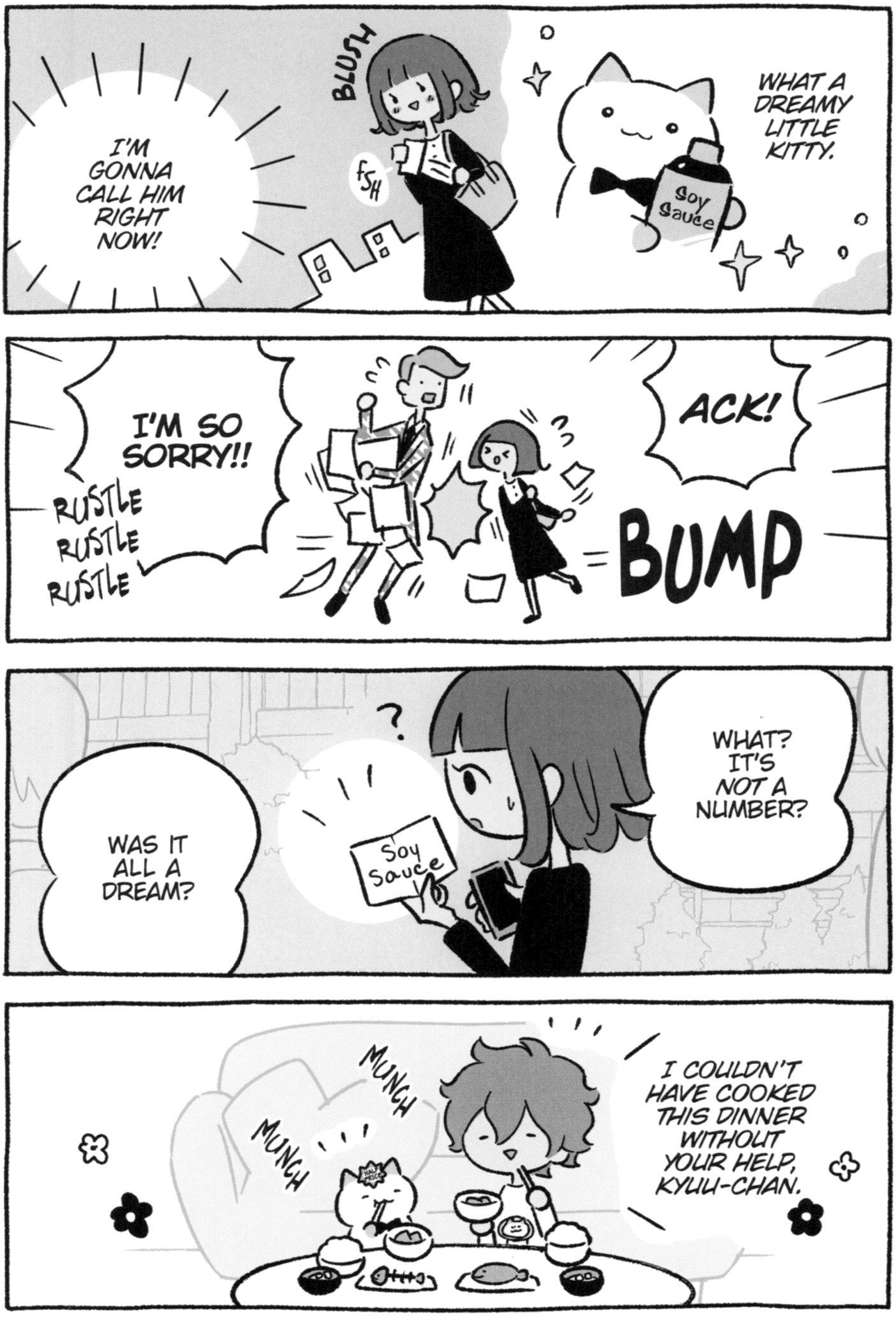
WHAT A DREAMY LITTLE KITTY.
BLUSH
Soy Sauce
I'M GONNA CALL HIM RIGHT NOW!
FSH
ACK!
I'M SO SORRY!!
BUMP
RUSTLE RUSTLE RUSTLE
WHAT? IT'S NOT A NUMBER?
Soy Sauce
WAS IT ALL A DREAM?
I COULDN'T HAVE COOKED THIS DINNER WITHOUT YOUR HELP, KYUU-CHAN.
MUNCH
MUNCH

THE STATE OF THE LUNCH

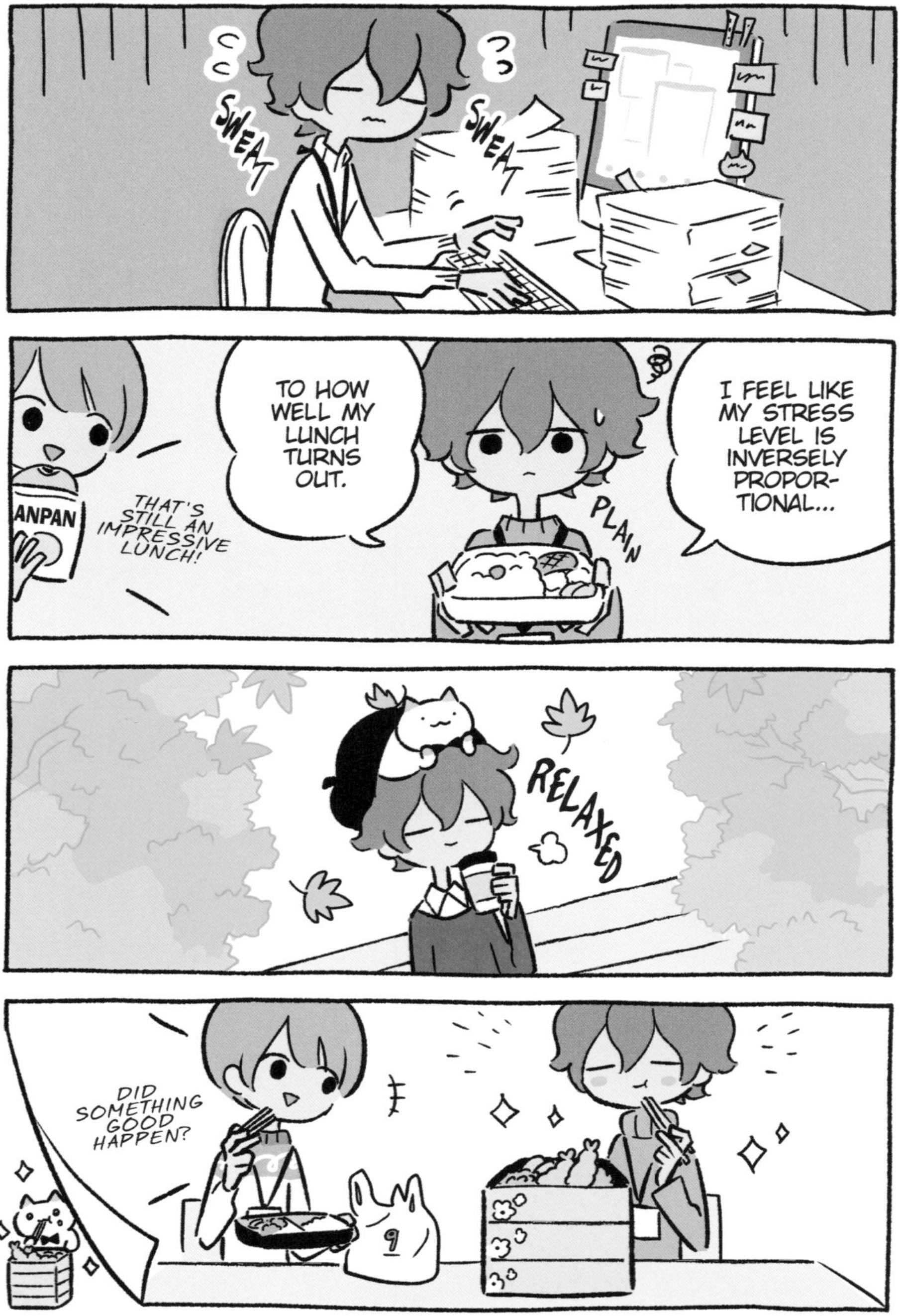
SWEAT
SWEAT
I FEEL LIKE MY STRESS LEVEL IS INVERSELY PROPORTIONAL...
PLAIN
TO HOW WELL MY LUNCH TURNS OUT.
THAT'S STILL AN IMPRESSIVE LUNCH!
ANPAN
RELAXED
DID SOMETHING GOOD HAPPEN?

PEAR NET

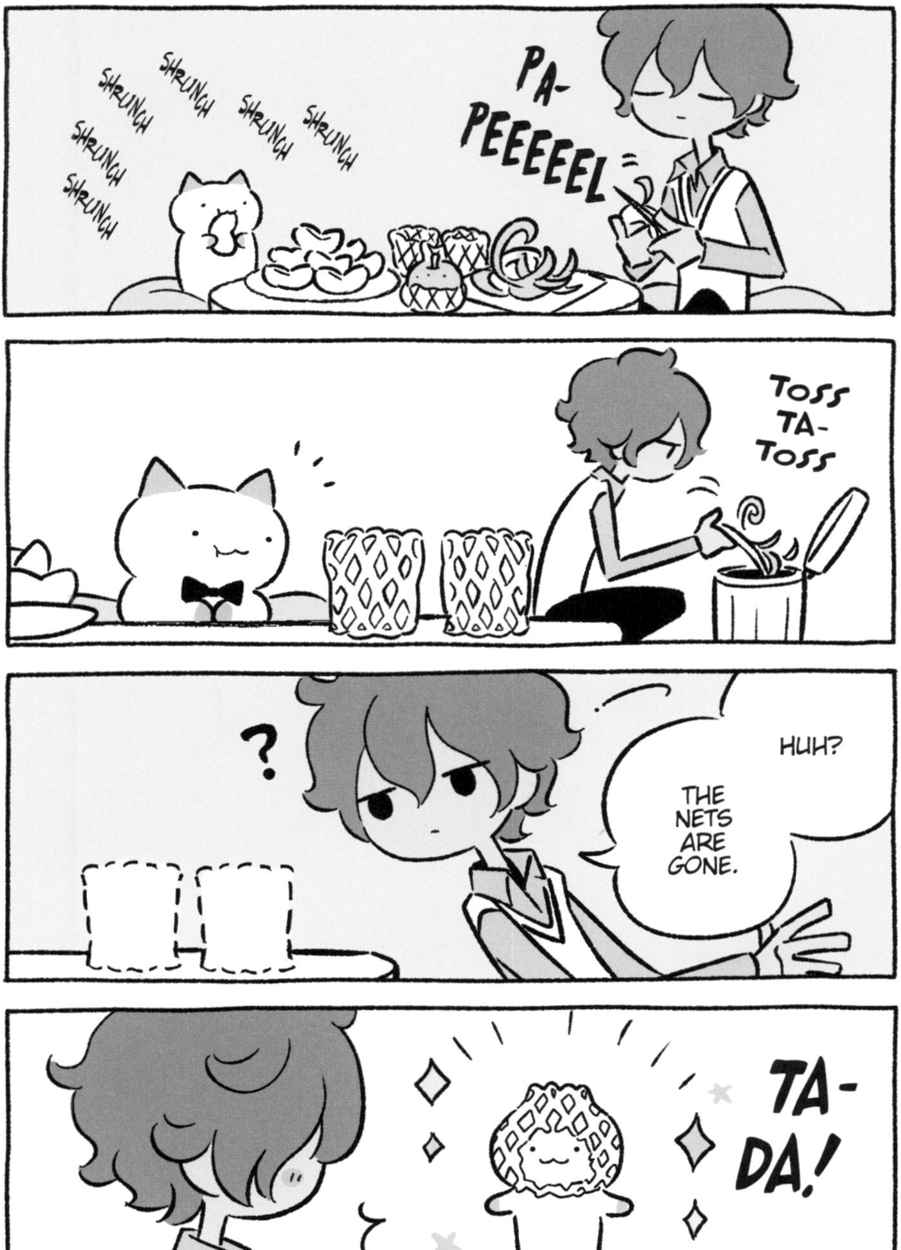
PA-PEEEEEL
SHRUNCH
SHRUNCH
SHRUNCH
SHRUNCH
SHRUNCH
SHRUNCH
TOSS TA-TOSS
HUH?
THE NETS ARE GONE.
TA-DA!

FULL OF AIR

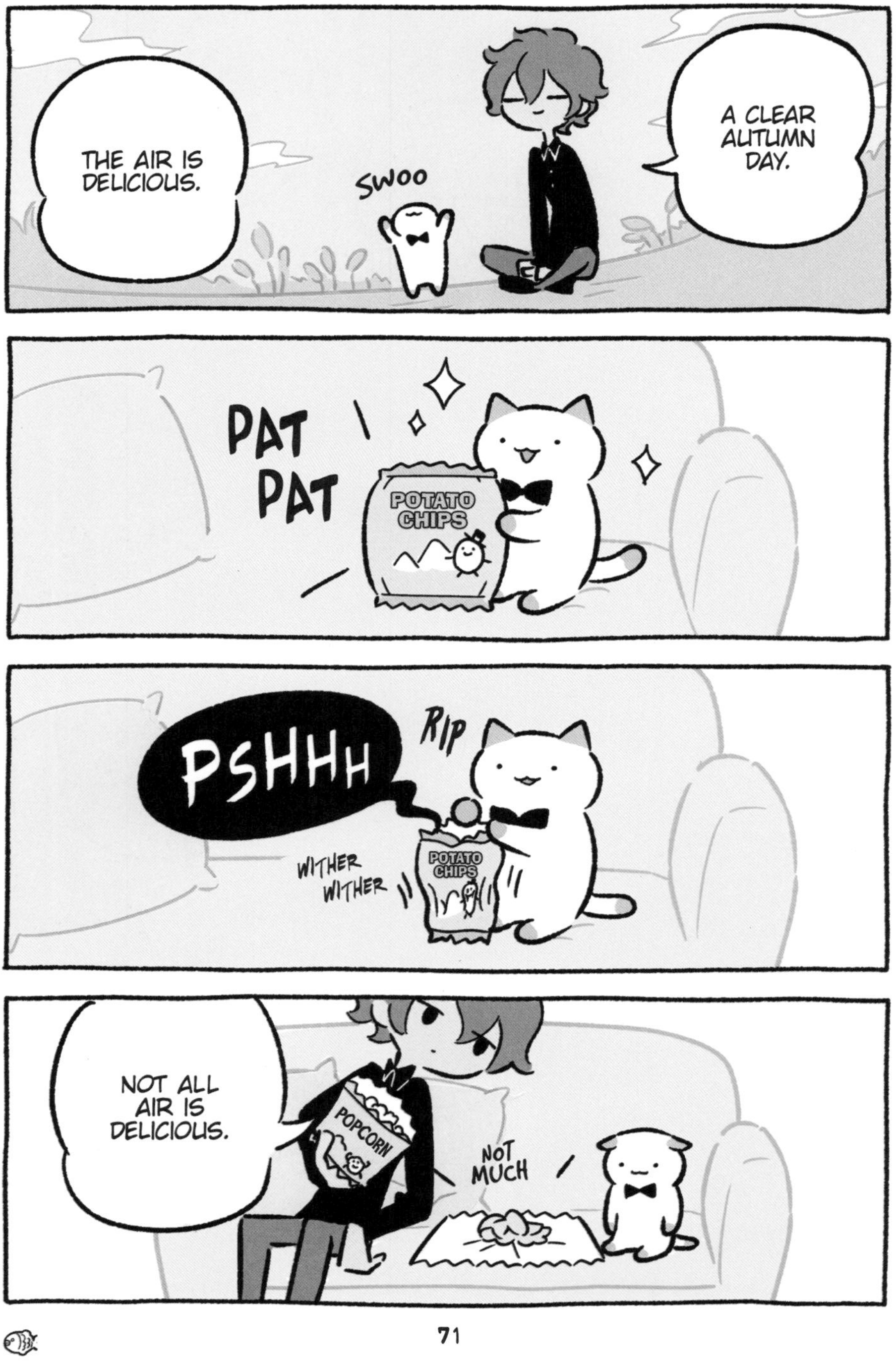
A CLEAR AUTUMN DAY.
SWOO
THE AIR IS DELICIOUS.
PAT PAT
POTATO CHIPS
RIP
PSHHH
POTATO CHIPS
WITHER WITHER
NOT ALL AIR IS DELICIOUS.
POPCORN
NOT MUCH

SLEEPINESS TEST

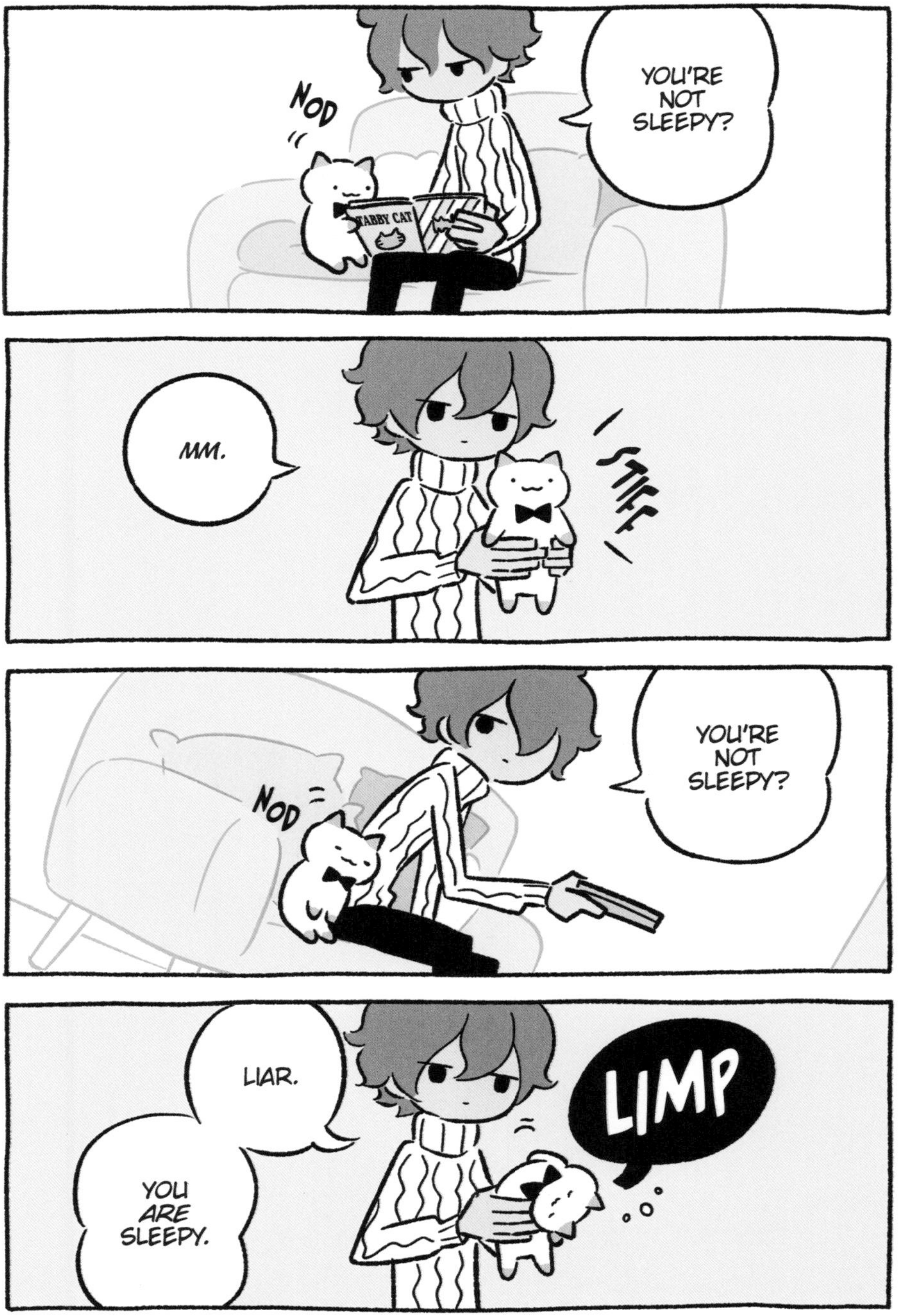
YOU'RE NOT SLEEPY?
NOD
TABBY CAT
STIFF
MM.
YOU'RE NOT SLEEPY?
NOD
LIMP
LIAR.
YOU ARE SLEEPY.

TOGETHER EVERYWHERE

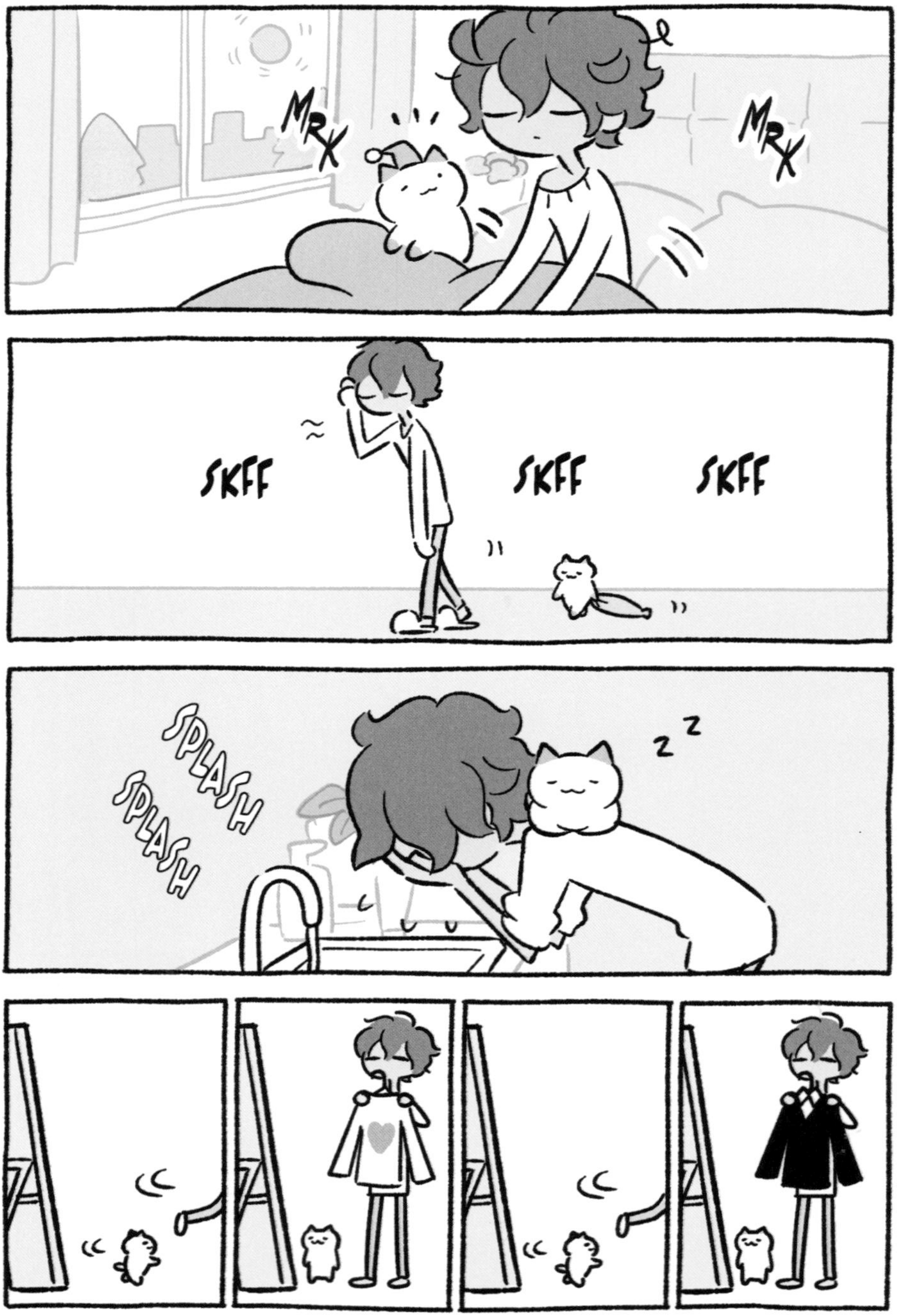
MRK
MRK
SKFF
SKFF
SKFF
SPLASH
SPLASH
Z Z

THE LITTLE SOY SAUCE GIRL

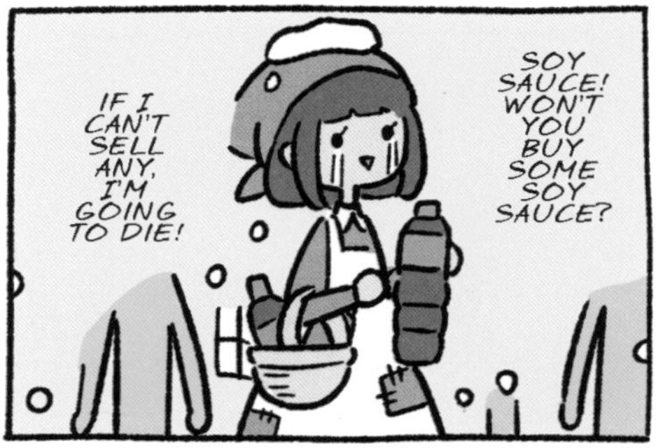
SOY SAUCE! WON'T YOU BUY SOME SOY SAUCE?
IF I CAN'T SELL ANY, I'M GOING TO DIE!

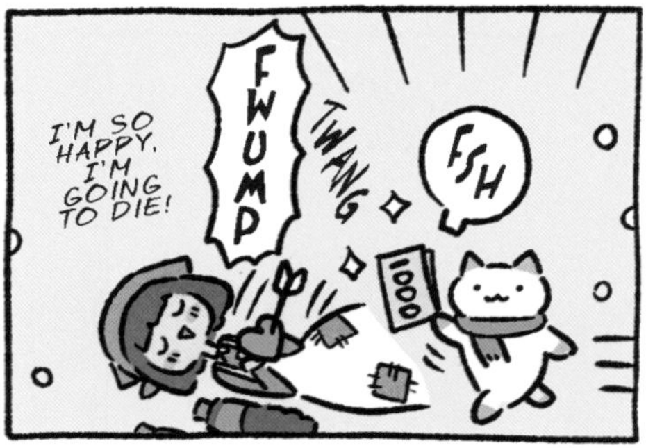
FSH
1000
TWANG
FWUMP
I'M SO HAPPY, I'M GOING TO DIE!

A SCARING PRO

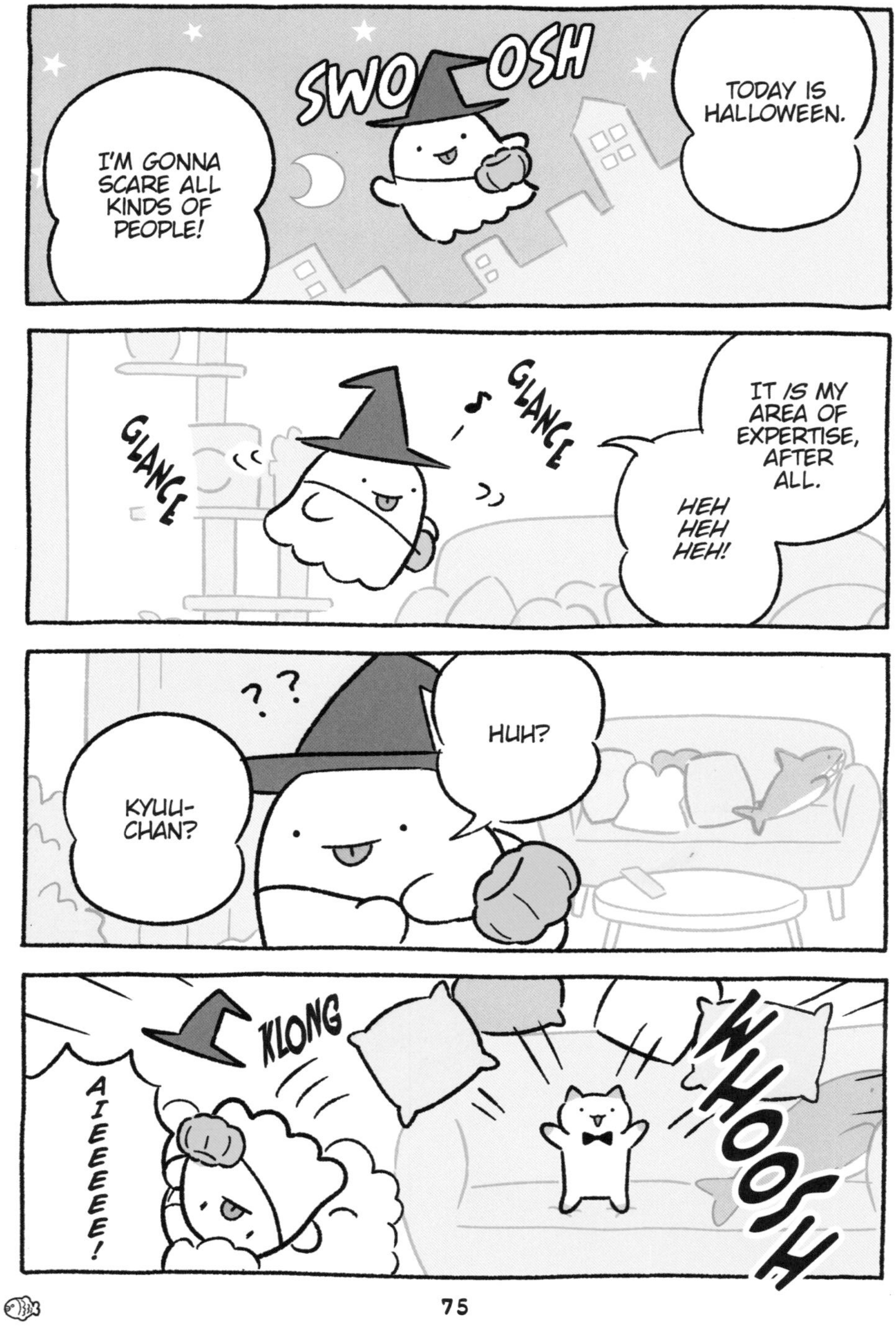
TODAY IS HALLOWEEN.
SWOOSH
I'M GONNA SCARE ALL KINDS OF PEOPLE!
IT IS MY AREA OF EXPERTISE, AFTER ALL.
HEH HEH HEH!
GLANCE
GLANCE
HUH?
? ?
KYUU-CHAN?
WHOOSH
KLONG
AIEEEEEE!

NEWEST MODEL

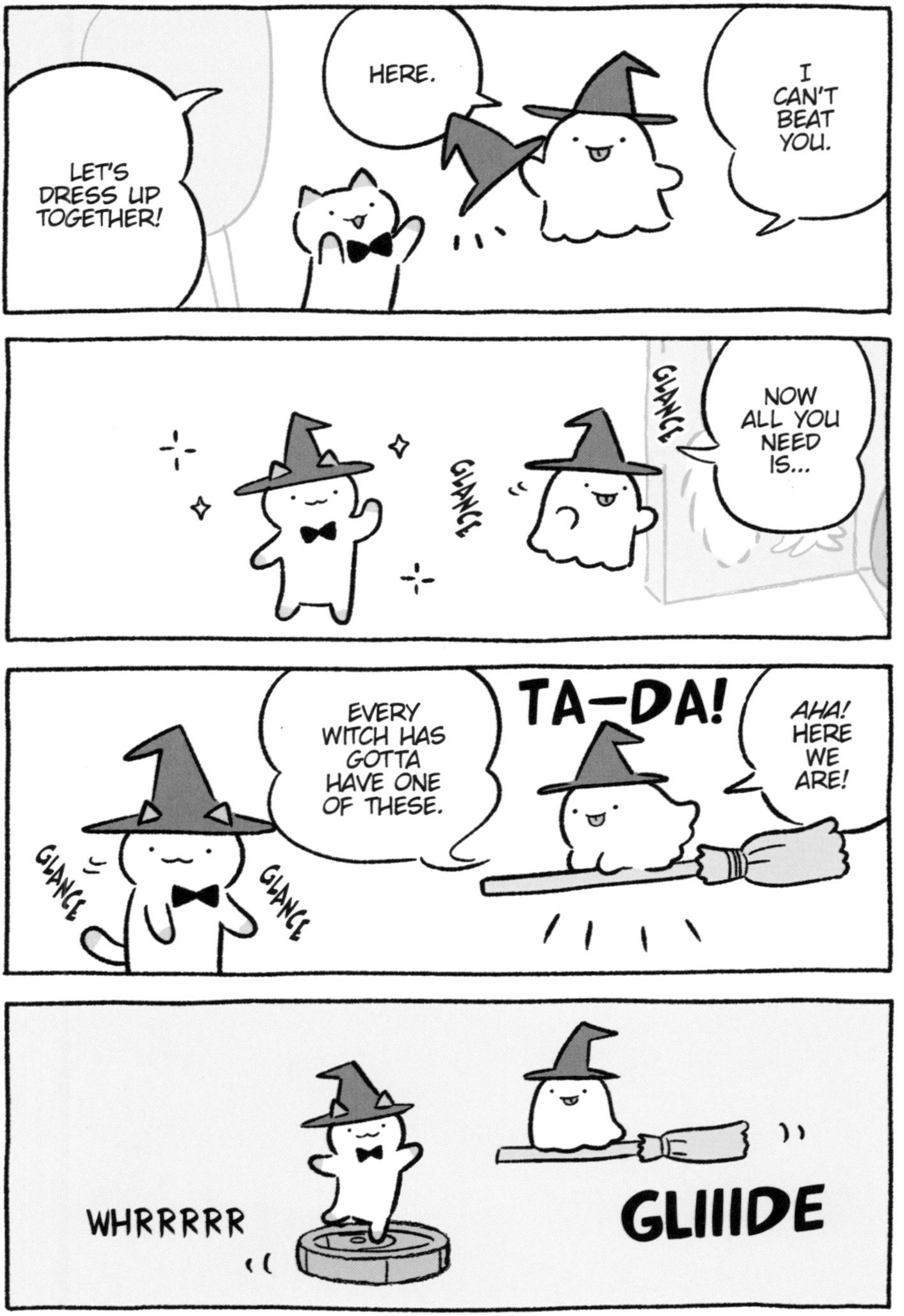
I CAN'T BEAT YOU.
HERE.
LET'S DRESS UP TOGETHER!
NOW ALL YOU NEED IS...
GLANCE
GLANCE
AHA! HERE WE ARE!
TA-DA!
EVERY WITCH HAS GOTTA HAVE ONE OF THESE.
GLANCE
GLANCE
GLIIIDE
WHRRRRR

PUMPKIN HEAD

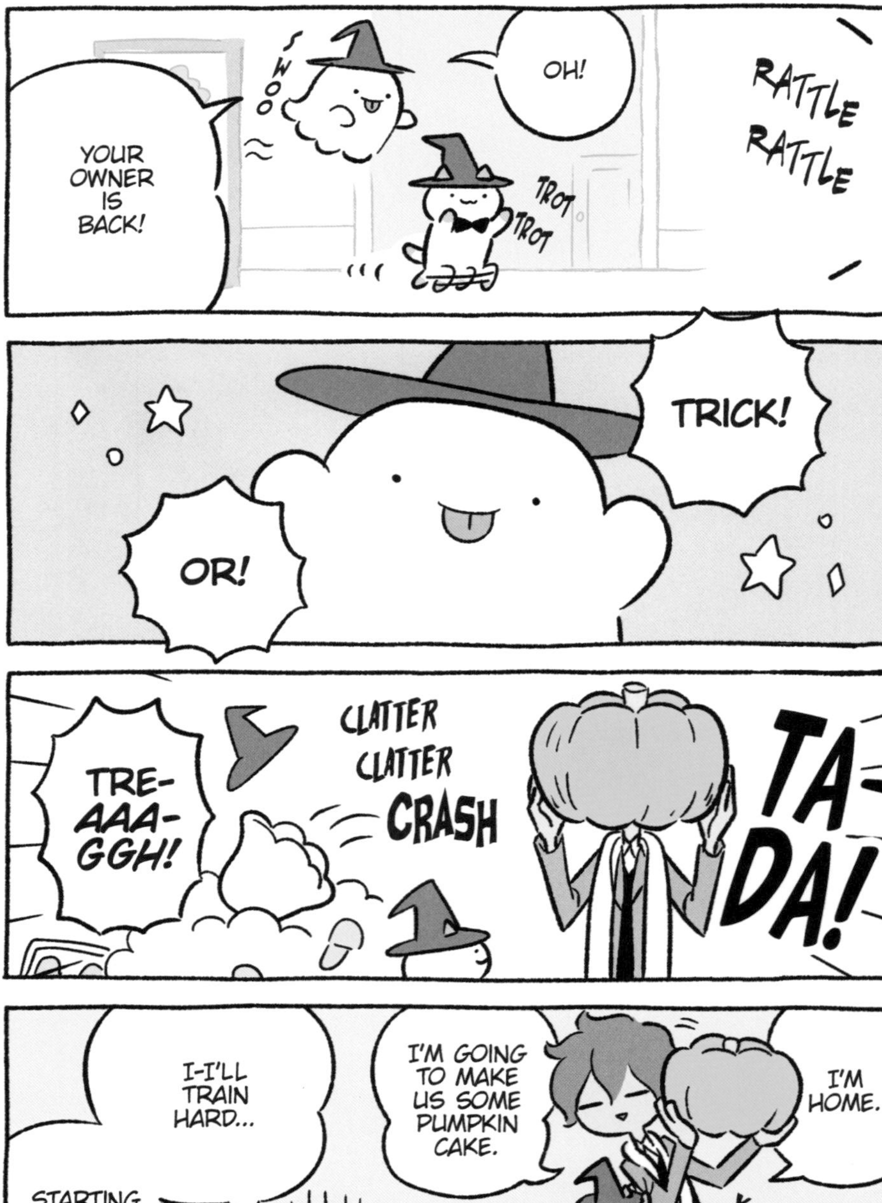
RATTLE RATTLE
OH!
SWOO
TROT TROT
YOUR OWNER IS BACK!
TRICK!
OR!
TA-DA!
CLATTER CLATTER CRASH
TRE-AAAA-GGH!
I'M HOME.
YOINK
I'M GOING TO MAKE US SOME PUMPKIN CAKE.
I-I'LL TRAIN HARD...
STARTING NEXT WEEK.

PARTY

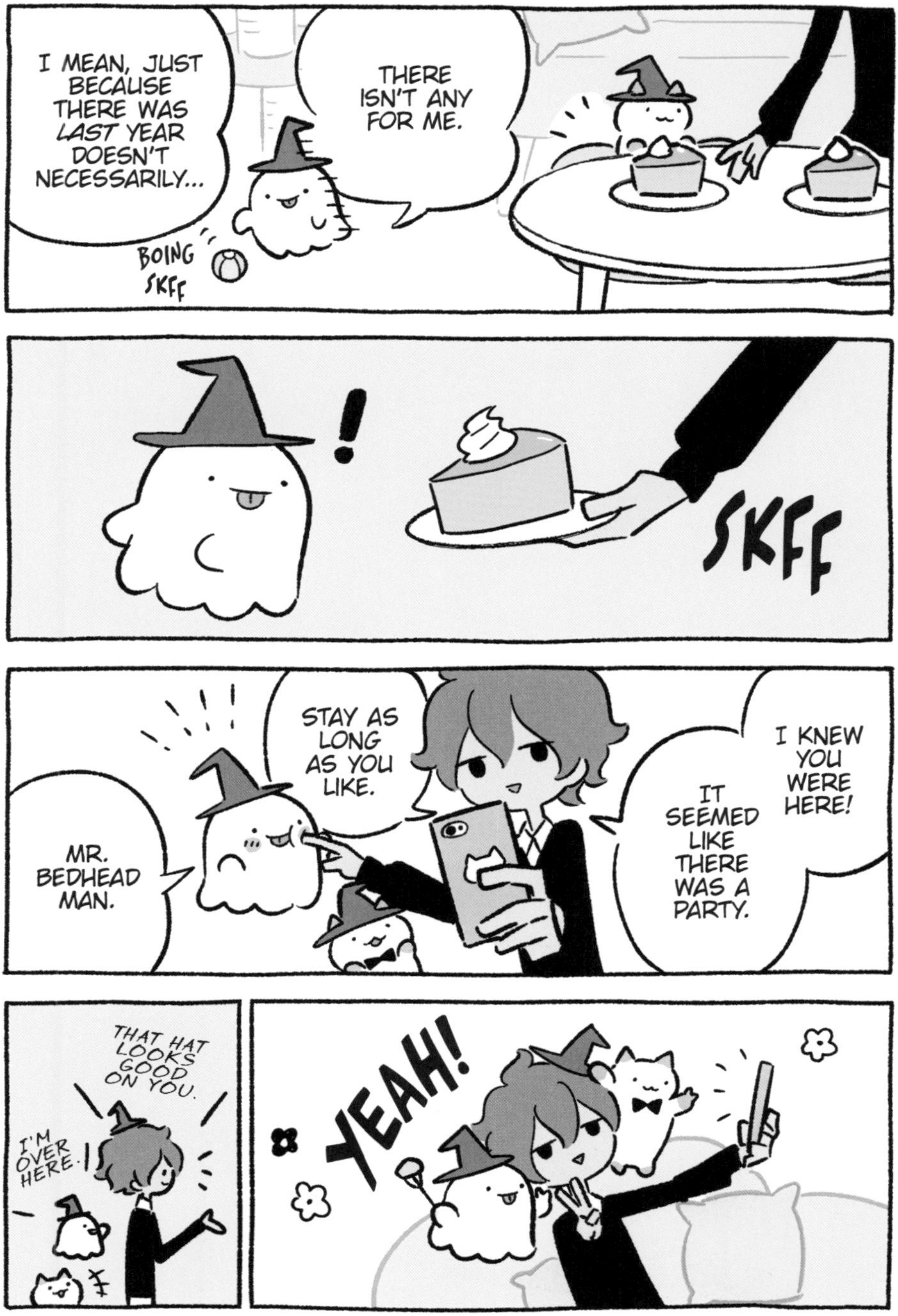
THERE ISN'T ANY FOR ME.
I MEAN, JUST BECAUSE THERE WAS *LAST* YEAR DOESN'T NECESSARILY...
BOING
SKFF
!
SKFF
I KNEW YOU WERE HERE!
IT SEEMED LIKE THERE WAS A PARTY.
STAY AS LONG AS YOU LIKE.
MR. BEDHEAD MAN.
YEAH!
THAT HAT LOOKS GOOD ON YOU.
I'M OVER HERE.

WAGER

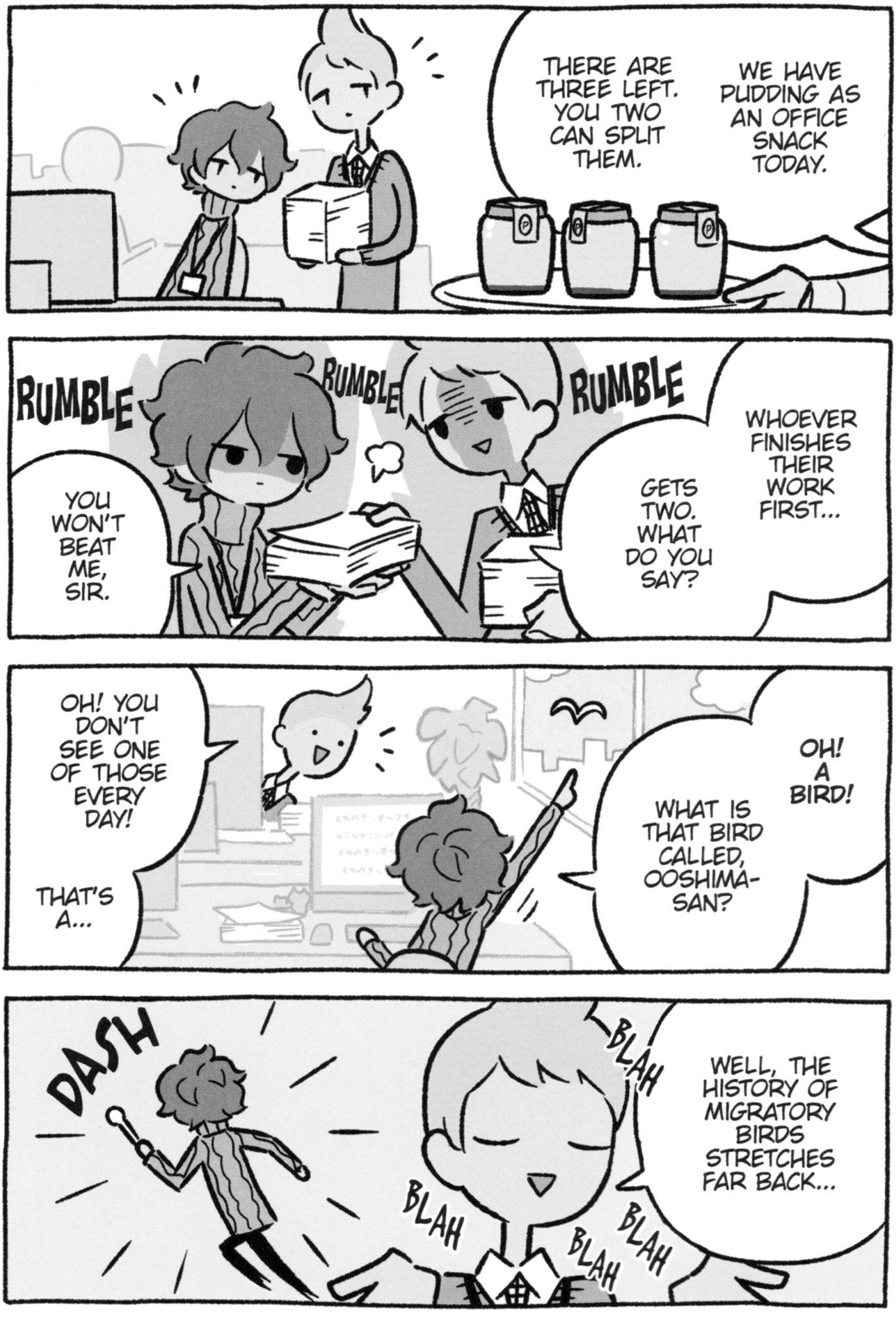
WE HAVE PUDDING AS AN OFFICE SNACK TODAY.
THERE ARE THREE LEFT. YOU TWO CAN SPLIT THEM.
RUMBLE
WHOEVER FINISHES THEIR WORK FIRST...
GETS TWO. WHAT DO YOU SAY?
RUMBLE
YOU WON'T BEAT ME, SIR.
RUMBLE
OH! A BIRD!
WHAT IS THAT BIRD CALLED, OOSHIMA-SAN?
OH! YOU DON'T SEE ONE OF THOSE EVERY DAY!
THAT'S A...
BLAH
WELL, THE HISTORY OF MIGRATORY BIRDS STRETCHES FAR BACK...
BLAH
BLAH
BLAH
DASH

JUST MISSED HIM

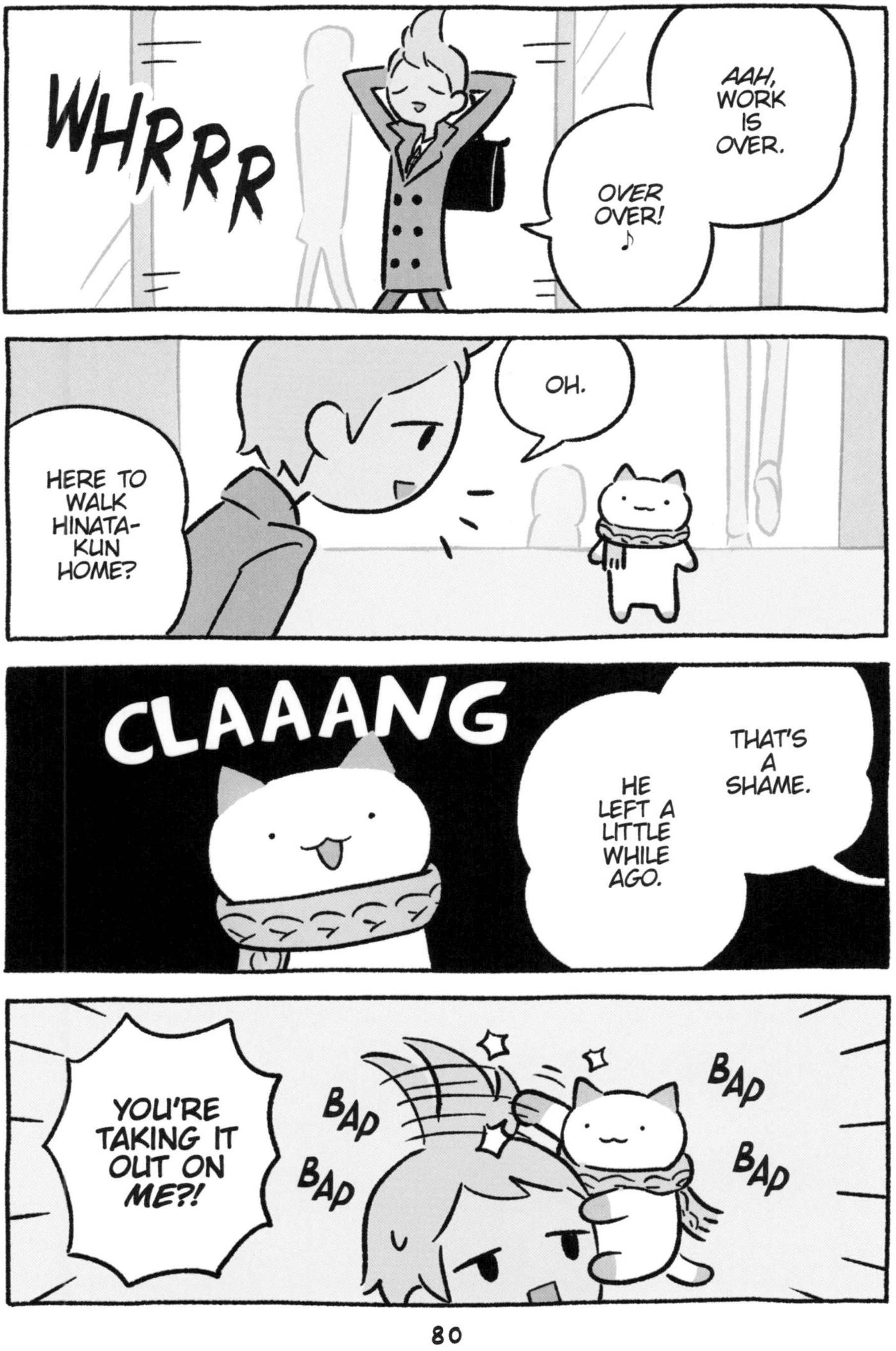
AAH, WORK IS OVER.
OVER OVER! ♪
WHRRR
OH.
HERE TO WALK HINATA-KUN HOME?
THAT'S A SHAME.
HE LEFT A LITTLE WHILE AGO.
CLAAANG
BAP
BAP
BAP
BAP
YOU'RE TAKING IT OUT ON *ME?!*

EMOTIONAL ROLLER COASTER

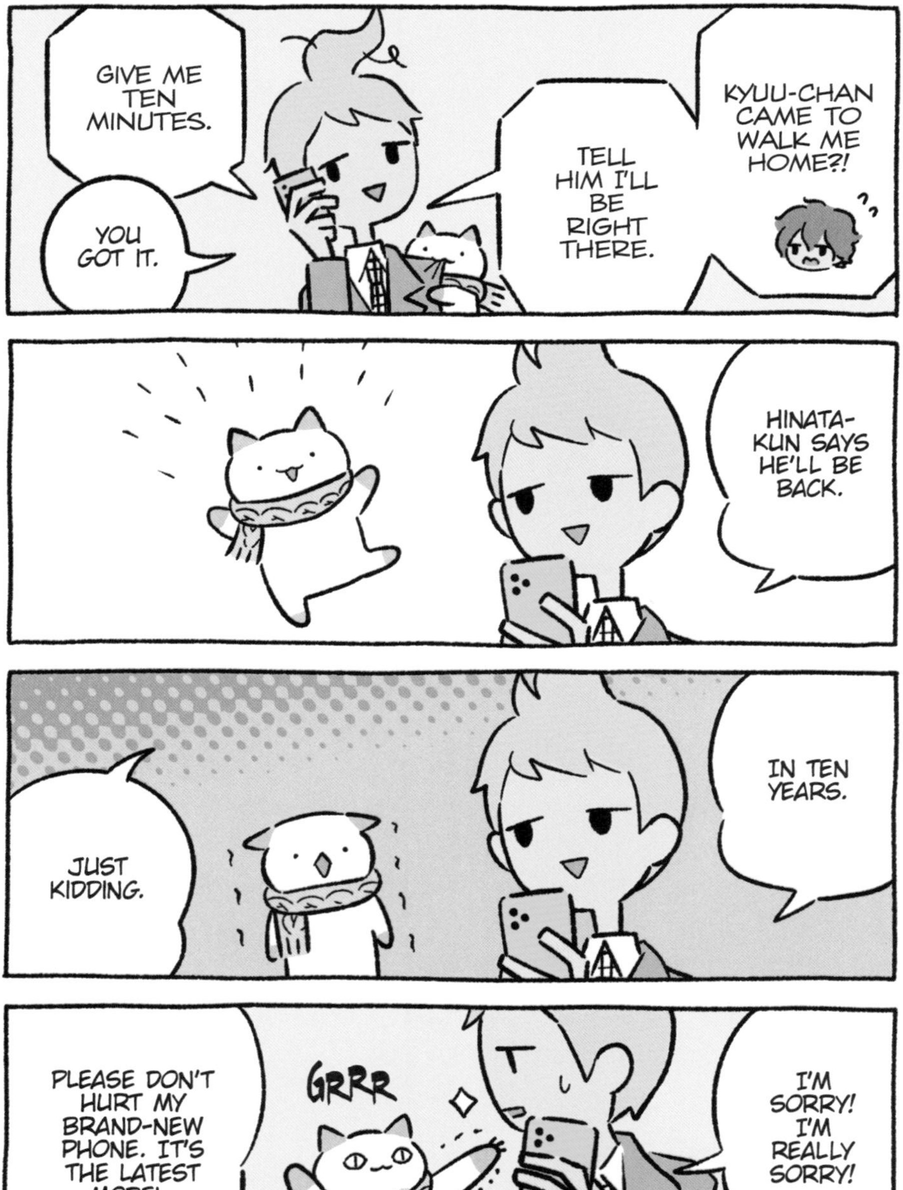
KYUU-CHAN CAME TO WALK ME HOME?!
TELL HIM I'LL BE RIGHT THERE.
GIVE ME TEN MINUTES.
YOU GOT IT.
HINATA-KUN SAYS HE'LL BE BACK.
IN TEN YEARS.
JUST KIDDING.
I'M SORRY! I'M REALLY SORRY!
GRRR
PLEASE DON'T HURT MY BRAND-NEW PHONE. IT'S THE LATEST MODEL.

HILARIOUS BANTER

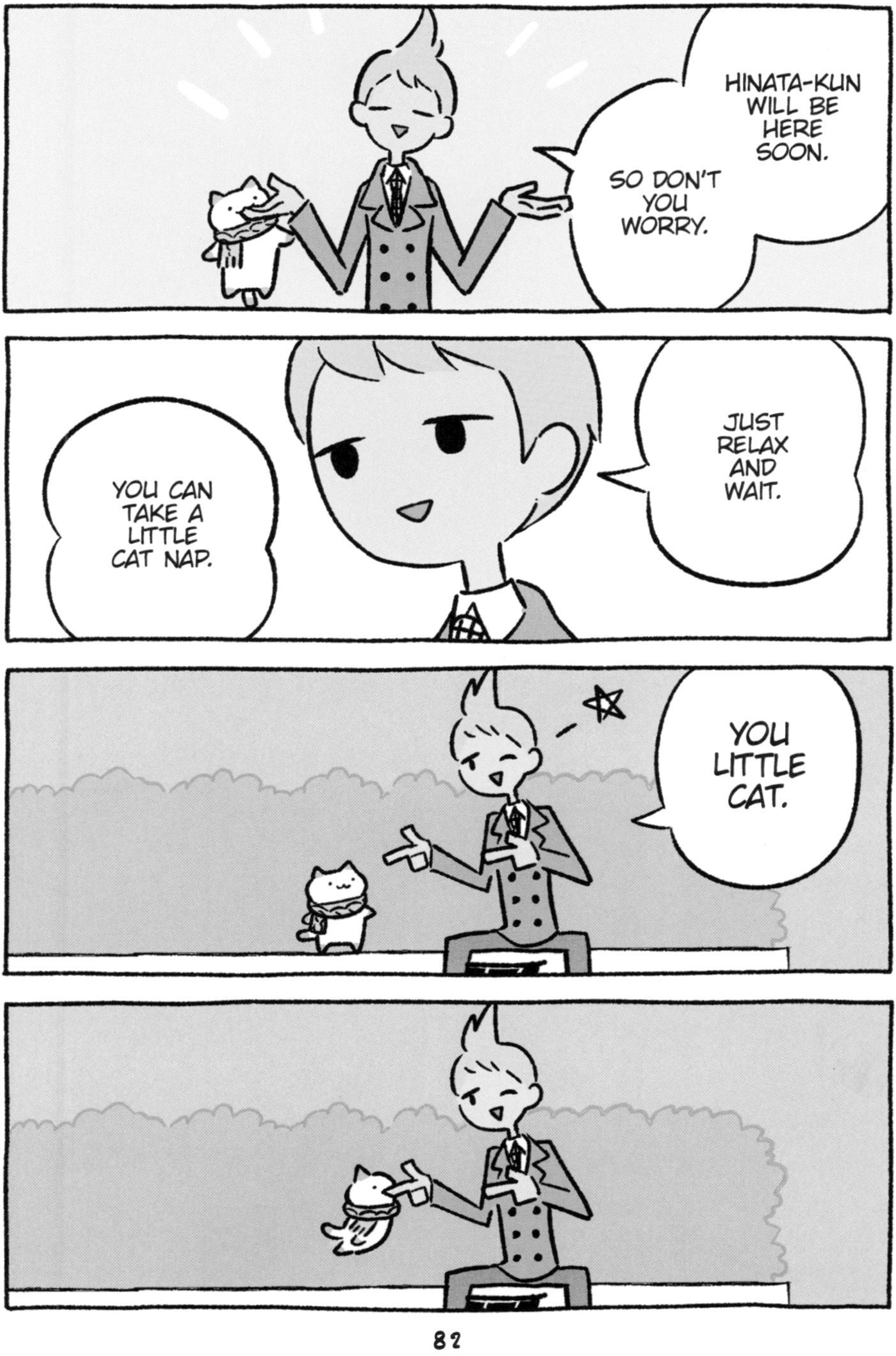
HINATA-KUN WILL BE HERE SOON.
SO DON'T YOU WORRY.
JUST RELAX AND WAIT.
YOU CAN TAKE A LITTLE CAT NAP.
YOU LITTLE CAT.

I WANT TO PET YOU

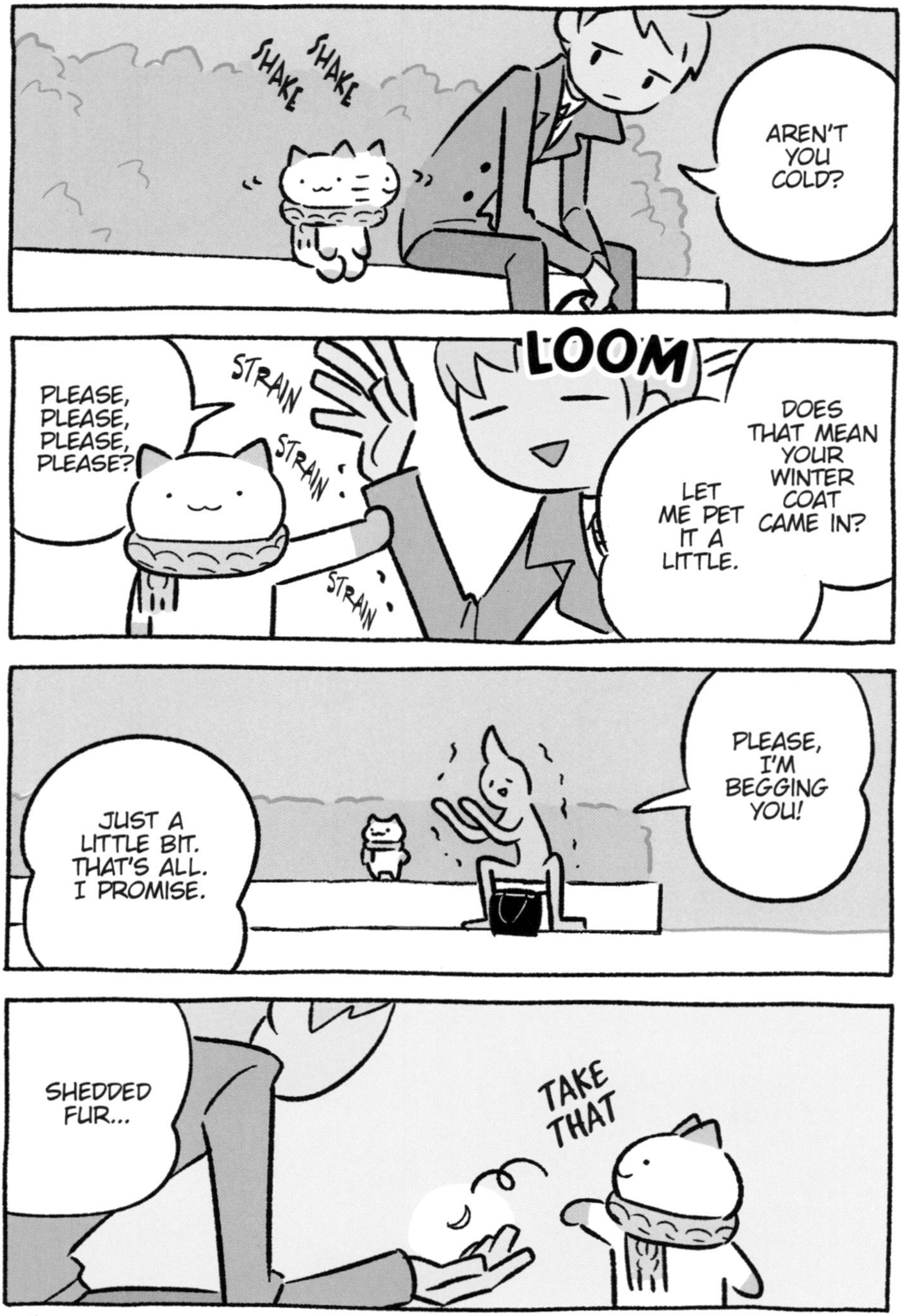
AREN'T YOU COLD?
SHAKE
SHAKE
DOES THAT MEAN YOUR WINTER COAT CAME IN?
LOOM
LET ME PET IT A LITTLE.
STRAIN
STRAIN
STRAIN
PLEASE, PLEASE, PLEASE, PLEASE?
PLEASE, I'M BEGGING YOU!
JUST A LITTLE BIT. THAT'S ALL. I PROMISE.
TAKE THAT
SHEDDED FUR...

REUNITED

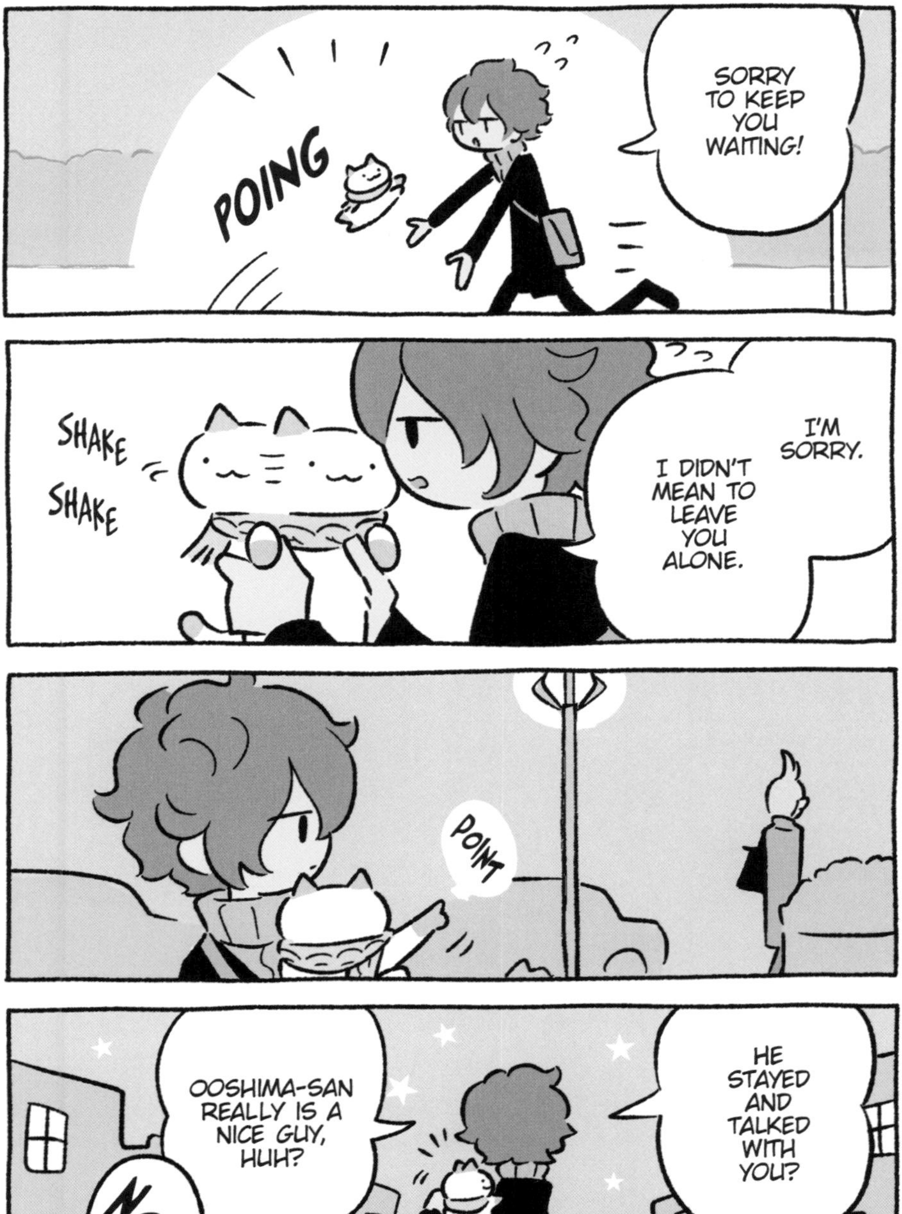

SORRY TO KEEP YOU WAITING!
POING
I'M SORRY.
I DIDN'T MEAN TO LEAVE YOU ALONE.
SHAKE SHAKE
POINT
HE STAYED AND TALKED WITH YOU?
OOSHIMA-SAN REALLY IS A NICE GUY, HUH?
NOD

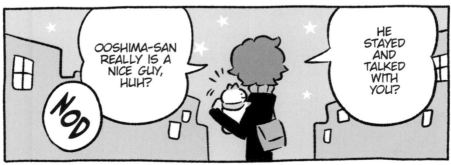

HOT POT

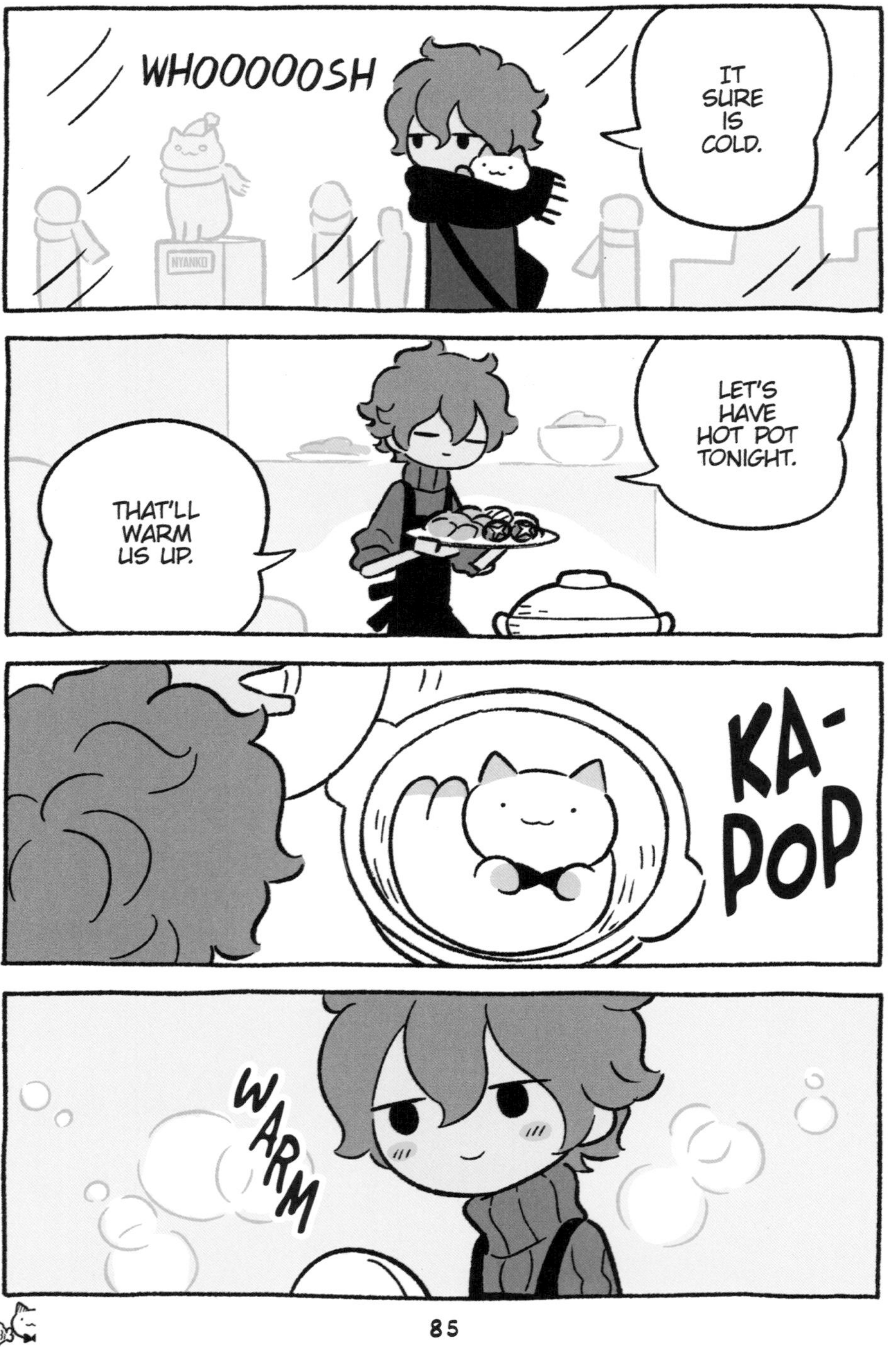
IT SURE IS COLD.
WHOOOOOSH
NYANKO
LET'S HAVE HOT POT TONIGHT.
THAT'LL WARM US UP.
KA-POP
WARM

EARS

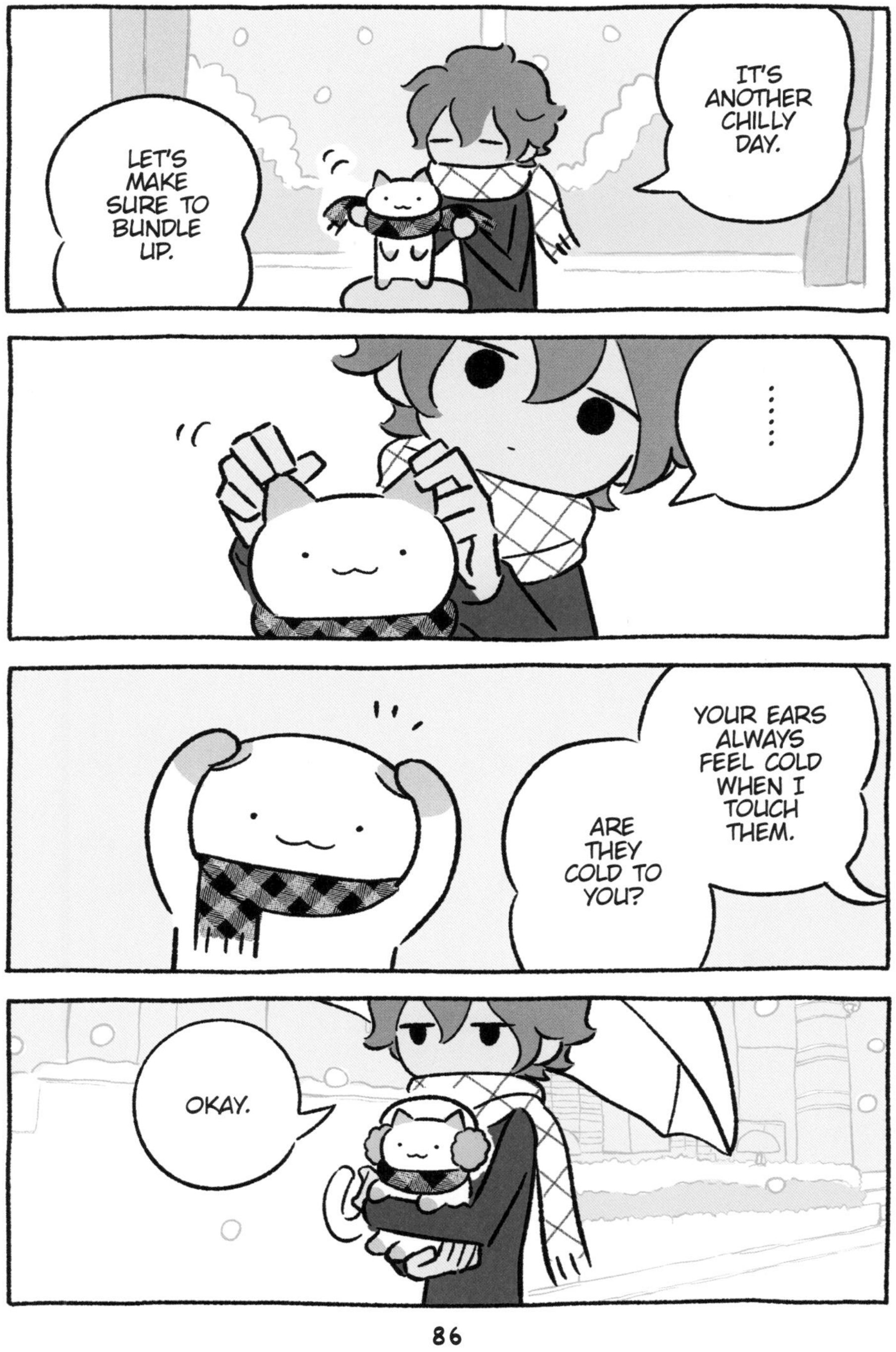
IT'S ANOTHER CHILLY DAY.
LET'S MAKE SURE TO BUNDLE UP.
......
YOUR EARS ALWAYS FEEL COLD WHEN I TOUCH THEM.
ARE THEY COLD TO YOU?
OKAY.

REALIZATION

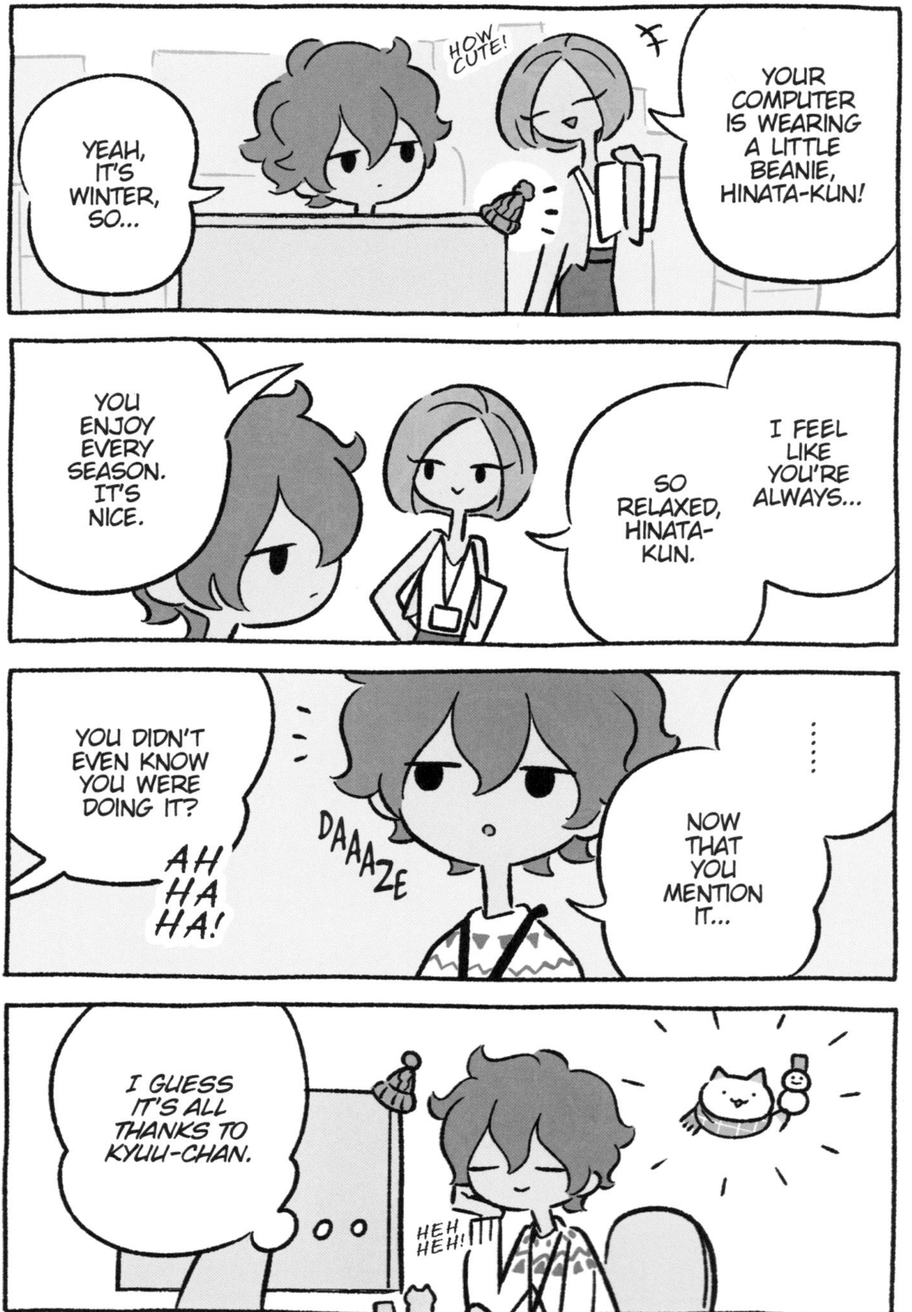

YOUR COMPUTER IS WEARING A LITTLE BEANIE, HINATA-KUN!
HOW CUTE!
YEAH, IT'S WINTER, SO...
I FEEL LIKE YOU'RE ALWAYS...
SO RELAXED, HINATA-KUN.
YOU ENJOY EVERY SEASON. IT'S NICE.
......
NOW THAT YOU MENTION IT...
DAAAZE
YOU DIDN'T EVEN KNOW YOU WERE DOING IT?
AH HA HA HA!
I GUESS IT'S ALL THANKS TO KYUU-CHAN.
HEH HEH!

FLAG

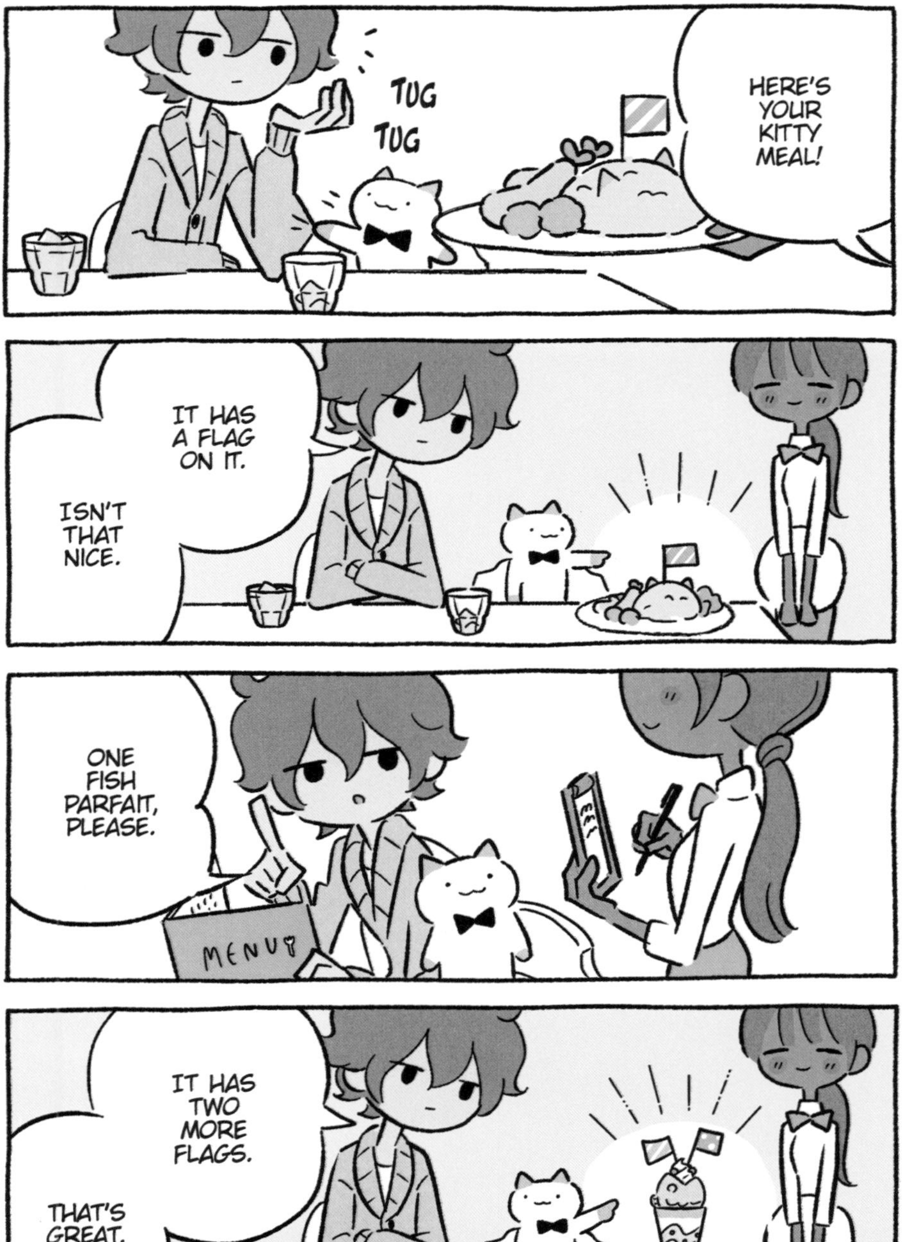
HERE'S YOUR KITTY MEAL!
TUG
TUG
IT HAS A FLAG ON IT.
ISN'T THAT NICE.
ONE FISH PARFAIT, PLEASE.
MENU
IT HAS TWO MORE FLAGS.
THAT'S GREAT.

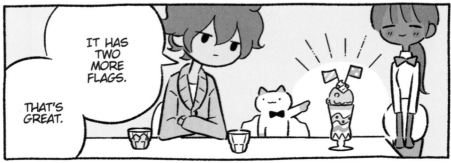

MIXED IN

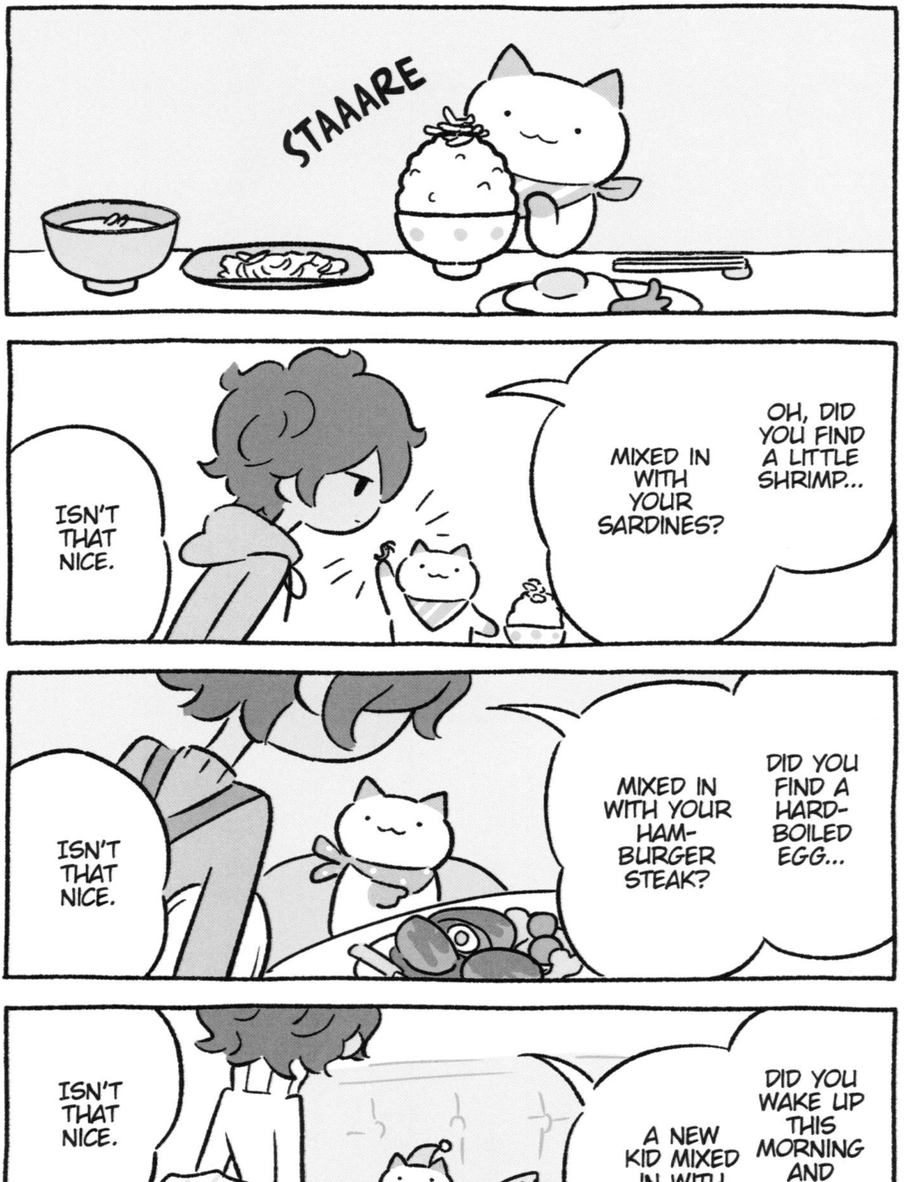
STAAARE
OH, DID YOU FIND A LITTLE SHRIMP...
MIXED IN WITH YOUR SARDINES?
ISN'T THAT NICE.
DID YOU FIND A HARD-BOILED EGG...
MIXED IN WITH YOUR HAM-BURGER STEAK?
ISN'T THAT NICE.
DID YOU WAKE UP THIS MORNING AND FIND...
A NEW KID MIXED IN WITH YOUR FAMILY?
ISN'T THAT NICE.

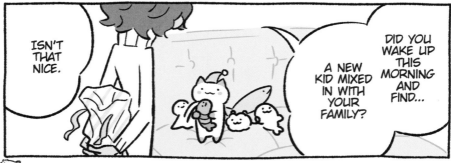

THE ONES IN THE SHADOWS

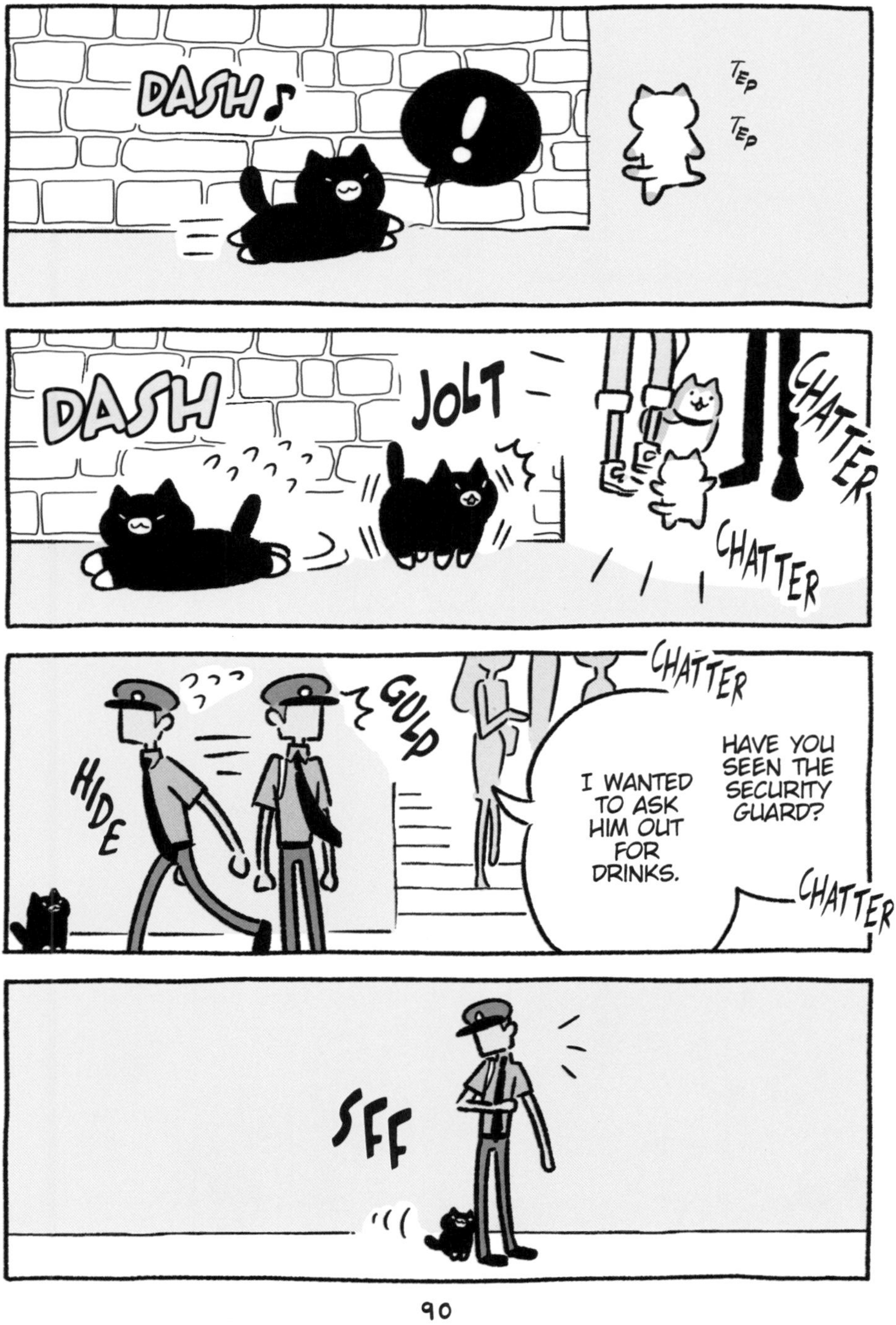
TEP
TEP
!
DASH♪
CHATTER
CHATTER
JOLT
DASH
CHATTER
HAVE YOU SEEN THE SECURITY GUARD?
I WANTED TO ASK HIM OUT FOR DRINKS.
CHATTER
GULP
HIDE
SFF

GUARD MAN

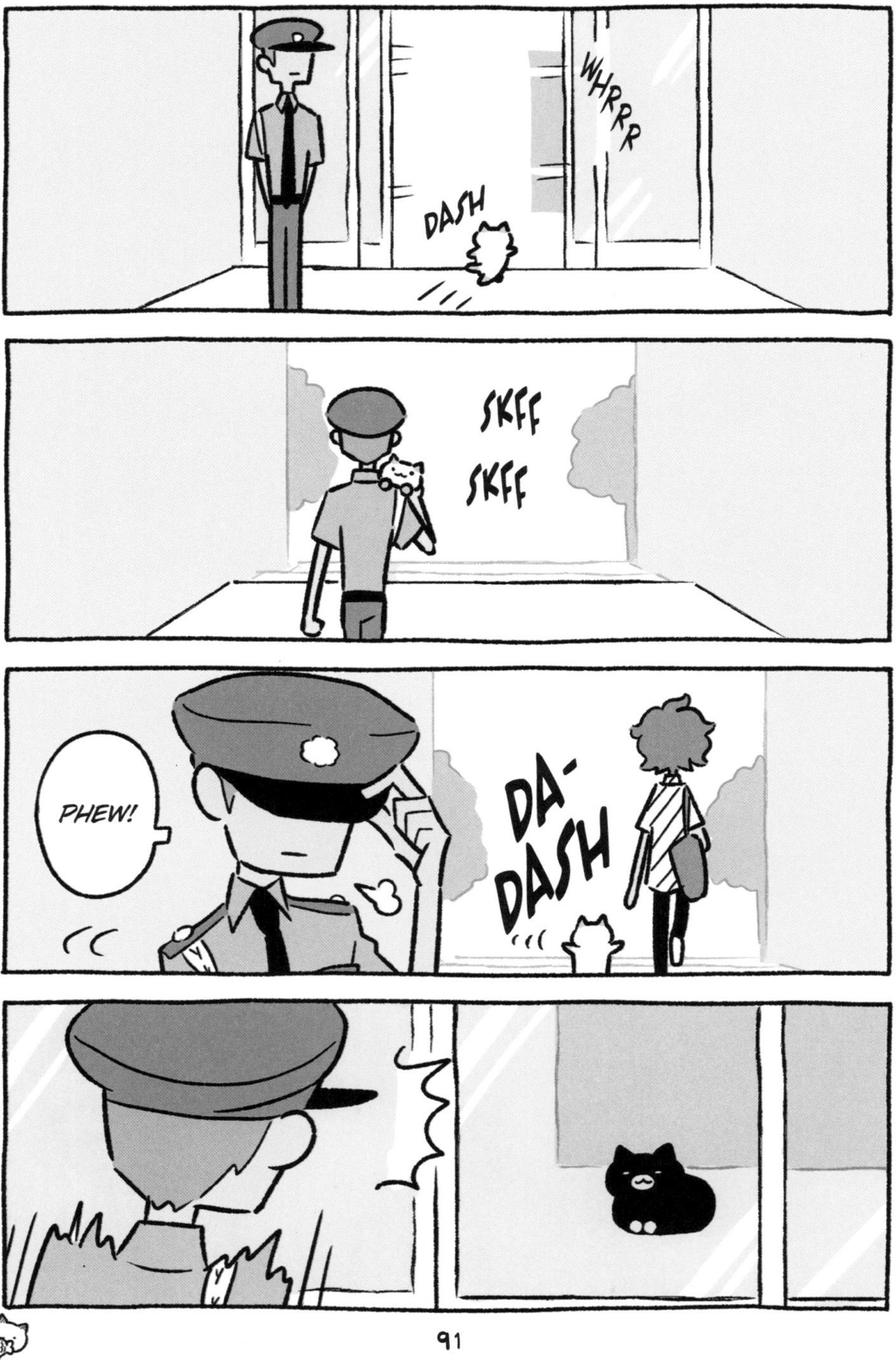
WHRRR
DASH
SKFF
SKFF
DA-DASH
PHEW!

WAITING

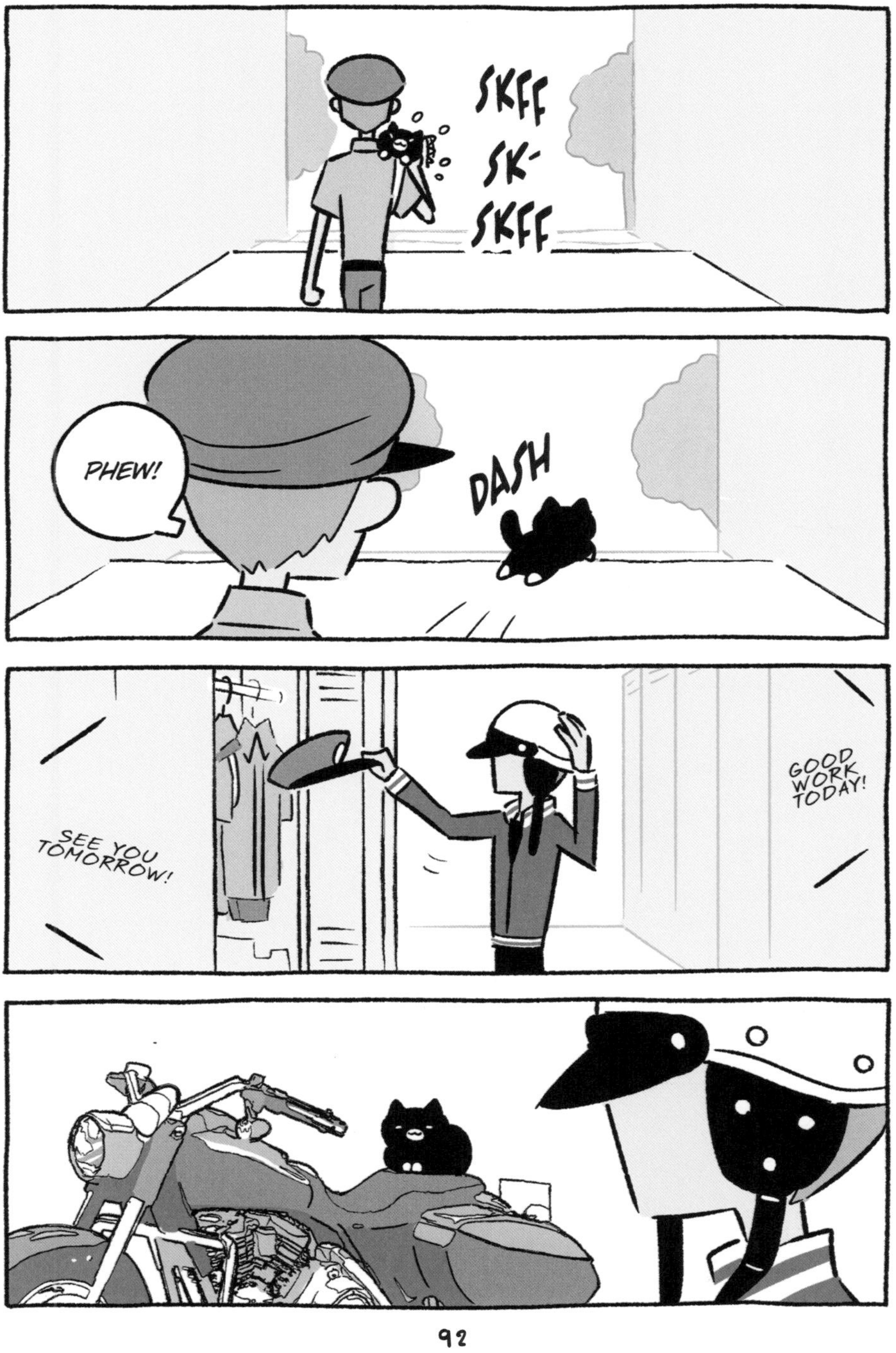
SKFF
SK-
SKFF
DASH
PHEW!
GOOD WORK TODAY!
SEE YOU TOMORROW!

A PLACE TO CALL HOME

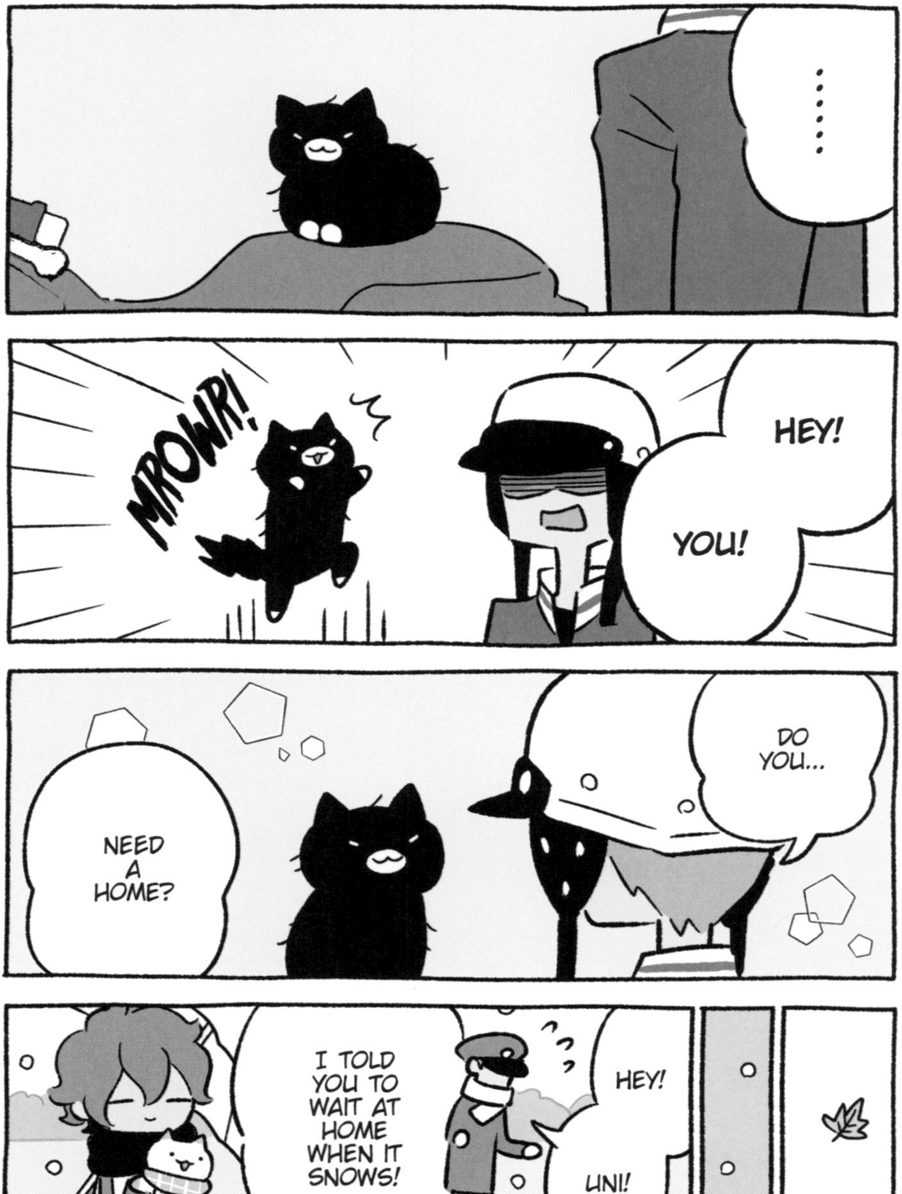
......
HEY!
YOU!
MROWR!
DO YOU...
NEED A HOME?
HEY!
UNI!
I TOLD YOU TO WAIT AT HOME WHEN IT SNOWS!

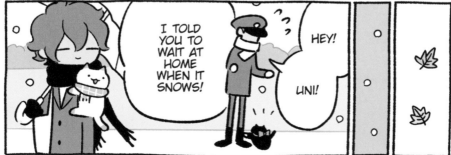

THE SECRET OF THE SHRIMP

LOOK CLOSELY...
THERE'S A ZIPPER ON ITS BACK.
TURN IT INSIDE OUT, AND...
TA-DA!
FRIED SHRIMP!

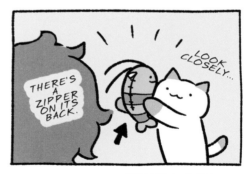

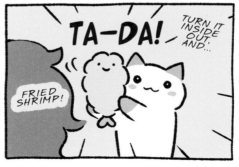

KOTATSU

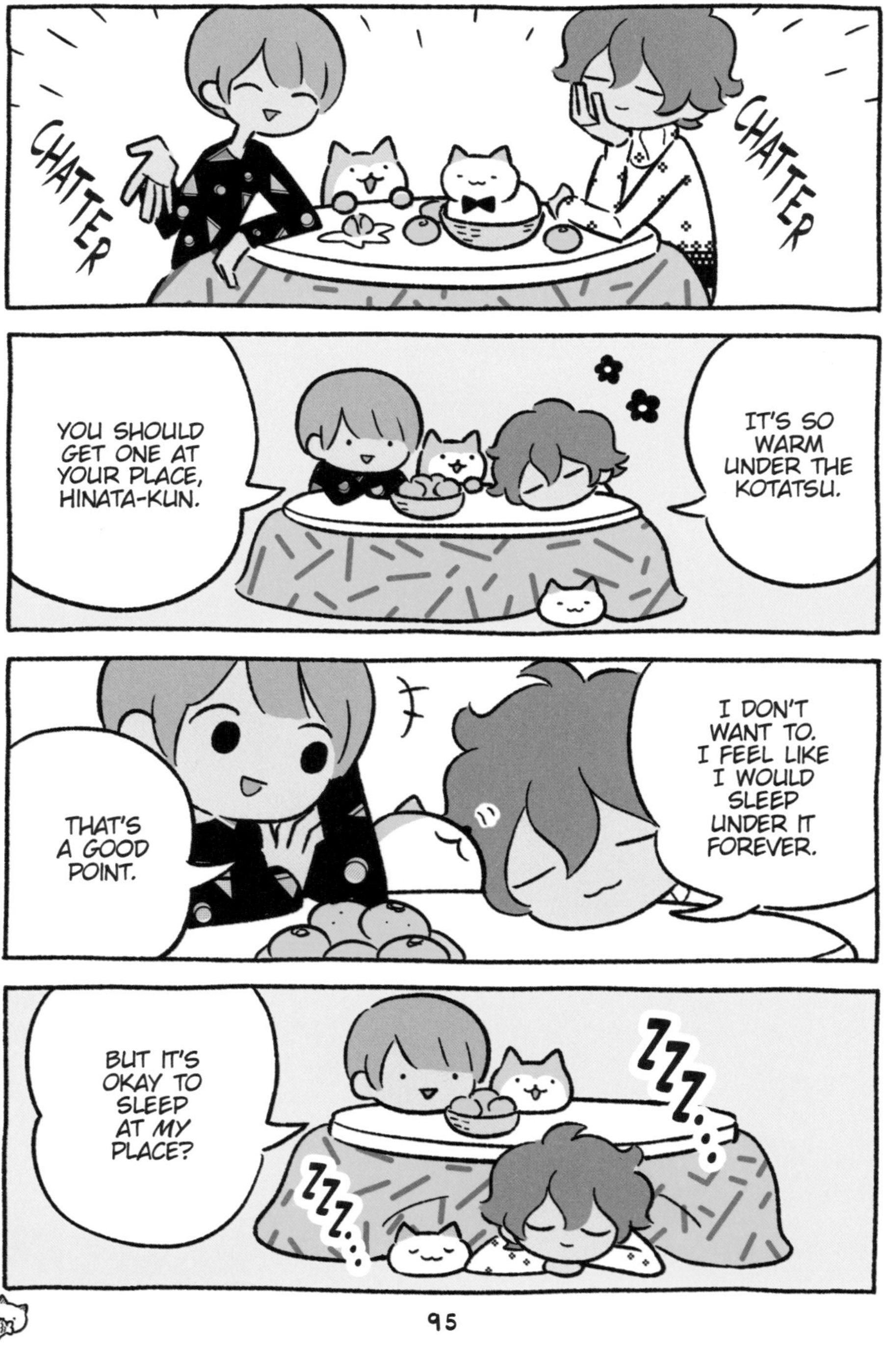
CHATTER
CHATTER
IT'S SO WARM UNDER THE KOTATSU.
YOU SHOULD GET ONE AT YOUR PLACE, HINATA-KUN.
I DON'T WANT TO. I FEEL LIKE I WOULD SLEEP UNDER IT FOREVER.
THAT'S A GOOD POINT.
ZZZ...
BUT IT'S OKAY TO SLEEP AT MY PLACE?
ZZZ...

SURPRISE ATTACK

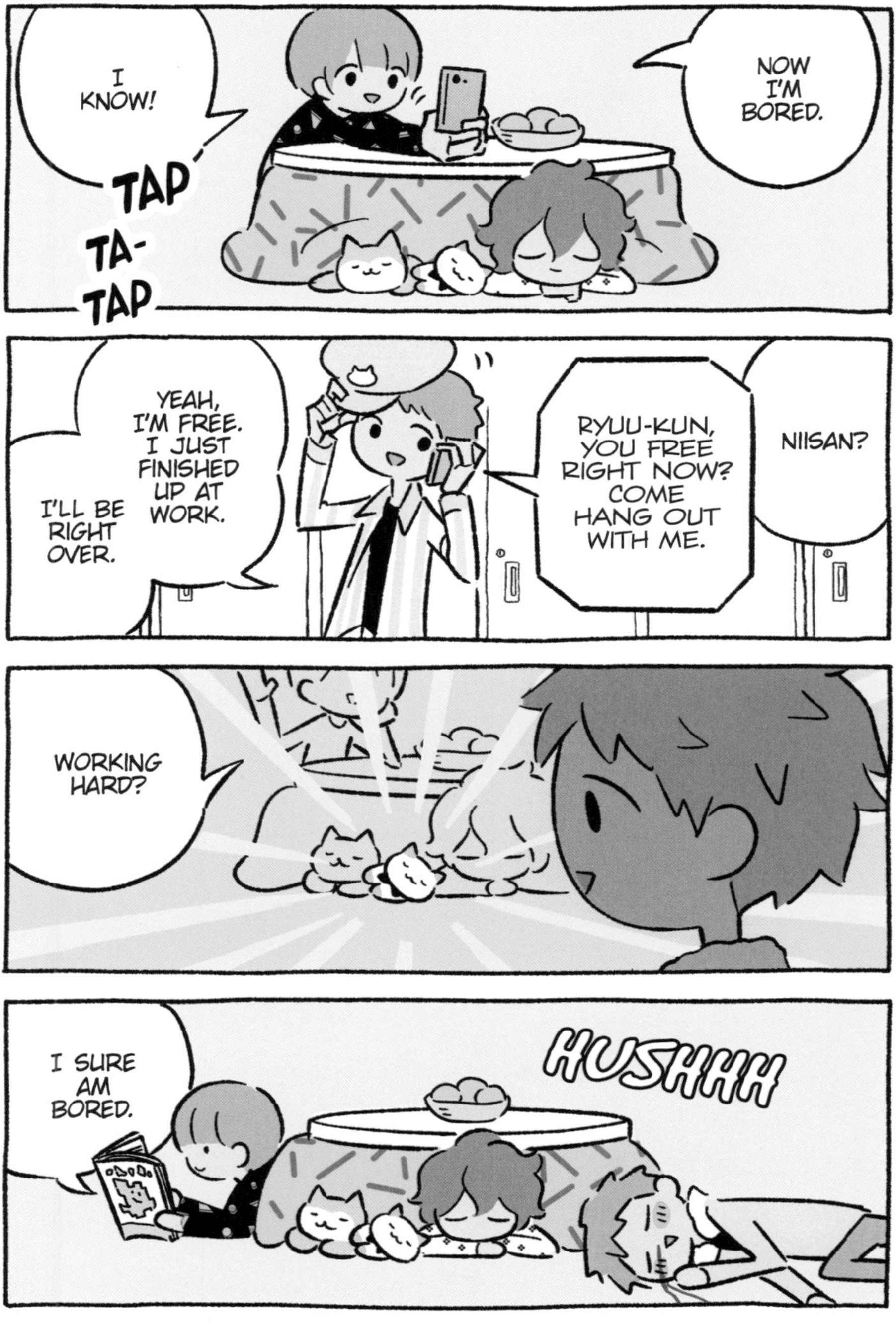
NOW I'M BORED.
I KNOW!
TAP TA-TAP
NIISAN?
RYUU-KUN, YOU FREE RIGHT NOW? COME HANG OUT WITH ME.
YEAH, I'M FREE. I JUST FINISHED UP AT WORK.
I'LL BE RIGHT OVER.
WORKING HARD?
HUSHHH
I SURE AM BORED.

STARVING

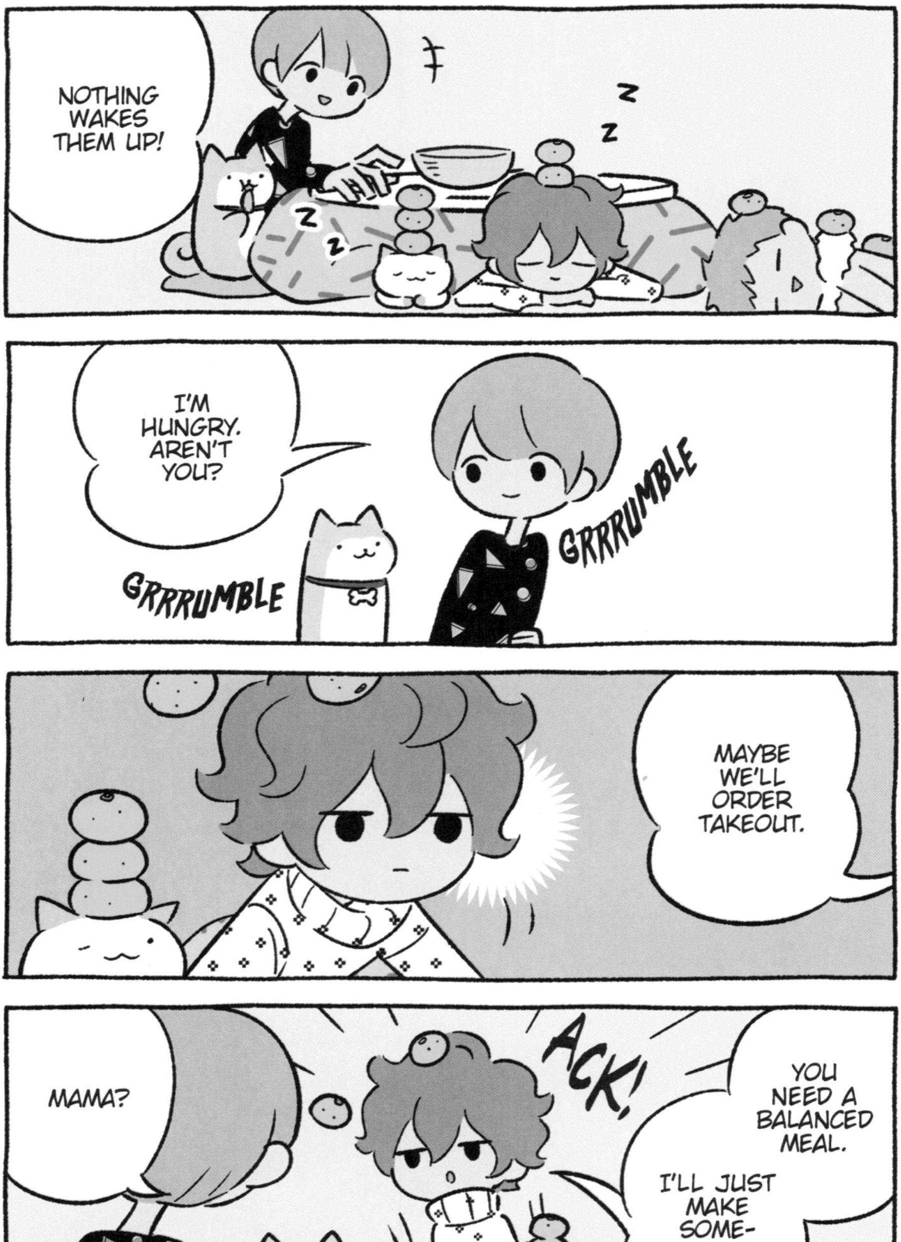
NOTHING WAKES THEM UP!
Z
Z
Z
Z
I'M HUNGRY. AREN'T YOU?
GRRRUMBLE
GRRRUMBLE
MAYBE WE'LL ORDER TAKEOUT.
YOU NEED A BALANCED MEAL.
ACK!
I'LL JUST MAKE SOME-THING.
MAMA?

MARSHMALLOW

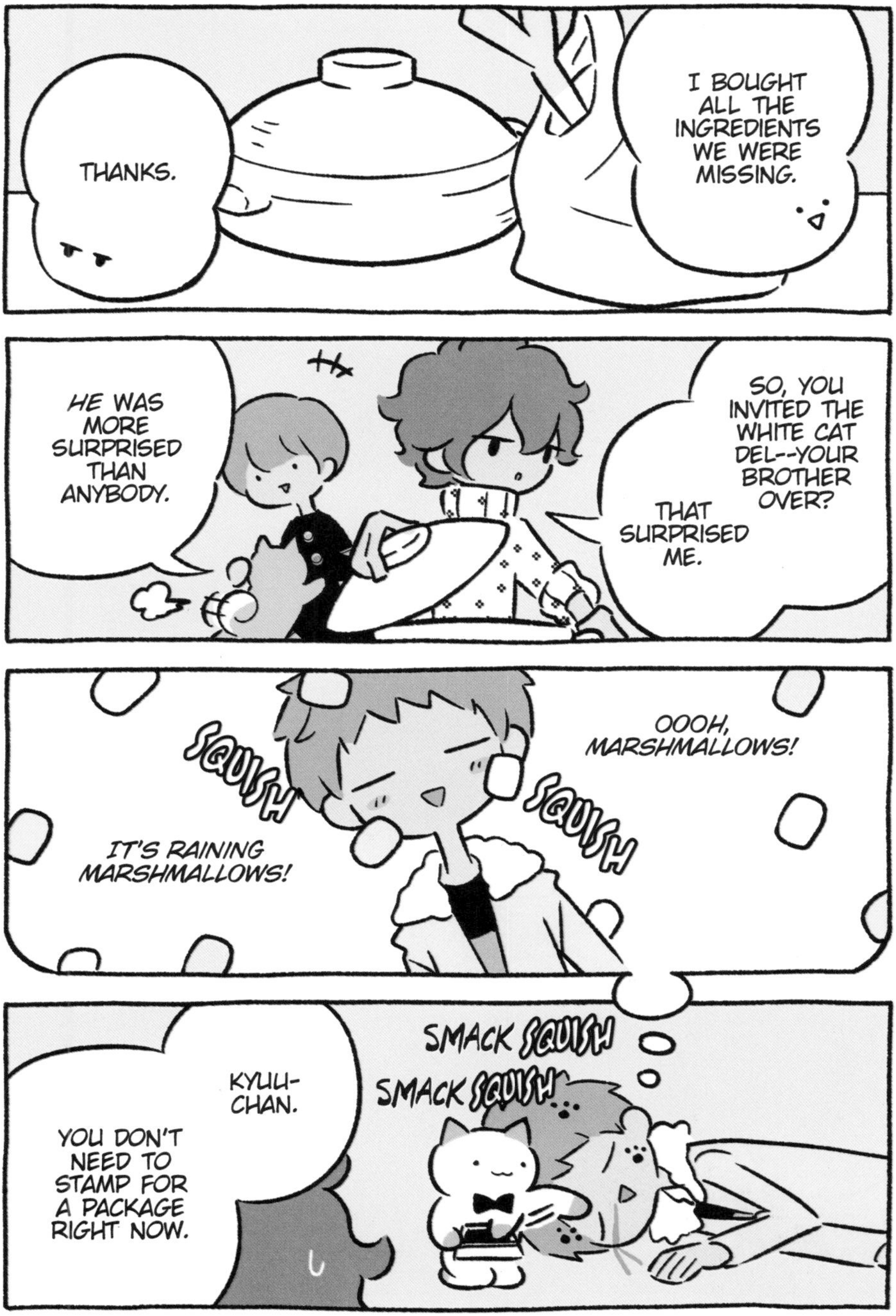

I BOUGHT ALL THE INGREDIENTS WE WERE MISSING.
THANKS.
SO, YOU INVITED THE WHITE CAT DEL--YOUR BROTHER OVER?
THAT SURPRISED ME.
HE WAS MORE SURPRISED THAN ANYBODY.
OOOH, MARSHMALLOWS!
SQUISH
SQUISH
IT'S RAINING MARSHMALLOWS!
SMACK SQUISH
SMACK SQUISH
KYUU-CHAN.
YOU DON'T NEED TO STAMP FOR A PACKAGE RIGHT NOW.

CONDITIONED RESPONSE

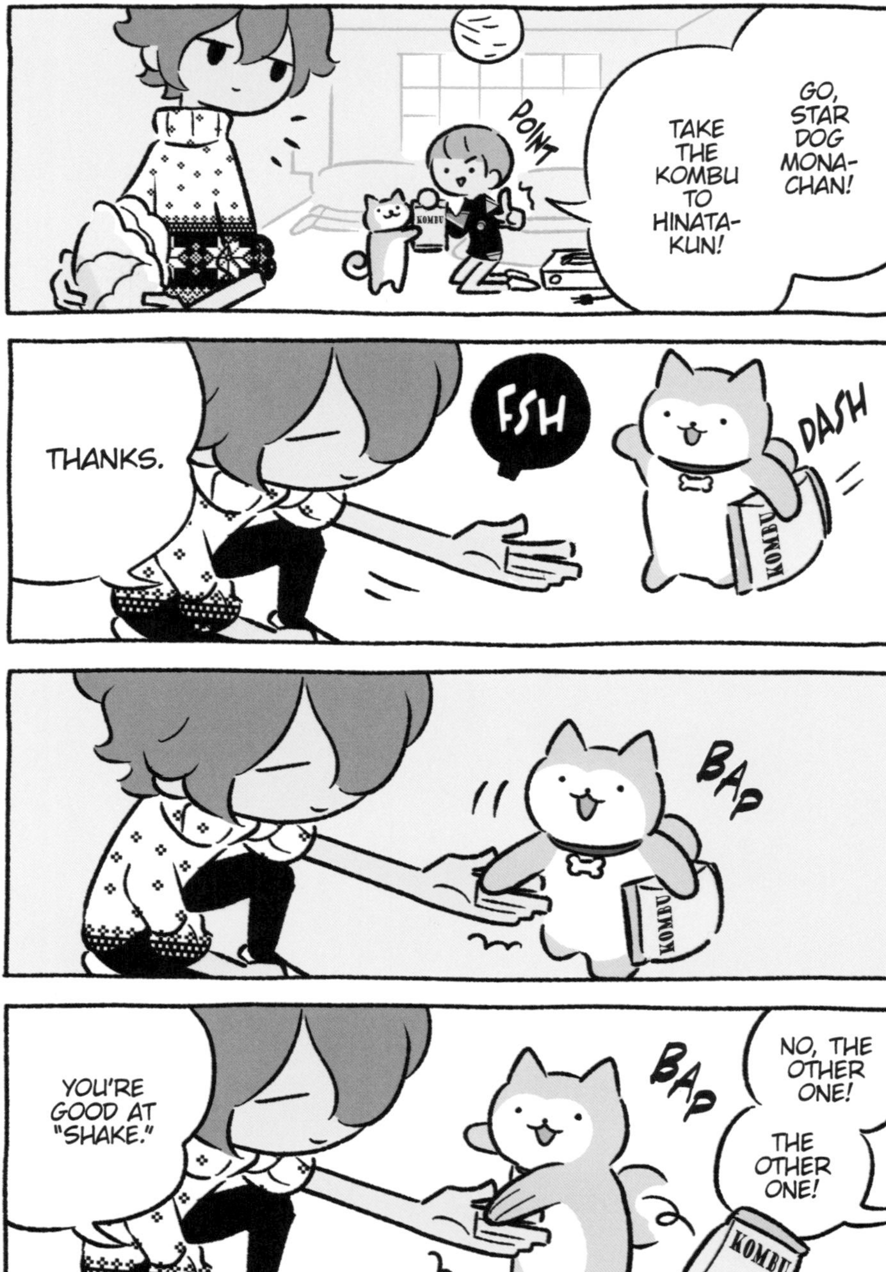
GO, STAR DOG MONA-CHAN!
TAKE THE KOMBU TO HINATA-KUN!
POINT
KOMBU
DASH
FSH
THANKS.
KOMBU
BAP
KOMBU
NO, THE OTHER ONE!
THE OTHER ONE!
BAP
YOU'RE GOOD AT "SHAKE."
KOMBU

CHEAT CODE

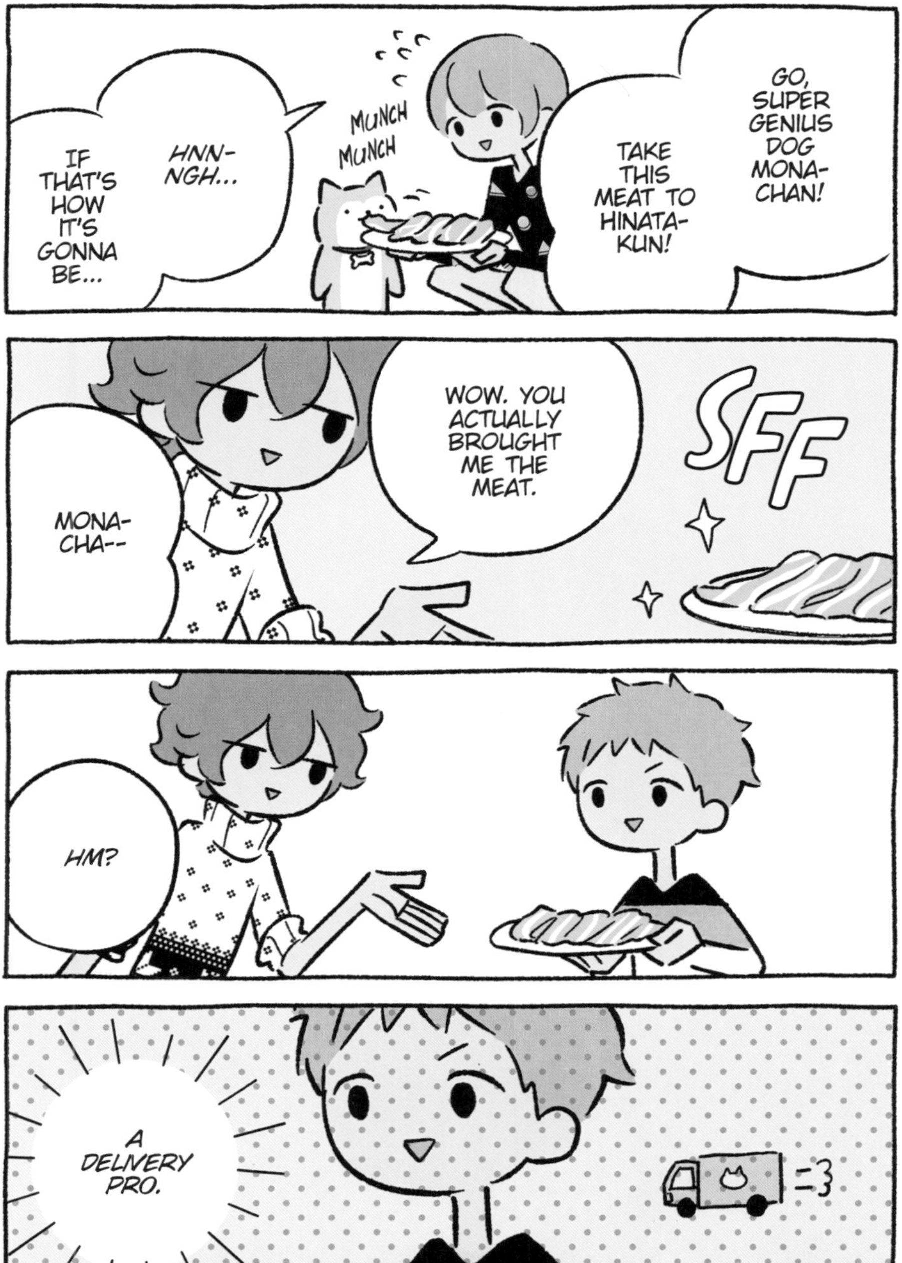
GO, SUPER GENIUS DOG MONA-CHAN!
TAKE THIS MEAT TO HINATA-KUN!
MUNCH MUNCH
HNN-NGH...
IF THAT'S HOW IT'S GONNA BE...
SFF
WOW. YOU ACTUALLY BROUGHT ME THE MEAT.
MONA-CHA--
HM?
A DELIVERY PRO.

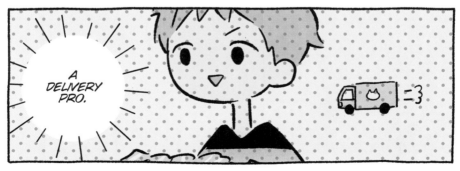

OFF THE CLOCK

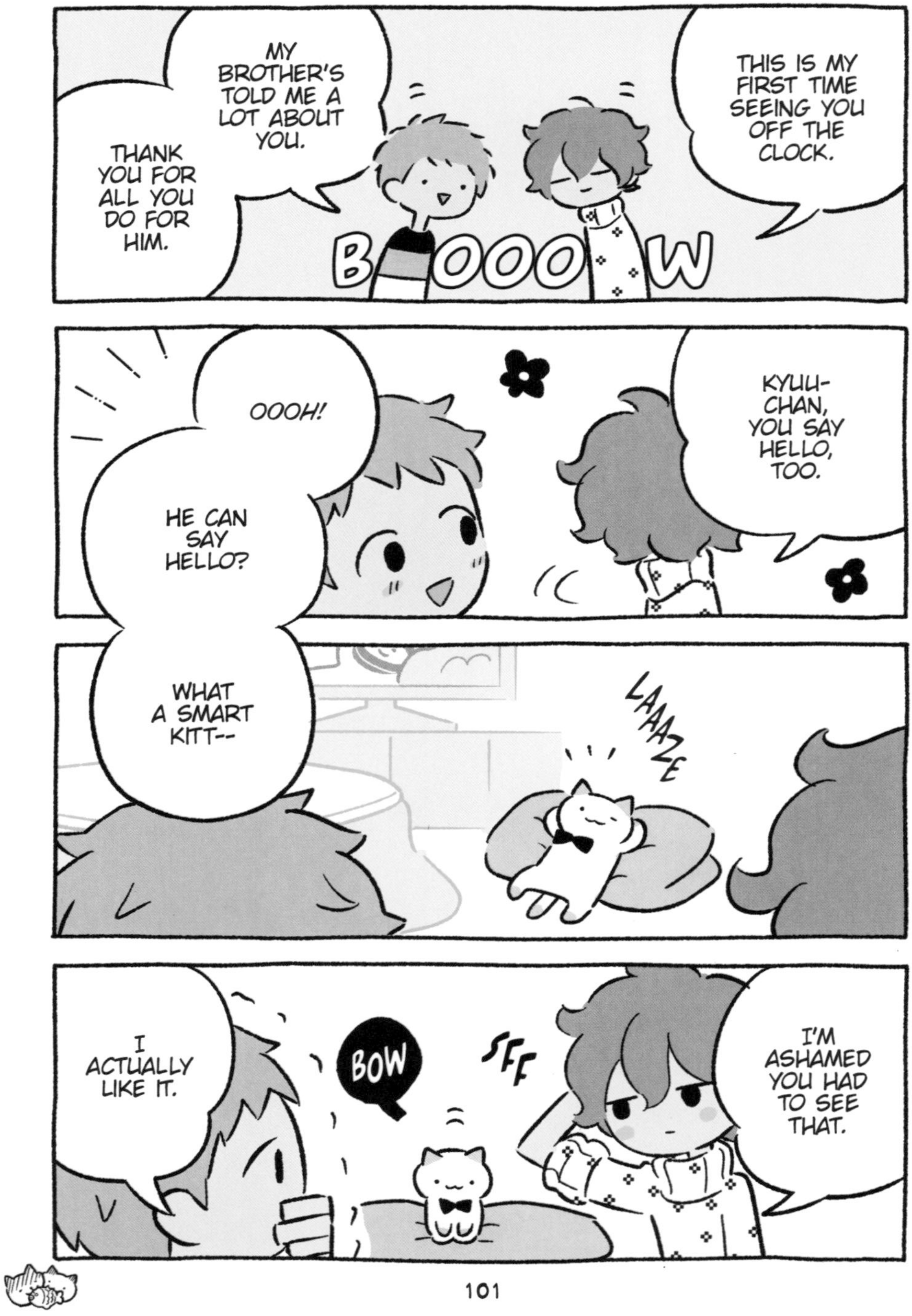
THIS IS MY FIRST TIME SEEING YOU OFF THE CLOCK.
MY BROTHER'S TOLD ME A LOT ABOUT YOU.
THANK YOU FOR ALL YOU DO FOR HIM.
BOOOW
KYUU-CHAN, YOU SAY HELLO, TOO.
OOOH!
HE CAN SAY HELLO?
WHAT A SMART KITT--
LAAAAZE
I'M ASHAMED YOU HAD TO SEE THAT.
SFF
BOW
I ACTUALLY LIKE IT.

REASON

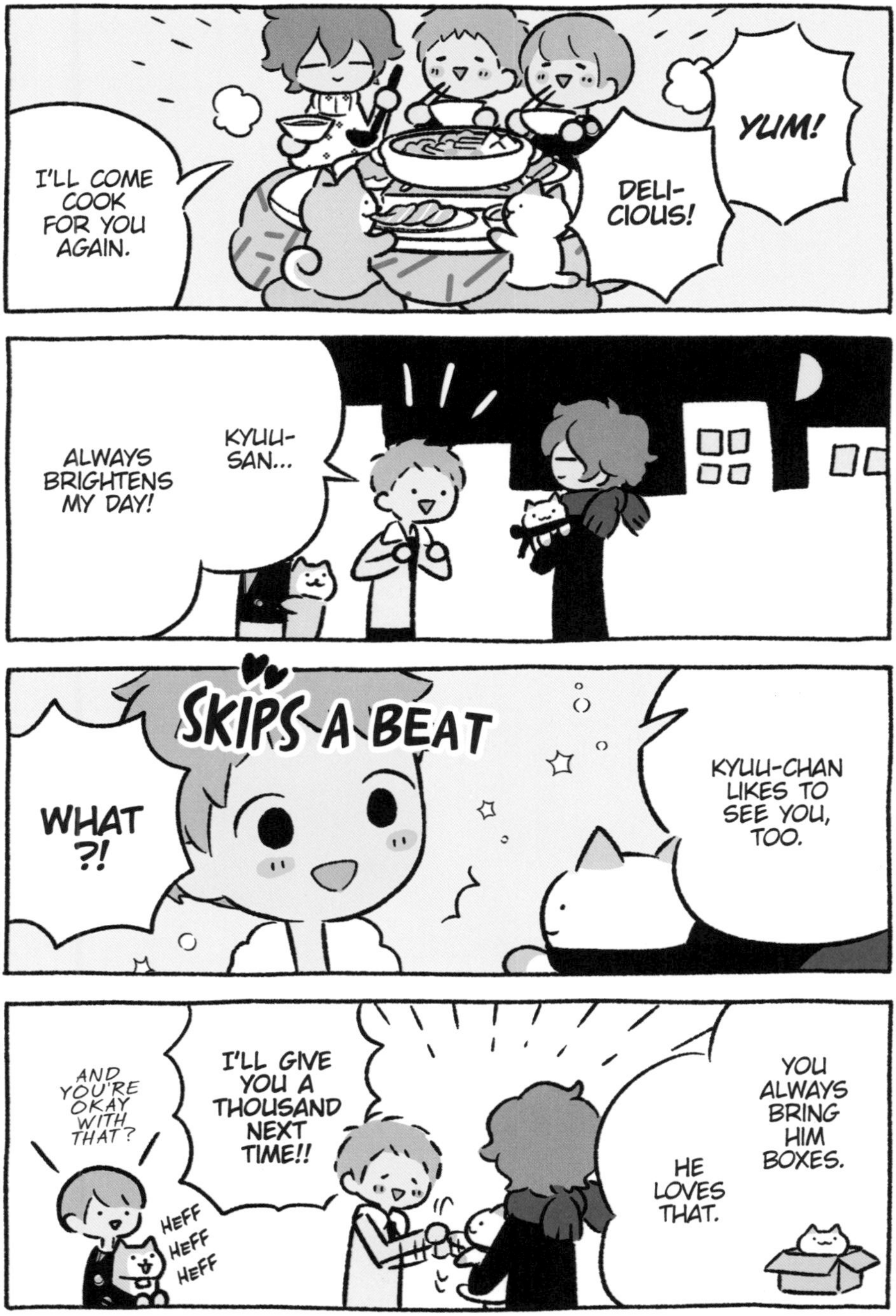
YUM!
DELI-CIOUS!
I'LL COME COOK FOR YOU AGAIN.
KYUU-SAN...
ALWAYS BRIGHTENS MY DAY!
KYUU-CHAN LIKES TO SEE YOU, TOO.
SKIPS A BEAT
WHAT?!
YOU ALWAYS BRING HIM BOXES.
HE LOVES THAT.
I'LL GIVE YOU A THOUSAND NEXT TIME!!
AND YOU'RE OKAY WITH THAT?
HEFF HEFF HEFF

A LITTLE TRIVIA(ZUKI)

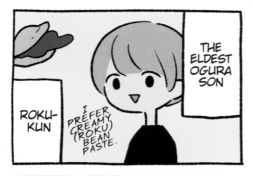

THE ELDEST OGURA SON
I PREFER CREAMY (ROKU) BEAN PASTE.
ROKU-KUN
THE SECOND OGURA SON
I PREFER CHUNKY (RYUU) BEAN PASTE.
RYUU-KUN

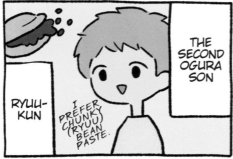

SURPRISE BOX

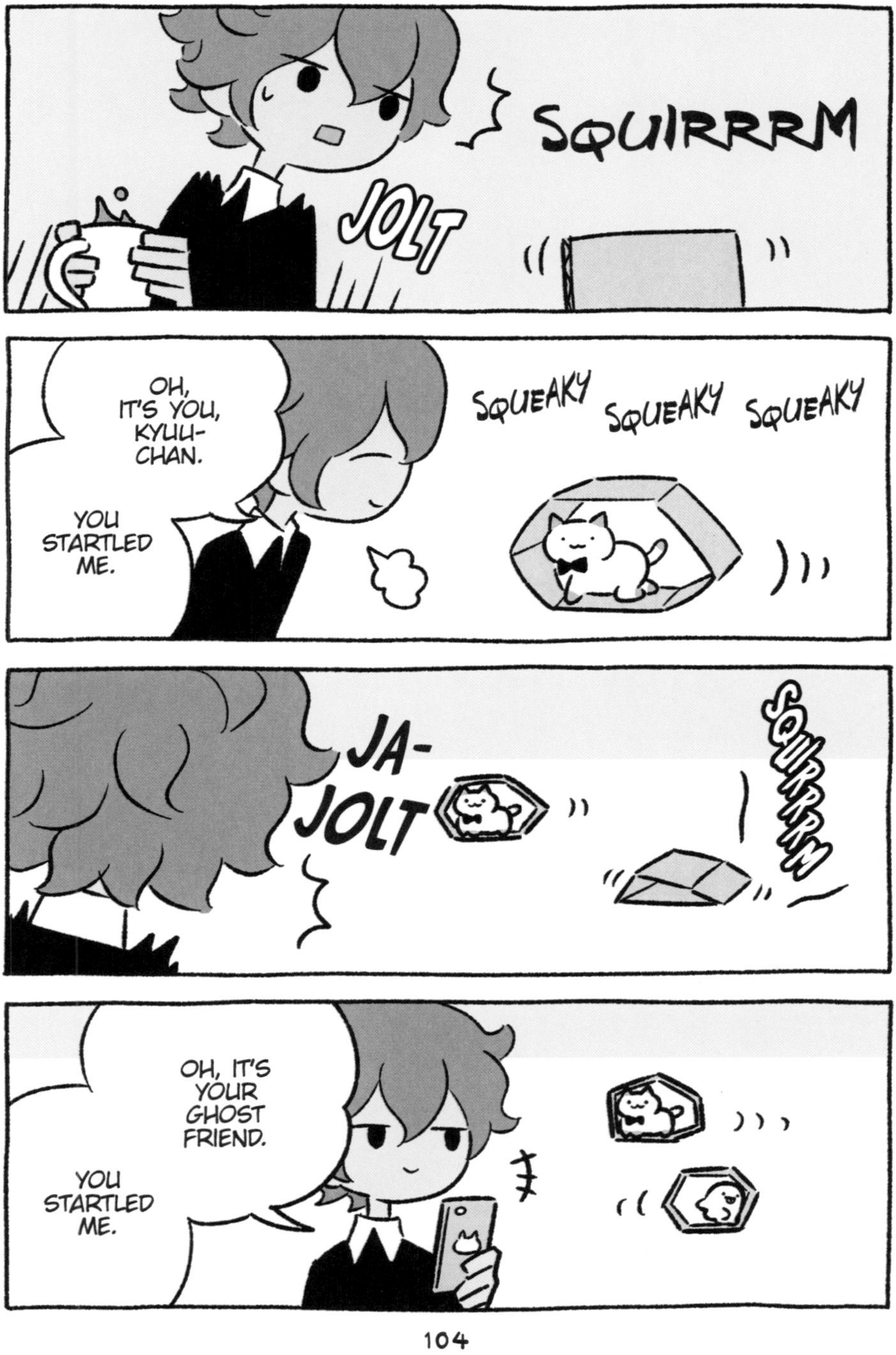
SQUIRRRM
JOLT
SQUEAKY
SQUEAKY
SQUEAKY
OH, IT'S YOU, KYUU-CHAN.
YOU STARTLED ME.
SQUIRRRM
JA-JOLT
OH, IT'S YOUR GHOST FRIEND.
YOU STARTLED ME.

MIXED UP IN

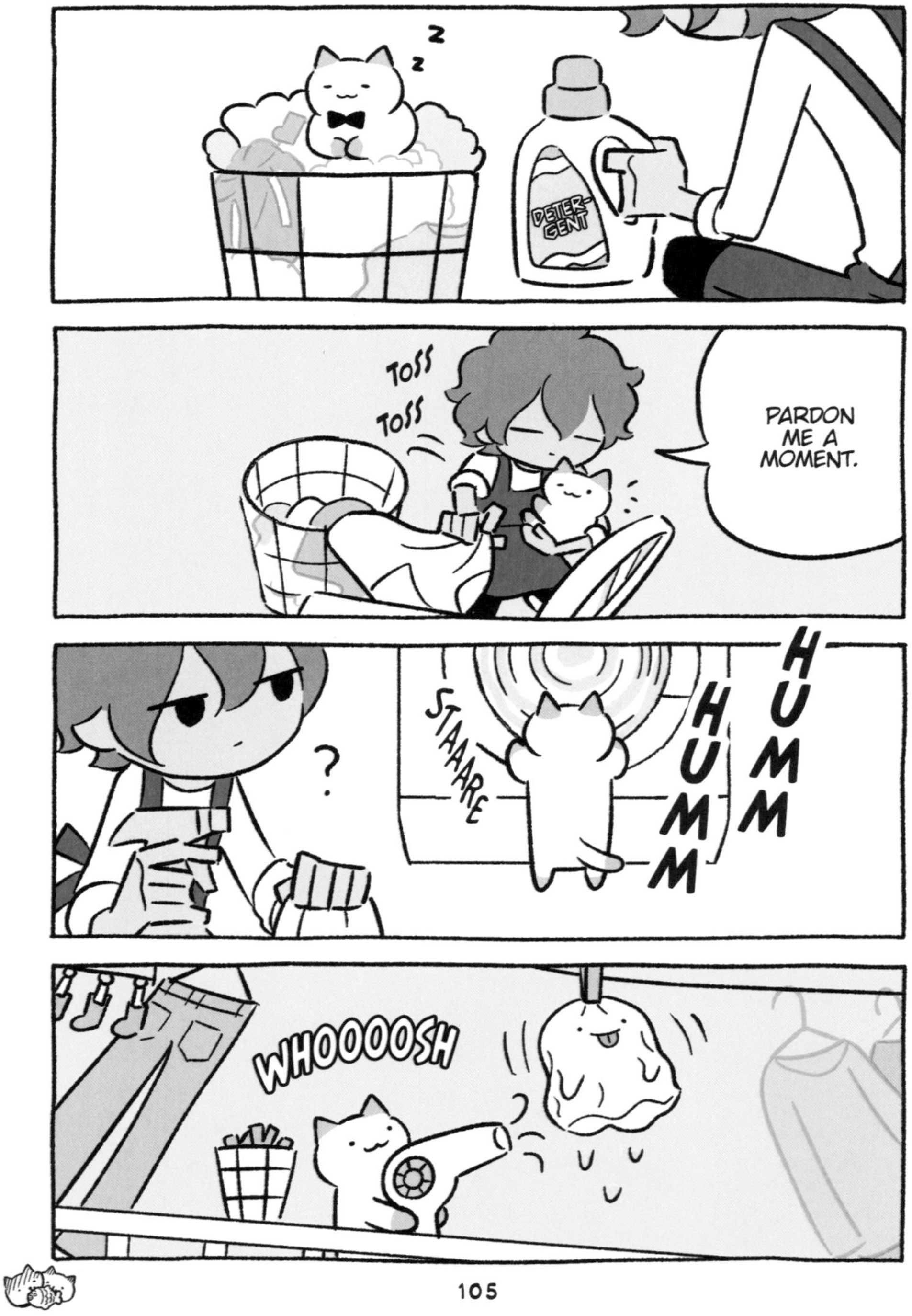

DETER-GENT
PARDON ME A MOMENT.
TOSS TOSS
HUMM HUMM
HUMM HUMM
STAAARE
WHOOOOSH

LUCKY

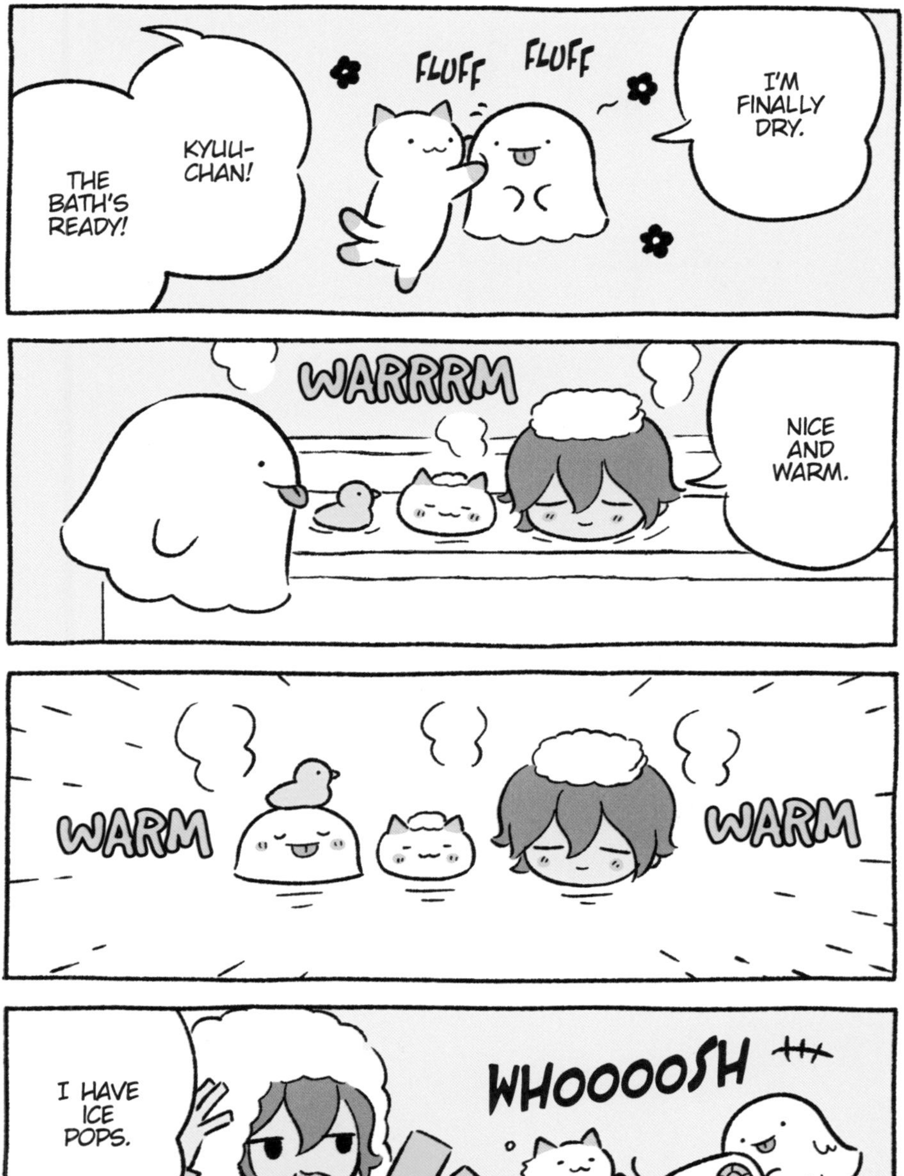
I'M FINALLY DRY.
FLUFF FLUFF
KYUU-CHAN! THE BATH'S READY!
NICE AND WARM.
WARRRM
WARM WARM
WHOOOOSH
I HAVE ICE POPS.
Chill

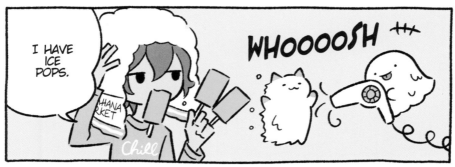

PINK SENSOR

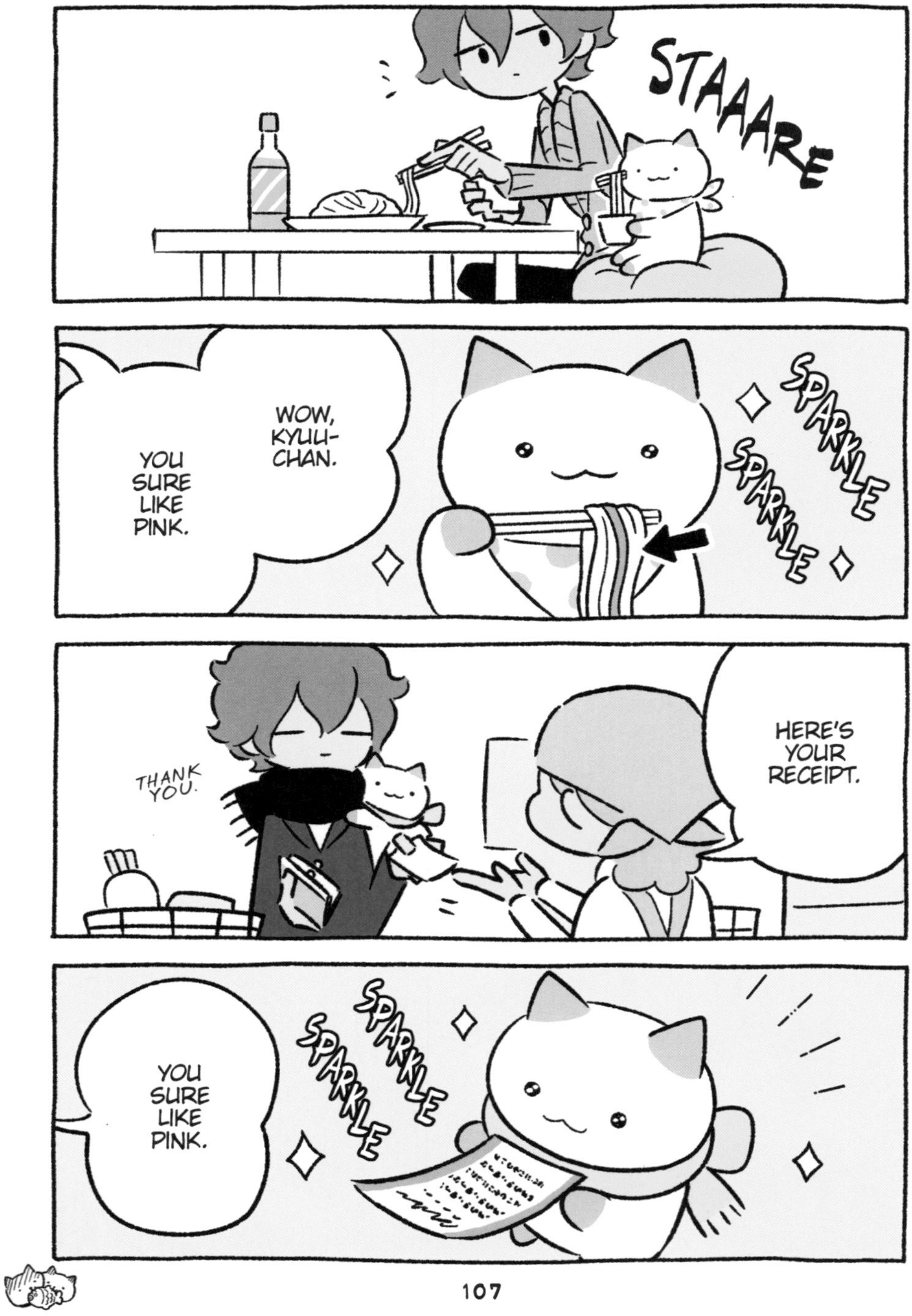
STAAARE
SPARKLE
SPARKLE
WOW, KYUU-CHAN. YOU SURE LIKE PINK.
HERE'S YOUR RECEIPT.
THANK YOU.
SPARKLE
SPARKLE
YOU SURE LIKE PINK.

STRANGE LANGUAGE RADAR

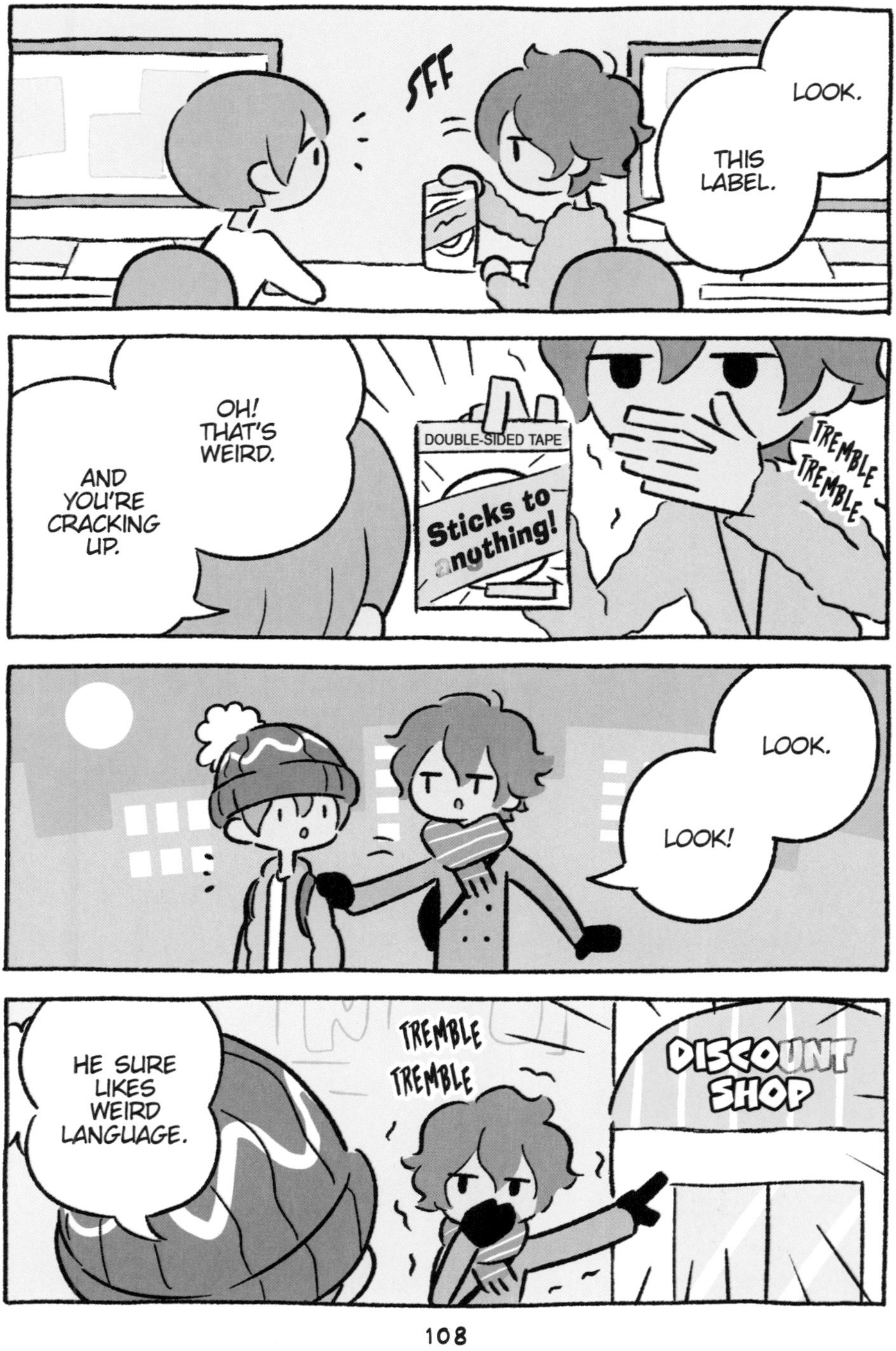
LOOK.
THIS LABEL.
SFF
TREMBLE TREMBLE
DOUBLE-SIDED TAPE
Sticks to anything!
OH! THAT'S WEIRD.
AND YOU'RE CRACKING UP.
LOOK.
LOOK!
DISCOUNT SHOP
TREMBLE TREMBLE
HE SURE LIKES WEIRD LANGUAGE.

STYLISH GLASSES

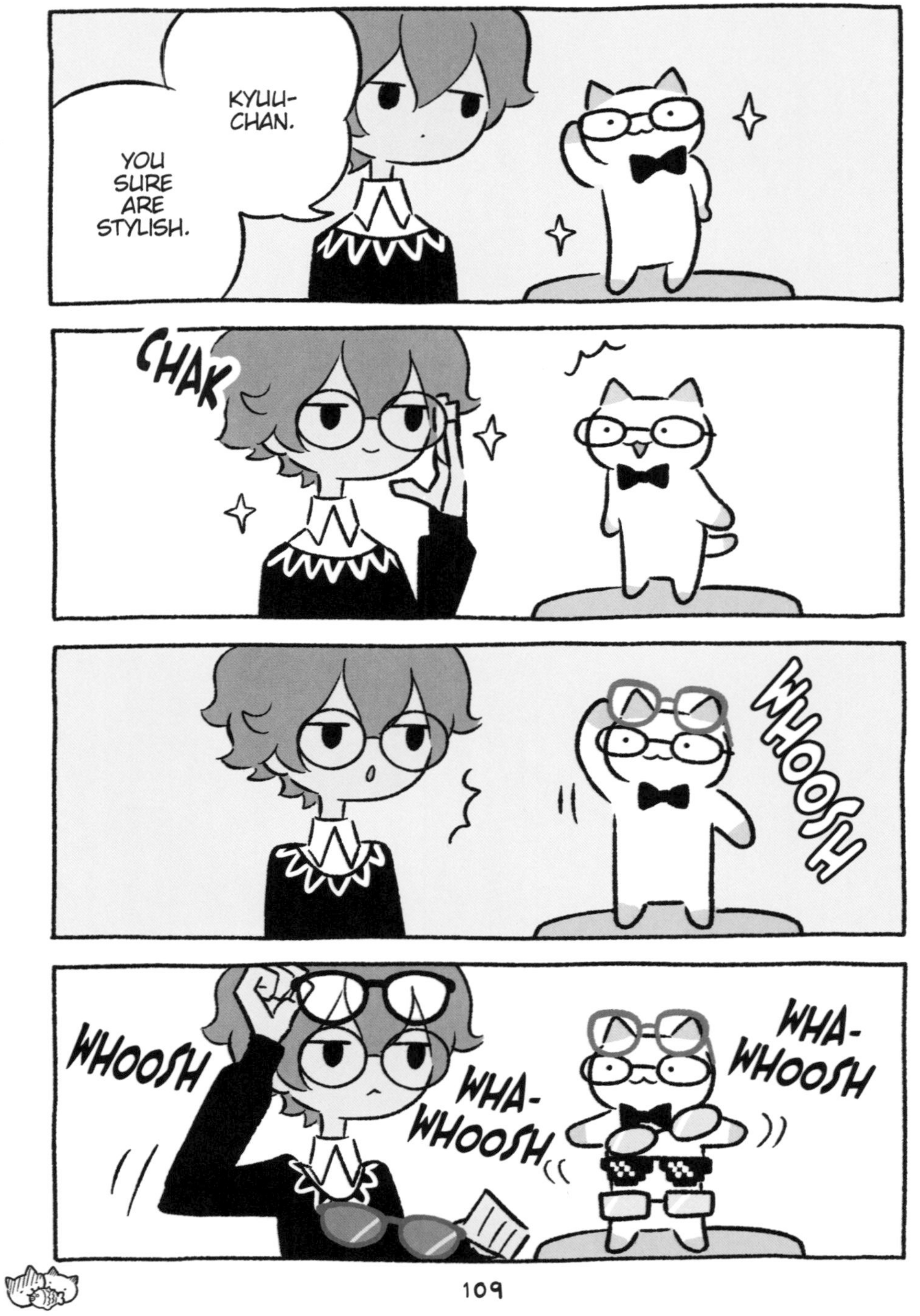
KYUU-CHAN.
YOU SURE ARE STYLISH.
CHAK
WHOOSH
WHA-WHOOSH
WHA-WHOOSH
WHOOSH

WHITE CAT

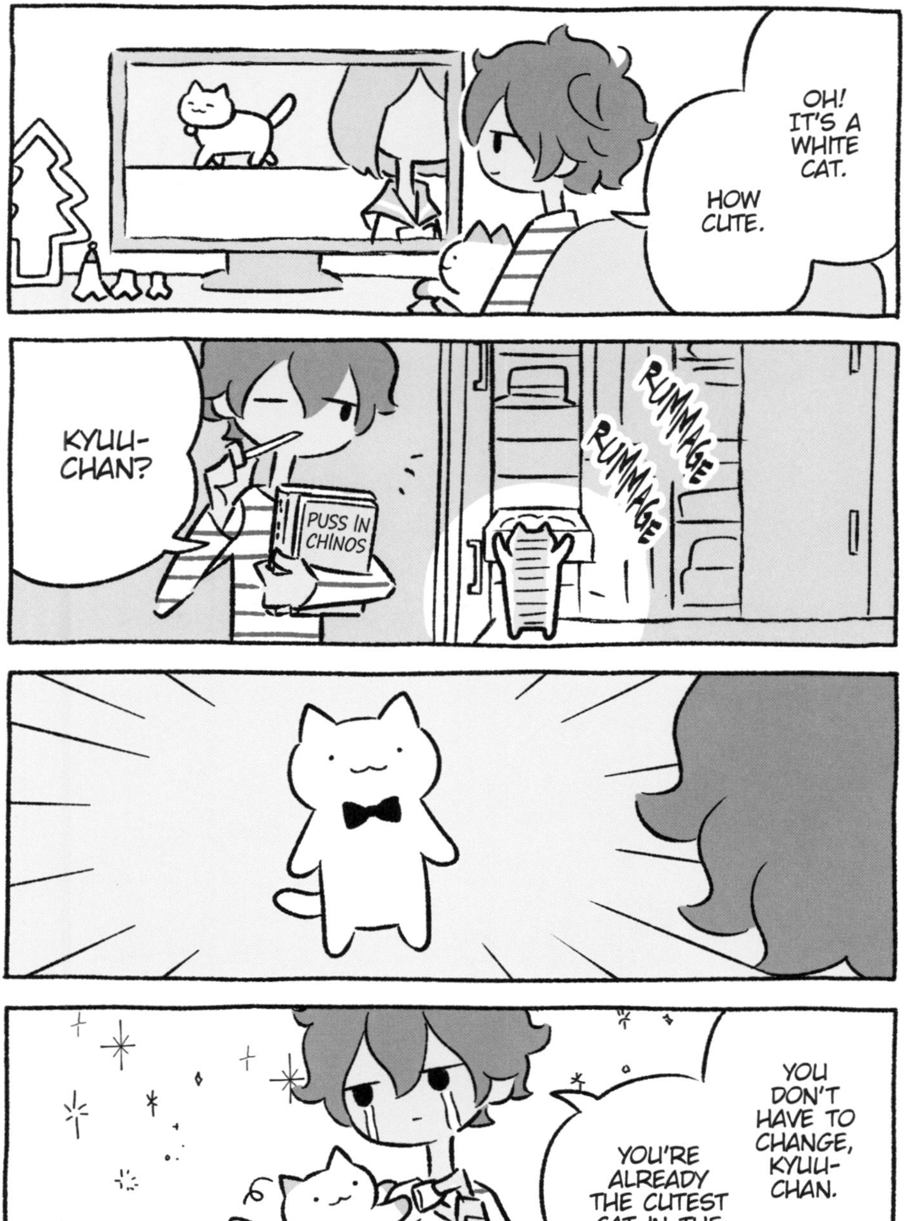
OH! IT'S A WHITE CAT.
HOW CUTE.
RUMMAGE
RUMMAGE
PUSS IN CHINOS
KYUU-CHAN?
YOU DON'T HAVE TO CHANGE, KYUU-CHAN.
YOU'RE ALREADY THE CUTEST CAT IN THE WORLD.

POPCORN AND...

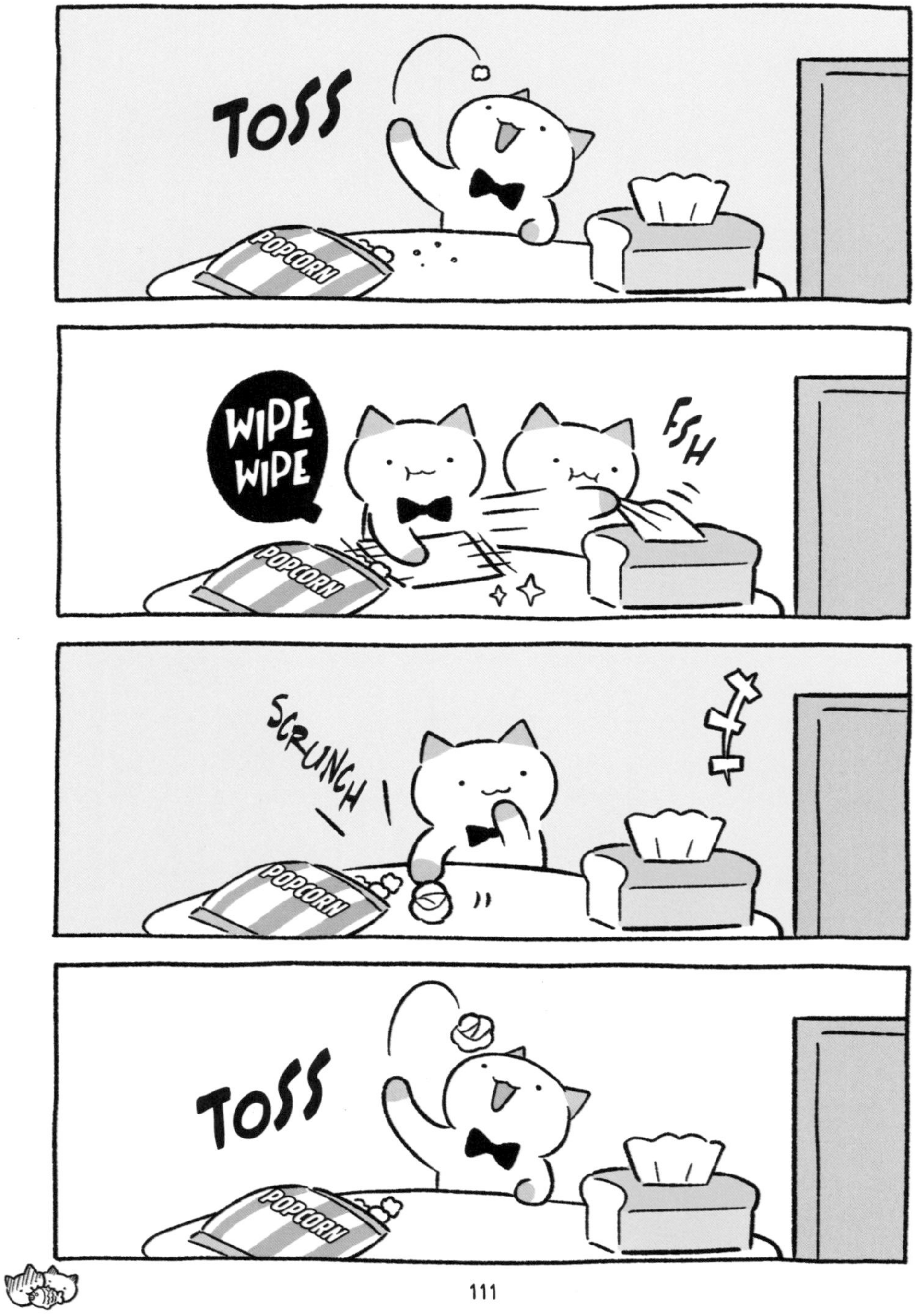
TOSS
POPCORN
FSH
WIPE WIPE
POPCORN
SCRUNCH
POPCORN
TOSS
POPCORN

SKATING RINK

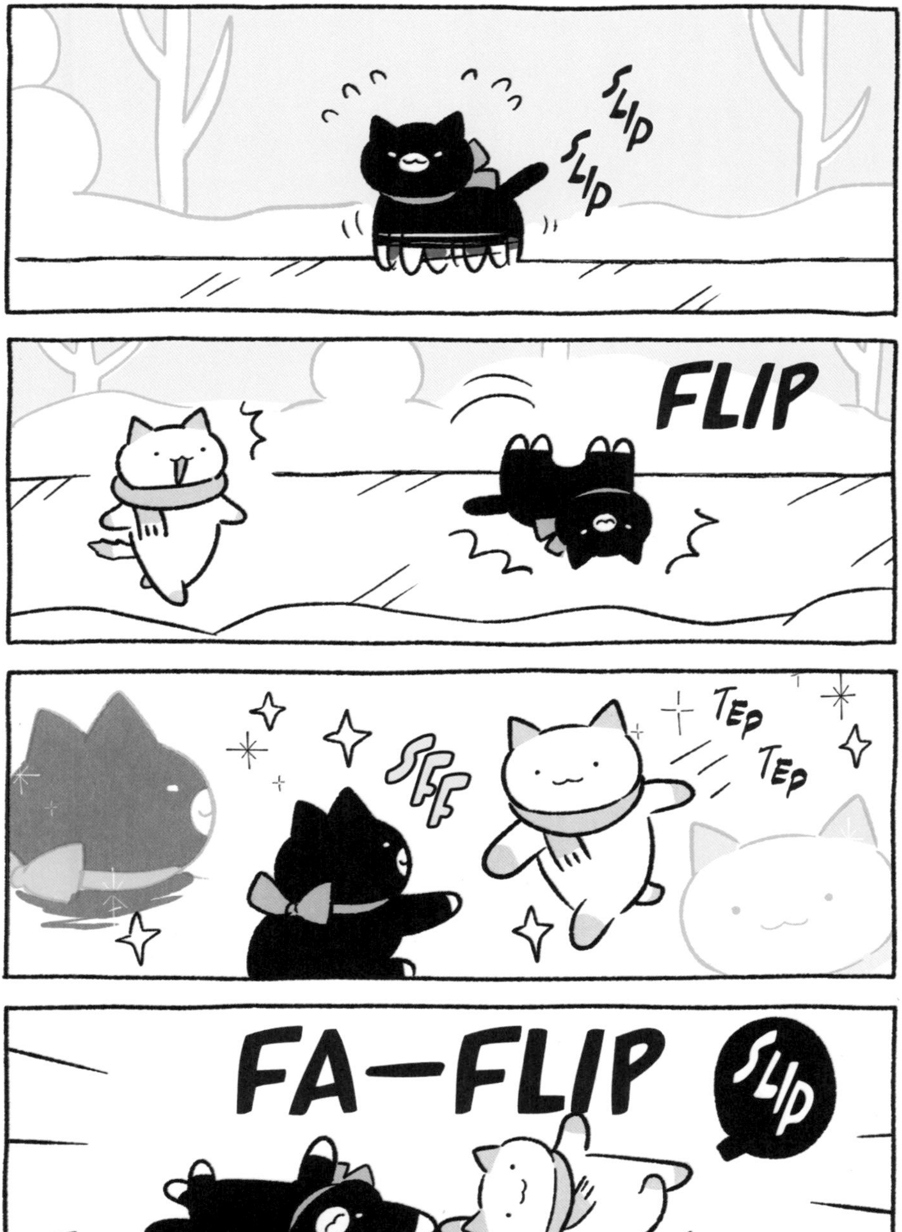
SLIP SLIP
FLIP
TEP TEP
SFF
SLIP
FA-FLIP

SNOWDRIFT

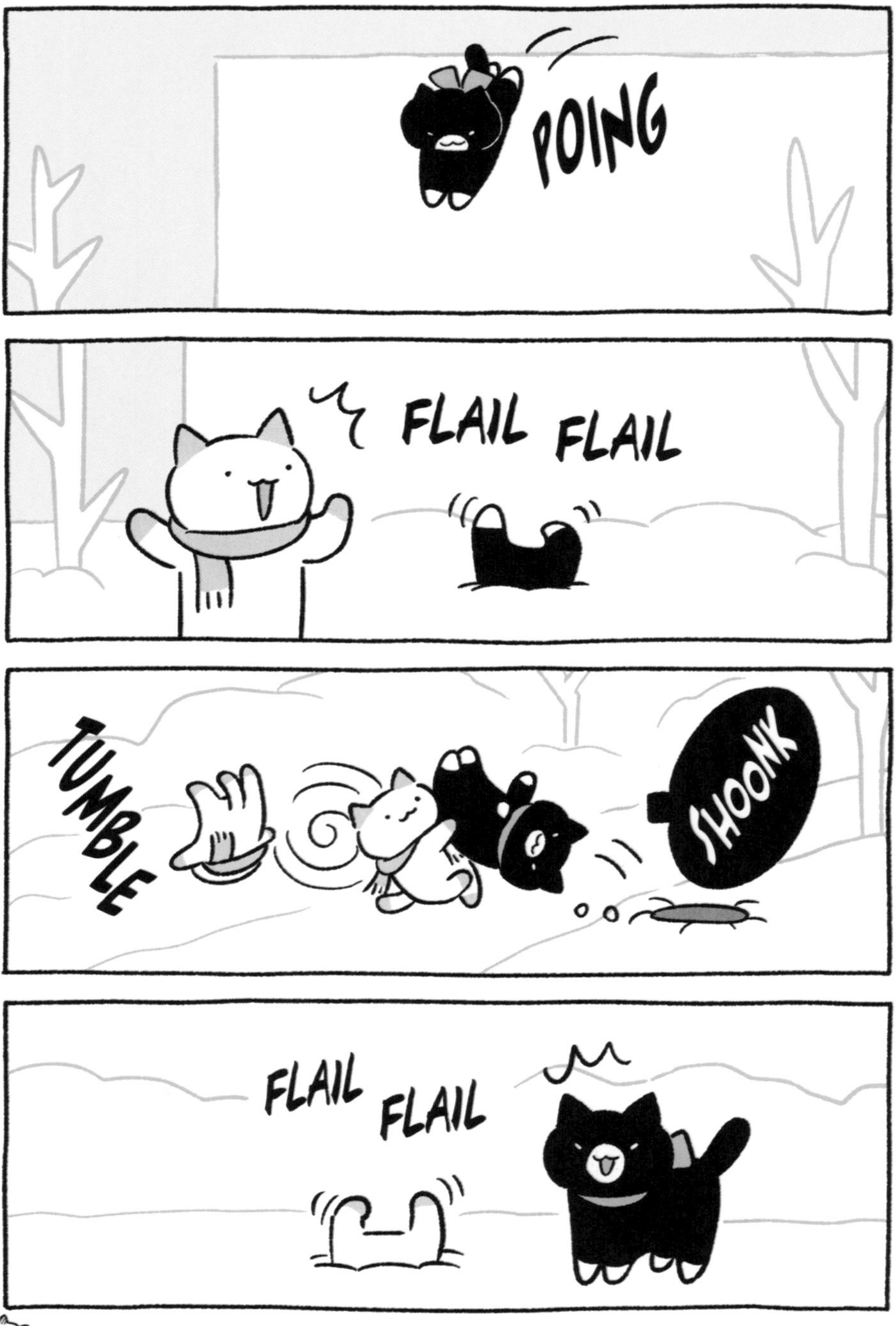
POING
FLAIL FLAIL
SHOONK
TUMBLE
FLAIL FLAIL

SNOWMAN ARTISAN

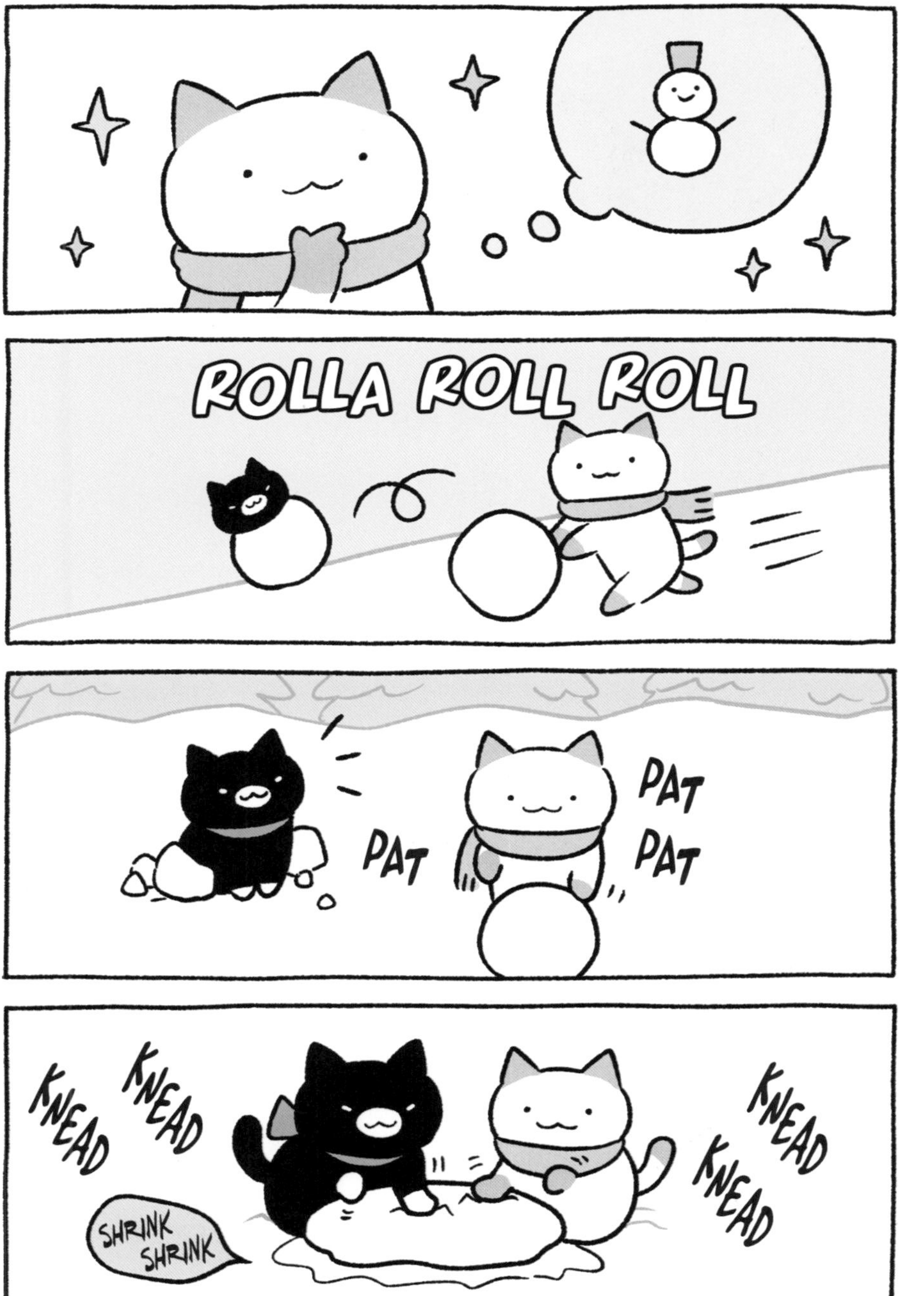
ROLLA ROLL ROLL
PAT
PAT
PAT
KNEAD
KNEAD
KNEAD
KNEAD
SHRINK SHRINK

IT'S SNOWING

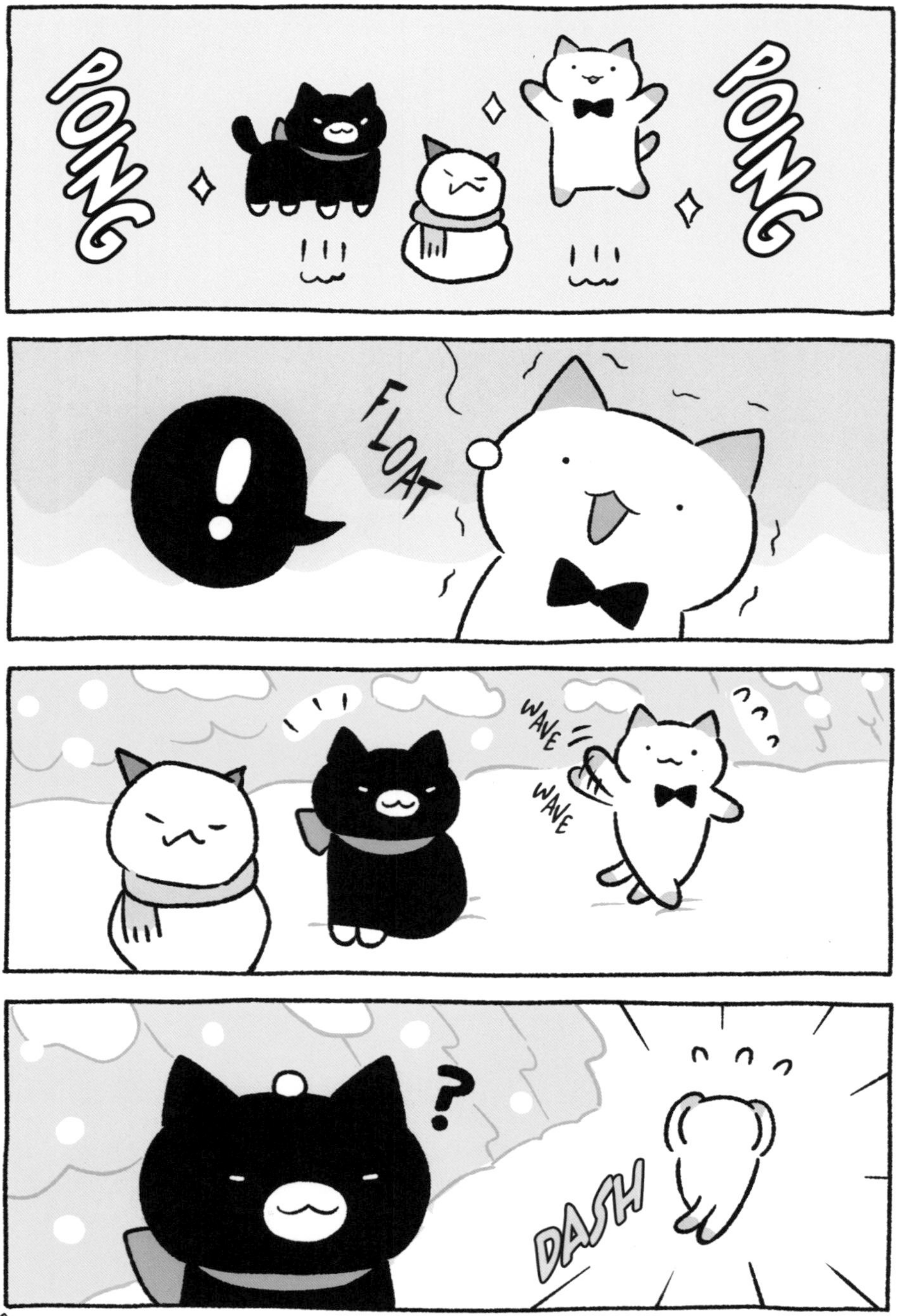
POING
POING
FLOAT
!
WAVE
WAVE
DASH
?

QUICK PACE

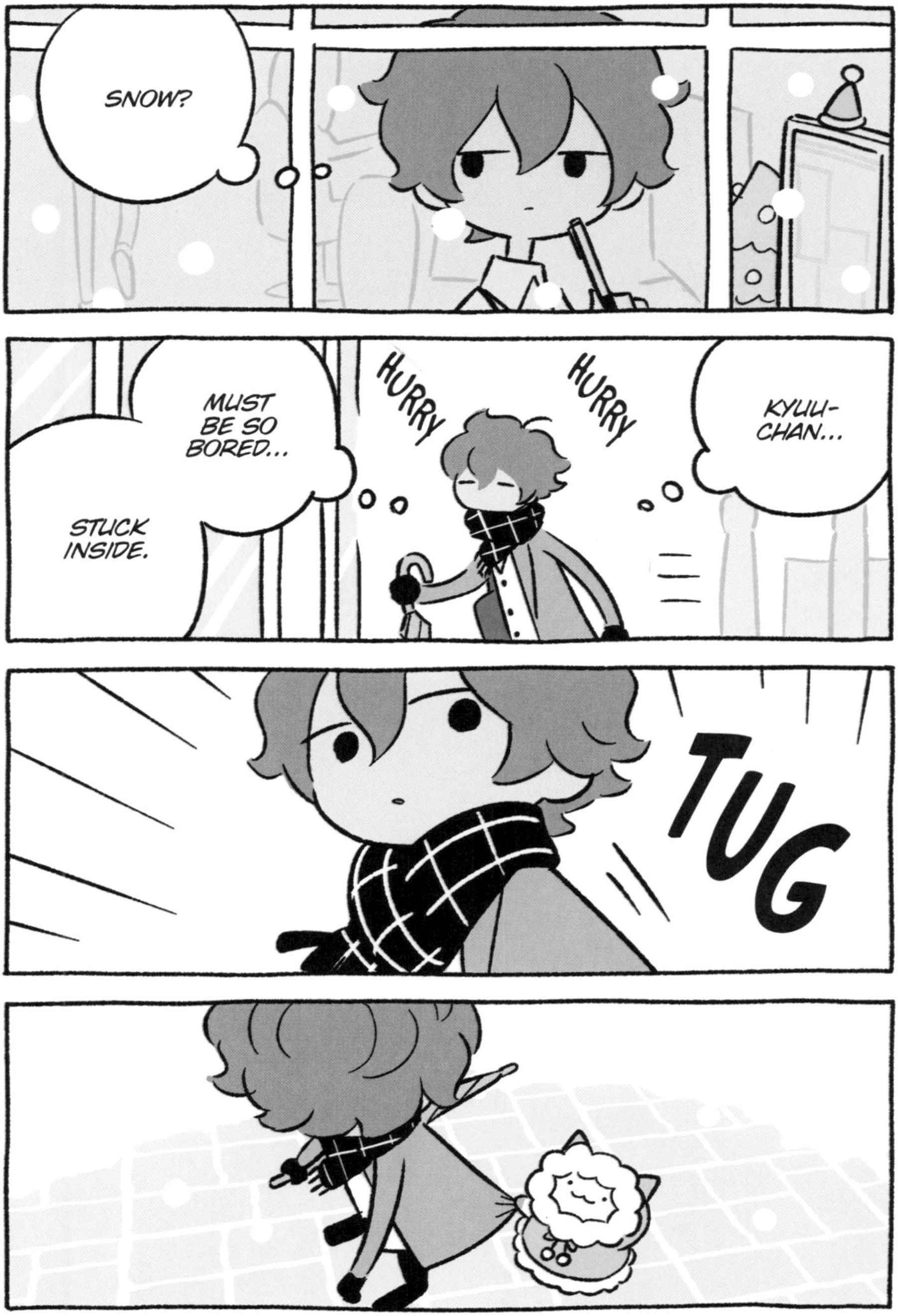
SNOW?
KYUU-CHAN...
HURRY
HURRY
MUST BE SO BORED...
STUCK INSIDE.
TUG

CHARADES

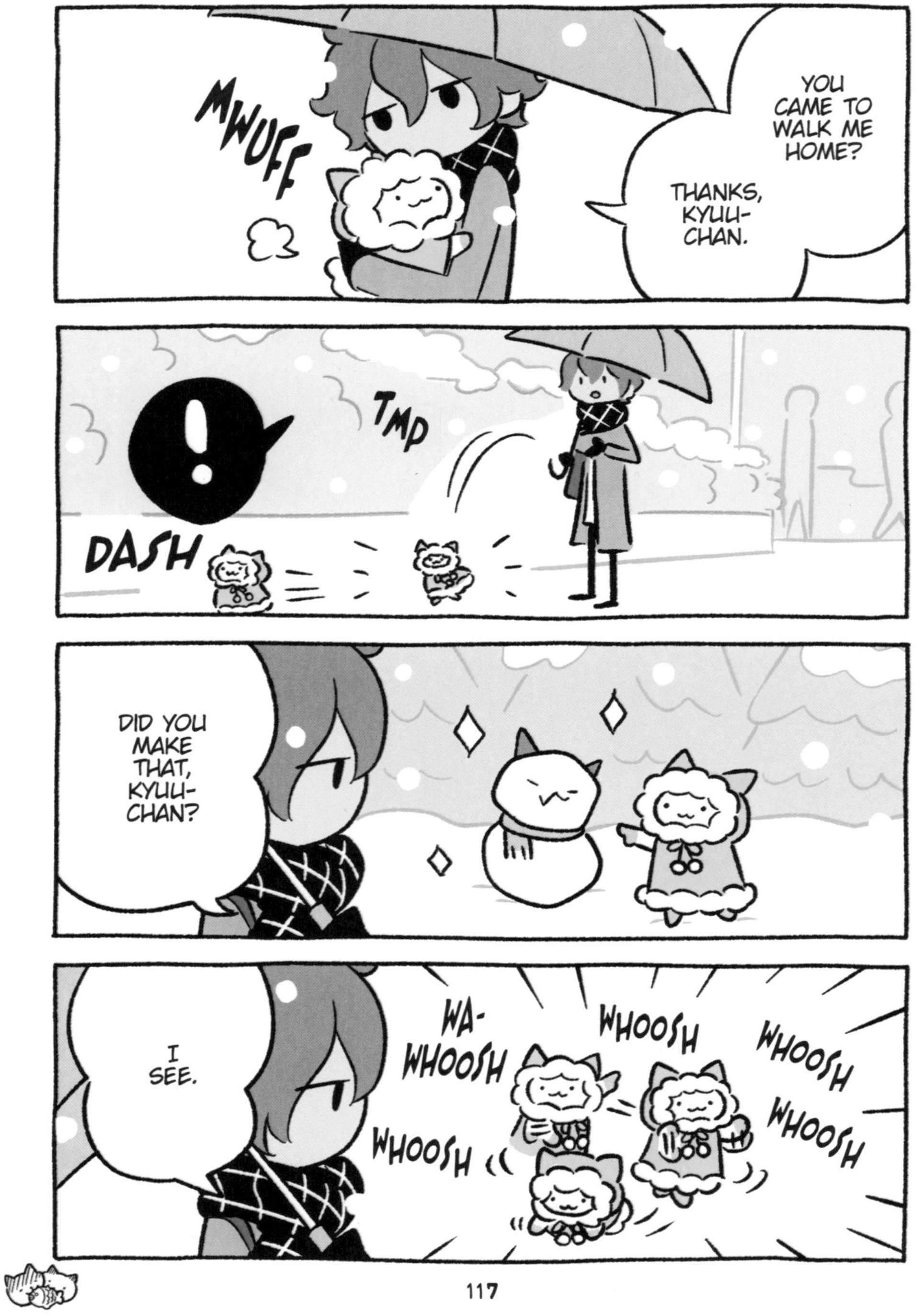
YOU CAME TO WALK ME HOME?
THANKS, KYUU-CHAN.
MWUFF
TMP
!
DASH
DID YOU MAKE THAT, KYUU-CHAN?
WHOOSH
WHOOSH
WA-WHOOSH
WHOOSH
I SEE.
WHOOSH

A WORLD OF SILVER

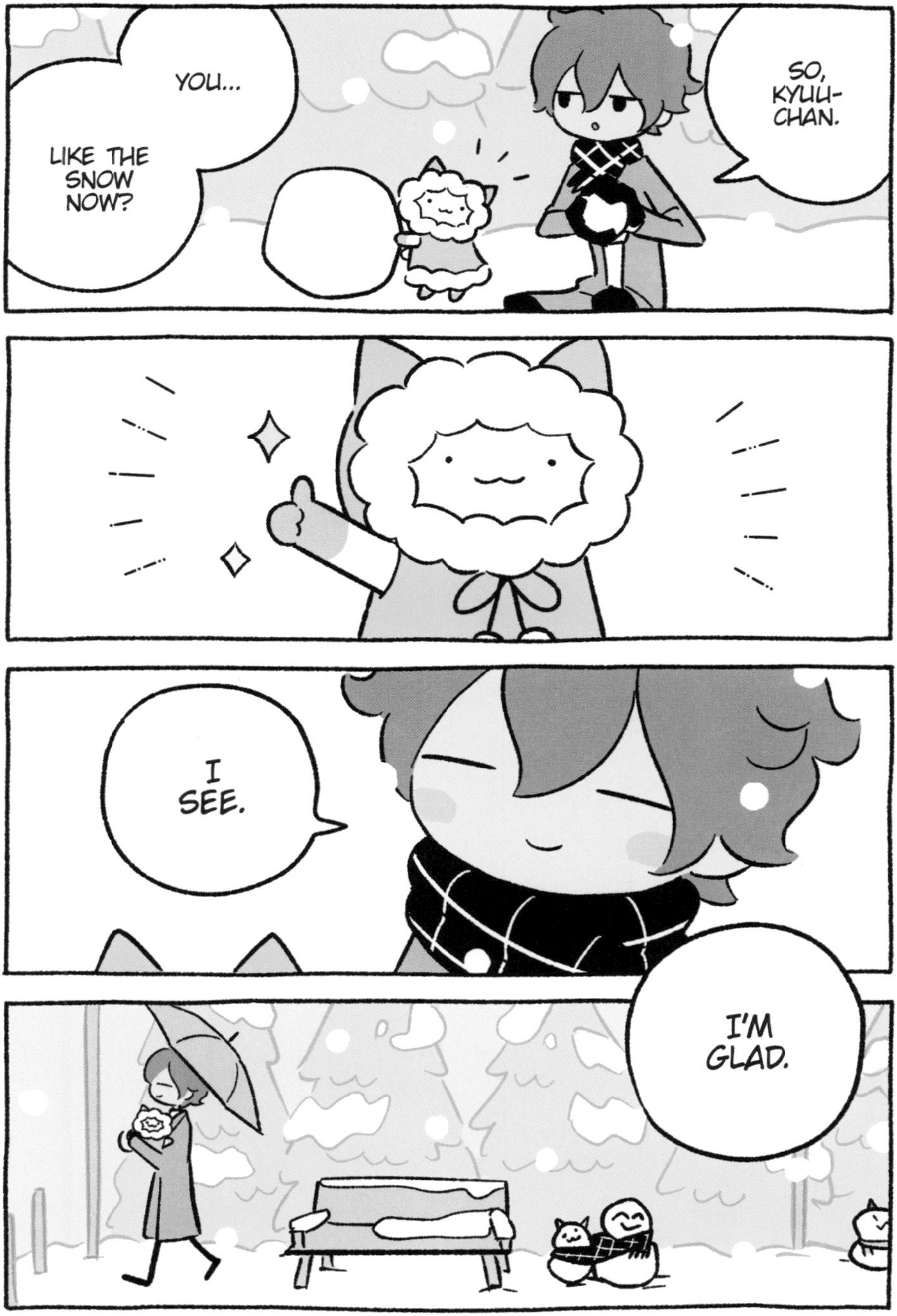
SO, KYUU-CHAN.
YOU...
LIKE THE SNOW NOW?
I SEE.
I'M GLAD.

BONUS MANGA

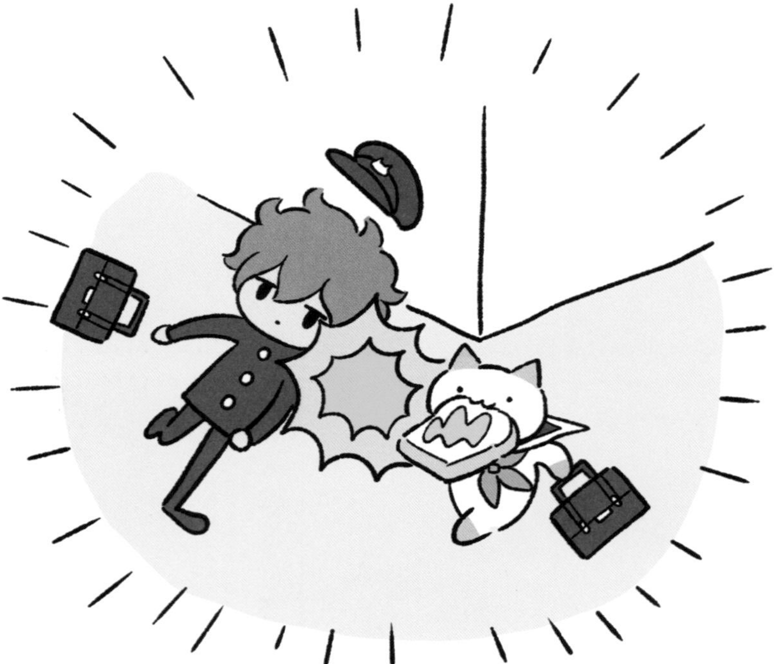

Crash

STARTLED

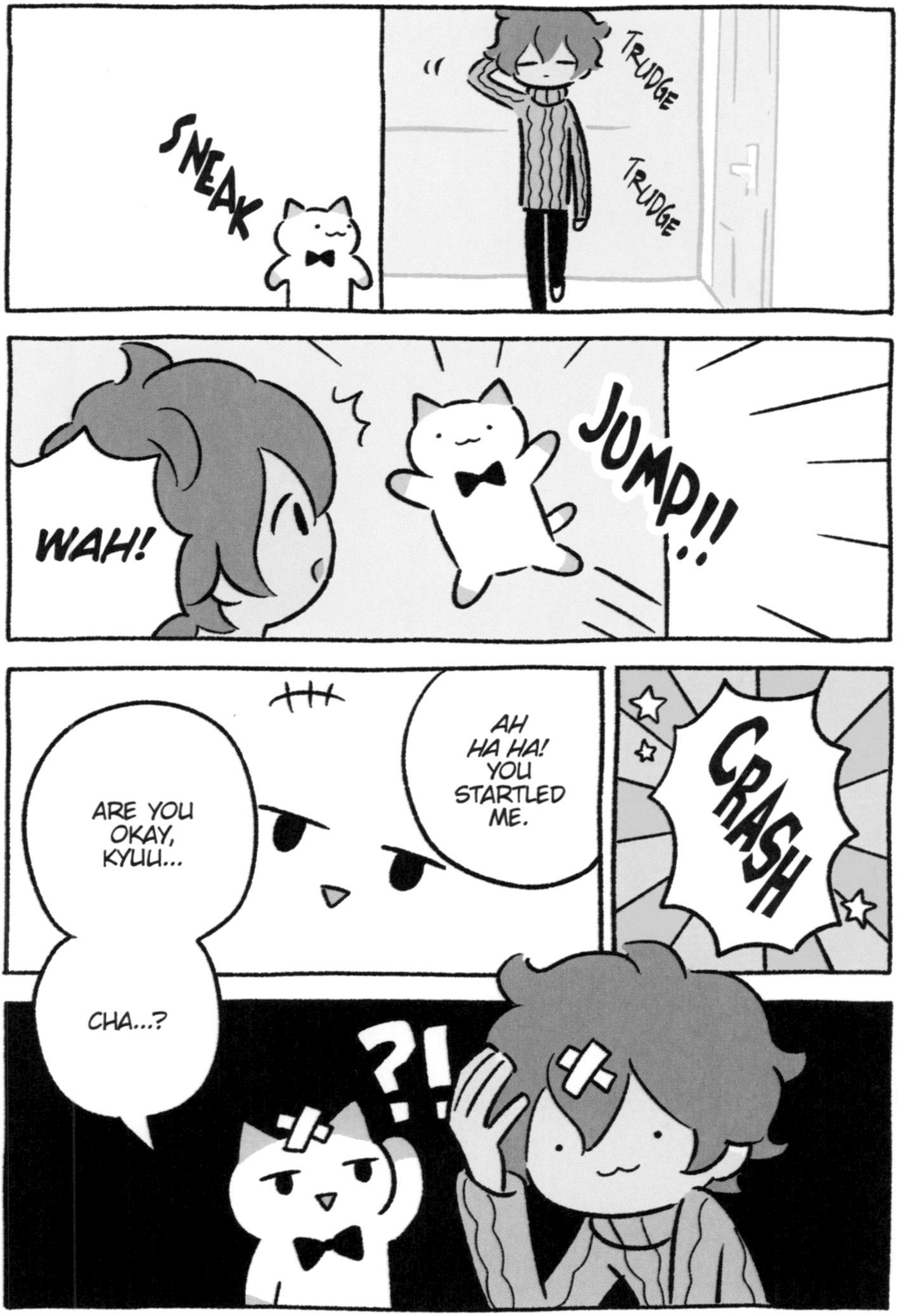
TRUDGE
TRUDGE
SNEAK
JUMP!!
WAH!
CRASH
AH HA HA! YOU STARTLED ME.
ARE YOU OKAY, KYUU...
CHA...?
?!

WONDER CAT AOI-CHAN

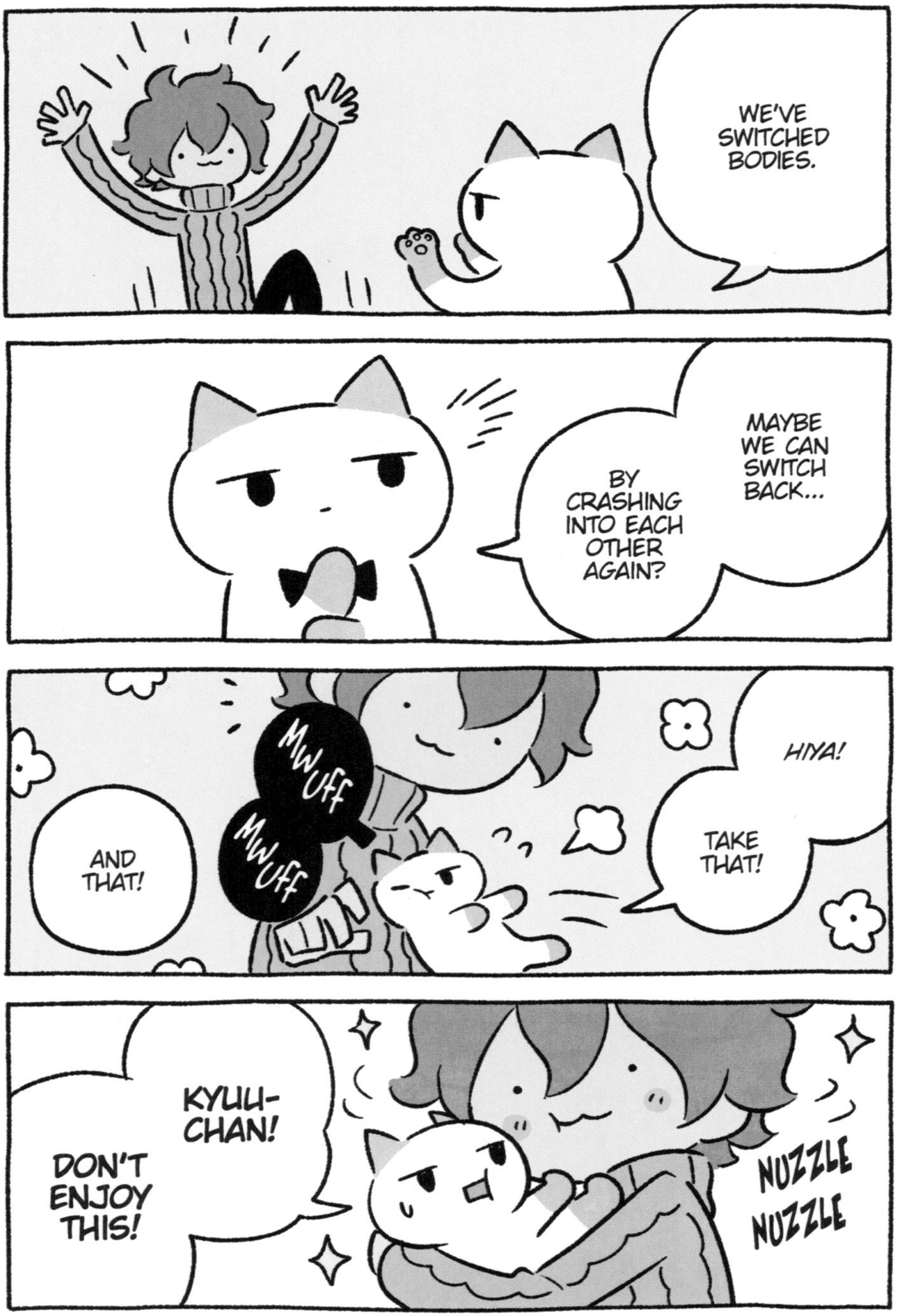
WE'VE SWITCHED BODIES.
MAYBE WE CAN SWITCH BACK...
BY CRASHING INTO EACH OTHER AGAIN?
HIYA!
TAKE THAT!
MWUFF
MWUFF
AND THAT!
NUZZLE NUZZLE
KYUU-CHAN!
DON'T ENJOY THIS!

BY FORCE

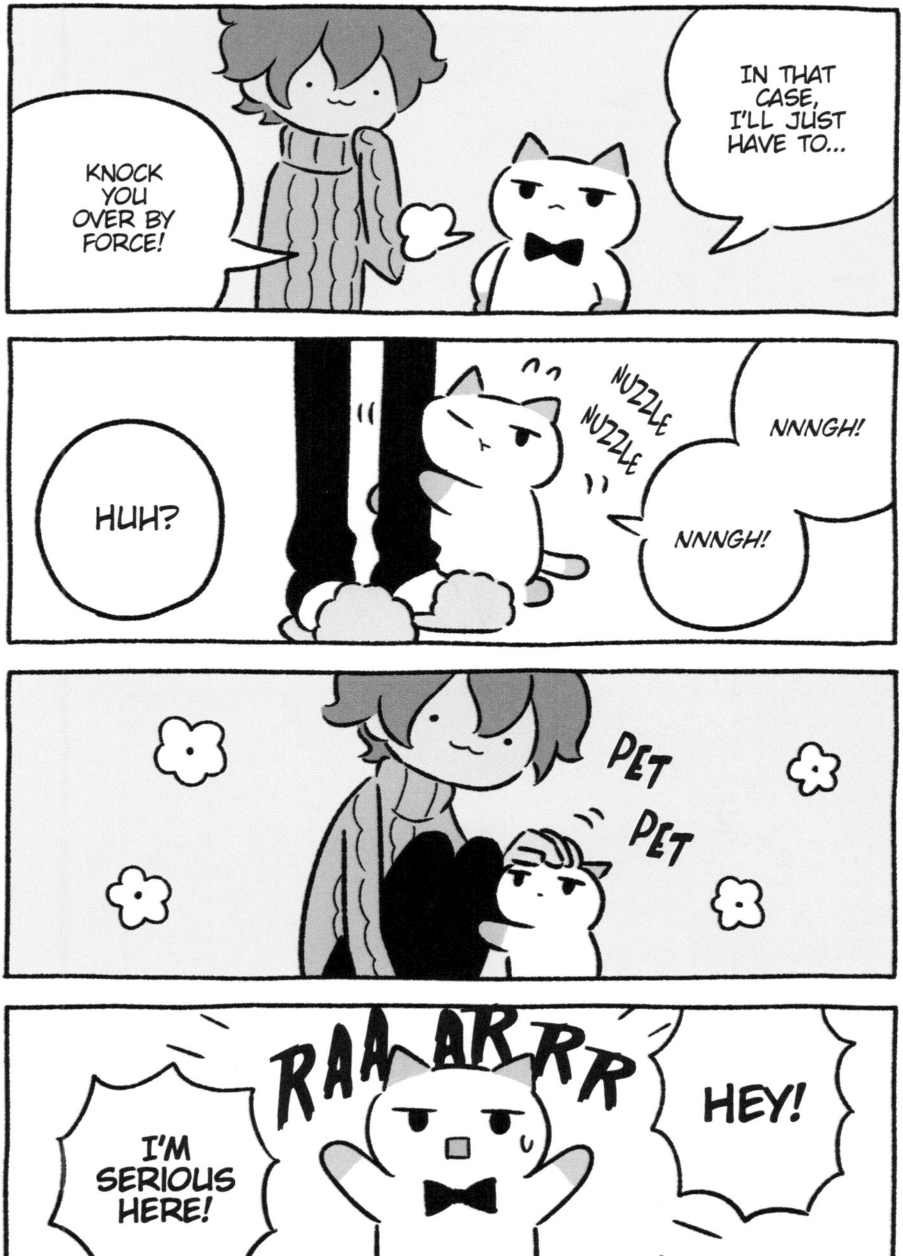
IN THAT CASE, I'LL JUST HAVE TO...
KNOCK YOU OVER BY FORCE!
NNNGH!
NNNGH!
NUZZLE NUZZLE
HUH?
PET PET
HEY!
RAAARRR
I'M SERIOUS HERE!

GREAT IDEA

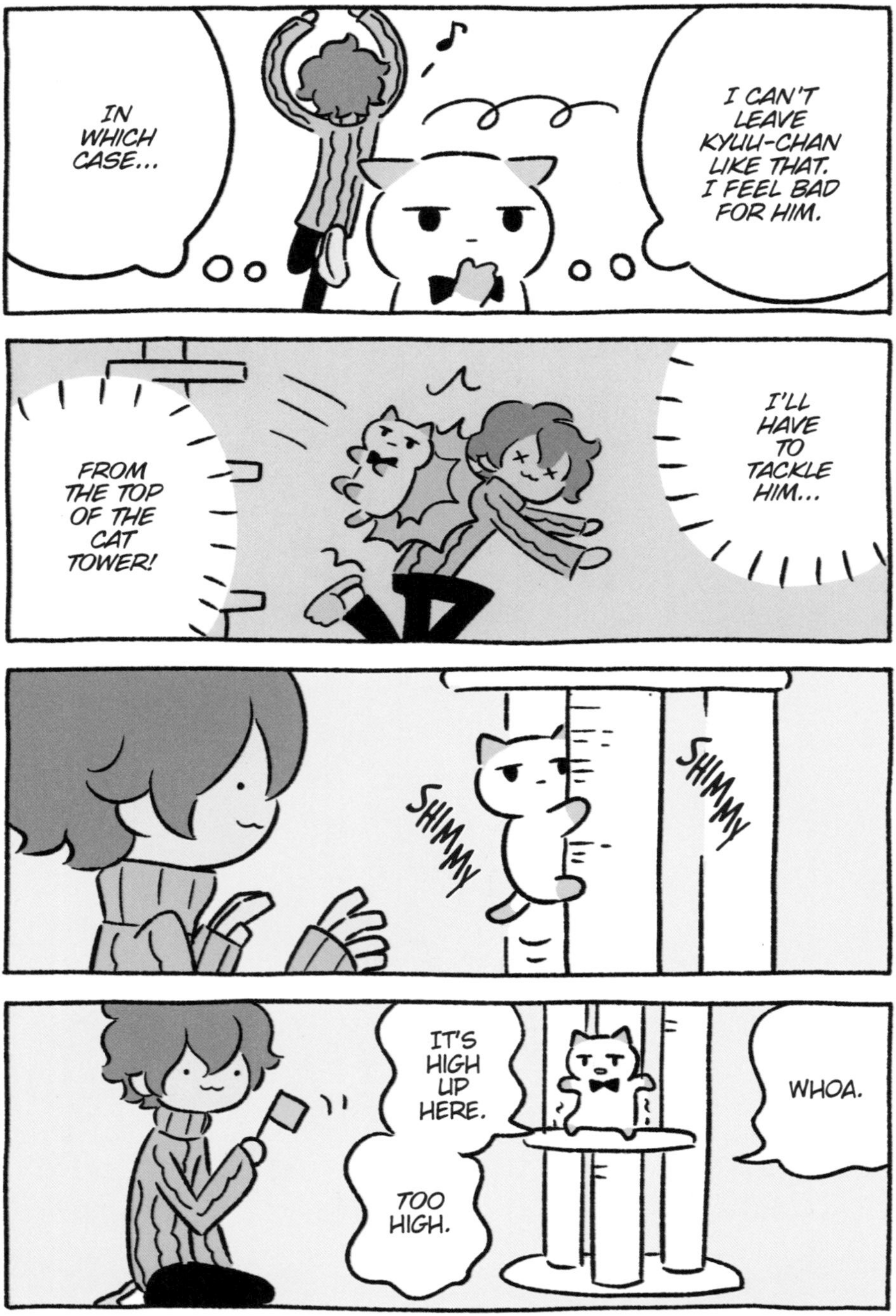
I CAN'T LEAVE KYUU-CHAN LIKE THAT. I FEEL BAD FOR HIM.
IN WHICH CASE...
I'LL HAVE TO TACKLE HIM...
FROM THE TOP OF THE CAT TOWER!
SHIMMY
SHIMMY
WHOA.
IT'S HIGH UP HERE.
TOO HIGH.

OPTIMISM

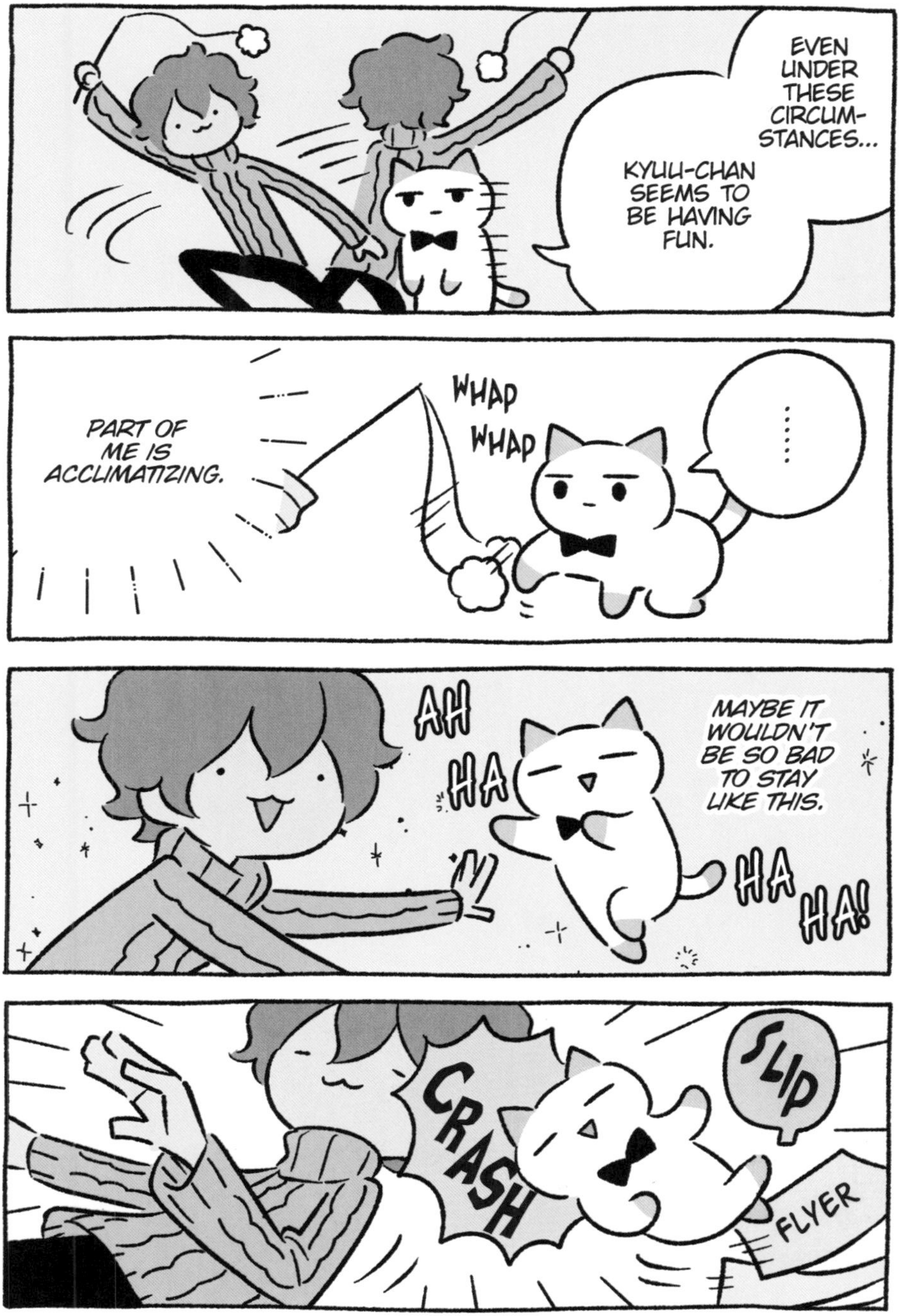
EVEN UNDER THESE CIRCUM-STANCES...
KYUU-CHAN SEEMS TO BE HAVING FUN.
......
WHAP WHAP
PART OF ME IS ACCLIMATIZING.
MAYBE IT WOULDN'T BE SO BAD TO STAY LIKE THIS.
HA HA!
AH HA
SLIP
FLYER
CRASH

MYSTERIOUS EXPERIENCE

GASP!
WHOOSH
WE'RE BACK!
WHOOSH
THAT STARTLED ME.
......
BUT...
IT WAS KIND OF FUN, WASN'T IT?

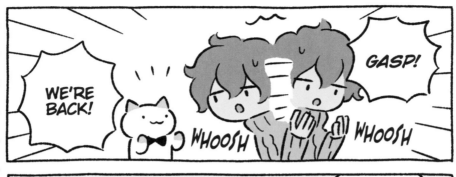

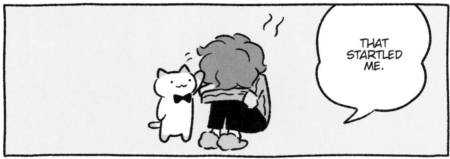

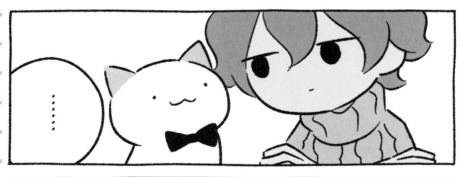

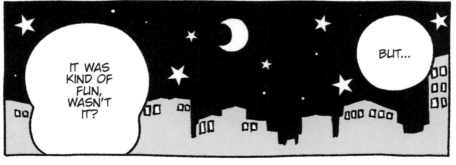

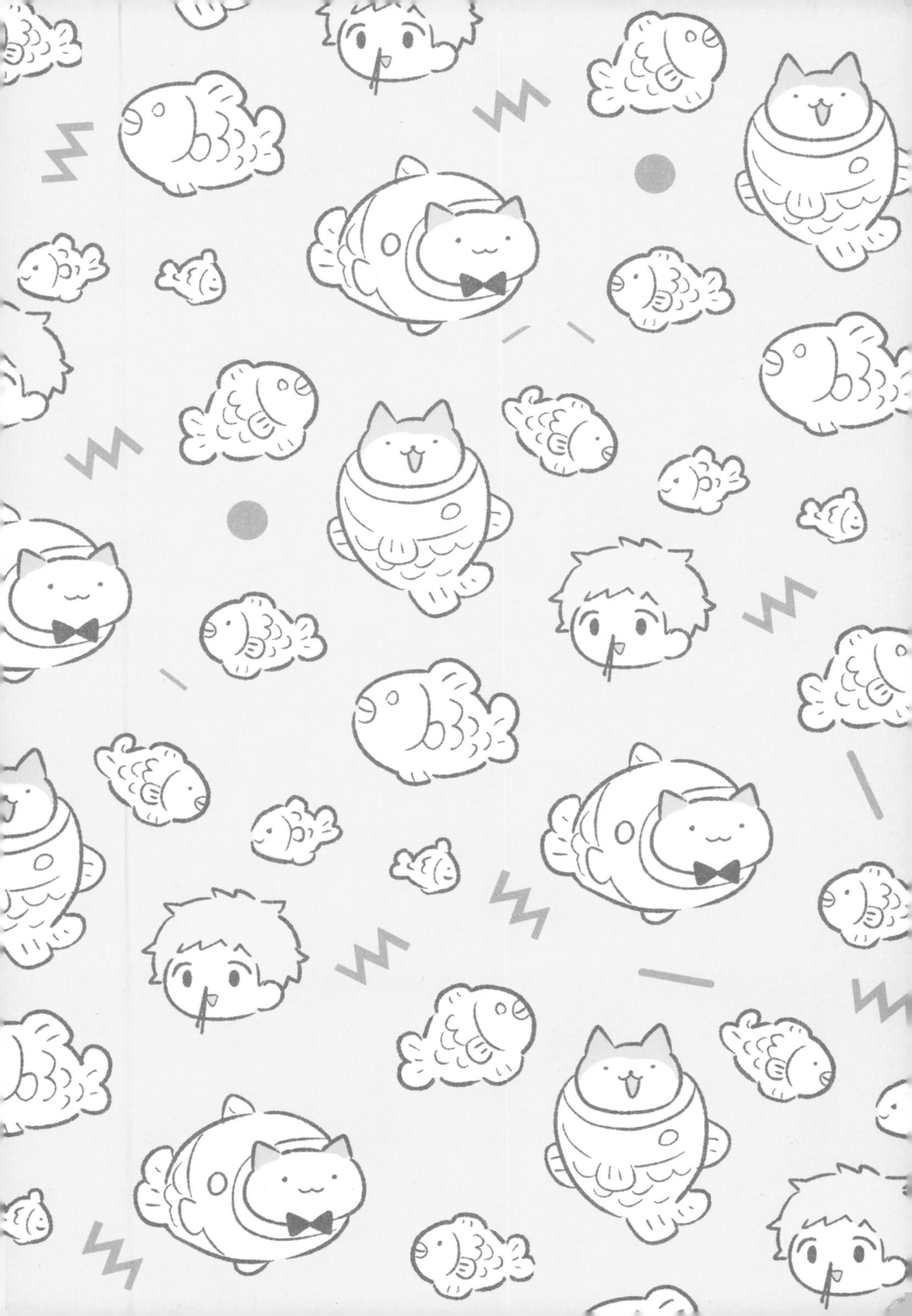

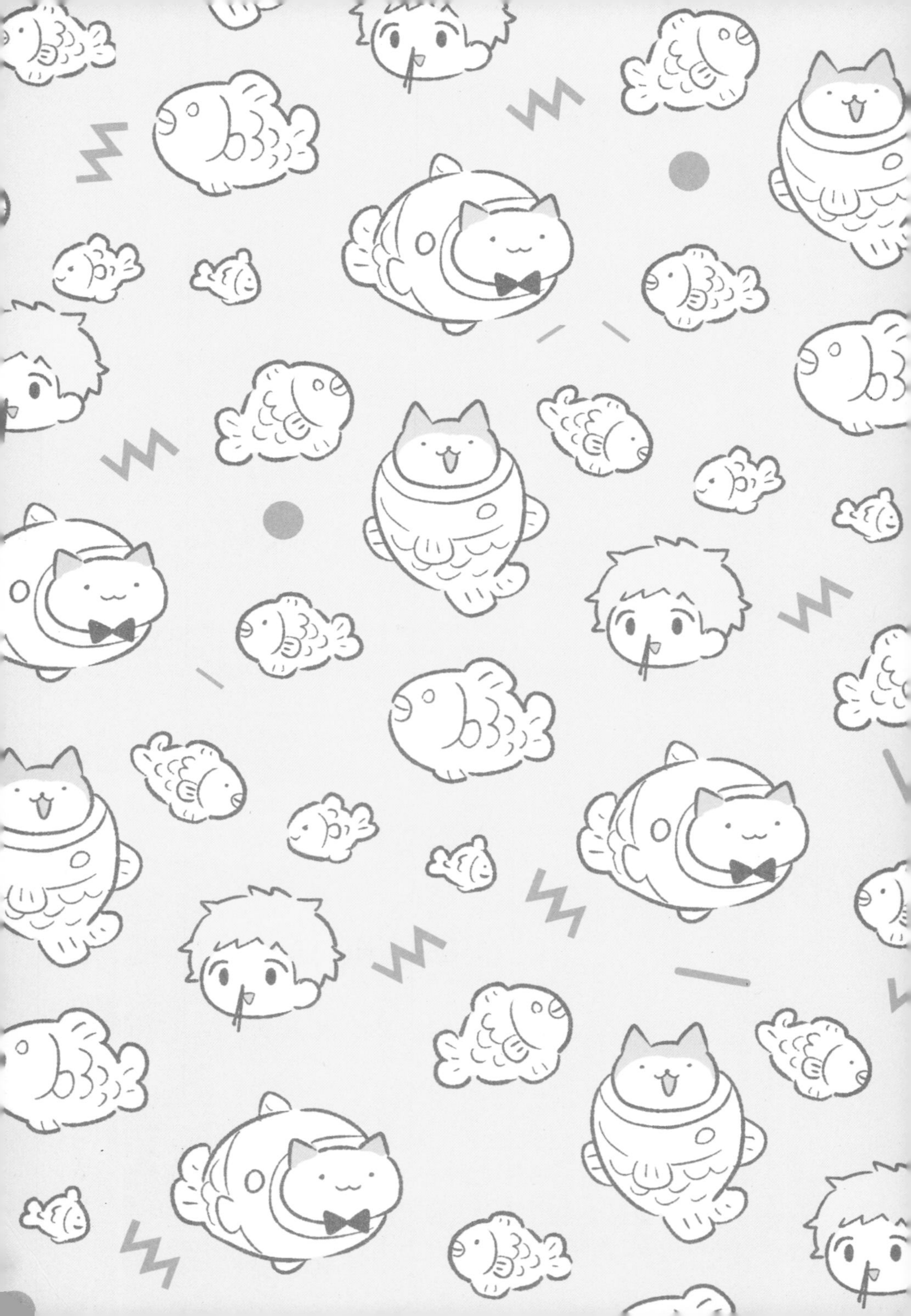

SEVEN SEAS ENTERTAINMENT PRESENTS

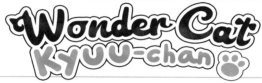

Wonder Cat Kyuu-chan

story and art by **SASAMI NITORI**　　　VOLUME 5

TRANSLATION
Alethea & Athena Nibley

LETTERING
Roland Amago
Bambi Eloriaga-Amago

COVER DESIGN
H. Qi

COPY EDITOR
Dawn Davis

SENIOR EDITOR
Peter Adrian Behravesh

PREPRESS TECHNICIAN
Melanie Ujimori

PRINT MANAGER
Rhiannon Rasmussen-Silverstein

PRODUCTION MANAGER
Lissa Pattillo

EDITOR-IN-CHIEF
Julie Davis

ASSOCIATE PUBLISHER
Adam Arnold

PUBLISHER
Jason DeAngelis

FUSHIGINEKO NO KYUU-CHAN VOL. 5
© SASAMI NITORI 2020 Printed in Japan
All rights reserved.
Original Japanese edition published by Star Seas Company.
English publishing rights arranged with Star Seas Company
through Kodansha Ltd., Tokyo.

Seven Seas press and purchase enquiries can be sent to Marketing Manager Lianne
Sentar at press@gomanga.com. Information regarding the distribution and purchase of
digital editions is available from Digital Manager CK Russell at digital@gomanga.com.

Seven Seas and the Seven Seas logo are trademarks of
Seven Seas Entertainment. All rights reserved.

ISBN: 978-1-63858-239-7
Printed in Canada
First Printing: April 2022
10 9 8 7 6 5 4 3 2 1

S0-AXJ-356

READING DIRECTIONS

This book reads from *right to left*,
Japanese style. If this is your first time
reading manga, you start reading from
the top right panel on each page and
take it from there. If you get lost, just
follow the numbered diagram here.
It may seem backwards at first,
but you'll get the hang of it! Have fun!!

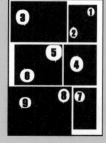